AFTER EVER AFTER

Rowan Coleman worked in bookselling and then publishing for seven years, during which time she wrote her first novel, *Growing Up Twice*, published in 2002. She left to write her second novel, *After Ever After*, and now lives in Hertfordshire with her husband and daughter.

Praise for *Growing Up Twice*

'*Growing Up Twice* is a fresh, warm and hugely enjoyable read . . . truly brilliant. Her captivating style leaps off the page, engrossing you from the first sentence' *Company*

'A fantastic first novel' *heat*

D0584035

Also by Rowan Coleman

Growing Up Twice

AFTER EVER AFTER

Rowan Coleman

arrow books

Published by Arrow Books in 2003

3 5 7 9 10 8 6 4 2

'Secret Love'. Words by Paul Francis Webster. Music by Sammy Fain. © 1953
(renewed) Remick Music Corp, USA. Warner/Chappell Music Ltd, London W6 8BS.
Reproduced by permission of International Music Publications Ltd. All rights reserved

First published in the United Kingdom in 2003 by Century

Arrow Books
The Random House Group Limited
20 Vauxhall Bridge Road, London, SW1V 2SA

Random House Australia (Pty) Limited
20 Alfred Street, Milsons Point, Sydney,
New South Wales 2061, Australia

Random House New Zealand Limited
18 Poland Road, Glenfield
Auckland 10, New Zealand

Random House (Pty) Limited
Endulini, 5a Jubilee Road, Parktown 2193, South Africa

The Random House Group Limited Reg. No. 954009

www.randomhouse.co.uk

A CIP catalogue record for this book
is available from the British Library

Papers used by Random House
are natural, recyclable products made from wood grown in
sustainable forests. The manufacturing processes conform to
the environmental regulations of the country of origin

ISBN 0 09 942769 9

Typeset by SX Composing DTP, Rayleigh, Essex
Printed and bound in Great Britain by
Cox & Wyman, Reading, Berks

For Erol and Lily, always

Acknowledgements

With huge thanks to Kate Elton for her wonderful support and amazing ability to know what I mean even when I don't! And to everyone at Arrow and Random House who has helped me come this far.

To my friends Clare and Graham Winter, the entire Smith family, especially Lynn and Rosie, and to Sarah Boswell and Amanda Hamilton for their superbly practical support. Thank you to Naomi and George Benson for being just next door whenever I needed a coffee or babysitting. Also to Sue Gee for offering such great inspiration and encouragement. Thanks to Lizzy Kremer, who is always there when I need her.

Especial thanks to my mum, who has been fantastic and who says I couldn't have written this book without her, and I have to admit I agree. And my final and greatest thanks to Erol and Lily, who give me so much love and joy every day.

Prologue

'I must say,' Dora said, looking at her reflection in the mirror, 'I never thought it would be possible to find a colour that would suit both a black woman and someone like me, you know, someone who permanently looks like they're in need of a blood transfusion.' Her expression of mild astonishment dimmed into a scowl as she remembered that a small crown of dark red rosebuds had been entwined into her glossy bottle-black bob. Camille stood beside her and together in the mirror they looked like the yin and yang bridesmaids, or maybe Superbridesmaid and her not quite evil twin.

'I know,' Camille said with a self-approving glance. 'Say what you like about the stuck up old bag, she's got great taste,' she said with a giggle.

'Shhhhhhhhhh.' I looked hastily over my shoulder. 'She'll be back any moment with the dress!' I pulled my mother-in-law-to-be's oversized white towelling bathrobe around me even more tightly and breathed in deeply and then out deeply trying to remain calm and poised – a calm and poised bride-to-be.

'What is this colour anyway?' Dora said, ignoring me. 'Is it puce?'

I remained calm and looked at her, a picture of serenity.

'No. It is not puce. It's Winter Cranberry,' I said with deliberate calmness, tapping my foot and looking at the clock.

'Where has she gone with that dress? It's almost twelve; we're supposed to be at the church by one.' I closed my eyes and imagined Fergus in his hotel room, tying his cravat or trying to. I pictured him in the cranberry and gold brocaded waistcoat and smiled, thinking how dashing he was going to look in the long frock coat and Mr Darcy-style boots. Then I remembered that if my mother-in-law-to-be didn't get a crack on I'd be marrying him in my knickers.

Suddenly it all made sense. My eyes flew open.

'That's it!' I said. 'She's run off with the dress! It's the last chance she's got to stop her precious son from marrying a commoner from a council estate!' Dora rolled her eyes, took a cigarette out of her fur-trimmed muff ('muff!' she'd giggled when mother-in-law-to-be had handed it to her) and put it to her lips. My jaw dropped in horror; any form of cigarette para-phernalia was strictly forbidden in the double-fronted 1930s Art Deco palace, Castle Kelly – Fergus's birthplace. The thinly brittle façade of calm I had constructed for myself shattered at my feet.

I am afraid of Georgina, mother-in-law-to-be. She's one of those women who look twenty years younger than they should and who dress better than I do. She's all that and more, queen of her castle and her family, and then suddenly Cinders here breezes in from the cellar after her son, and she doesn't like it. Not one little bit. I mean, she's not tried to throw me in a dungeon or anything, she's been perfectly polite up to a point, but you can just see it in the ice-cold gimlet eyes: *You are not good enough.*

Dora snorted with laughter at the look of horror on my face.

'Don't panic! I'm not smoking it, I'm just holding it; it helps me relax and forget you've got me dressed up like a Christmas tree.' She patted my hand. 'Anyway, she hasn't run off with your dress. Can you imagine what the glitterati of wherever-the-fuck we are, *Berkhamsted*, would say if the social event of the year didn't happen?'

I nodded, breathing in, breathing out. Dora was right. Georgina might have been taken aback by Fergus's sudden announcement of his plan to marry a girl he'd hardly even mentioned let alone brought home for her seal of approval, but once the news had sunk in she had waded into the breach in full organisational battle gear, clearly determined to camouflage the unsuitability of the marriage in as much glamour and style as she could manage.

'Well, you'll need help, dear, you can't possibly manage by yourself, what with no mother of your own,' she had said, and I had been grateful to accept before I realised exactly what she meant – and it wasn't 'I'll book your tickets to the Bahamas, no problem'.

'Yeah, don't be mad,' Camille said, twirling one of her wedding-special ringlets. 'Have you *seen* those shoes? No one buys Jimmy Choo shoes that they will never wear again unless they plan to go through with it. Anyway, she couldn't run in those heels and that woman is *not* leaving *those* shoes behind. Not unless she really has got a heart of stone.' She flashed me her traffic-stopping smile. 'What colour is puce, anyway?' Camille asked me, 'I always thought it was green.'

Dora snorted.

'No, you're thinking of puke,' she said. 'Puce is more your Winter Cranberry kind of colour.'

'I'm sure you're right,' I said, breaking into their conversation. 'I mean, she's Fergus's mother, right? He is the fruit of her loins and he is just the most wonderful man, the best and kindest man. He must have some of that from her. He can't have inherited all of his loveliness from his dad. And look at his dad! He's lovely too and he married her. She must, somewhere deep inside, have a soul.' I tried to conjure up an image of Georgina as a young mother nursing her only child, but somehow it wouldn't come.

'Yeah. Cor, Fergus's dad is top banana. I fancy Fergus's dad,' Camille announced, so that anyone just on the other side of the door would be able to hear her. Everyone I know fancies Fergus's dad, Daniel, because he looks like Fergus but sort of silvered and with a real Irish accent and an endless line in cuddly cable-knit jumpers. Somehow he and Georgina have stayed married for a million years or something, so she can't be *that* bad. Either that or she is *really* bad in a feminist reworking of Bluebeard kind of way.

Deep calm breaths.

'Stop panicking.' Dora sat next to me on the bed. 'The only thing that can stop this wedding now is if one of Fergus's ex-lovers turns up mid-ceremony and shouts 'No! He's already married! To me! And these are his twins!'

I stared at her in horror.

'Joke! It's a joke! I'm only joking.' At last she showed some sensitivity to my total sense-of-humour bypass on the subject and with a rare gentle smile leant her forehead against mine. 'You know, your mum would be so proud,' she whispered, before squeezing my hand. Our eyes locked for a moment and Dora let me stare at her for as long as I needed to, to battle back the threat of tears.

'So listen,' Dora said, breaking the moment with a wink to Camille. 'You know all about sex, right? Anything you need me to brush up for you now?'

Camille settled on the bed behind me.

'Yeah, any extra positions you think you might need to know, you know, to keep your marriage nice and spicy?' she said with a giggle.

'How about how to bring that overlong blow job to a speedy end?' Dora interrupted her. I shook my head, laughing. 'No?

4

Sure? You know there is nothing worse than that fifteen-minute lockjaw feeling?' She picked up an empty champagne bottle and shoved the neck of it into her mouth, making her cheek bulge.

'Ohfferthuckffakegetonwiffit!' she said, rolling her eyes.

I laughed and pushed her away, reaching for my glass of flat champagne.

'No, I have no complaint in that area. Didn't I tell you two why I am marrying this man? Because he's hung like a very large horse and so dirty in bed that the first time he shagged me I thought we'd get arrested . . . Oh hi, Georgina.'

Fergus's mother shut the door behind her and looked at me, flaring her nostrils as if she had come upon a terrible smell.

'Just joking about, you know . . . Hen humour . . .' I trailed off, avoiding eye contact with either smirking bridesmaid.

I watched Georgina compose herself, looking as if she were trying her best to shut out the reality of her future daughter-in-law.

'Right, here we go. Come on now, Katherine. Spit spot,' she said, unzipping the dress from its plastic bag.

'I'd thought you'd lost it!' I tried to joke in a poor attempt to dispel the tension, but her face never cracked, maybe because of the Botox. I took off the dressing gown and the cold air raised goosebumps on my arms and legs.

'Brrrrr,' I said with a hapless smile, suddenly feeling that my ivory basque and gold lace-topped stockings were the most inappropriate things imaginable.

'I have never understood why you couldn't have waited until the summer, at the very least, if not have had a proper engagement,' Georgina told me, neatly dispensing with any pretence at friendliness. 'A February wedding, I ask you. It makes it almost impossible for one to find anything worth wearing.' I looked at her already decked out in a lilac and grey ensemble from some boutique in Kensington where you have to ring the bell to be let in, and they only do that if they like the look of you. I thought briefly of my mum in faded jeans and a cheesecloth smock and wondered what she would have made of all this.

'Hands up, come on.' Georgina barely managed to suppress a snap, clearly impatient with my reverie. Dora caught my eye, pulling down the corners of her mouth in a sympathetic grimace. I remembered that technically I was getting married to this woman too today, so I stood my ground, just a little bit.

'Well, we didn't want to wait. Anyway we *had* planned to go away and get married . . .' I tried not to sound wistful as I remembered Fergus persuading me to let his mother take over with her plans.

'Think of it like this,' he'd said. 'She hasn't got a daughter, only a son, and you haven't got a mother. It will be perfect for both of you. Give you a chance to get to know each other. I just know that when she gets to know you she'll adore you.'

'That's what I'm afraid of,' I'd said, but as it turned out I had nothing to worry about on that score. Through the short wedding preparation period Georgina had frog-marched me from designated store to designated store overruling my choices on flowers, decorations and colour scheme until finally we came to the frock, at which point I was so determined to dig my heels in that I almost didn't let her bully me into her choice of impeccably tailored gown. But it was beautiful and worse than that she was right – it was the right dress.

'You look great,' I said to Georgina meekly, conciliatory as I lifted my hands over my head and became lost to all, for a brief moment bound in the comforting muffle of acres of cream netting. She blinked in response, or maybe because she was going to anyway.

'Right, breathe in. Have you put on a few pounds?' Georgina asked me as she buttoned up the back of the dress. I avoided looking her in the eye and thought about my period that had been due two weeks ago and was surely late due to pre-wedding stress. In fact, I was so certain that I'd relax the moment the ring was on my finger that I'd stuffed Camille's muff full of tampons in readiness. There wasn't room in Dora's, it was full of fags.

'Right,' she said, nodding decisively. 'Very nice.' She wheeled a full-length mahogany-framed reproduction Victorian mirror round to meet me. I looked at the stranger in the mirror, blinked and looked at Dora.

'Well, look who's the fairest of them all,' Dora said with a slow smile. 'Bloody hell, mate, you look fucking incredible.' And for once I didn't think she was taking the piss.

'You do, you look wonderful.' Camille's eyes were bright with tears. 'Oh God, I'm going to cry again!'

I looked at myself. My dyed red hair had been returned to its natural deep brown and it fell undressed and in loose waves around my shoulders. I had had nightmares about the dress ever since the moment I'd let Dad pay for it. In my memory Georgina had tricked me into buying a huge ballooning edifice, and I woke up sweating, seeing myself getting stuck halfway down the aisle like a huge puffball mushroom. Now that it was on I felt like Grace Kelly, like Cinderella going to the ball. Like Calamity Jane when she gets her posh frock on and makes Buffalo Bill fall in love with her, because men don't fall in love with girls wearing trousers. Like a woman worthy of Fergus Kelly's love – the one for him.

Georgina looked me up and down and nodded.

'Well, come on.' She rolled her eyes. 'We haven't got time for moping about. The car's due in five minutes and you haven't got your fur-trimmed bolero jacket on yet!'

I was laughing as I slipped the jacket over my bare shoulders.

'Kitty?' My father's voice sounded on the other side of the door. We all froze.

I looked at Dora and Dora looked at Camille. Camille gave

me an encouraging smile, mouthing, 'Don't worry, it'll be okay.' At least I think that's what she mouthed.

Fergus had despatched his best man to go and pick Dad up and bring him here because Dad couldn't go anywhere on his own. He wasn't agoraphobic exactly – he could make it to the local shops and back; he was just terrified of pretty much everything new.

'Kitty, is it all right to come in?' As usual he sounded hesitant and unsure, and as usual it irritated me. I composed myself.

'Yes, Dad. Come in!' I called out. I almost didn't want to see his face when he saw me, I almost wanted to turn my back and run in the opposite direction.

'My word,' Dad said, and in that split second I prayed that he'd say anything, anything at all except for what I knew he was about to say. 'You look just like her . . .' I watched him lost for a moment, his face a picture of remote reverie. He'd said exactly the wrong thing.

'Thanks,' I said, trying to hide my disappointment. It wasn't that I didn't want to remember her, it was just that every other day of my life had been about her death and I so wanted this day to be about my life. I know that Mum would have wanted it too. Dad took my hand and squeezed it; his was a little sweaty.

'She's here, you know, she's with us even now,' he said, his eyes brimming with tears. I closed my eyes on the last image I remember of my mother and tried to chase it away with happier ones. 'She would have loved this day.' He dropped my hand and turned his face to the wall, shutting the world out. I glanced awkwardly at the others in the room and laid my hand on his shoulder.

'I know, Dad, and she'd want us to be happy,' I said briskly to him. 'So let's make her proud, okay?' Slightly taller than him in my shoes, I turned him back to face me, straightened the

8

cravat I could see he felt so uncomfortable wearing and smoothed down what was left of his hair.

'Ready?' I said, wishing that I could ask him if he'd remembered to take his antidepressants, but not wanting Georgina to hear.

'Ready,' he said a little uncertainly.

'Come on, girls, let's roll!' I said excitedly. 'I'm getting married in ten minutes!' I sang, and as we left the house Fergus had grown up in, the winter sun broke through the clouds and made the rain-soaked pavements shine as if they were laid with gold.

In the last second before he stood up, Fergus drained both his champagne glass and then mine, whispering, 'What's yours is mine an' all that . . .' I smiled. I knew how much he was dreading this moment, how he'd holed himself up for weeks on end fretting about getting it just right.

'Look, relax, all you have to do is thank the bridesmaids, say what a babe I am and sit down,' I'd told him, secretly much more worried about my dad's effort and his best man's hilarious line in dirty 'gags', as he referred to them.

'No, Kits, you don't get it. This is my moment to tell everyone what you mean to me. And I'm not blowing it.'

As it had turned out, Dad hadn't done so badly. He'd gone through the book I'd bought him and pretty much read 'Father of the Bride Example Speech A' verbatim, and I was grateful for the bland pleasantries and borrowed anecdotes. He'd even omitted mentioning my mother beyond how much we both missed her, and I knew it cost him, but on today of all days, my perfect day, I didn't want the spectre of her death hanging over us. If Dad didn't understand then I knew that Mum would.

'A speech.' Fergus's clear voice cut through the murmur that filled the hall as he prepared himself. 'If there was ever a reason that I nearly didn't propose it was the thought of standing up in front of two hundred of my friends and family and making a speech . . .' Fergus winked at me and I knew he was thinking of the empty beach and guest list of two that we had had to forgo.

'Get on with it then!' Colin the best man shouted, and a rumble of chuckles rolled around the room. Colin perked up, visibly heartened after his joke about the sex mad mother-in-law had fallen so flat.

'Um, right.' Fergus studied his dog-eared cue cards for a moment, his black hair falling over his winter-sky-blue eyes, and my heart leapt to his defence. My Fergus, so constantly confident, now suddenly shy and vulnerable.

'So, anyway. I had to think of reasons that were good enough to make it worth my while . . .'

'She's up the duff!' Colin hollered and the stony silence that greeted him sent him back into his shell as a failed stand-up. It *was* funny, really. No one here, not even Georgina's stuffed-shirt heavy mob, believed that a twenty-first-century couple would get married over an unplanned pregnancy. And that wasn't the reason at all, not at all. I tallied up my tear-fuelled tantrums over the last couple of weeks and was certain that I was in the midst of a particularly prolonged bout of PMT.

'Ha, no.' I saw that my husband's long fingers were trembling. 'No. It's simple really. In the last thirty-odd years I have often wondered what kind of woman would make me want to marry her. When I was about eight I decided it was Princess Leah in her gold bikini.' Two hundred people smiled. 'And she pretty much headed the field for the next ten years or so. But truth be told, as I grew into a man I never thought I'd fall prey to the big "C". Commitment. Things happened and eventually I stopped believing in love. I thought that that kind of love existed only in storybooks and on movie screens and I knew I didn't want to settle for less.

'It seems foolish now, but I had a kind of a "vision" of my perfect woman. I mean, I didn't know what she looked like, or what her name was, I only knew that when I met this person I'd know her, know that she was my soulmate. After a long time looking I thought I'd never find her.' Fergus caught my hand and held it tight. 'And then I met Kitty and I knew I'd found her. I thought it would probably weird her out too much to tell her that in the first half an hour after we'd met, so I tried to keep it to myself. In fact I more or less sat on the information for all of a week and then I couldn't keep it to myself any longer. Imagine, then, how happy I was, how lucky and blessed, to know that Kitty felt the same way about me.' I smiled up at him, nodding.

'Kitty makes me laugh, laugh so much I can't breathe. She makes me sing, and I mean literally. You know you're happy when you find yourself attempting a Craig David song in a tuneless baritone first thing in the morning and you don't even know who Craig David is. Then you know you've found someone you have to hold on to. Although my neighbours might not think so. I really can't sing.' A ripple of laughter swelled at the back of the room and spread through the guests until it broke against the top table. Fergus seemed visibly heartened.

'Kitty makes me hold my breath. Every day when I know I'm going to see her again, even if she's just been in the next room, I'm so excited about the prospect that I forget to breathe. She's simply the most beautiful person I know, and today more than ever.'

The guests let out a collective 'ahhhh' and a ripple of applause swept around the room. Fergus pulled me to my feet and put his arm around my waist, drawing me into the strength of his body.

'Most of all, Kitty inspires me. She makes me want to be more than I already am, she makes me want to strive to be the kind of man that she deserves – and that's why I asked her to marry me. And because if I had to make a speech, at least I knew I could use it to tell you about the magic that this woman has brought to my life.'

A whoop of cheers and laughter hit the ceiling and filled the room. Even Dora gave a little smile.

The corners of Fergus's mouth curled up as he kissed me.

At last, I thought. At last, I'm saved. My prince has come.

Chapter One

It's raining. Gene Kelly skips off the kerb opposite my house and splashes in a puddle, happy again, apparently, and, what's more, ready for love. I blink hard twice and look at the faintly luminescent hands of Ella's cow-jumping-over-the-moon night light-and-clock combo. Four twenty-five a.m. I am not surprised to see Gene, it's usually around this time that I start to hallucinate. I rub my eyes (one at a time) and return my gaze out of the window to the rain-soaked street now empty of musical stars and quiet again, *so* empty and *so* quiet in a way I'd never known in my native Hackney. One year on and small-town life is still taking some getting used to.

Ella has been asleep for twenty minutes or so, the side of her face half lost against my breast and her small fingers closed tightly around the neck of my nightshirt, gently snoring in dream-free abandon. I really should go back to bed now, but if I get out of this stupid rocking chair that Fergus had made for me to nurse her in, there's a chance that it may creak. It doesn't always creak, usually only every twelve or so rocks, but I lost count when I was getting her back to sleep and I can't be sure what number I got up to. And even if I get out of the chair successfully and manage to lower her into the cot without waking her like it says in The Book; (*Chapter One: Everything You Need to Know about Motherhood, page 32: . . . maintain body contact with your baby for as*

13

long as possible as you lower him into the cot. This enhances the feeling of well-being and reduces the trauma of separation. Well, that's all very well, but they don't tell you how you don't wake your baby up whilst standing on tiptoe and attempting a bend at the waist that would tax the abdominal muscles of a twenty-year-old who *hadn't* recently acquired a whole new layer of padding to their stomach. But I digress.) even then there's a creaky floorboard by the door, to add to which, even if I do manage to remember where it is and even if I do succeed in skipping over it without landing on the other creaky floorboard in the hallway, I might breathe out and that would wake her up again.

During the day, six-month-old Ella can sleep through the TV, the radio, the workmen, emergency service sirens – not that you hear them so much round here – but for some reason as soon as the sun sets, and especially when her mother thinks it might be time to get some sleep, she becomes a Ninja light sleeper, ready to leap into action at the slightest snap of a twig. In fact, so convinced am I that any attempt to return her to her cot will be futile, I'm tempted just to stay in this ridiculous chair all night and go to sleep dreaming about Gene, even if I do wake up with a dead arm and a crick in my neck that would have me looking permanently to the left. However, The Book, which, let's face it, is the nearest thing I have to maternal advice, says you can't totally abandon your normal life to cater to your baby's every whim (*lie*), so as my normal life is lying in the dark staring at the ceiling waiting for Fergus's next snore, I should try to return to the bedroom.

I hold my breath, rise silently from the chair, tip myself and Ella precariously over the cot rails and lower her on to the mattress, feeling the ever increasing threat of a recurrence of my birth-related back injury shoot down my spine. Ella screws up her face and whimpers a little, but then her fist uncurls and her breathing becomes even again. I look at her for a moment, feeling that peculiarly new emotion, that overpowering helpless love that was born the day she was; but then I do tend to love her *even* more when she's asleep. Crossing my fingers I leap over the nursery threshold with the grace and light footfall of a ballerina. No creaks greet my bare feet as I land. I stand for a second more and listen for movement from the cot. When I hear none I think 'Oh good, she's still asleep,' and 'Oh God, I hope she's still breathing,' at the same time. I resist the urge to make the dangerous return journey to double-check and breathe out a barely audible sigh of relief.

Ella's wail crescendos like a siren call into the night and even though I can't see him I just know that Fergus is turning his back on the bedroom door and stuffing his head under the pillow.

'Okay, darling, I'm coming,' I say wearily.

Ella and I settle back into the stupid chair and I put her on the breast in direct contravention of the rules given by The Book on page 142 (*NEVER use the breast to comfort or quiet your child*). As her sobs subside into snuffles, Gene Kelly and the other one, the one that might be Princess Leah's mum, start to tell me they've danced the whole night through. Good for them.

Not so long ago the only reason I'd have been up all night would have been the pharmaceutical speed that Dora somehow acquired through some dodgy contact or other. We'd be dancing all night in some club, and then we'd get breakfast in a dingy café on the way home, and then we'd go for a walk down by the River Lee and the ducks would make us paranoid. Even more recently I'd be up all night with Fergus, talking and kissing and making love, yes, really doing it that way, the by-the-book romantic way. Now we're lucky if we get five minutes before breakfast and even then I'm fairly sure it's got more to do with his morning hard-on than me. It's just, what's the word . . . perfunctory.

When did all this happen? When did I start on the path that brought me here, hollow-eyed and missing in action? Or rather missing myself in the middle of the action.

Let me think . . . I'd known Fergus for two months before he asked me to marry him, another three months before the wedding and then, well, Camille forced me to take the pregnancy test the week after we got back from honeymoon and by then I was almost eight weeks gone. Another seven months and a bit for Ella to appear on the scene and she is now six and a bit months old. It has taken me something like eighteen months to come to this.

Under two years to go from city girl to nursing.mother, dyed-in-the-wool single chick to married and frumpy. It took me ten seconds to fall in love with Fergus but has taken me eighteen months, a marriage certificate, a mortgage and a baby to reach the first clear-minded thought since the moment I met him.

I don't really know who he is.

I know he's not an international crime baron, or a spy, I know he doesn't have a secret and glamorous life. I know he's an IT consultant in the City. I know he's got an Irish grandmother on his father's side which he sees as justification to describe himself as a Celt and occasionally adopt a faux Irish accent that used to drive me mad when we first met and still does but in an entirely different way. What I mean is, what I think must have happened is that shortly before Ella was born the storm blew itself out of our whirlwind romance and left me dumped like my old friend Dorothy in a strange land where I don't understand the language. The land of marriage, motherhood and my new home town of Berkhamsted. Smalltown Land. Smalltown Middle-Classville. Landrovertown. You get the picture.

Now Fergus.

I can remember very clearly, the way that women do, the night that I met Fergus. It had been raining like it is tonight, but different rain. Summer rain, light and cooling in the city. The sort of rain that might precede a thunderstorm. I remember every detail the way girls do remember everything about the day they meet their true love.

We'd finished work about an hour earlier, or at least I had – finishing on time in the human resources department of a major record label was difficult, especially with our borderline personality-disorder boss, but Camille made an art of working late, and not because she was dedicated to her work. Camille was still working on a spreadsheet she should have finished hours ago, a routine consequence of her endless office-hours phone calls to her mum, with whom she enjoyed the kind of mother–daughter intimacy that I had only daydreamed about. (*But Mum, do I need two eggs or three? Do I sift the flour? Mum, Mum, what do you think about invisible panty liners? The black ones?* That sort of thing.) Still, I consoled myself when jealousy crept up on me, if my mum were still alive there would be a good chance I wouldn't make it to parties on time, so there's always a bright side.

'Oh God, oh God, wait for me,' she'd cried as I blotted my lipstick and checked my evening outfit inch by square inch in my make-up mirror. I looked at the back of her head. She was never ready on time. Never in the five years I'd known her.

'Come on, Camille, if we don't leave soon all the celebs will be gone!' Maybe it wasn't fair to pick on Camille too much. If it hadn't been for her we'd never have got invites to this latest industry party. Camille knew everyone who counted and everyone who counted was in love with her. From executive producers to post-room boys, Camille had inside tabs on everyone and everything at Starbrite Records.

Which was great, because we only worked as assistants in the human resources department and our brushes with glamour would have been few and far between without her contacts.

17

There was no mystery to how she did it: her hundred-watt smile and 'it could be you' eyes swung it every time. Maybe if her fan club knew just how much she loved her boyfriend they wouldn't have put out quite so much with the freebies and VIP passes, but Camille had an ingenious way of never letting it come up.

'I know, I know, I've just got this one last set of figures to put in and then I'm . . .' She caught sight of one of her cornrow plaits over her shoulder. 'Hey, listen,' she said, changing her own subject with her usual continuity carefree aplomb, 'what do you reckon to me going blonde the next time I get a weave done?'

I shook my head at her and shoved her out of her chair. 'Budge over. I'll finish this and you get ready.'

She smiled at me gratefully, probably certain that my infamous impatience with tardiness of any kind would force my co-operation eventually and result in me finishing her work for her.

'Cheers, you're a doll, but really – blonde, maybe? Like her from Destiny's Child?'

I gave her a quick appraisal and tried to imagine her with blonde hair instead of the shiny black plaits that framed her oval face now. Camille was a beautiful girl, slim and sexy in a way that belied her couch potato loved-up weekends. She somehow emanated a bronze glow that made her dark skin faintly luminescent, powering the sparkle in her almond-shaped, amber-coloured eyes. I couldn't see how blonde extensions could improve on that.

'Maybe something different from plaits, but not blonde. Stick to the natural look, babe,' I'd said. 'It suits you.'

'Natural-ish look. One day my own hair will grow long enough to do something with . . .' she said wistfully, and applied the lipgloss that was the only cosmetic she wore, or needed to wear.

Dora had been with us that night; she'd been waiting in the foyer with her dark glasses on and her mac pulled conspicuously around her body like protective armour. Other departing Starbrite Records people raised eyebrows in her direction as they left, probably wondering if she was one of the over-the-hill (over twenty-one) hopefuls that occasionally hung out in the lobby desperate to give an impromptu concert to a passing executive, receptionist, cleaner – whatever. I just put it down to her eccentricity, the same attitude to life that had made her dye her eyebrows blue when we were fifteen and that had made her dye her naturally honey-blonde hair black two weeks before that night.

Things had happened to Dora when she was a child, things that meant she ended up in care, things which made her and me the weirdest two kids at school and instant soulmates, protecting each other from the jibes of the lacy-topped socks girls and their permed perfection. We told only each other about the things that had happened to us, and because of that I understood her perfectly. I never questioned her latest tangent in lifestyle, because that was the kind of person Dora was: a ship sailing close to the wind but always coming back safe to the port of our friendship after every near miss.

All my life I have half pretended that I'm a very intuitive soul, but I don't remember knowing that by that time Dora was already caught deep in addiction. I think it was partly because it was never like I'd seen it in films, dramatic, horrifying and didactic. She looked well, she held everything together okay, and she earned good money, so I suppose she didn't need to go robbing old ladies to support her habit, not when heroin was only twenty quid a pop. Can you imagine? I always thought it was so much more expensive than that. Anyway, I tell myself that the change in her was so gradual as to make it almost imperceptible. Honestly, though, there is also the fact that I was too busy waiting to be in love to notice at first. We all drank a lot and we all dabbled sometimes, looking for something else to temporarily occupy that empty space we imagined was allocated for the contentment a relationship would bring.

Then, after Fergus, I was too busy *being* in love to notice, putting my heart and soul into living the dream I had dreamt about so often. After almost thirty years of waiting for my lightning bolt to strike, the delight of romantic electrocution made me miss all the signs of her addiction, largely because I simply didn't see her quite so much and when I did I was being part of a couple, a kind of benevolent sister letting her indulge in her latest range of oddness. I simply didn't know about it until she was admitted to hospital. And I feel bad for that. I let Dora down.

Dora was always odd, had been from the first time I'd hung out with her at lunch break at Hackney Downs Primary School and she'd pierced her own ears with a safety pin, a cork and a bottle of TCP, the scent of which was still discernible about her person for the rest of the week. Not *so* weird – teenagers do go a bit mad, you might think – but we were only seven. So Dora in shades and a mac on a summer's evening wasn't an unusual thing. To let myself off the hook, maybe I wouldn't have noticed even if I had been on the ball, all present and correct.

'Worried you'll be spotted by the Feds?' I asked as we exited the lift into the lobby. 'Or maybe the Mafia is after you again?' She peered at me over the rim of her cat's-eyes glasses and pushed her dyed black fringe out of her eyes.

'You may laugh, but some of us were born to be arrested.' We did laugh, and Dora strode out into the damp evening air with us, where the last remnants of the summer's day we'd missed, pinned behind hermetically sealed double glazing, sizzled on the pavements.

This launch wasn't your usual kind of affair held in whichever was the latest hippest club or music venue. It was to celebrate the sudden, surprise commercial success of one of our singer-songwriters, a guy called Simon Shaw who had been languishing unheard and unplayed almost since he'd been signed and until he was almost due to be dropped. And then some anglophile indie fan in LA had chosen one of his tracks to feature in the latest teen flick and he had become an overnight Stateside success, prompting the instant renewal of his contract and the swift re-release of his back catalogue. Camille had told us that Nick Cavell, the boss of us all and God to many a teenage hopeful, had told her that he expected the fuss to be over as soon as Shaw won an Ivor Novello award, so they wanted to make as much cash as possible right now. It seemed that Simon was unaware of the Machiavellian machinations that turned behind his back, though, as he believed fate had finally delivered him the break he deserved after years and years of paying his dues. Despite this he wanted to 'keep it real'. So the champagne, the discreetly provided coke, the party-compulsive celebrities, the godlike executives and the likes of us, the hangers-on, were all transferred to a warehouse conversion in the Docklands where an old school friend of Simon's, an aspiring artist, had managed to put together a show. Simon wanted to spread his good luck around.

It was an impressive space and the art was fairly impressive too: huge canvasses of compelling colour. The artist guy hung around them with his girlfriend, looking on nervously as a scantily clad soap actress eyed one painting, biting her thickly glossed lip and absent-mindedly adjusting her thong. Following our usual routine, the three of us made a beeline for the bar and collected as many free bottles of beer as we could carry before finding a niche that would afford the best view of the proceedings at the top of a wrought-iron spiral staircase with a balcony that overlooked the sequined throng.

'What does this Simon Shaw geezer look like then?' Dora asked me as she shed her mac to reveal a very revealing red lace-trimmed dress, the sort of affair you'd see going for £9.99 at Walthamstow market. 'I might want to sleep with him. I've recently realised I've never shagged a famous person.' Dora had never yet been turned down by anyone she had taken a fancy to; it was her instant display of her double-jointed contortions that usually swung it.

'He's sort of, well, blondey, mousey, blue-eyesy kind of average, really,' Camille said. 'He's terribly nice, though. We had a lovely chat in the lift the other day.'

Dora and I exchanged an 'it figures' look, or at least I think we did; she still had her shades on.

'Well, I'm off to shag someone fitting that description. I'll see you chicks later.' And she headed off into the crowd, leaving me to reflect that the time we spent together at parties and clubs before she went off on her own private missions had dwindled down to almost nothing.

'Look!' Camille squealed, 'is that David Beckham?' I peered at the back of a curiously shaved blond head in a white suit and gave it the benefit of the doubt.

'Yes, I reckon it is – which means Posh must be around here somewhere . . .' We avidly scanned the crowd for a hint of Dolce & Gabbana.

As the evening wore on and the bubbles in the bottled French beer gradually seeped into my bloodstream, I wandered with Camille from clique to clique, riding on the coattails of her instant acceptance and meeting and talking and flirting and somehow waiting for *something*.

It was just after midnight when it happened; it was 12.02 to be precise. I'd been standing apart from a crowd on the raised balcony just under the curves of the wrought-iron spiral staircase as it continued up to some of kind of loft space, waiting for either Dora or Camille, whoever turned up first. I'd been looking at the city lights flicker across the river. It was the evening before the longest day and the last streaks of a fabulous sunset still lingered just behind the skyline, waiting for the onset of night to finally extinguish the heat of the day.

For a moment I forgot the quiet roar of the crowd and myself and my endless wait as I watched the shadows wash over the dark river water.

'All right?' I span on my heel and looked at a tall man who was returning my gaze with the kind of enquiring curiosity that might have been considered impolite. Did I look drunk? I was about to open my mouth to assure him that I *was* all right when his jaw dropped and his eyes widened. I looked over my shoulder but there was no one there.

'Oh . . .' he said with a half-smile, as if he'd been expecting someone or something. 'Um, sorry, it's just that . . .'

I prepared myself for the 'Don't I know you from somewhere?' chat-up line, thinking that if he was going to trot it out it could have been much worse. In that first second all I noticed was his height and the breadth of his shoulders and the slope of his cheek. He had the kind of physical presence that makes you instantly flustered and teenagey.

'I beg your pardon?' I said, an uncertain smile hovering on my lips as I desperately composed myself in readiness for another game of flirtation. It's so strange, but in retrospect, in that moment, I thought I was facing my usual type. A predator, a smooth operator who would whisk me away for a night of empty passion with a bunch of pretty words I chose to believe until the next morning and a week of empty answerphones – like any one of my previous ten ex-boyfriends. The type that was wildly beguiling and exciting to begin but which invariably seemed to end up as uncommunicative, angry, mad or just plain cruel. I couldn't have been more wrong.

23

He paused, and then shook his head with self-conscious embarrassment, his initial composure lost in semi-shyness and uncertain charm.

'Sorry, what I mean is that you look like someone. Someone I've been waiting for . . .' He glanced over his shoulder at the glittering throng. 'It must be all these famous people, it makes you think you're seeing double all the time.' I wondered if I should feel offended or sorry for him. The poor man had obviously been stood up by some stupid cow who didn't know what was good for her.

'She didn't show then?' I said with an understanding smile. He blinked at me.

'Who? Kylie Minogue?' He turned and scanned the crowd. 'I know, I told Si she wouldn't.'

I laughed. 'No your date, the one you thought was me.'

He looked back at me with a quiet smile, as if enjoying his own private joke, and brushed off my query with a shrug. 'This girl just asked me when my next film was coming out and if she could have my autograph. I told her I work in IT solutions. I've never seen anyone disappear so quickly.' He bit his lip. 'Who do you reckon she thought I was? Not Brad, too blond – maybe Pierce?'

I smiled and shook my head.

'Mmm, maybe from behind . . .'

We both laughed then, the way two people new to each other do. A little louder, a little more carefully delighted than usual, just testing each other.

'I know what you mean, though.' I took a step nearer to him. 'I work for the record company that threw this bash. Usually when I say that, people start singing or rapping or tap-dancing or all three, and then they find out I do admin in the HR department and can't be bothered any more.'

We grinned at each other stupidly and I remember that I

glanced around briefly, as I always did when I met someone, looking for celestial signs. I think I might have seen a shooting star or perhaps it was the blinking lights of a plane heading for City Airport – one or the other – but either way I took it to be a good omen.

'I'm crap at social functions,' he told me cheerfully, running his fingers through his longish black hair. 'Rubbish at meeting people. It's because all I do all day is spout technical crap that actually means nothing at boardrooms full of people who pretend they know what I'm talking about until all of us are blue in the face and bored rigid. It's the kind of job that can seriously compromise your social skills. I only came to this party 'cos I used to go to school with Mr Humphries over there . . .' He gestured vaguely at the crowd.

'I beg your pardon?' I said, trying to see who he meant, and thinking that his social skills seemed fine to me.

'Oh, Si I mean. Simon Shaw. We always used to call him Mr Humphries. We all thought he must be gay, what with his guitar playing and poetry society. I went to an all-boys school,' he said as if by way of explanation.

I laughed. 'Well I hope he's not gay, for my mate Dora's sake,' I said. I took a step closer to him, and his gaze was so intense, the moment so inexplicably loaded, that I froze under it like a rabbit caught in headlights. It was then, in that short second, that I noticed the improbable blue of his eyes.

'Um,' he said, stiffly polite, clearly as taken aback as I was. 'So, you work at Si's record label then. Cool. Do you get to go to all the do's?'

I shook my head cautiously. That was the second reason many people wanted to know me, free access to celebrity bashes.

'No, I wouldn't if it wasn't for my colleague, Camille. She knows everyone.'

His eyes lit up with recognition. 'Oh, Camille! Lovely girl.'

I was not surprised.

'Are you a friend of her too, then?' I asked him. If he was he couldn't be single. Camille would have had me sitting across a dinner table from him long before now.

'No, not a friend exactly, I met her outside the loos, we had a chat about how hot it was and she told me to come up here, said it was a bit cooler, with a beautiful view.' He looked momentarily hesitant and then, with an almost imperceptible shrug, he looked me in the eyes and said, 'She was right, about the view I mean.'

I smiled then, and tried not to laugh, but he caught my look and grinned to himself.

'Too much?' he asked.

I half shrugged and shook my head. My new friend squirmed and I could tell that chat-up lines weren't really his thing. I remember I liked that about him.

'I'm sorry, I haven't introduced myself, have I? All those years of private education wasted. Mum'd be tearing her hair out if she could see me now.'

He held his hand out to me. 'I'm Fergus, Fergus Kelly. Yes, dad Irish, but I've lived in England all my life.'

I took his hand, amused by his pre-emptive strike against the routine of small talk. 'Kitty,' I said. It was the nickname my mum had given me as a little girl and I had clung on to it long after she had gone, until somehow it had seeped out of the school yard and on to my graduation certificate, my CV and my phone bill.

'Kitty, short for what?' he asked. No one had asked me that in years.

'Katherine,' I said, feeling kind of slighted.

'Mmmm, I like Kitty better – it suits you.' He let go of my fingers with a touch of reluctance and an awkward silence interrupted what was already a halting conversation. Even in the

26

dim lighting I noticed his cheeks colour slightly as he cast around for something, anything, to say.

'Well, it's good to know your name. There's nothing worse than waking up with someone the next morning and realising you don't know their name.'

I stared at him and the smile froze on his face, transforming into the perfect expression of horror.

'Oh God, did I say that out loud? Jesus.' For a second he regarded his feet in disgust. 'You know that you're . . . really nice looking. I mean, you look like a nice person. I mean, you're pretty too, not just nice as a person because I don't know you as a person, but you look nice. Really . . . nice.' He paused and swallowed hard. 'Look, what happened is this. Have you ever done that thing when you start thinking of something to keep up a conversation with this really pretty girl you've just met and this really stupid crass line from a copy of *101 Chat Lines* that your mate keeps in the loo pops up and you *immediately* dismiss it but it's there just waiting for you to open your mouth so you can fuck the whole thing up? That's what happened, honestly. I mean, I'm not a pig. I was only going to say I thought you looked nice in that dress, but then the whole evil tongue thing . . .' He ran out of steam and I couldn't help but smile at his embarrassment. 'But don't worry, I really don't expect you to sleep with me or even talk to me from now on. Ever again, actually.' He shook his head in frustration and I began to laugh.

'Security?' he shouted, waving his arms theatrically. 'Can someone remove me from this woman's presence immediately?' A number of fashionable people glanced up at him for the brief moment they could spare from themselves and then ignored him. 'I told you I was no good at chat-up lines.' His smile disarmed me and my heart sort of melted, right there.

He didn't leave. He held his ground, his cheeks flushed and hot.

'Do you want me to go?' he asked, touchingly hopeful. I shook my head.

'No, no. I don't think so . . .' I smiled again and together we turned our backs on the party and walked over to the plate-glass window that looked out on to the city.

'Kitty, look at those stars. Can you remember the last time you saw a cloud of stars like that over London? It must be something to do with light refracting off the edge of the earth, don't you think?'

I glanced at his profile, marvelling at how quickly he became at ease again and watching his boyhood shadow re-emerge in a moment of childlike fascination.

'Yeah, that's exactly what I thought,' I said happily, and for a moment we both tipped back our chins to bathe our faces in the light-filled cosmos; the party, the glass, the city lights all seemed far, far away. After a few moments my heartbeat, which had soared after his almost inappropriate declaration, slowed to a manageable rate and I felt comfortable.

He turned, taking my hand, and looked into my eyes.

'Do you want to talk about music and film and all that malarkey?' he said mildly. 'Because I'm pretty sure I can't get to the end of that without telling you my favourite film is *Deep Throat* or that my all-time classic book is *Confessions of a Driving Instructor*.'

I laughed and I shook my head. 'I don't think we'd better risk it right now, not while I'm quite liking you.'

We watched each other intently for a moment.

'Good call,' he said. He took the beer bottle from my hand and set it on the floor. 'Kitty, you've guessed by now that I'm not terribly good at talking to incredibly beautiful women, so I'm just going to tell you that for the last five minutes I've been dying to kiss you. If you slap me now I'll take that as a no.' He looked as nervous as I felt, but he didn't wait for my assent. We

28

both knew that I didn't need to speak any more, my consent formed in the gradually diminishing space between us. His hand snaked around my waist and pressed firmly against the small of my back, bending me to his kiss, and another shooting star soared above us. I was lost and found all at once.

'Bloody hell, Kitty, you've pulled a shag!' Dora exclaimed loudly in my ear and we broke apart, both glowing from the kiss. I felt as if the last fragments of that sunset had entered me to escape the onset of the night. I shone with it.

'So have I pulled a shag,' Dora stated proudly. 'It's singer-songwriter Simon Shaw.' I looked at the fuzzy blondish man who stood next to her and determined that she had indeed pulled the man of the moment, but that his album cover photo had been seriously digitally remastered.

'Well done, Dors,' I said, knowing that she'd want me to override good manners with praise for her quarry, although Simon Shaw seemed pleased to be admired in this way. I got the feeling that sexual admiration had been thin on the ground for him before he got famous.

'Well done yourself, Kitty. Not bad.' Dora gave Fergus the once-over.

'Fergus, mate,' Simon Shaw said, holding out a hand to Fergus. 'Glad you could make it. I saw you a while back, but that publicity bird kept wheeling me around to all these showbiz types.' He looked guiltily pleased with himself.

'No worries, Si. I've been talking to the love of my life here.' Fergus said it lightly, but as he picked up my hand again I felt a lightning bolt lighten my head and turn every passing plane into a shooting star; how many more signs did I need?

'Fergus and I went to school together,' Simon told a patently uninterested Dora. 'I wanted all my old mates here tonight, not to show off or nothing. You know, keeping it real.' Before we could reply, Dora pulled him off into the crowd and I guessed that I wouldn't see her again that night. To be honest I was glad to have at least one friend discharged from my responsibility.

'Kitty, will you come with me for some coffee? I know this great café.' Fergus said, suddenly irrepressibly excited.

'Um, well, okay,' I said. It wasn't that I wasn't sure if I wanted to spend more time with him, it's just that after his recent Freudian slip I hadn't expected him to actually want actual coffee.

'I was right, I did recognise you. I *knew* it was you,' he said to himself as he led me down the steps.

'Oh yes, it definitely is me.' I answered quietly.

And that was how we met.

Chapter Two

The shooting pain down my left arm and the pins and needles fizzing in my fingers combined with the dead weight on my chest confirm that I am having a heart attack. Some small part of me feels quite relieved, for although I'll be doing most of my parenting from heaven at least I'll get some sleep and maybe my mum'll be able to give me some tips.

Suddenly the weight is lifted from my chest and the life-giving scent of coffee is wafted under my nose. I open my eyes and try to dismiss a vague sense of disappointment that I'm still alive. I see Fergus with Ella slung casually over one shoulder snoring happily and the 'World's Best Mum' mug he bought me steaming in the other hand.

'Morning, Mrs Kelly,' he says, with an indulgent grin. I resist the urge to look over my shoulder for my mother-in-law. 'You're mad, you are. Why didn't you come back to bed once she'd gone off?'

I want to speak but my mouth is stuck together and someone has laid bricks on my eyelids.

'You know . . . Ninja thing,' I say, making reference to our private joke about her light sleeping. I reach for the coffee and creak out of the chair, which gives a companionable creak in return as it rocks gently backwards. Stupid bloody chair.

'I must do something about that chair . . .' Fergus mumbles to himself as he transfers Ella to her cot with one fluid carefree movement, eliciting not even the slightest stir from her prone form.

'Burn it?' I suggest, and I stretch my aching back and scowl at him. 'How do you do that?' I ask him, frustrated, once again, that he has the edge over me on this parenthood business.

'It's because she can pick up your stress, babe. Try and relax,' he tells me helpfully. I'll give him try and relax. I push a tangle of greasy hair out of my eyes and pad out of the room, shaking my fingers back to life. Fergus follows me and slips his arm around my waist. I tense, instantly.

'Why don't we go back to bed now, sweetheart?' *Back* to bed? I think. 'I've got another ten minutes before I have to leave for work . . . Just enough time for a stress relieving quickie . . .'

I sigh hard and push his hands away.

'Fergus,' I whisper as loudly as I can, '*if* I do get into bed and *if* that little angel in there doesn't activate her extrasensory perception and decide that now is the moment that she simply *must* have a nappy change or a feed or twenty-two renditions of "Somewhere over the Rainbow", or the "Waggle the Elmer the Elephant rattle" game, or the "Watch me roll over" game, or the "I want to refuse food for thirty minutes and then cry because I'm hungry" game, or, or, or *something* . . .' I take a deep, wide-eyed breath . . . *if* she doesn't do any of that and I make it into bed, I can assure you the very last thing I'll be doing is partaking in a "quickie" with you!' The very thought of it makes me contract what's left of my pelvic floor muscles in horror.

'Okay, darling, okay. I'm sorry.' I know that he is mortified by offending me so and that the last thing he wants is to upset me. He draws me to him for a hug but my body is still rigid with tiredness and tension, and no matter how much I want to respond I just can't. It's almost as if each one of my nerve endings has been insulated, and trying to get my body to react to him in the way it used to is like wading through some thick and glutinous liquid. It's hard for Fergus, I know; it used to be our thing, sex. It used to be my thing, a kind of awareness in every part of me, but since Ella it has been resolutely dormant. It's not something you know you have until it's gone.

Fergus brushes my hair away from my forehead as if he doesn't notice that it's thick with grease and baby sick.

'It's just that I fancy you so much and, you know, we don't get to do it much these days, do we?'

I sigh, remembering the feeling of intimacy between us and lean into him a little, inhaling the sharp citrus scent of his aftershave.

'You smell nice,' I say. 'Are you having an affair with a thin woman with no stretch marks?' I look up at him, half joking but half not.

'No, I'm having an affair with this ravishingly beautiful woman who has a few lovely stretch marks and an arse that drives me wild. She happens to be my wife.' He kisses the top of my head and I follow him down the stairs, glad that we have somehow made up without ever quite falling out.

'Isn't it today that you're off to see the girls?' he says.

My stomach knots. I'd forgotten. I'd arranged this lunch ages ago with Camille during one of her weekly, hour-long, work hours London news bulletins. I'd let her persuade me that I needed a life outside the house and that it'd do me good to have a break from the baby for a while. It was Camille's idea – a sixth-month celebration of Dora's sobriety, and Dora had taken the plan to her heart. Although I couldn't face clubbing with the anti-drug, health food zealot that Dora had become by necessity since her last bout in rehab, I had let them both talk me into making a visit to town for lunch. Georgina was primed to watch over her granddaughter, although the builder could have done a better job, and now Fergus was handing me fifty pounds.

'Is that enough?' he says. 'Better have another twenty.'

I sigh, trying to remember when my own money had run out and I had become entirely dependent on Fergus. Sometime soon after I told Starbrite Records I wasn't going back to work, I guess. It's not that I'd especially noticed my pay cheque going into my account every month as most of it evaporated before the end of that working day; it was just that now my account languished redundantly in the black (courtesy of Fergus) I sort of missed my weekly angst-ridden, breath-holding trips to the cashpoint.

I take the money and tuck it into my pyjama pocket wondering, as I follow Fergus down the stairs, if I could accidentally drop it in the washing machine and not have to go out at all.

'Now, when Crawley gets here, tell him he's to sort out that bloody bathroom today or he's sacked,' he says, referring to the builder he's employed to turn this Victorian terrace from an old-lady's time capsule into a decent living space.

To say that I was rather shocked the day he drove me here and presented me with the keys is something of an understatement. It was about two weeks after I knew I was pregnant. We were newlyweds and I still expected every day from that day forward to be like every day before then: perfect.

'A proper home for the lad,' Fergus had said, nodding at my tummy. 'Can't bring a baby up in a Docklands flat, and I thought Berkhamsted, why not? I grew up here. Loved it, fresh air and only a short commute.'

I'd looked at the crumbling red brick, the overgrown garden and the varieties of peeling wallpaper and burst into inconsolable tears. I hadn't been pregnant long enough then to know that inconsolable tears were pretty much par for the course. Fergus had shepherded me into the entrance hall, his arm around my shoulder, and let me weep into his coat until finally I could catch my breath again.

'It smells of pee,' my voiced wobbled as I looked up at the dusty ceilings.

'Darling.' Fergus spoke into my hair. 'Don't worry. We'll get builders in, we'll make it wonderful, we'll triple our capital in no time. You know, you'd never get a place like this for this money in Berkhamsted unless it needed a little bit of work done on it and it's near my mum's, which'll be great for you when the baby's here. And think of all the space for the lad to play footy in. After a good airing you won't even notice the pee.' As Fergus ushered me from room to room detailing each one of his already extensive plans for the place I tried to see myself, to see Fergus and the barely imagined baby there and I just couldn't. I felt that I didn't belong there; it was too big, too old, too far away from everything I knew, and I knew I would hate it.

'It's just not me, Fergus,' I said, turning to face him.

'I know what you mean, but think about it. *You're* not you any more, are you? Not the you that lived in pokey old flats and slaved away from nine to five. You're free of that, Kitty. You're my wife now and you'll be a mum soon. Think of how good it'll be for the baby.'

I looked through the dirty kitchen window down the hundred-foot garden and spotted what I thought were some apple trees and maybe some rose bushes deep amongst the thicket of weeds and thistle. A sudden flash of memory took me back to the small patch of flowers my nan had let me grow on her allotment; I used to go there with her every Saturday during the summer when I was seven, the summer after my mum died. I'd weed and water them and smell them and pick some to take to Mum's grave. Geraniums I think they were. That was the summer just before Nan died. After that there was just Dad. It might be nice to have a garden . . . I'd looked up at Fergus, his sweet face set with the absolute certainty that he was right.

'Look, Fergus, it's a nice idea,' I'd said. 'And I can see the house would be lovely with a bit of work, but I won't know anyone here, will I? And, well, no offence, but your mum gives the impression that touching a baby would bring her out in hives. I think I'd rather be in your, our, flat. With Camille nearby and Dora and the places that I know. And anyway, when I go back to work it'll be much easier if I can drop the baby off at a nursery nearby rather than miles and miles away. I don't think six-month-olds should commute too far, do you?'

I'd smiled up at him and had been greeted with an oblique look of anxiety.

'Fergus . . . What is it?' By that time I'd learnt exactly what that look meant. 'What have you done?'

Fergus had smiled resolutely and put his arm around me.

'It's just that I thought, I was so sure you'd fall in love with it when you saw it and places round here go, literally, in hours . . . and look at it, Kitty. A garden for the baby, not just a concrete balcony, a real family home with space for more kids one day, and anyhow if my work keeps going the way it is you won't have to worry about going back to work. Just look at it, don't you feel that this is exactly the right place for us?'

I'd stared around at a kitchen totally devoid of any plumbing and wondered if Fergus really knew me at all.

'No, Fergus, for you maybe, but not for me. Big house, renovation – that's not me, I'm not your Carole Smillie type. I like our flat – it's bright, it's small and there's a contract cleaner.'

Fergus's face had fallen and I'd sighed. He was so full of determination to be exactly the right kind of husband, and I had only half-baked daydream ideas of what it meant to be the perfect wife. I'd attempted a compromise.

'Well, maybe . . . I *would* like a garden to work on, I guess. A place I could make my own. Maybe in a few months when I've had a chance to think about it we could look for somewhere similar. Let's go home and talk about it . . .'

Fergus had given me that lopsided grin, which I have since come to understand means that he doesn't take me seriously.

'The thing is,' he'd said sweetly, 'that I've made an offer and got the mortgage in place.' He held my shoulder and kissed me hard and fast. 'All I have to do is tell the solicitor to go ahead and exchange. Tell me I can make that call, because I know this will be the best thing for us, I just *know* it.'

I'd stared at him, the shadows of the house looming over my shoulder.

'But Fergus, you've bought a house . . . a *house*, without asking me?'

'No, I wasn't going to buy it if you really *hated* it. I just wanted to get the whole scary and stressful bit out of the way first. Listen, I don't want you to worry about a single thing, okay? Not ever again, not when you have me to look after you. Come on, Kitty, take a chance! What do you say?'

I couldn't say anything; it was all I could do to stay on my feet as I felt the earth reel from under me.

'I just . . .' I'd stuttered, and turned on my heel and headed for the front door, desperate for fresh air, desperate to get out from under those three floors of crumbling brick. 'I just don't believe you, Fergus. You can't do things like that, you can't.'

I'd stumbled as I'd rushed out of the front door and Fergus had caught me, putting his hands on my shoulders to steady me. As we had looked at each other for a moment it had felt as if we were strangers seeing each other for the first time.

'Kitty, please. I'm sorry. I thought . . . I thought I was being all dashing and romantic. I thought you wanted the perfect family life for your baby, the life you never had. This isn't what

I'd planned at all . . .' He'd given a wry smile. 'I thought you'd be weeping in my arms with joy by now.'

I'd taken a deep breath and waited for the nameless panic to subside. Everything he had said sounded rational, logical, and if there was one thing I knew about him it was that he loved me and I loved him. I'd told myself it was just change I was afraid of and if anyone's life needed change it was mine. I'd told myself marriage was about trust and giving. Above our heads the oppressively grey sky had lightened a little to let the sun break through its cover in strong assertive slants.

'Maybe it's a sign,' I'd thought. 'Maybe it's meant to be, and if I know one thing for certain it is that Fergus *is* my fate and we *are* meant to be.' I'd studied Fergus's face and seen how much he wanted this and realised how much I wanted him to have it.

'Okay.' I'd taken another long look at the façade of the house. 'Tell your solicitor to go ahead.' I'd felt curiously relieved for a while, and for the long months after that that it took to complete I managed to almost forget about it. After all, that's what it's all about, isn't it? Having your protector, your knight in shining armour to look after you. Fergus was all I'd dreamt of since as long as I could remember, and I was sure I'd love the house eventually.

Except we've been here for the best part of a year now and I still feel like a stranger here.

Fergus bundles me back up the stairs to bed, planting a firm kiss on the top of my head before bounding down the stairs and off to work. It still makes me smile a little, the way that having a wife and baby at home makes him feel so much happier to slog out his existence in the City, although I never imagined how much he'd be out of this house he wanted so badly. The way things are at the moment, he's more of a guest than a resident.

I listen to the quiet creaks and breaths of the house without him and feel its emptiness. Today I know that in a few minutes Mr Crawley and Tim will be here and the house will be filled with noise and activity again, but soon, soon there will be just Ella and me in these long days without Fergus. What will it be like then, I wonder?

I don't sleep. I lie under the duvet with my eyes tight shut letting the fizzle of exhaustion creep across my temples, listening for the faint sounds of Ella's breathing on the monitor and waiting for the inevitable entrance of Mr Crawley and his cohort. They have a key, so when they do arrive I won't necessarily have to get up, but Ella seems to be in love with Mr Crawley and I have found that whilst she is mesmerised by watching him work I can usually get four, sometimes even five, spoonfuls of fruit purée into her before she flings up her hands, arches her back and starts to growl. I can only call it growling. I've looked it up in The Book but I can't seem to find it listed in the index, not under growling, aggressive animal noises or even experimentation with vocalisation. It's just growling.

I look at the clock – 8.30 – and close my eyes.

I'm not sure how long has passed before Ella's siren wail crowbars me awake, but I'm up and in her room before I've even opened my eyes. The cow jumping over the moon tells me its 8.32. As soon as she sees me she stops crying abruptly and breaks into a cheery grin, stretching her arms out in anticipation of being picked up.

'Hello, pickle,' I tell her. 'Sleep well, did you? Because Mummy didn't . . .'

She very helpfully holds her feet up for me as I change her nappy, examining her toes with the clinical interest she exhibits for every new-found object about her person. Bored with her toes she proceeds to cheerfully pick one baby wipe after the other out of the pack, delicately dropping it to the floor like a lady who expects her hanky to be returned to her by some dashing young man.

Below I hear the door slam and then Mr Crawley runs through the itinerary for the day with his apprentice. Ella suspends her actions in rapt attention at his voice before releasing her limbs in a carefree expression of joy, firing off a machine-gun round of baby laughter.

'Wagawa!' she says happily.

'Wagawa,' I agree with her, wondering if babies really ever do say 'Agoo' like it says in The Book and if they do, why doesn't Ella and *why* does she growl?

The continuous background hum that is the absence where my mum should be amplifies for a moment and I actively wish she were here to ask. Fergus's mum is not quite the same, particularly as I have serious doubts that she is human, let alone maternal in any way. In fact if it wasn't for Fergus's marked lack of any superpowers I'd say he had been dropped to earth in a meteorite and that she'd taken him in against her better judgement. Apart from anything else, how did Fergus's dad ever get her to do anything as patently unhygienic as have sex with him? I mean, Daniel's a sexy man, you just have to look at him to see it. Georgina looks liked she'd need a sterile environment and ten square metres of clingfilm to get it on.

I remember that Fergus told me about supervising Mr Crawley and quickly dress and take Ella downstairs.

Ella screams with joy at the sight of Mr Crawley and I hold back a scream as I watch young Timothy, Mr Crawley's nephew or something, spread plaster dust across my kitchen.

'Mr Crawley! This area is where I sterilise Ella's stuff, you know, and feed her! I'm fairly certain her nutritional needs don't include bits of brick!'

Mr Crawley appears from behind a worktop and looks at me down his aquiline nose, lifting an aristocratic chin.

'I'm terribly sorry, Mrs Kelly. Timothy, clear that mess up at once and get upstairs and prep the bathroom.'

'I'm terribly sorry, Mrs Kelly,' Tim repeats in quiet tones, and picks up one of my dishcloths to address the mess. I smile and console myself with the thought of having a working bath and shower again and not having to wash myself inch by square inch in the tiny bathroom sink. Having made a half-decent job of clearing away his mess, Tim scuttles upstairs and I pour Mr Crawley a cup of coffee as Ella sits in her high chair and gazes at him with an adoration that would have Fergus spitting feathers if he knew.

Mr Crawley is unlike any builder I have ever met or seen or thought of as possibly existing. He's posh. He's very posh and terribly well spoken, as is young Timothy, who's bordering on about eighteen and who I imagine won his role on the team by being expelled from the same local boys' school that Fergus attended with Simon Shaw. For example, Mr Crawley has brie and grape sandwiches for lunch, and it is because of him that I had to unpack Fergus's London flat coffee maker as he always refuses instant and had preferred instead to bring his own flask of Columbian coffee until I bought some in especially for him. He and Tim have fifteen-minute breaks twice a day, and at lunchtime (which is never longer than an hour and often shorter) they discuss the news in *The Times* or *play chess*. When I'm trying to make sense of it all I imagine that Mr Crawley once headed up an immense corporation and one day decided that the pressures of high finance just weren't for him and packed it all in to become a builder. Or he was a Nobel award-winning novelist with insurmountable writer's block or that maybe being a builder just pays better than either of those options. But one thing I do know: you'd only ever find a posh builder in Berkhamsted.

Whatever the reason, he is a nice man. Fergus, who hardly

ever sees him, can't believe this and routinely inspects his work looking for signs of shoddiness, and fully expects to be ripped off. I have no such worries; in fact the only thing I worry about is the day Mr Crawley packs up his belongings and moves out for good. How will I get Ella to take solids then? Besides, I'll miss him.

I take Ella, sticky-mouthed and triumphant at her latest conquest over the dreaded spoon, into the living room to breastfeed her. I enjoy the weight of her in my arms and settle back into the sofa and listen to the noises of the house. The morning seems springlike and it reminds me of something. Oddly it takes me a while to search the memory out.

The year that Brian Harvey, the stereotypical builder, came to fix our roof.

I was six then and we lived on this estate on Stamford Hill, a big block of post-war flats. Not a high-rise but a maze of long buildings connected by communal balconies and no more than four or five storeys high. Yes, it was five I think, but anyway, we lived on the top storey and the roof leaked.

Dad had been on to the council to get it fixed for weeks and weeks but that was the seventies and nothing much happened very fast then, so one day he came in and told my mum he'd met this bloke down the pub who said he'd do it for a good price.

'I don't know, Don,' my mum had said. 'We should just wait for the council, shouldn't we?'

It was a wet spring and it seemed to me that it rained constantly; pots and pans were positioned all around the flat but the worst of it was in my room. I used to like the tympanic symphony that played for me as I went to sleep, but Mum worried about my chest.

'If we wait for them, we'll be waiting until the cows come home and anyway this little one deserves a quiet night's sleep in her own bed without fear of drowning!' He picked me up as he said it and swung me under his arm. 'Hey, little pickle? What do you think?' And I laughed the same tinny machine-gun laugh that Ella does now.

We settled into his telly chair in time for *Doctor Who*.

'I think we should get it fixed, Dad,' I'd said, rubbing the palm of my hand along his stubble.

'There you go then. Kitty thinks we should get this bloke to look at it. Don't worry, love, it'll be fine.'

My mum had regarded us both from the doorway and smiled, shaking her head.

'Well, I can't argue with both of you, can I?' she'd said, and then she'd gone into the kitchen to make chips. I remember her peeling and cutting potatoes. Who actually makes chips any more?

The morning Brian was due to arrive I'd heard Dad getting ready to leave; it was still dark outside. He always left early, before six, to get to the bus depot where he worked as a mechanic. I used to imagine he was like Cliff Richard at the beginning of *Summer Holiday*. All singing and quiffs. I'd heard the murmur of Dad's voice talking to Mum before he left and I'd closed my eyes and feigned sleep as he crept into my room and brushed a kiss against my forehead.

'Love you, pickle,' he'd whispered and finally I'd heard the latch on the door click to. I'd waited for a few seconds and then run into my mother's room, leaping on to the bed.

'Kitty! Good God, child, you're like a herd of elephants!' she'd said like she always did. I'd giggled as she'd pulled me under the covers to tickle me.

'It's early, darling,' she'd said, winding her arms around me and curling me into the curve of her body. 'Come on, let's go back to sleep.' I'd tucked my chin over the edge of the quilt and looked for faces in the turquoise peacock-patterned wallpaper, waiting until her breathing became even again. Then, once I'd known she was asleep, I'd turned around ever so quietly and watched her sleep like I did every morning. I'm glad I had that time to watch her in those days, because now I remember every little detail of her face: the soft brown wave of her hair, her wide and inviting eyebrows and the long gentle curve of her mouth.

Later that morning the builder had arrived, and if I had to put a finger on it, pinpoint a specific moment, I'd say that that was the day that she had begun to die.

Chapter Three

'Right, off you go then,' Georgina says, eyeing up my ensemble of loose shirt and jeans as if I am wearing a red latex number and thigh boots. It's not my fault that she's the only grandmother in the world who pitches up for babysitting with her suspiciously still-red hair neatly coiffed and a figure-hugging top over a slim-fitting pair of suede trousers. It's not fair, it's anti the laws of the universe – I should be the glamorous one, not sodding Boadicea here. Someone should do something. I drag my attention away from her Cuban-heeled boots and zone back to whatever it is she's talking about.

'Break'll do you good,' she finishes, whatever it was, and cleaves Ella from my arms, beginning to rock her in exactly the way she doesn't like to be rocked. 'We'll sort you out, won't we poppet, we'll teach you how to have a nap when Grandma says so.'

Ella looks exactly how I feel, and I search for any half-decent reason why I can't go out.

'Um, I've decided, we have, Fergus and I, that we aren't doing that leaving them to cry thing. We don't think its very kind?' I say, anxiously picturing my little Titan howling her lungs out for hours whilst her grandma has a fag in the back garden. She'll go all red and her face will be wet with tears and she won't understand why I haven't come home.

45

'So I'd prefer it if you didn't, you know, just leave her.'

Georgina sighs about as theatrically as a person can sigh. 'In my day . . .' she begins, but just at that moment Mr Crawley enters the room and Ella launches herself at him with the assurance and desperation of a trapeze artist escaping from a dragon.

'I just wanted to say the kitchen is spic and span now, Mrs Kelly. I got Timothy to give the fridge a bit of a wipe out while he was there.' He nods at the elder Mrs Kelly, who presses her lips together.

'Thanks, Mr Crawley, that's really good of you,' I say. 'Tim doesn't want a job as a cleaner, does he?' I laugh half-heartedly.

Georgina has already offered me the services of her cleaner, and my refusal to take her on has caused some kind of offence. Now she edges past Mr Crawley and makes her way to inspect the kitchen, calling out behind her, 'Have you made up the bottles, then? I can't be bothered with all that nonsense.'

'Yes!' I lie. In fact I have defrosted breastmilk, but as she is disapproving of breastfeeding at all it seems simpler to lie and pretend it's formula.

I look anxiously at Mr Crawley and he leans a little closer to me and whispers, 'Don't worry, Mrs Kelly, I won't let your little pickle cry on her own.' I am so grateful that he is going to be here that I almost cry myself. He takes my hand and pats it. 'And I've got a funny feeling that we've got *just* enough work on to mean that we shan't be leaving until just after you get back. Now remember, you are going out to have some fun, there's nothing to worry about here.'

I nod and repeat his words over and over in my head until I've collected my keys, kissed and hugged Ella until she squirms angrily for release and finally shut the door on Georgina singing, 'And WHEN the bow BREAKS the BABY will FALL.' I can picture Ella wincing.

*

When I get to the train station ticket office I have five minutes to spare, my carefully applied first-time-out make-up is halfway down my face, the heat is pulsating from my cheeks and sweat prickles my forehead.

'London!' I pant at the ticket office man, sounding maybe more desperate than I need to.

'Travel card, madam? Single or return?' I stare at him wondering who he's talking to and then remember that I am a madam, and not the glamorous sort that goes to work in lingerie but the sort that is middle-aged and frumpy. I look at the clock; another minute ticks by. 'Come on, come on, Kitty,' I think to myself. 'You know this stuff, you've lived in London nearly thirty years.'

'Um?' I look at him hopelessly.

'Travel card,' he tells me with kind authority, and I thrust one of Fergus's notes at him hoping it will be enough, scooping up the change and the ticket and racing on to the platform just in time to make the foot-high leap on to the train before the doors close and it pulls out of the station.

I find a window seat and breathe, grateful that this off-peak train is almost empty except for some tracksuit-bottomed lads who are making their daily pilgrimage to Hemel Hempstead, Mecca of the terminally highlighted, in order to walk up and down the high street all day.

As the last remnants of Berkhamsted slide out of view I feel a moment's panic about leaving Ella and force myself not to phone and see how she is, because I know that if I hear crying then I'll be pulling the emergency cord and jogging across country to get back to her, and then Dora and Camille really will think I've gone insane. I sit back and let the rocking of the train calm my nerves. I'm shocked and a little guilty to find that once the train gathers speed I am excited; excited to be going home once again, to a place big enough that no one knows me, where I could feasibly head off down some turning and never come back again if I felt like it. Of course I'd never do that, but just to know I could is somehow freeing. I like the idea of belonging to no one, even if the reality of it scares me half to death. No, lunch with Dora and Camille is all the excitement I need right now, maybe more than, in fact.

The thought of lunching with the ladies reminds me of my recently forgotten and now radically dishevelled personal appearance. In fact, since Ella I've been so involved in her that I've even forgotten I've got one.

A quick inspection in my make-up mirror reveals facial mayhem, but I manage to fix it up pretty good with one of Ella's baby wipes and I reapply as much mascara as I am able to between the rhythmic judders of the carriage. I brush my sweat-damp hair out and briefly toy with the idea of tucking my loose shirt in. I might have risked it, but when your two best friends are both a size ten there's really not much point in kidding yourself. I sigh and anxiously wish that at some point in the last few months I had broken my rule about not shopping for new clothes until I'm thin again, and gone and bought something to wear that isn't so last millennium, especially as all the signs suggest that I may *never* be as thin as I once was again and I wasn't even thin when I was thin. Oh God, I don't know what I'm talking about either.

But I do know that I'll have to show up to lunch with two of the capital's most stylish (if in Dora's case a little *avant garde*) occupants looking like the Michelin man in a voluminous red (*red!*) silk shirt that Fergus's mother bought me after the birth. ('Nice and roomy, dear.') I run my fingers through my hair and tell myself that my friends won't care what I look like, even though I know that even the best of girlfriends are always ever so slightly chuffed at outdoing their mates on the clothes front.

Gradually the green-grey rush of the countryside loses out against the crowded graveyards and trackside factories that precede the grimy and ragged lace edge of the city as it unfurls its skirts in greeting. I press my face against the glass, waiting for the sign that says 'Euston 1 Mile', and resist the urge to kiss the glass as I finally come home again with a rush of relief. This is it, this is where I will feel like myself again. Where I can be me.

Camille has offered to meet me at the station, and although I know everywhere north of the river like the back of my hand I've accepted her offer, grateful for her tactful acknowledgement of my general lack of practice with the world and, more importantly, other adults that aren't my husband. I tap my foot impatiently as the train crawls the last few metres of the journey into the platform and wait at the door pressing the 'Open' button beside it long before the train finally comes to a halt. When I step off the train the last lingering fragments of any apprehension I had are sucked out of me by the vacuum of London air, thick with the carbon monoxide I have missed so badly.

I practically run to the ticket gate. I would run, but as my body is now in a permanent state of exhaustion, a speedy and ungainly hobble is all that I can manage, pressing my forearm over my chest in an ill-fated attempt to stop my breasts wobbling and the catch on my nursing bra from coming undone. I feel it click open and I am forced to stick my hand inside my shirt and do it up as I walk along, looking as if I am giving myself a good fondle.

Good as her word, Camille stands just beyond the ticket barrier dressed in a long jade-green shift dress, wearing a pair of low-heeled mules with silk flowers at the toes. As I take in her outfit, followed by her new weave, which is short, flicky and foxy, I begin to slow down. Even on my best shirt Ella has left a shadow of regurgitated milk and my sandals are thick black flat ones with a Velcro fastening that has curled up at the end. My jeans bite into my waist and my hair hasn't been styled since the day I got married. I feel like Cinderella covered in ashes, only *after* the ever after bit.

Camille spots me and furiously waves both arms. I marshal my smile and go to her, trying to remember that in real life I'm a happy and confident person, the hub of our little family trio.

'Babe! Babe!' she shouts eagerly and I find my practice smile melting into an expression of genuine pleasure.

'Oh my God!' she yells, flinging her arms around me. 'You look fantastic! Are you sure you had a baby?'

I laugh and hold her tight.

'You are very sweet,' I say. 'But you are lying, I look like a dog. *You* on the other hand look amazing. Look at your hair!' I turn her this way and that as she flutters her lashes for me and flicks her flicky bits. 'My God, Alex must think he's died and gone to heaven!'

Camille bites her lip and looks a bit sheepish.

'Well, there's a bit of a story there. Come on, I'll tell you all about it when we get to the restaurant.'

Twenty minutes later we're sitting at the open-fronted door of Cava, a little Spanish place in the City, near to where Dora works and not far from Fergus's offices. I wonder about going to see him later and surprising him and I have to force myself not to picture him taking his secretary over the desk in between memos.

Dora is late. Camille checks her watch and anxiously searches the passing crowd of super-thin straight-haired girls in tiny-waisted skirts, looking for our friend.

'Don't worry, Cam, I'll spot her no trouble in this lot. She'll be the one in the latex rubber catsuit,' I grin, looking forward to seeing Dora's latest incarnation.

Camille raises an eyebrow.

'I think you'll be more shocked by her latest transformation than any of the previous ones,' she says half to herself as she scans the crowd. 'I offered to call for her, but she said no, she had to finish some stuff up before she left for lunch. I do trust her, you know that I do, but it's just that, well, Dora pretty much defines flaky, doesn't she? Who ever knows what Dora will do?'

I nod. Neither of us wants to talk about her when she isn't there, but both of us are thinking the same thing.

I was just going into labour when Dora was going into intensive care. Although I knew nothing about it until a couple of days later, it seems that Dora was on the brink of exiting this world for ever just as Ella entered it, but Dora was lucky.

It seems wrong to think of her as lucky, but in reality it was Dora's ready access to the cash that got her into this trouble that saved her. If she had been your average addict mugging people for mobile phones or prostituting herself, the chances are she would have been dead or dying before she got into a rehabilitation programme. At least she had enough credit on her gold card to allow Camille to book her into a private unit called the Abbey, and the sheer trauma of the experience was mildly alleviated by a fleeting friendship with a model and soap actor. She was there for twelve weeks. In the last few months since she'd come back into the world I'd seen her only once, when she came to see Ella for the first time. Her blonde roots had shown an inch thick through her black hair dye and her natural slimness was painfully accentuated. Despite that, though, she'd seemed happy, and we had talked for the first time in months the way we used to. Dora and me against the world. It was Dora who taught me how to fight the inevitability of fate, and I was grateful and glad to see that once again she was engaged in that fight too.

She had held Ella at arm's length and eyed her speculatively.

'I can see why *you* love her and everything,' she'd said, slowly. 'But I've got to tell you, mate, I just don't see it myself.'

We'd both laughed but I really don't think she was joking.

I look at Camille's concerned face and think how my two separate best friends have gradually become closer to each other than I am to either of them. Once I was the hub on which our friendship turned. Now I feel more like a spare wheel. I don't know if Dora has ever told Camille about her childhood in care, but I do know that Camille knows more about Dora right now than I do, and that makes me feel guilty.

'But she's all right now, going to the meetings and all,' I say, partly to reassure myself. 'Told me she got asked out by some really old crusty guy and she totally binned him and it was only when she got home that she realised he was a really famous sixties rock star!'

I laugh, keen to show that I am still a part of Dora's life. She does call me every week, but in reality our conversations are short and restless. There is really pretty much nothing that we have in common any more, except for the fact that we've loved each other for such a long time and need each other the way everyone in the world needs somewhere to come from and somewhere to go back to.

'Oh yeah, I heard about that.' Camille takes her eyes off the passing crowds to look at me. 'I think she's all right, but we thought she was all right before we knew anything, didn't we? I mean, when I was a kid you knew if your best mate was hooked on smack. They had spots and really greasy hair and they acted like Zammo off of *Grange Hill*. No one tells you that they can appear, well . . . normal, more or less. I want to trust her, I need to, I think. She hasn't got anyone else to show they have faith in her.' I look studiously at my cutlery before Camille adds, 'Well, except you, of course.'

Suddenly something in the crowd catches her eye.

'There she is!' Camille waves wildly, half standing in her chair. I scan the crowd looking for Dora, but her transformation is so complete that she is practically standing in front of me before I see her.

I stare at her. The black-haired bob and cut-price chic have vanished. The Dora that has approached our table has totally reinverted herself into, well, herself. Her natural blonde hair has been cut into a spiky cap, which suits her pointed chin and big green eyes. Her normally ash-white skin is slightly tanned and she is wearing a City-chic summer trouser suit that shows off her long legs.

'Bloody hell, do I know you?' I smile with delight, hugging her close, feeling her thinness sharply against the padding of my curves.

'Mate!' Dora holds me away from her and studies me. 'You look good, glowing and everything. Lost a bit of that extra weight since I saw you last . . . still got those enormous breasts, mind you. Blimey, how do you get out of doorways?'

We laugh and sit down, still holding hands. I look from Camille to Dora and feel at home.

'Oooh, let's order wine,' I say happily. 'I'm such a cheap date these days that I'll be pissed after half a glass . . .' I look up from the wine menu to see both Camille's and Dora's smiles fixed on their faces.

'What?' I ask them. They exchange glances. 'What?' I repeat. Dora screws up her mouth.

'Booze, mate, not allowed booze,' she says with a half-smile. 'It's the programme I'm on. I'm not allowed *any* addictive substances except fags and caffeine.' Dora lights up as she says this and I cringe at my own thoughtlessness. Dora shrugs. 'It's cool, I'm so detoxed that I reckon my liver's gone into shock.' She reaches into her bag and pulls out her packet of Marlboro's. 'Mind you, I fully expect to croak it from lung cancer any time soon.'

I smile uncertainly and Camille catches my eye encouragingly.

'Well, then – it's not as if I'm not used to being teetotal either.' I look up at the waiter who has appeared at our table. 'Two large bottles of mineral water, please.' I look at Dora. 'Are you allowed sparkling or are all those bubbles evil or something?'

Dora laughs and the tension passes.

'No, go for it.' She smiles at the waiter and studies his arse as he retreats. 'Anyway, enough about me; how's Prince Charming? How's the baby? Tell us about your new life in the *count*-ry.' Dora enjoys exaggerating the first syllable of the word. She leans back in her chair and takes a deep drag on her cigarette.

I think about my new life. I get up, I look after Ella, at some point during the twenty-four hours in each day I must sleep otherwise I'd be dead by now. That's it. I look at them, waiting expectantly, and wonder exactly how much they'd really care about Ella's attempts at crawling, or that her hair is gradually beginning to curl or that when I sing to her she seems to hum along, if a little bit tunelessly. I know that really it won't mean a thing to them, and I know that it's not because they are heartless or that they don't care. It's just that since Ella's birth I've been living in a parallel universe, like a piece from a different jigsaw puzzle that just happens to fit into their world too. If you look at the big picture as far as Dora and Camille are concerned, I don't make any sense any more. I smile and wave the minutiae of my life away in a single gesture.

'It's great. Fergus is great. Ella is great. Everything is great really. It's great. I'm tired, but, you know . . . it's great.' I shrug and cast about for a change of subject. 'Camille – tell me about your hair! You said there was a story?'

Camille claps her hand over her mouth and laughs. 'Oh my God . . .'

Ten minutes later Dora and I exchange disbelieving but unsurprised glances.

'You're joking,' I say. 'You're mad. I know how much you earn and you are mad.'

'Yeah, but I didn't think it'd cost that much.' Camille shrugs. 'I mean, I didn't check how much it would cost but you know how you have an idea of cost in your head? I thought it'd be about eighty quid, max.' She raises her hands with a 'what can you do?' gesture.

'So, let me get this straight.' Dora lights a new cigarette from an old one and then vigorously puts out the stub. 'You told Alex that you were having this weave and that it would cost thirty quid, even though in your little world you'd decided it was going to cost you eighty quid, which you still can't afford anyway. You go to the salon, not any salon mind, but one on the King's Road. You go there without bothering to check the price first and then when you go to leave they charge you one hundred and sixty-five pounds. That's *one hundred and sixty-five pounds*!, and you have to have it done again in six weeks?' She downs the remnants of her water like she once would have a straight whisky. 'I tell you, you should come to NA with me, mate. I'm sure we can get you in on the grounds that you're addicted to spending money you don't have.'

Camille picks up her glass and gives a little shrug.

'Well now, it would have been all right, I mean, not all right but okay, except that when I went to pay neither of my cards went through, both maxed out.' Camille giggles. 'So I phoned my mum but she told me if I couldn't pay for it I had to sit right back down and have it taken out. Well obviously that wasn't an option, and by now everyone's looking at me and I'm trying my best not to die of embarrassment. So, in the end I had no choice. I had to phone Alex, pull him out of a meeting, explain the situation to him and get him to pay over the phone! Nightmare.'

I laugh. Camille's cheerfully fatalistic telling displays exactly what kind of a nightmare she thought it was, a fluffy sort of nightmare that actually qualifies as a dream. A dream boyfriend, that is.

'How much does that man love you? If you were my girlfriend I'd have sacked you years ago!' I tell her, banging my palm down on the table.

Camille smiles ruefully.

'Well, he was pretty fed up, but you know us. Nothing keeps us mad at each other for long. I think it's because he's away a lot, it keeps it fresh . . .' She diverts her gaze to the middle distance, gently touching her hair. 'We sure made up good and proper that night. I tell you, *this* was worth every penny . . .'

Dora and I exchange glances and silently mouth 'yuck' to each other.

'I bet you hide shopping from him too, don't you? And then bring it out a couple of weeks later and say you've had it ages,' I say mischievously.

Camille is unrepentant. 'Yeah, of course I do! Don't you?' She looks from me to Dora.

'No fucker to hide it from,' Dora shrugs, happily lighting up another cigarette with the embers of the last one. 'And anyway, it's my money, I earn it, I'll spend it on what I like as long as I don't have to go to a bloke in Dalston to get it and it isn't gonna kill me.'

Camille and I smile uneasily. It has always been Dora's policy to joke about her problems and sometimes, like now, I feel it's designed more to make other people squirm than to make herself feel better.

'What about you, Kits? Now you're a lady of leisure, do you have to account for every penny to Prince Charming?'

I laugh it off, squirming from the truth.

'No, don't be mad. We share things. I mean, I'm not earning at the moment but I will be soon, when Ella's a bit bigger maybe . . . Fergus and I have agreed,' I lie. In fact we have disagreed about it heartily for the last six months. I want to work, not because I want to escape my baby but because I need to; it's part of me. I've always had to look after myself before; a virtual orphan as a child, I dragged myself up.

And that's the problem. Fergus is obsessed by his mission to make sure that for the first time in my life I don't have to worry about anything at all. When we first got together it sounded like a dream come true. In fact, the more protective he became the more vulnerable I let myself be. But now I find that I miss getting out there and making a contribution to my world that I can see in hard cash.

Fergus is certain that I'm trying to put a brave face on it and that really I just want to be looked after. And I do, but I want to look after him too. We haven't had a stand-up row about it, it's just that every time I bring it up, he puts his arms around me, kisses me on the top of my head and tells me everything's fine, and it is. But what I don't think he sees, what I don't think he realises, is that I feel as if I'm fading from the world, gradually becoming invisible as what used to be me seeps into other people lives.

As much as I love being with Ella, there will be a time when I need to detach myself from the background hum of our lives and be visible in the world as myself again, as an individual, and I'm fairly sure it doesn't mean I'm a bad mother or a selfish person. I just need to be a person, an occasional individual person, and Fergus can't see that – not yet.

I find myself nodding like one of those dogs in the back of a car and I force my neck to a standstill. 'It's cool. I don't feel like the little woman or anything,' I say out loud. 'You know Fergus: the world's sweetest bloke.'

'Yeah,' Camille agrees. 'And the world's fittest bloke. I tell you, I'd let Alex support me any day of the week.' Her eyes sparkle as she says it.

'You already do!' Dora says and we all laugh. Camille glows, and not for the first time in my life I wonder how she stays as much in the first flush of love as if she and Alex had met only yesterday.

'Dors!'

All three of us turn our heads sharply as two other women enter the room. I squirm uncomfortably in my chair. It's one thing to feel big and frumpy with your two best mates, it's another thing entirely when unknown thin people arrive on the scene. They don't know that I too used to be thin and that I've recently had a baby. They'll think that I've always been fat! I suck in my stomach, although it makes no impression, hidden as it is under the voluminous shirt, and I can feel the solid folds that were left behind after Ella's eviction.

'Oh, all right!' Dora raises her cigarette in greeting and turns back to me, lowering her voice. 'That's Alice and Karina. Really her name's Karen but she's moved to Ladbroke Grove and gone all West London. Alice is a trustafarian, spent all of Daddy's cash on cocaine. He's cut off her allowance and now she has to model to pay her rent, poor cow.'

Dora's smile is paper-thin. 'Karina is a PR exec, vodka. Her enlightened company forced her to attend NA after she threw up on the CEO's desk during a board meeting. Personally I think they're both lightweights, but knowing them helps me keep sight of the big picture.' Dora's smile widens as her new friends approach the table.

'Ladies, how are we?' she says with a rarely seen charm she reserves only for people she doesn't like much. I smile at them nervously. Alice looks like she's been San-Tropezed from head to foot, her skin a tawny gold and her hair streaked with blonde. Karina's perfectly straight brown hair falls exactly to her shoulder-line and grazes the tops of her rounded shoulders. Why don't they look like shit? I've been off any kind of toxic substance, including peanut butter, for over a year and I look like shit. Where's the justice?

'And this is Kits.'

Dora introduces me and I haul myself back into the moment. I sit back in my chair certain that surely I, the married one with the baby and the lovely home, should have the moral high ground over three ex-addicts – four if you include Camille's kamikaze flirtation with credit – but for some reason I feel as if these walking wounded have left me standing out in the cold, excluded from their fascinating complex of 'issues'.

'Oh my God,' Karina says matter-of-factly as she slips into a chair. 'I saw Julian last night and . . . we finally did it!'

I blink as Dora screams enthusiastically and reaches across the table to hug Karina's modest shoulders with one arm, extending her lit cigarette over the ashtray with the other. Even Camille seems to know what they're talking about.

'Soooo?' Dora plonks back into her chair. 'How was it?'

'Please,' Alice rolls her eyes. 'Don't encourage her. I've heard every single detail on the tube along with half of London . . .'

Karina grins smugly.

'Put it this way, I haven't felt this sore since my first session of advanced yoga.' She points her cigarette at her feet and then back to her face. 'These toes were behind these ears only last night!' The explosion of laughter washes over me and retreats without sweeping me up in its exuberance.

I brush my hair off my shoulder and lean forward into the conversation.

'So you've got stubble rash where you can't see, have you?'

Karina smiles fleetingly in my direction and rushes on as if I'm not there. As I listen to her exploits, to Dora's sweetly sarcastic commentary and Camille's enthusiastic giggles, I feel jealous, far away and jealous. This used to be me. I used to be Karina, the one who rushed in with the tales of terrible boyfriends and stupid sex. I used to be the person who had my friends in fits of hysteria as I told them about my latest conquest. I used to be the one constantly fluttering like a butterfly, excited and flushed by the promise and the hope of new love. At last Fergus had fulfilled that promise and had ended once and for all that constant edginess, that eternal waiting – yet somehow I miss it. Somehow I thought I could come back up to London and, abracadabra!, I'd still be the same person I was before Fergus and Ella. Somehow, I thought that everything that had changed in my life wouldn't matter any more, not to the real me, not to my closest friends. But it does. In a flash of understanding, I realise I'm not me any more. I'm not me in my big house and posh kitchen in Berkhamsted, and I'm not even me in a London café with my best friends. I'm not me any more. Karina is, and she's not even very good at it.

'Are we ordering food?' I say clumsily over the conversation so that I look rude and, what's more, greedy. The waiter has returned to our table about eight times since Alice and Karina have arrived but so far has been unable to get a word in.

'Oh, God. Food!' Karina giggles. 'I always forget food.'

Dora throws me a look, rolling her eyes, and says, 'Yes, Christ, I'm starving. Bring it on. Kits, what do you fancy?'

I've already decided on a spinach and ricotta lasagne, but before I can order, Alice, who has been trying not to stare at my breasts for the last few minutes, interrupts me.

'Um, Katie, is it? Sorry to butt in, it's just I think that . . . well, are you leaking?'

I stare at her for a beat and then down at my shirt. A dark wet flower has blossomed over my left breast and a companion patch is just coming into bud over my right. The waiter politely excuses himself once again and I close my eyes in shame. I had felt them begin to feel a little heavy, but I never imagined that this would happen. It was time for Ella's last feed about an hour

60

ago, but as I haven't been anywhere without her in six months I'd forgotten this could happen. I am soaked through and I have nothing to change into. I can feel the heat radiating from my face and I bite back tears.

'Oh God, I'm so sorry. Oh fuck. Look . . . Oh God, I'd better go . . .' I push my chair away from the table and stand up, for once yearning for the invisibility that usually stalks me.

'Don't be mad,' Dora says, catching my hand. 'Come on, I'll take you to the loo and we can stick your boobs under the dryer.'

She smiles encouragingly but I shake my head and the threatened tears begin to run down my cheeks.

'No, it'll just stain, I'd better go.'

Dora holds on to my hand, looking at me, silently asking me not to leave. I am acutely aware of Karina and Alice staring at me as if I am the fucked-up one.

'Please, Dora. I want to go,' I say in a low voice, and she releases my hand, unable to hide her disappointment.

Camille picks up her bag. 'I'll go with her,' she says to Dora.

'No!' I shout, making her jump and stare at me, her eyes wide with surprise. I lower my voice. 'No, I'll be fine. I can look after myself, okay. I'm fine. I just need to go. I'll call you both . . .'

Dora hugs me briefly, careful not to press her linen shirt against the wet silk of my top.

'I'm sorry,' I tell her.

'Okay.' Camille looks exasperated. 'I'll call you tonight, okay?' She kisses me quickly.

'Sorry, I'm sorry,' I repeat as I gather up my belongings. 'Just hormones and fatigue and all that. I'm fine. Really.' I race for the doorway.

Just as I reach the exit a burst of laughter sounds from the women I've left behind. I *know* they aren't laughing at me, but even so I feel like the little girl stuck in the middle of a circle of crowing children all those years ago after Mum was killed. Only this time Dora isn't here to beat them all up for me.

Chapter Four

I look at my surroundings and guess that I am about a five-minute walk from Fergus's office. I know that I could go home now, holding my bag across one breast and my hand over the other, and try to pretend it has all gone swimmingly, or I could call him and rely on him to make me feel better like he always does.

I fumble for my mobile phone, grateful that lunchtime is over and that the streets are largely deserted.

'Fergus Kelly, please,' I say, barely holding on to my composure. As I listen to the ring tone, I pray that it will be him who picks up and not his PA, Tiffany.

'Fergus Kelly?'

Thank God. 'It's me,' I manage to squeak.

'Kitty? What's up? Where are you? Has something happened?'

I gulp for air, angry with myself for wanting to cry but unable to stop it.

'Um, I'm on Appold Street and it's nothing really, but, well, I . . . I . . . can I come and see you just for a minute?' I clutch the phone like a last straw.

'Oh baby, course you can. You walk down to my offices and I'll come and meet you, all right?'

'All right,' I say, and five minutes later everything is all right again. Fergus puts his arms around me and rests his chin on my head before tipping my chin back and kissing me until I feel a slight and familiar movement in his trousers. I push him away, smiling, and raise an eyebrow.

'Are you pleased to see me, then?' I manage to joke, even if I am slightly aggravated that even when I am patently in such a state the only thing he can think about is sex.

'I can't help it, darling, you always turn me on.' He takes my hand and begins walking slightly awkwardly, making me smile. 'Come on, tell me all about it.'

When we walk into his office a few minutes later I do feel better, but embarrassed.

'I can't believe I freaked out like that,' I say under my voice, nodding at the obliviously pert Tiffany who isn't the fluffy blonde her name suggests, rather a sleek brunette with razor-sharp hips. She returns my greeting with a studied lack of interest, and I can feel her eyes burrowing into my back as Fergus closes the door on us.

I swallow the jealous question that is sitting heavily on my tongue like a fat toad and press on with the conversation. 'I mean, you know, there are all these women and, except Camille, they're all fucked-up big time and yet they're all poised and perfect and there I am red as a beetroot with sodding breast milk all down my front.'

I catch Fergus grinning at me.

'It's not funny!' I say, smiling. But he shakes his head, and runs his fingers through his blue-black hair.

'Yeah, it is. And anyway, just imagine them licking the toilet floor in desperation 'cos they've dropped a couple of granules of coke. At least what you are going through is natural, and it will get better, and you have Ella and me. They have to deal with their problems all their life.'

I nod, sighing heavily.

'Mind you,' Fergus continues, 'you'll have a rebellious daughter on your hands pretty much for ever.'

I smile, thinking of Ella's latest assertion of independence, which involves happily kicking me in the chest every time I try to dress and change her.

'Yeah, you're right,' I say, with a smile. Suddenly an image of the new Dora pops into my head. 'She seems all right, though. Good, even,' I say out of context, but Fergus picks up my thread with his usual intuitive ease.

'Yeah, I thought so,' he says.

I look at him. 'Did you? When?'

He stares at me blankly for a moment and then his face clears.

'Oh yeah, didn't I tell you? I ran into her the other day – she's working round here, PA for some CEO, isn't it? I didn't recognise her at first, what with the hair and all.' He makes a vague gesture around his head and shrugs. 'She looks good.' He smiles and I fight down yet more irrational jealousy. I know that Fergus forgets his own head on a daily basis, let alone chance encounters with one of my friends. I know that there is no other reason why he wouldn't tell me about it, and probably Dora just thought it was too boring to mention too.

'Oh right,' I say flatly. 'Well, she does.' I pull myself together. If the delectable Tiffany isn't going to make me break my resolution not to test Fergus on his fidelity, then Dora certainly isn't.

I push back my shoulders. 'I'm sorry, you must be busy, I'll get off. Have you got any, you know, tissues or something?' I stare glumly at my shirt and hug my aching breasts.

'Don't worry about leaving. We're in a bit of a lull and I was planning on leaving early anyway.' Fergus goes to the hook on his door and brings out a clean shirt still in its dry-cleaning plastic. 'It's a bit quiet today and I want to spend a bit more time with my girls before it hots up again next week.' He hands me the shirt. 'Here, you can change into this.'

He opens the office door a crack.

'Tiff, the wife's just getting changed and then I'm off. Can you redirect all calls to the mobile? Cheers.'

He shuts the door and leans against it as I unbutton my shirt.

'There's always a bright side,' he says and I avoid his eye. 'A striptease from the missus.'

I drop my shirt on the back of his chair, conscious of my engorged breasts straining against the demure white lace of my nursing bra. Fergus's eyes are riveted.

'You are gorgeous,' he says with quiet concentration. I smile awkwardly and attempt to dissipate the tension in the room.

'This is soaked through too,' I say, feeling the material of my bra.

'Well, take it off for a bit then.' Fergus walks over to me, his eyes travelling the length of my body. Standing close to me he runs the back of his forefinger over the swell of one breast.

'Fergus!' I whisper, trying to appear scandalised instead of a nervous wreck. I let him reach behind and unhook my bra, lifting it off my shoulders and catching the weight of my breast in each hand. To stop this now would be too big a rejection.

I look at the door.

'Don't worry, no one will come in,' he says. 'God, they're so heavy.' He pushes me against his desk and sits on the chair putting his mouth to one nipple.

'Let me taste them,' he whispers before he suckles.

'Fergus I . . .' I'm certain that what he's doing isn't right, but before I can finish my sentence I am stopped by the juddering pleasure his attention gives me. He lifts his face away and smiles.

'You taste sweet,' he says, and he returns his attention to the other breast. Gradually his kisses travel up to my mouth and I feel him unbutton my trousers.

'Fergus!' I whisper a faint protest as I realise that he plans on going all the way.

'Sorry, darling, I can't stop now,' he mumbles and he pulls my knickers and jeans down to my knees and turns me to face the window. I briefly wonder if the rows of grey-tinted glass windows opposite can see in here before I feel him push his way into me. I am surprised, surprised that it doesn't hurt the way I expect it to and surprised that it feels so good, so good in fact that I quickly stop analysing the sensation of his movement and start to enjoy it. It's over quickly and afterwards both of us are sticky, hot and satisfied.

He holds me close in the curve of his body for a second and cradles my breast for a moment longer before turning me back to face him and kissing me deeply.

'My God, we need to do that more often,' he says, with heartfelt conviction. 'You are the sexiest woman on earth.'

I laugh and try to push him away. 'I know, I want to do it and everything it's just that I'm so tired and . . .'

Fergus presses his fingers to my lips. 'I'm not criticising you. I know that having a baby makes everything different. I know it and I wouldn't change it for the world. I'm just saying that making love to you as often as we used to is something I miss.' He drops a kiss on my forehead and reaches for a box of tissues from his desk, taking some and handing me the box.

We dress in silence, exchanging glances and smiles, giggling sometimes like a couple of kids. If I had known that this would happen up here I would never have come to his office, but I'm glad that it did happen and I am relieved that we have redis-covered the sense of intimacy that seemed to be lost before it could become old and comfortable.

Finally, when we are halfway presentable, Fergus puts his arm over my shoulder and kisses my temple.

'I love you, Kits. Our lives might have changed for ever and ever, but I'll always love you, no matter what. Don't forget that.'

I smile back at him as I remember how much I love him.

Sunlight streams in through the train window as we travel home and, as I close my eyes, the speeding shadows it casts through the track-side trees flicker and dance through my lids.

I lean my head on Fergus's shoulder and smile as I feel the warmth of his lips brush my forehead. This is what it was all about. This is why I married him, because he and only he has ever been able to banish the dark shadows and the bad dreams. Only Fergus has filled the spaces that I didn't even know were empty. One thing I've realised today is that I'm not that madcap Kitty that I used to be, and so what? After all, that Kitty spent most of her nights wishing she could be like me, wishing that her life could be turned inside out. And now it has and mostly it's wonderful – lonely sometimes and different and scary, but wonderful. I just have to try harder to make it work, that's all. I just have to try harder.

'*Berkhamsted*, this is *Berkhamsted*.'

The automated train announcement breaks me from my reverie. Knowing that we have only a few moments more before the chaos of our lives drives its invisible wedge between us again, I take his hand and kiss it.

'I love you so much,' I tell him. 'Spending time alone like this is just what we need. We should arrange for your mum to have Ella regularly. I'm sure she'd love it and, well, I'm sure Ella'd get used to her *eventually* . . .'

Fergus digs me in the ribs with his elbow before standing and hauling me to my feet.

'That's a great idea, I'm really glad you thought of it.'

As we emerge from the station into the warm evening air, for the first time in months I feel peaceful and I feel myself.

As we reach the front door, Fergus stops me and leans forward to kiss me one last time before we dive back into the mayhem of a partially renovated house and young baby. I am lifting my mouth to meet his when Ella's scream rips into the closing space between us and tears me out of Fergus's arms, hurtling me towards the locked door. Her cries reach a frantic crescendo as I fumble to fit the key into the lock.

'Kitty, calm down! She's probably just overtired or something.' Fergus takes the key from my trembling fingers and opens the door. I race into the living room and find a strange man taking my daughter's temperature, while Georgina and Mr Crawley look on.

'What's going on?' I demand, reaching for my daughter. Ella sees me and stretches her arms out to me, bucking to be free and literally screaming. I have never seen her so upset, her eyes so wide, her small face such a picture of fear and pain. I take her in my arms and she buries her hot and wet face into my neck, her whole body shaking with hiccupping sobs.

'Its okay, darling,' I say, clutching her, even though I have no idea if it really is. 'It's okay.' I look at Georgina, feeling furious with her already.

'What's happened?' I state the question with a cold anger that has risen suddenly through me to chill the warm evening air.

Georgina flicks her hair off her shoulder and visibly bristles.

'Well,' she points at Ella. 'She started screaming and wouldn't stop. I rocked her and so on,' she gestured, as if she was talking about trying to start a car. 'And then I noticed that she was very hot.' She stared at Mr Crawley. '*He* said to give her some paracetamol and see what happened but what I want to know is who *is* this man to be telling me to how to look after my own granddaughter and . . .' She turns to Fergus but I stop her in her tracks.

'What's *wrong* with her!' I cut across her and address the man I presume is a doctor, gastric flu, measles, meningitis and worse all galloping through my mind. This is my first baby – she only has to cough and I'm certain she's on the brink of death. I've never seen her like this before.

'Not too much, actually,' the doctor tells me, his voice deliberately calm. 'She's teething. It's very common for a baby to get a temperature at this stage, and in fact the dose of Calpol we gave her twenty minutes ago *has* done the trick.' He nods at Mr Crawley. 'Her temperature's come down and I think the worst thing wrong with her at the moment is that she's missed her mummy.' His tone is kind but I feel his absent criticism keenly.

I press my cheek to hers, rock her, until gradually her sobs quieten to intermittent shudders and gulps and she hangs on to two ropes of my hair, one in each fist, for dear life.

'Are you quite sure?' I quiz the doctor, thinking of the tales of misdiagnosis I've heard of.

'Yes, she's got no other symptoms, except sensitivity around the mouth and general clinginess. No rashes, nice soft tummy, no glands up. I have a feeling that her temperature will settle down now, but if not, give her another dose of paracetamol in four hours, and if she develops any other symptoms let me know and I'll come out immediately.'

He smiles to himself, an 'overprotective mother' smile, I'm sure, and begins to gather his belongings. I am torn between wanting to cry with gratitude, kill Fergus's mother and die of the overwhelming guilt I have felt since I took my baby back in my arms. I had forgotten her, she'd needed me and I hadn't been here. I hadn't even really missed her until the moment that I'd heard her cry. Fergus squeezes my shoulder and kisses the top of Ella's head.

'Poor little darling, aren't you?' He says to one of us or maybe both. 'Thanks for coming out, Doctor, I'll show you out.' He leads the doctor out into the hallway.

'Shhhh, shhhh, my baby,' I whisper to her. At last her

breathing has grown even and she watches Georgina with soulful wet eyes from the safe haven of my arms.

'Why didn't you call me?' I ask Georgina, incredulous. She looks uncomfortable and defiant.

'Because I didn't want to worry you. I wanted you to have a break. I suspected it was nothing to worry about,' she lies. 'Anyway, I thought you might have called in *here* or come home a bit earlier,' she tells me haughtily. I glare at her.

'To be fair, Mrs Kelly did suggest calling you but we both decided it would be a shame to spoil your day out,' Mr Crawley says awkwardly. 'And I had a feeling that really it was nothing.'

I smile, knowing how very unfair it is of me to be angry not with him but only with Georgina.

'I know you meant well, but she's my baby. I always want to know, even if there's nothing wrong. She's mine.'

I turn back to Georgina.

'I think you'd better go,' I say quietly. 'Ella needs some peace.' Fergus re-enters the room, a diplomatic smile already in place.

'Well, he seems like a nice chap, never had him before. He was saying, darling, that we should get her registered there permanently. I told him you'd be taking her for her jabs but . . .'

'Fergus, I was just telling your mum I thought she'd better go,' I say over his attempt to pretend there isn't an atmosphere as thick as soup in the room.

'But I . . .' She turns to her son. 'Fergus, I was only trying to help. I just wanted *her* to have a nice time. I did what I thought was best. If she *had* been ill the doctor was here, and I didn't see the point of worrying . . .'

Fergus puts his arm around her shoulders and guides her into the hallway.

'I know, I know . . .' he's saying, and I am furious at him for being so understanding. I sit in a chair and without thinking of

Mr Crawley's presence I reach under Fergus's shirt, unhook my bra and put Ella to my breast.

'I do think she was trying to be helpful,' Mr Crawley says at last. 'It's just that she's not very good at showing it, and she's a bit of a panicker. She wasn't to know that I've had four kids of my own and six grandchildren. She thinks I'm just the builder.'

As she suckles, Ella's hand releases my hair and grabs her own ear. It occurs to me that after all Mr Crawley really is just the builder, but for some reason I feel more comfortable with him than I do with my own mother-in-law.

'I know, I know. It's just that I'd have wanted to know. Now I feel like I've abandoned her, and worse, I feel like she feels like I abandoned her. The Book says that babies remember these things, you know . . . Mind you, The Book says it's okay to leave them screaming their heads off until they finally pass out in misery, so The Book's talking out of its arse, frankly.'

Mr Crawley smiles and crouches briefly by my chair.

'Of course you feel like that, that's how she's designed to make you feel. You're her mother.' He raises himself up, his knees creaking. 'Not as young as I used to be. Well, I'll be off now; I've a very nice bottle of wine chilling in the fridge and a date with Radio Three. Puccini night.'

I smile at him. 'You and Mrs Crawley settling in for a romantic night in, then?'

'Oh well, you could say that. Mrs Crawley died nine years ago. Breast cancer. But I always think of her when I hear that aria from *Madam Butterfly* . . .' He looks wistfully into space for a moment. 'But I keep myself busy, that's the main thing. Right then, I'll see you in the morning.' He shuts the door behind him and I can hear Fergus's voice as he questions him on the progress of the building work.

Ella is now peacefully asleep and as I watch her head lolls back a little and the tiniest smile transforms her face. The Book would say it was wind, but fuck The Book, from now on I'm going to ignore it.

I had never guessed that Mr Crawley was a widower. I have taken to confiding in him without a thought, but I have never once asked him about his own life. Since Ella, my own life, as small as it was, has expanded in my eyes until it has obliterated the whole of the world and everything in it. I've lost sight of everything but the way I've been feeling, or rather haven't been feeling.

'She is trying, you know,' Fergus says after closing the front door on Mr Crawley. He sits on the arm of the chair and strokes Ella's sweaty hair with the back of his finger. 'She finds it hard, she's a seventies mum. All this . . . you know, actually showing affection to your kids, it's a bit alien to her. But she does care.'

I avoid his eye, concentrating instead on Ella's sweetly rounded face, now relaxed into sleep, and I gently rise from the chair.

'Well, she might care, but there is no way I'm leaving my baby with her again. No way.' I take Ella up to her nursery leaving a silent and crestfallen Fergus behind.

Chapter Five

Mum and I are washing up. I'm standing on the little wooden stool Dad made for me with my hands in the warm soapy water, smoothing the bubbles up my arms, pretending it's bubble bath, or Imperial Leather like in the adverts. The sun bounces off the gleaming taps. Mum stands behind me, reaching round me for the plates and cups, rinsing them through and placing them on the draining board. Every now and then she plants a kiss on the top of my head and then she flicks a little puff of bubbles on to my nose. I giggle and splash water over my shoulder at her. We both laugh and I feel her hands lift me off the chair and begin to spin me around and around and around. At first the bubbles on my fingertips shimmer in the sunlight like snow, flying off as we gather momentum, like clouds now, like clouds and we're flying. Then all at once the sky becomes black and all the joy has turned to terror. The bubbles have gone and so has Mum and I'm just spinning, faster and faster, and I can't stop and there's something there waiting for me to stop. And it's blood now, blood flowing from my fingertips, and I can't find my mum and I shout, 'Mum!'

'Jesus, darling, Kitty?'

I blink in the darkness, feeling my own senses rushing back into reality. I'm breathless, my heart hammering in my chest, my face wet with tears.

'Oh Fergus!' I say with a whimper and I plunge into his embrace, burying my head in his chest, sobbing. After a while the darkness of the room recedes a little, lightened by the faintly orange glow of the streetlights and the night light in Ella's room.

I sit up, pushing my hair roughly back from my face.

'Sorry, I'm sorry. I'm all right now. Let's go back to sleep.'

Fergus pulls me down to lie beside him.

'Dream about your mum again?' he asks softly, taking my face in his hands as he wipes away real tears with the balls of his thumbs. I nod mutely and look into the soft shadows.

'Darling,' Fergus says quietly. 'What was it this time, do you think? Overtiredness?' He strokes my face with the back of his hand and kisses my neck. I know he is trying to be kind, but this isn't how I want kind to be.

'So, what was it, do you think?' he repeats, with an encouraging smile. 'Cheese?'

'No, Fergus, I don't think it was cheese.' I say quietly. I want to say, 'I think it's the traumatic circumstances of losing your mother when you're a very small girl, of finding your mother dying, not cheese, you insensitive idiot.' But I don't because it would hurt Fergus to think he is being any less than thoughtful, and because I know he's trying to make light of it all – he thinks he can chase away the shadows that way. So instead I tell him another reason, but it's still true.

'I think . . . I think it's because now I have Ella, now I have her and I love her so much, I know just how really awful it must have been for Mum to know . . . that she was going to leave me and that there wasn't a thing that could be done about it. Knowing – the knowing must have been the worst.' I turn my back on Fergus and he hugs me into the curve of his body, his arm resting lightly on my breasts.

'Maybe she didn't know so much,' he says gently, his fingers finding their way under my pyjamas. 'Maybe it was over too quickly for her to know.'

'No, she knew. She knew,' I say, for a moment picturing the end and then chasing the image out of my head as quickly as it has appeared. I feel Fergus's stubble graze the back of my neck, making me shudder.

'Well, don't think about it now,' he whispers. 'Let me help you feel better.'

I turn in his arms and smile against his cheek.

'I'm sorry, darling, I'm just so tired. I really need to go back to sleep, is that okay?' I can't hear him sigh but I know that he does. I turn away from him once again and close my eyes, concentrating on regulating my breathing, but it's a long time before I sleep.

Fergus has left without waking me, the spring sunlight is streaming through the curtains and Ella is not crying. Ella is *not* crying.

'Oh my God,' I say out loud. Dragging back the bedclothes I rush into her nursery. In the split second it takes for me to get there I picture her white and still. Picture her dead. She's not, of course, she's lying in her cot playing with her toes, and when she sees me she laughs. I pick her out of her cot and hug her close to me until she struggles to be free.

'I can't believe that you slept all night!' I tell her. 'It's over. The long months of sleepless torment are over. I can tell people my baby sleeps through the night!' I dance around the nursery making Ella shriek with laughter, hoping that the last uneasy remnants of last night will evaporate in the sun.

Determined to feel energised and optimistic, I decide that today I'm going to make a start on my garden. The sky is blue, the caprice of April is giving way to the sporadic warmth of May and I'm going to weed. After we'd moved in, and during the seemingly endless last months of my pregnancy, I had nothing to do but avoid tradesmen, eat too much and stare at the garden. I'd looked at the long, yellowed and weedy grass and the overgrown trees and I'd dreamt of a place for my baby and me. In the absence of any other purpose I'd imagined a long summer where I floated about in a white dress and planted a herb garden as my baby gurgled and giggled under the shade of a tree. Of course, since Ella has been born I've been too tired to even open the door to the back garden – the moment I put her down she screams like a banshee, and a *white* dress? With my hips, I don't think so; but I've clung on to the dream, and today is the first day I have the time and the energy to do anything about it. I get The Other Book, Alan's book, the one that I've been reading religiously, one laborious paragraph/fifteen-minute baby power nap at a time, and bound down the stairs. Then I bound back up again to get Ella's monitor and bound back down.

'Morning.' Mr Crawley walks in through the back door. 'How's that baby? Any more teething trouble?'

I smile at him, resisting the urge to hug him with joy.

'Not so far, and guess what?'

He lowers his chin and smiles at me.

'What?'

'She slept through the night!' I omit the fact that I didn't, and smile brightly. 'Maybe this is it, maybe she'll start to sleep though from now on and I'll never be tired again!' I whirl around, laughing. 'God, I sound like a sleep-deprived Scarlett O'Hara.'

Mr Crawley takes his smoked salmon baguette out of his bag and puts it in the fridge.

'Well, I'm pleased for you, but in my experience it's not usually so easy . . .'

I shrug off his experience and ignore it.

'Yeah, well, according to Scary Poppins, if I haven't got her

77

sleep-trained by three months she'll be holding up banks and walking the streets selling her body for drugs by the time she's eighteen, so frankly, who cares?' I open the miscellaneous stuff cupboard and take out my first ever piece of gardening equipment, my only piece of gardening equipment actually, but I'm sure they'll come in handy.

'Well, watch your fingers with those.' Mr Crawley raises one eyebrow as Tim joins us fifteen minutes later.

'Come along, young man, we've got a bathroom to grout today,' he says, his only admonishment a slightly hurt and let-down tone. Tim's cheeks pinken and he gives me an apologetic shrug as they disappear upstairs.

I have my pristine and unused long-armed shears in my hand when the front doorbell sounds. I'm not sure what I'm supposed to do with them, but I wholly resent the intrusion on what was to be my cathartic attack on the overgrown garden. I pause for a second and look longingly at the back door before I turn to answer it, sighing huffily as I go. When I open it a scruffy young man in green overalls greets me. It occurs to me that I am still a young woman too, technically at least, and I make a mental note never to refer to anyone the same age as me as 'young' ever again.

'Mrs Kelly?' he asks. He's Welsh.

'Yes?' He's obviously some kind of workman but I can't work out which kind. All of the relevant ones are in the house right now and we won't need a decorator for ages yet.

'Ah good, I'm Gareth Jerome, Jerome's Gorgeous Gardens?' He rolls the 'r' in gorgeous and looks as if he expects me to let him in.

'I'm sorry, am I expecting you?' I ask.

'Oh yes. Mr Kelly booked me a couple of months ago to start on your garden, we agreed I'd get going as soon as the weather picked up. There's a lot of clearing to do, is that right? Of course, I should have started planting months ago but it's not too late yet, you'll still have a really beautiful garden come the summer.' He smiles with obvious pleasure at the thought and I look him up and down and seethe. Damn bloody Fergus, he *promised* me that the garden would be all mine! I shake my head. The last thing I need is a cuckoo unbalancing my already precariously placed nest.

'Look Mr . . . Jerome? There's been a misunderstanding. We don't need a gardener. I'm doing the garden and . . .' The phone begins to ring and I know exactly who it is. And I would have anyway, even if there were more than one person in the whole world who ever phones me these days.

'Will you excuse me for one moment,' I tell him and go to pick it up.

'Well?' I ask in lieu of saying hello.

'Ah, he's arrived, I see. Thought he might do, what with it being sunny and all. You see, the thing is . . .' Fergus does his usual trick of riding roughshod over my evident anger and displeasure in the hope that his amiable charm will evaporate my mood. It infuriates me, and worse still it diminishes all of my concerns to nothing but girlish foolishness, as if nothing I think or feel is to be taken seriously.

'Fergus, you promised! Don't you remember the conversation? You said moving out of London would be the best thing for all of us and I said okay as long as I get the garden to myself? Remember? The garden is mine! I've got plans and everything!' I pick up my piece of grid paper that I have lovingly filled with my designs under the detailed instruction of Alan and wave it at the receiver as proof. Gareth Jerome shuffles his feet awkwardly on the doorstep and turns his back on me to gather his long reddish brown hair into a ponytail. I glare at him. I mean, who has long hair these days? Does he think it's the eighties?

'Darling.' Fergus's tone is conciliatory but not remotely

cowed. 'I know what we agreed, but I just thought there is so much crap out there – it's so overgrown and all that – I just thought that maybe he could help with the clearing of it all and leave you to do the fun bit. I mean, if you just start to clear in the few moments that Ella is asleep you'll never get anywhere will you? Will you? Look how long it's taken you to get to chapter three in your gardening book – nearly six months!'

I sulk silently for a few moments, belligerently resisting the logic of his argument.

'You could have discussed it with me,' I mumble.

'I meant to, but you know how busy I've been. Dad recommended him, sorted it out for me and then I meant to tell you, but something happened and it just went out of my head until the sun came out today and I suddenly thought, "Oh shit, I'm for the high jump."'

I smile but try to keep it out of my voice.

'Can we afford a gardener?' I feel it's my duty to mention cash, although it never seems to bother Fergus and since I quit my job I have had nothing to do with it.

'Yes, we can afford a gardener,' Fergus says deliberately.

I sigh and look at the lanky figure of Gareth Jerome. He doesn't look like he could prune a hedge let alone get through the jungle of overgrown thicket out the back. Maybe he's wiry.

'Okay, but when it's cleared he goes and I'm in charge, agreed?' I raise my voice for Gareth Jerome's benefit.

'Agreed. You know that I love you, don't you?'

The inevitable smile rushes into my voice, along with a brief reprise of that feeling that sometimes seems as distant in miles as Fergus is these days.

'Yes, I love you too. I'll see you later.'

He always manages to convince me out loud that he is right, even if my heart is convinced that he is wrong.

Goodbyes said, I return to Gareth Jerome. Of course I know

I shouldn't be suspicious of all Welsh people just because the last boyfriend I had before Fergus was Welsh and possibly the most low-life, double-dealing, two-timing, evil-minded, manipulating man I have ever met, but logic doesn't often come into it when you're dealing with an ex-hangover, and I remember once going out of my way home for weeks to avoid a shop called 'Anne's Antiques' just because Anne was the name of the man I loved's new girlfriend, so really, being slightly resentful and mistrustful of this stranger is me being fairly well adjusted in my book. It's the very same lilt in his voice that used to send me bananas with Trevor that puts me right on edge now.

'Did you get that?'

He sighs and nods, looking disappointed, and, tipping his head to one side, watches me with a relaxed scrutiny. With his long straight hair and earthiness, he's somehow faintly medieval, slightly wolfish.

'Not really what I do, manual labour, being a fully qualified landscape gardener, but I suppose as I've not got too much on at the moment, what with the business being new and all . . .'

I shrug and let him in. He makes his way to the kitchen and looks down the length of the garden and then gives me the same assessment, making me wish for once that I'd washed my hair and put on a top that was not resplendent with baby sick; he has amber-coloured eyes.

'You really need a tree surgeon for that,' he says, nodding at a sprawling cherry tree. 'But I guess I can do it. Yeah, it's got potential, that's for sure . . .' He sighs again, wistfully, and I clutch my grid paper to my chest protectively.

'I'll get my stuff and get stuck in.'

Mr Crawley, who has come down for one of the mini-bottles of Evian that he keeps in the fridge, sees Gareth Jerome, opens his mouth and then closes it again.

'Do you know each other?' I ask, and Gareth Jerome holds out his hand to Mr Crawley, nodding.

'No, I don't think so. Heard of you, obviously,' he tells Mr Crawley, who returns the greeting with an oddly grim smile.

'All right?' Gareth Jerome asks him.

'I'm very well, thank you,' Mr Crawley says, and then he turns on his heel and exits the kitchen without another word.

Gareth Jerome begins to bring through his tools, and, suddenly robbed of my purpose, I carefully fold my garden plan back into page seventy-three of The Garden Book and turn to the European laundry mountain which erupted suddenly shortly after Ella's birth and which has never seemed to diminish since.

My spirits plummet to the tips of my toes and I reach for the iron.

I iron one of Fergus's shirts, which I think is reasonable considering that in my adult life, which began at the age of sixteen when I'd finally felt I could leave Dad to it, I had sworn to never, never iron again. I had promised myself daily during all the years betweens Mum's death and the day I got a residential place to gain a B. Tech in business studies at college that as soon as my life was my own I'd never touch a domestic appliance again.

Dad liked everything done around the flat the way Mum had done it. No, that's too mild. He wanted – demanded – that everything around the flat should be exactly the same as when she was alive, everything. And I loved him and I wanted everything to be exactly the same too, as if keeping laundry day on a Monday and fish day on a Friday would somehow recreate my mum out of the empty spaces left by her absence. So I tried at first to help him voluntarily, and everyone said how good I was, a proper little lady looking after my dad, and I was proud of that. But then seven turned into ten, and by the time I was eleven I dreaded going home from school, dreaded letting myself into the long list of chores that Dad would have left out for me. The long list of tasks that I had to have finished before he got home from work. Iron Monday's washing on a Tuesday; dust and vacuum on a Wednesday; clean the bath and loo on a Thursday; and every weekend to do the shopping and change the bedclothes, ready for the laundry on Monday. I tried telling him once that Mum never changed the bedclothes every week but every other week. He was furious, accused me of calling my mother a slut and sent me to bed crying my eyes out. After that, every night, straight after our tea, I'd wash up the pots and pans and go straight to bed to read one of my books to escape to any place but that place. It was around about that time he stopped kissing me goodnight.

Then, as I grew older, the battle of wills began, the arguments and accusations. I was ungrateful and selfish, he was domineering and lazy. We co-existed, furious with each other twenty-four hours a day for each one of my early teenage years. Even that, though, was better than the last few months I'd lived with him.

By the time I was fifteen I didn't argue about the housework any longer because I didn't have a choice. I'd let myself in from school and there he'd be, sitting in the corner in exactly the same place he'd been when I'd left that morning, staring at the telly. By that time I had to do everything around the house because there was no one else but me. By that time he was slowly trying to kill himself, and I refused to be dragged down with him. A lot of the people round there thought I was heartless, uncaring and hard to leave him when I did, like I did; to go to the lengths of finding a way out when I was so young. But what they didn't know, what they didn't realise, was that I had to go then, I had to. I was saving my own life.

So, to be an ironing expert – not to mention cooking,

cleaning and washing aficionado by the age of eight – seemed very unfair to me both at the time and for ever after. In fact, no sooner was I settled into my shared room with an ex-public school girl called Sara from Dorset than I made it my task to instantly forget all thoughts of housework for ever, and the pair of us, free at last of our entirely different oppressive regimes, practised as much slovenly behaviour as was possible without contracting a flesh-eating disease. My general tidiness did gradually improve over the years, but the ingrained resentment I felt towards any kind of domesticity had never left me. I have always suspected, even now, that I should be out playing in the park instead.

I'd explained this to Fergus not long after we'd met, and he had held me all night long, silent and shocked, as most of the people that I've told the story to normally are, but not so afraid by it or horrified that he couldn't look me in the eyes. If by that time I *had* had any doubts about how much I loved him, it was his unflinching certainty that whatever had happened to me in the past would make no difference to our future that made me believe that I really could be happy.

Then, after I left work, and after we'd left London, his understanding over my stance on ironing subsided somewhat. Out came the whole 'I've got to commute and work all day while you stay at home with the baby' speech, and although the motherhood thing was equally as hard (equally! Ha!) and important as his job, it was his job, after all, that was paying the mortgage, and the very least I could do for him was make sure he had a shirt to put on in the morning. And I agreed, secretly thinking that after giving birth to his baby, suffering stitches, losing any hope of a good night's sleep, seemingly for ever, and gaining a stone that didn't seem to be going anywhere any time soon, it did seem the very *least* thing I could do for him. But I agreed to do it as I supposed he had got a point, even though the thought of him being half right made me baulk and, what's more, anxious. Somehow, to have laughing arguments over ironing was something I'd never considered a consequence of marriage, but I'd shrugged off the discomfort and told myself to grow up. Marriage is about compromise; all the magazines say so.

And so every morning he has one clean ironed shirt hanging on the bedroom door, but everything else, including all my clothes, can stay creased, just like me. Well, it's a compromise, isn't it?

I wait a long time for Camille's message service to pick up her number. She must be in a meeting or, more likely, on the phone to her mum.

'Hi, Cam. It's Kitty. Look, I just wanted to say I'm sorry for running off yesterday. I just, well, you know, suddenly got hot flushes and went a bit bad. Apparently it's quite normal, but I'm sorry anyway because I was looking forward to seeing you and Dora. Will you tell her I said sorry? I'd call her too but I'm really pushed for time.'

I let the lie crackle and fizz down the line. 'So, call me then, we can catch up,' I say despondently, unable to keep the down notes out of my voice, and hang up.

Camille will call me back, I know, this afternoon maybe, or tonight. And so will Dora sometime in the next couple of days and we'll talk, and laugh and gossip, but really everything's changed. Yesterday showed me that, and now I have at least to try to let myself go with the flow, otherwise I'm going to go insane. I have to embrace my new life; I have to actually live it.

Today is the day that I am definitely going to the One O'Clock Club, Berkhamsted's premier and, as far as I can make out, only secular mother and toddler group. I'm definitely going in this time. I'm not just going to *say* I'm going and then decide to stay home to watch *Crossroads* at the last minute. I'm not even going to get Ella ready and put her in her pushchair and then go to the garden centre instead to browse happily alone. Or even wheel her right up to the town hall door and stand there for five minutes until another mother comes along and catches my eye with a friendly smile, sending me scarpering in the opposite direction as fast as the buggy will allow me.

This time I'm definitely going in. After all, I am one of them. They are no different from me, no more competent, professional or able than I am. Ella and I can go to the mother and babies club too. I'm sure that we can, and anyway, Mr Crawley says that once I've met some other mums I'll realise what a good job I'm doing and I'll stop worrying about everything I can think of.

So, today's the day, and after all I can't go with dirty hair.

Unable to wait for the bathroom to be finished I wash my hair in the kitchen, trying my best to ignore its distinctive sink smell, and as I wrap a tea towel round my head I watch Gareth — mentally dropping his surname in a bid to think of him in more friendly terms — as he fills green plastic bag upon green plastic bag with weeds. Every now and then he'll stop and crouch down, fingering a plant with the kind of intimate care I reserve only for Ella and Fergus, take a notebook out of his top pocket and jot something down in it.

'He's having opinions,' I think to myself. 'He's planning my garden, damn him, secretly. Well I'm not having it.' I wring my hair out in the sink and head into the garden. Despite the spring sun, the chill of the morning air greeting my damp hair sends a shiver down my back. He stands to greet me, tucking his notebook back into his overall pocket. He's not really skinny, I notice, just exceptionally tall, taller even than Fergus, I think, whose chin fits perfectly on the top of my head.

'How's it going?' I ask, looking pointedly at the notebook pocket.

'Piece of cake.' He shrugs his shoulders and looks around at the few square feet he's cleared so far. 'Grunt work, that's all. Not the creative stuff I usually do.' He sounds defensive. 'I reckon you'll need to lay new turf, though. This grass has gone to pot. Do you want me to rotovate this when I've cleared it and get it ready?'

I open and close my mouth. Do I? I haven't got to lawns in my book yet.

'Ummm, well, er, yes, I suppose I do. I mean, I do, definitely. Yes please.'

He seems to suppress a smile and nods in affirmation of my hesitant command. Crouching again, he beckons me over, and lifting the branch of an overgrown conifer out of the way, says, 'See here? *Viola odorata*. Sweet violets, a delightful little plant. Shy but tenacious and really very beautiful.'

As I crouch down next to him and try to think of the last time I heard a man's voice say 'delightful' without sounding camp, I imagine that I can sense his glance brushing my cheek. I look up quickly but he is still examining the plant.

'There's still quite a lot of lovely plants in this garden that you could preserve if you wanted to, some really marvellous rose bushes at the back there and a lovely Clematis over there.'

He looks at me with a level assurance that I find obliquely disconcerting. There's something about him, his poise and personality, that seems familiar. Maybe he reminds me of a film star or someone I once knew. No, that's not it . . .

'It seems a shame just to pull them out after they've struggled so long to keep growing in amongst all these weeds,' he continues with a half-smile.

I hold his amber gaze for a moment, mildly distracted by the dramatic sweep of his dark brows, and silently curse him for knowing more than me, although, granted, next-door's cat knows more about gardens than I do, and I nod my head.

'Well, leave what you think is worth leaving, then, and I'll incorporate them into my plan if I agree, okay?'

He nods and softly bites his lip, turning his face away from me for a moment. He's trying not to let me see he's laughing at me, damn him. He takes a second to compose himself and then turns back to face me.

'Okay. Cool. Whatever you say.' He smiles at me then and it's all I can do to stay balanced on my heels. In that second every aspect of his face, his body and his presence conspires against me and knocks the wind out of me. I feel my heart race, my skin tingle and fizz, my stomach tie into knots. All the sensations I believed to be null and void spring suddenly, stupidly, back into life. Gareth Jerome is a very attractive man and I now know where I recognise him from: from girlhood dreams and adult fantasies. Gareth Jerome is my type.

I blink at him, stupid with shock and shame, and scramble to my feet, turning back towards the house and shouting, 'I'll make you a coffee' over my shoulder. Whatever happened to me then was written all over me, and he saw it. He saw, and what's more it made him smile.

First of all, I hate men like Gareth Jerome. Good-looking men who know it and think it'll get them whatever they want with the flash of some dimples and a bit of feigned sincerity, and secondly, I am suddenly aware of my wet hair hanging lank round my shoulders and yesterday's milk-stained T-shirt and my still-too-tight jeans. I stand at the kitchen sink and compose myself. Although a steaming pot of fresh coffee bubbles on the hot plate, I take a jar of instant out of the cupboard and spoon it into my worst mug.

This Gareth Jerome, he comes in here, he takes over my garden, he flicks his hair around like some bloody male model and then he goes and acts all handsome, and frankly I don't have time to be worrying about my hair and eyebrow stubble regrowth.

I don't want a man I'm going to find attractive hanging round the house, it's just not on, it's far too Lady Chatterley, and I especially don't want one who's going to think he's got a bored, sexually repressed housewife on his hands. Doesn't God know I've been spending the last few months trying to fancy my husband again, and the last thing I need is some other man to go and kick-start the engine? It's obviously some kind of anomaly in fate's grand plan for me, and I'll just have to take it into my own hands to correct it. I force myself not to look out of the window at him and peer steadily into the larder until I can be sure that my cheeks have returned to their normal pallor.

Gareth Jerome. My type. Out there in my garden. That kind of roguishness, a brash kind of confidence in his own occupation of space. And the way he looked at me back there when he smiled. All that in those few seconds made me feel, just for a moment, the way I did that first night with Fergus. Just for a moment he looked at me like I wasn't married and a mum. He looked at me like I was just me. It's frightening, it's wrong and, what's more, it's damned inconvenient.

Or it could be hormones. This is the thing about hormones. Before you get pregnant you are pretty au fait with them. You know when they're going to get you, when the rise in the level of your oestrogen or whatever is going to turn you into a snappy-happy drama queen. You sort of know that one week a month, when the diet goes out of the window, you will buy a pair of turquoise pumps that are a size too small and shout angrily at your boyfriend, best friend, boss, because it's Tuesday and you just can't take another Tuesday.

Then, when pregnancy happens, it takes you a while to realise that that one week of the month has extended to every week of every month for nine months and then seemingly for the rest of your life. Yes, Gareth Jerome is fairly good looking. Handsome even. Before the atypical, kind, caring, generous and sweet

Chapter Six

It has taken me the rest of the morning to get us ready to go out, and at last I'm changing Ella into what I hope is going to be her last outfit of the day on the kitchen floor, an idea which she is heartily against.

'I know, darling, I know you don't like to wear clothes, but I'm afraid it's the law.' She attempts to poke out her own eye in defiance of the law and kicks me in the chest.

'Right little live wire you've got there, love.' Gareth Jerome looms above the kitchen worktop. I jump and hastily scoop Ella up into my arms.

'Oh, right, yes. Well, she knows what she likes, and it's to be naked, mostly.' I zip up her coat and do my best impression of a cool smile and glance out at the garden. Most of the grass has been cut back and the vague outline of what was once a bed-bordered lawn is slowly beginning to emerge.

'Looks like you're doing a good job,' I say grudgingly.

Gareth stretches his arms wide, opening his shoulders and revealing his throat briefly to the sun.

'Well, I am good at my job and it's a nice day. Added incentive. After all, that dank dark winter seemed to go on for most of the year.' He pauses for a moment and leans against the kitchen bench. He's rolled his overalls down to his waist and tied the arms around his hips, revealing long and lightly muscled arms.

'Look, I know you've got your plans and all, but while I've been out there I've been brimming over with ideas. How about I make you a plan up, free of charge, mind, and then we sit down and compare ideas together. If you don't like it, I'll scrap it, no worries.'

He returns his gaze to me and I studiously examine the rotten wooden fence that is barely separating our garden from the neighbours'. I expect that after a few days I'll stop being impressed by hawk-like eyes and raven hair and get over it, much the same way that I eventually had to stop the heart hammering, stomach-churning paroxysm that overtook me every time I saw Fergus or else I would have died, literally.

I imagine sitting down with this Gareth Jerome, and I wonder what the harm in getting some expert advice outside of a book might be and decide it's okay. I'll just steal any of the ideas I like and do it myself. Sort of horticultural espionage.

'Okay then. I suppose. When you come back tomorrow?' I realise that between now and then I will have to finish colouring in my plan and read the chapter on 'Planning and Planting' in order to look professional. He flashes me that smile again and I manage to stiffen my knees in time.

'Here we go!' I say brightly to Ella as I wheel her out into the harsh daylight.

'Have a good time!' Mr Crawley's head appears out of an upstairs window.

'Yep! Yep, we will!' I say, waving up at him, sounding as if I'm about to be put to death in a gladiator's arena, but I have to look at it this way: either it's the One O'Clock Club in the town hall or it's a half-naked Gareth in my garden. The way I'm feeling today the One O'Clock Club is an altogether safer proposition.

'And I meant what I said about those auditions. You'll really enjoy it!' Mr Crawley calls before closing the crumbling sash window.

'Yep!' I say again, to myself this time, my voice a strangulated squeak.

If it wasn't happening to me it would be funny. There I was yesterday, trying to recapture just a little bit of my old life, looking for just a moment of familiarity, and here I am today with a crush on my gardener, a trip to a toddler group and the promise of a part in the local amateur dramatics society's latest production. I couldn't make things much more different if I tried.

It was Mr Crawley's idea, of course, this whole auditions thing, and, I suspect, part of his secret plan to rehabilitate me into real life, just at it was he who had brought the One O'Clock Club leaflet and left it out for me to read. I was hiding in our living room from Gareth when Ella had started to scream at the top of her lungs. By the time I reached her nursery, Mr Crawley and Timothy were singing 'Ohhhhk-la-hom-a!' to her with what seemed to be practised gusto, and she was giggling with abandon as Mr Crawley polkaed her around the room.

'Oh, thank you,' I said, smiling at them, and upon seeing me Ella instantly burst into tears as if she'd just remembered what a terrible mother I am.

'Oh, darling, darling.' I failed to pacify her and lifted her on to her changing table, knowing that this particular performance wouldn't be over until she'd been changed and fed. At least it wouldn't have been if it wasn't for Mr Crawley and Timothy's impromptu launch into 'I'm just a girl who can't say no'. I giggled too, then, more with relief than anything else, although Mr Crawley's mid-west falsetto was pretty funny.

'You two show a remarkably extensive knowledge of musical lyrics?' I questioned, briefly wondering if a gay May-to-September romance might explain all of Mr Crawley's more unusual traits.

'Ah, well, the Berkhamsted Players, you see, Mrs Kelly. I am a stalwart member, and Tim here has picked up a bit along the way. Mostly chorus, I'm afraid, although I did play Fagin in the 1999 production of *Oliver!*, which was rather favourably reviewed in the *Gazette*, I might add.'

I saw the genuine pleasure in his smile and hefted Ella back into my arms, whereupon she reached for my hair and yanked it joyously.

'So, this year it's all "surreys with fringes on top", is it?' I asked, my head at a forty-five degree angle.

'No, no, that was last year. This year it's *Calamity Jane*. We did wonder about doing two musical westerns back to back but, well, frankly our coffers are low and it saves on costumes.'

I bit my lip as I took Ella down the hall to my bedroom and deposited her like a frog in a lily pond on the floral cover. She contemplated the whole sitting unsupported business for a few seconds before lunging forward on to her chin and proceeding to crawl backwards, which is the only direction she's been able to master so far − to her certain doom, given half the chance.

I was surprised that Mr Crawley had followed me into the bedroom instead of returning to his work in the bathroom.

'You should try out for it,' he told me with an encouraging smile.

'Try out for what?' I asked

'The Players, the Players' *Calamity Jane*. I reckon you'd stand a good chance, you can carry a tune. I've heard you sing to the little one and I know the director would love to be able to cast a Calamity under the age of forty-five and not menopausal, although I'm fairly sure Mrs Ponsenby wouldn't agree, smug old cow.'

I let my jaw drop at his first ever display of anything other than charming good nature and laughed swiftly, lifting Ella from the precipice of the left-hand side of the bed and returning her to the relative security of the right.

'It's just that it's not really my cup of tea, *am dram*.' I had referenced my mental picture of Myself, dressed cute and out clubbing, before remembering that, according to recent events, what I automatically considered to be my favourite way of passing the time actually had nothing to do with me any more. I sat down, dizzy with the vertigo of days falling away from me, and picked Ella off the edge of the bed just in time once again. She squealed in frustration.

'Okay, I'll think about it,' I said, wanting him to leave, catching sight of a stranger's profile reflected plumply in the bedroom mirror.

He watched me closely for a moment and then, talking softly, he said, 'It's only that you've been here, in Berkhamsted, nearly a year now, haven't you? And I think I'm right in saying that the only people you know are Mr Kelly, his family and us. Oh, and the little one, of course. I just think it would do you good to get out a bit. That's all it is.' He smiled at me gently as he closed the door behind him.

I think, somehow, that during that conversation he had assumed my assent and was certain I would go. And I suppose that I will go. It'll be different, it will be me, the new, married, country-town me.

I wheel Ella across the high street and decide to take a detour past Boots. I don't need to cross the road as the town hall is on this side, but I decide I can't be early and I can't be on time. What if I get there and no one's there? And what do I say when I get there? What if they're all huddled around in a group looking at us as we stand in the corner waiting for someone to talk to us? For God's sake, it feels like the first day of school! I'll have nothing to say to these women – I'm just not one of them.

I am about to turn the buggy through a three-point turn when I catch my reflection in Boots' plate-glass window and it halts me abruptly. A brown-haired, slightly rounded face looks back at me. Not a stranger's face, but mine now. It's not a hideous face, in fact it's quite pleasant in its way, and whichever way you look at it it's definitely me. In a way it's sort of comforting to know that I'm not that wild, red-haired, lipsticked, mini-skirted girl any more. It doesn't matter really that Gareth Jerome jangled me just a little bit back then in the garden because it's not Kitty Simpson any more, it's Kitty Kelly, mother and wife. I curl the end of my hair around my finger and look at it closely, the last tiny bit of red hair dye which I had been growing out since the moment I met Fergus, because he told me he thought that my naturally brown hair would suit me better, still stains the very ends of my hair.

'The last tiny bit of the old me,' I say out loud to Ella, who twists her head in her hood impatiently to look at me. 'The very last little ickle bit of me,' I say, bending over her to tickle her under her chin as I redirect us back to the One O'Clock Club. She bats my hand away with a chuckle and smiles at me.

I stroke her cheek and remember the first time I saw that smile.

It was after we left Simon Shaw's party. Fergus had promised me coffee and toast in the last working man's café left in the Docklands. He'd led me by the hand past a blur of what might have been celebrities – I didn't know and I didn't care – and up to the river's edge. I'd felt as if I were floating. The lights along the river blossomed like fluorescent flowers and I'd resisted the temptation to sing out loud.

We'd leant against a railing and his hand held mine simply, almost demurely, as we watched the water. Eventually I'd stopped worrying about how I looked in profile and became lost in the formless movement and reflected colour of the water. So

I'd jumped when Fergus's voice had cut with knife-sharp clarity into my new soft-focus world.

'Will you come back to my flat, Kitty?' he'd said with a lightning-swift change of plan, taking a step closer to me. I could see that his pupils had dilated almost enough to entirely obliterate the violet ring of his iris. He'd pointed along the walkway. 'I live just down there. I've a river view balcony.'

'What about the great night café that you know?' I'd asked, afraid, not of being found dead in a ditch the next day, but of the speed and strength of force with which my body had decided that it wanted to go back to his before my mind had had a say in it.

He'd sighed and looked out across the river.

'Well, we could go there, it's true. But . . .' He'd paused and looked away from me.

'But? But what?' I'd asked, tucking my hand through the loop of his arm.

'Well, it's less likely that you're going to let me kiss you all over in the middle of a café,' he'd said with a grin that was stopped dead by the intensity in his gaze.

'Blimey, why don't you just say what you mean?' I'd said, my voice trembling with laughter and my stomach turning over.

'I'm sorry, I'm sorry,' Fergus had laughed, turning to face me, placing each one of his hands on my hips with careful precision. 'Let's go to the café. I'll stand you a sausage sandwich.'

I'd watched him for a moment, noticed the space between his brows and the small tear-drop shadow under his bottom lip.

'No, let's go back to yours,' I'd said almost absent-mindedly. 'I think I'd rather you kissed my naked body all over.' I'd turned and walked away from him, swinging my hips as sassily as I was able to considering I'd just gone pillar-box red and could hardly believe myself.

'Um, Kitty?' Fergus had called after me. I'd gathered my wits and glanced over my shoulder seductively.

'Uh-huh?' I'd said, attempting the temptress look.

'That's great . . . it's just that my flat's the other way?' His grin was like a beacon. He was delighted with me and I was delighted with myself.

I'd run back into his arms and kissed him while I'd laughed until eventually we'd made our way to his flat.

It was only when we had entered his apartment building that I'd begun to feel nervous.

We'd watched each other silently in the lift, and I'd wondered if, half hoped that, he might kiss me then, but he hadn't, only kept his eyes on me until the lift bell chimed and the doors slid open. He'd led me down a short hallway, opened his flat door and then stood back to let me enter. For all his chivalry, I instinctively knew that this was how he preferred all of his guests to see his home for the first time: empty of the clutter of people, even him. It was a beautiful home, designed down to the last detail to reflect its exterior modernism, and best of all the far wall seemed to be made up almost entirely of glass which looked on to a broad terrace that looked out over the river.

'Wow,' I'd said as I walked in and a succession of spotlights illuminated the room.

'Oh well, you know,' he'd said, shrugging, a smile of pride belying his offhand tone. He'd crossed to his open-plan kitchen area and begun to work a large and impressive coffee machine. I'd walked to the glass wall and sighed.

'You must never get annoyed living in a place like this.' I'd thought of my own tiny flat, as insipid and as instant as my supermarket own-brand coffee.

'Well, I wouldn't say that exactly. The bird next door insists on sunbathing totally nude. Drives me mad,' he'd said as he made me coffee. I'd stared at him with open mouth for a beat before I'd realised that he was joking.

'You're joking,' I'd said, shaking my head.

'Of course I am. It doesn't annoy me at all.'

I'd laughed and threatened to throw a cushion at him. 'You're still joking! You are joking, aren't you?'

He'd grinned and wrapped his arm around me, pulling me close to his chest, and I'd tipped my chin upwards hoping now for that first kiss. He'd regarded me for a moment and then seemed to let out a held breath before releasing me apologetically.

'I'm joking.' He'd gestured to a large empty terrace.

'Do you want to go outside?' he'd asked. I'd looked at it, plant free and bare save for a shiny table and chair set. 'Coffee'll be five minutes and I can bring it out to you.'

I'd shaken my head, not wanting to spend time out on the terrace for the same reason he hadn't wanted to go to a café.

'Nope, I don't think I do. Do you mind if we stay in here?' He'd shaken his head and I'd followed him over to a pair of long toffee-coloured suede sofas, positioned at right angles around a large white rug.

'You must never spill anything,' I'd said for the sake of something to say. I'd sat down first and hoped that he would sit down next to me, but instead he'd taken the opposite end of the other sofa, leaning right back into it to look at me.

A few moments of silence had passed before he'd said, 'It's you, it really is you.' His voice had been soft with awe, yes, definitely awe. I remember it so well because it was the first time in my life I had ever elicited that response from someone, except when I'd tried to explain the circumstances of my mother's death, that is, and that's a different kind of awe altogether, awe mixed with lurid fascination. But then, in Fergus's eyes it was just awe and maybe even wonderment. I remember feeling as if I might be made of gold.

I couldn't think of anything to say to him and I'd bowed my head and stirred my coffee.

Several seconds had passed, and I'd felt his gaze on me before I'd found the courage to look up again.

'Let's talk,' he'd said suddenly with cheerful bravado. 'Tell me, tell me all about you – from birth to present.'

I'd paused, considered giving him the whole truth, and then decided that I'd hold back on that version, at least for a little while. I had the pre-edited first-timer version of my childhood down pat by then. Something about growing up, about my dad and me and art college, and then the secretarial course that was only ever meant to be a stopgap, about Dora and Camille, a holiday I'd once had in New York, the only interesting place I had ever been, and how much I wanted a puppy.

'What about your mum?' he'd asked. 'You don't mention her much.'

'Mum died. I was quite young. I . . . I was quite young,' I'd said and he'd let it go. And he'd told me about Simon Shaw getting caught with a hard-on at the back of class at school, and how he'd always wanted to work with computers from the first moment he'd set eyes on his Sinclair C-60, about his mum and how much he loved Dublin, and a moon dance he'd once been to in New Zealand. We'd laughed and talked some more and laughed. We were hoarse and still sofas apart when the sun rose. I had been desperate to kiss him.

'This is like one of those films, like *Truly, Madly, Deeply*, when they talk all night and don't make love until the next morning.' I'd felt the blush in my cheeks that my heavy-handed hint had instigated.

'Yeah, sort of,' he'd agreed, still watching me. He'd gone to the wall then to turn off the spotlights so that the full impact of the sunrise filled the room. I'd held my breath as he'd returned, but he'd returned to his position on the opposite sofa. He'd looked at his hands for a long time and swallowed.

'Would you do something for me, Kitty?' he'd said, voice tight. 'You might find it a little strange.' Butterflies had hatched in the pit of my stomach and I'd prepared for the inevitable catch.

'What?' I'd asked tremulously.

'Well, I . . . there's nothing I want more than to be over there kissing you, right now, all over. There's been nothing I've wanted more all night, well, except for one thing. Now you're finally here, I just want to look at you.'

I'd nodded and shrugged my shoulders,

'And?'

'Will you let me watch you just a little bit longer?'

I'd opened my mouth to speak, but he'd interrupted. 'Will you take off your dress?'

My mouth had shut and I'd looked away for a moment into the dawn, enjoying the tremble of excitement that ran from the tips of my ears to my toes. I couldn't think of anything to say, so instead I'd stood up, reaching behind me to unzip my dress. I'd thanked fate for putting a run in my last pair of tights and forcing me into hold-ups instead that morning, and let the dress fall about my ankles. I'd held my breath and looked at the fabric pooled at my feet for a long moment before lifting my chin. I'd seen Fergus swallow and bitten my lip. He hadn't seemed to be disappointed.

'The bra,' he'd ordered softly, holding my gaze. An imaginary chill had raised gooseflesh on my arms, and with a sense of showmanship that I didn't know I had I'd turned my back to him before unhooking my bra, sliding it off my shoulders and placing it on the sofa. I'd watched myself for a surreal moment as if I were someone else, half naked in a stranger's flat, before I'd turned back to him and let my hands fall away to my sides.

Agonising seconds had passed as his eyes travelled the length of my body before he'd sprung out of the sofa and taken me in his arms.

'I just can't wait for the rest,' he'd said, his warm hands running the length of my back and over my bottom before finally he'd kissed me.

Once our lips had met, any of the last barriers there may have been between us were swept away. He'd lifted me into his arms, making me feel as light as a feather, and lain me on the rug, kissing each inch of my face. His hands were in my hair, his mouth on my breasts, and I'd had to struggle to undress him. When at last we were both naked, we'd lain lips to lips, breast to breast, hip to hip, feeling the luxurious length of our bodies against each other.

'I'm a little nervous,' I'd whispered, although I'd discovered that I wasn't just as I'd said it.

'Don't be,' he'd told me, brushing my hair back from my face. 'I'm nervous enough for us both.' He'd smiled at me then, the smile of a stranger, yes, but one that was instantly full of love – love which I was certain I could reciprocate. I'd closed my eyes as he'd kissed me and I'd let myself slip into what I was sure was the first moment of the rest of my life.

And I was right, wasn't I?

I stop abruptly outside the doors of the town hall, waiting for the heat of the memory to cool on my cheeks. Another mother bustles past me with a cheery smile.

'Coming in?' she enquires pleasantly.

'In a minute,' I say, kicking myself for my own stupidity. Come on, Kitty Kelly! If you can give birth you can deal with a bunch of mothers and babies, for God's sake. They're not some power-mad totalitarian regime that's going to brainwash you into comparing soap powder.

'Come on, Ella,' I say with determination, and Ella sticks out her legs and waggles them in encouragement. 'We're going in.'

Chapter Seven

'Well, I don't care what you say, I'm sticking to Persil – that own-brand brought Lucas up all over, non-biological or not non-biological. Sugar, Katherine?' Claudia holds out a mug to me. 'What do you use?'

It has basically been 'the horror, the horror' since I walked in through the door. I was immediately swept upon and divested of my coat, Ella's personal details and the circumstances of her birth (Oh no, you pooooor thing. Don't even *talk* to me about stitches) within about five minutes. But Ella's eyes lit up at the sight of a tub full of plastic balls to roll about in and displayed social skills far superior to mine by lunging into them with wholehearted delight and biting another baby's bottom in a companionable sort of way. I blink at Claudia.

'Um, call me Kitty. I use . . .' I desperately try to picture the words on the side of the packet under the sink, but fail . . . 'Persil too. Definitely the best.'

Claudia nods at me sagely and I look around the rest of the group, all about my age, I suppose, hovering around the thirty mark. There is Susan Dunne, who was evidently blonde before the birth of her first child but now eight months on is black with a blonde trim; Kelly Grant, who must have been thin all her life until now and is still in denial about her maternity weight gain, judging by the straining zip on her jeans and the perilously tight buttons on her blouse – still thinner than me, mind you; Angela Harding, clearly a disciple of The Book – she's been fussing about getting her baby home for her forty-five minute nap at three-fifteen precisely since she walked in; and Clare Brown, a pretty girl, a bit younger than the rest of us, pleasantly plump with golden hair and green eyes. The group's only single mother.

'It happened on holiday.' She is telling me her birth story. 'One minute I was thinking that my back ached a lot and the next minute I'd had a baby!'

I stare at her, my mouth wide open.

'You mean you didn't know?' I ask, aghast, all soap powder perils forgotten.

'No! She didn't!' the whole group choruses like a Greek theatre group. They obviously like this story. Clare settles cheerfully into a bean bag, tipping her son up by his heels and shaking him until he's hysterical and as red as a beetroot.

'No idea,' she tells me, eyes glowing with a perverse kind of pride. 'I mean, I've always been, you know, "roomy" and all, and I kept on getting periods . . .'

'No!' I exclaim. 'That's so unfair!' I tell everyone else.

'I know!' Claudia chips in, her middle-class eyes round with the 'Take a Break' of it all.

'So then I'm in the hospital in Florida and this nurse goes to me,' Clare adopts a perfect accent, '"Honey, be prepared for a shock." I thought "fuck it, it's cancer or something", and she goes, "You're going to be a mommy." I nearly died. Ten hours later this little chap arrived and it's been bedlam ever since.' Her son, Ted, climbs up her legs and bites her thigh.

'Oh, you bugger,' she says with a smile, and Claudia and Susan exchange a raised eyebrow. I warm to Clare. I don't quite know how to put it, but she's like me. She's, well, she's council.

'What about the dad?' I say, clearly broaching a subject which the other members have chosen never to bring up. They all lean forward slightly, utterly failing to feign disinterest.

'Bastard denied Ted was his.' She contemplates her gorgeously blond baby. 'I tell you, if you put them side by side it's like peas in a pod. Went to court, did the whole paternity test thing, proved it was his and he is supposed to pay me a measly twenty-five quid a week. Never seen a penny of it. Wanker.'

She picks up Ted and hugs him. 'We don't need his money, do we, sweetheart,' she says with determination. 'I'm training to be a childminder, so once I'm registered we'll be all right.'

'Well, good for you,' I say warmly. Ella fixes her gaze on me and lunges in my general direction but the more she scrabbles on the floor the further away she gets.

'She can't go forward,' I say anxiously to Clare. 'Is she normal?'

Clare laughs.

'This one couldn't go forward for a month, in fact he went sideways. Did his head in, it did. The more he wanted something the further away from it he got, it was hilarious!'

I relax as I laugh along with her and wonder if I should go and scoop Ella up or let her get on with it.

Claudia hands me a shortbread biscuit. She's had two kids now and has appointed herself the group oracle.

'There *are* more of us, Katherine. But not everyone comes every week.' She says this like it should be a hanging offence. 'We all take turns in bringing biscuits and cakes, *some* of us bake, some of us . . .' she looks at the Tesco's own-brand packet of biscuits . . . 'don't. Now, as you're new, we'll give you a couple of weeks before it's your turn, okay?'

I smile at her through clenched teeth.

'Okay,' I say. My stomach tightens and my phobia about baking and home-making in general kicks in. I wonder just how bad it would look if I grabbed Ella and made a bolt for the door. Okay, so I'd lose the buggy and we'd have to leave town, but it might be worth it. I take a deep breath and watch Ella, who is lying on her back, arms akimbo, laughing her head off at the ceiling. I look at the ceiling but its comedy value eludes me.

'Calista! Get out of there at once!'

As Claudia retreats to marshal her daughter out of the waste bin, Clare rolls her eyes and raises an eyebrow in Claudia's direction. 'She reckons she's Miriam Stoppard and Delia Smith all rolled into one, that one. I bought the biscuits this week. I'm the only one here whose hubby isn't on £70K plus a year and can't be arsed to arse about with *dough*.'

I return her confidential smile, guiltily. She thinks I'm like her but I'm not, I'm a traitor.

'What about you?' she asks, inevitably.

'Um, well, yeah, I used to live in Hackney but I'm married now, living on Charles Street. Bit of a change, you know.'

Clare looks momentarily crestfallen, care lines suddenly sinking in her young face.

'That's great,' she says. 'You took a long time to come round to the group, didn't you? Your little one's how old now?'

'Um . . .' I can't think why I always have trouble answering this question; after all, I was there at the birth. 'Six months give or take. Yours?'

'Teddy? Eight months, and by Christ that child will be the death of me. He started crawling at five and a half months, pulling himself up at six and he can walk a few steps now. I swear I should be a size eight the amount of running about I do. I mean why? Why me? It should be Angela's little one, she ate oily fish three times a week for the whole pregnancy. I ate Maltesers.' She giggles and the knot in my stomach melts a little, warmed by the ember of what might possibly be a new friendship.

'Well, Ella only goes backwards, seems quite happy with that scenario. I'm fairly sure that given half a chance she'll still be doing it at twenty-one. Still, better that than still lying on her back and waggling her legs Michael Flatley style.' We laugh together.

'You know, it bloody knocks you sideways, doesn't it. This baby lark,' Clare says. 'Granted, it was a bit more of a shock for me than most, but I'd always had this idea it'd all be hearts and flowers and baby talc and it turns out you're knackered for ever, too tired to shag and you're not even allowed to use baby talc any more!'

I stare at her for a moment, kicking myself for the last five months of self-inflicted isolation.

'Clare,' I say sincerely, 'you are so right. And another thing . . .'

By the time I get in three hours later, Ella is flat out and I have this strange, fluttery, elated feeling in my stomach. I'm humming a happy tune, I have Clare's home number in my pocket, a date for coffee round hers this week and, best of all, the slowly dawning realisation that I'm not the only woman in the world who thinks she's a terrible mother and that she's doing everything wrong.

'How did it go?' Mr Crawley asks me, whispering for the exhausted Ella's benefit.

'Yeah, it was great. Really good, once I'd settled in,' I nod, all aglow.

'Good, I'm pleased. Well, the bath is plumbed in so you can use it tonight if you like. We'll be back in the morning to finish it off and start work on the patio.'

I wave them goodbye, looking around for Gareth, who must have left hours ago. I breathe a sigh of relief. Ella snuffles, still ensconced in her buggy, and I debate the merits of attempting to undress her and transfer her to her cot without waking her, like I'm sure Scary Poppins would.

'Oh, what the hey,' I say out loud and make myself a cup of tea instead, wheel her next to my chair and read a magazine until she wakes up.

When Fergus slams the door shut that night I am still humming, and I'm not even cross that he's forgotten not to slam the door shut again. I grin at him as he comes into the kitchen and he looks at me sideways.

'What's wrong?' he asks me cautiously, and then as Ella drums her legs happily at the sight of him, shouting 'Wagaaaaaaa!', he repeats, 'Yessss, what's wrong, what's wrong, what's wrong!' in a very camp, sing song voice as he scoops her out of her high chair and swings her ceilingwards. She shrieks hysterically.

I smile and he takes a step back, settling his daughter on his hip like a natural, and regards me, tipping his head to one side, five o'clock stubble shadowing his seven p.m. face.

'Nothing's wrong, everything is great. We went out today and made some new friends, and Ella ate all of her carrots and potato. You never know, she might grow after all. And I even had time to put my feet up today. And the bath's plumbed in.'

Fergus winds his arms around my waist and gives Ella and me a group hug.

'So we're happy, are we?' It's not until I hear the faint echo of surprise in his voice that I wonder if he has been secretly dreading coming home to me and my long list of grievances – and I can moan for England – every week night since Ella was born. I bite back on a reflux of resentment. No, it's not that, surely. He's probably just pleased that we seem to be getting ourselves together, even just a little bit.

'What about you?' I say, tipping my head back to look at him. 'You look tired.'

Fergus shrugs off my gaze and spins Ella round. 'No, well, yes. But I'm fine, fine. Work's fine, everything's fine.' He sets Ella down on the floor and kisses me. 'I sort of feel like I have two lives, but apart from that, it's fine!'

I study him for a moment. Maybe it's the long hours he's been putting in recently or the hour-long commute on a train stuffed full of stuffed shirts, but somehow he seems to have faded a little, become a little worn down.

Ella squeals as she backs herself into the fridge and snaps his attention away from me.

'Well, I sort of feel like I have no life to speak of,' I say, but the comment wafts over the top of his head as he crouches down to tickle Ella.

'Ha, yeah, I know!' he says jovially, which is his stock reply for everything I ever say that he hasn't really listened to.

'Please learn to go forward!' he says to Ella, before scooping her up again. 'You're going to back yourself somewhere I can't find you one day!' He swings her up by her arms and sets her down again facing the far wall. 'That should keep her busy for two minutes.'

In a bid to regain his attention, I step over Ella and kiss him on the cheek.

'You have first bath,' I say, with the kind of charitable generosity that six hours' sleep and a successful outing gives you. 'I'll stick a ready meal in the microwave and then we can talk over dinner?' I want to tell him about the club, and the Berkhamsted players and Clare. He squeezes my shoulder briefly and kisses the top of my head.

'Blimey, has someone come round and planted a chip in your head, Mrs Kelly? You've gone all Stepford.'

I laugh, shaking off the hurt I feel at his comment as childish, dismayed at the fragility of my own sense of wellbeing.

Fergus sees the look on my face and puts his arm around me. 'No, you have it. I know how long you've been yearning to be up to your chin in boiling water.'

My heart turns inside with love for him.

'You *are* my hero after all,' I tell him sincerely.

'I know, and I always will be,' he replies lightly. He kisses the top of my head and rescues the baby from backing herself into the vacuum cleaner. 'Go on.'

Forty minutes later and fully restored, I open the door of the nursery to find Ella already asleep, but it's only eight-ish. This is unheard of, it must be the carrots. Pulling my dressing gown close around me, I look down the stairs and listen to the faint sound of the TV. The baby's asleep, for once in my life I'm not so exhausted I can't speak, and we're both in the same building.

There's no excuse not to really.

I take a seat at the top of the stairs and begin to prepare myself mentally. I think about the night of the white rug again, the honeymoon, only last week in his office, but already they seem like distant dreams that never happened to me. I try Keanu Reeves and Russell Crowe in a leather skirt and then, suddenly, out of nowhere I'm thinking about Gareth Jerome crouching low on his long legs, fingering the soft down leaves of a sage plant as if they were . . .

I think about that poor rabbit with a septic eye on *Pet Rescue*.

I think about the Red Cross appeal advert that always makes me cry but which I have yet to donate to.

I think about Ella's nappy this morning. All sage plant allusions vanish and I am back to square one. Come on, Kitty, you can't wait until the next time you're in full view in your husband's office to get turned on, you have to get into it on a regular basis. Denise of *This Morning* fame says so and Denise is never wrong.

Calm, now, and collected, I decide the best way to approach this is to go in cold. It wasn't that long ago after all that Fergus used to light me up with a single glance, and I'm sure it won't

111

be too long now until he does again. Once I've got over the birth and the tiredness and lost some weight and found my feelings again. I've wondered over the last few weeks if I should try to explain this curious kind of numbness I feel whenever I think about sex, but I don't know how to, not without him taking it personally and thinking that I don't love him when I do. But it seems pointless trying to talk about something as intimate as that when he's too tired to muster a conversation about life's everyday things. I'm just hoping he won't notice and before long I'll get my groove back and everything will be just like it was before, but better.

I find Fergus not watching the end of *EastEnders*, but instead gazing absently at the TV, clearly thinking about something else. When he sees me he quickly rearranges his features into apprehensive pleasure, but in the fleeting moment before his face was a picture of . . . unhappiness? No, fatigue, that's all. Hard day at the office.

'Nice bath?' he asks, with ever so slightly off-key cheer-fulness.

'Almost orgasmic,' I say, inserting a calculated flirtatious note into my voice.

'Oh really?' he says with a smile. 'Maybe I can help you with that "almost" . . .' I let him pull me on to his lap and I relax into his kiss. I can't remember the last time we kissed like this. I'm glad to hear my own involuntary sigh as his hands move over my damp skin. Maybe tonight is the night. I pull open the buttons of his trousers, laying just enough of him bare to allow me to lower myself on to him. I tense just the moment before, like I think I always will from now on, hiding my face as I wince at the initial pain. He enters me and I gradually relax as I slowly move on him, sitting astride him. The warm palms of his hands stroke me from back to buttock, and as I kiss him deeply, I find myself wondering about making Ella some food myself instead of using jars. Maybe tonight's not the night. Fergus moans deeply and with some effort of will I force my mind back to the job in hand and look Fergus in the face. His eyes are closed and even here, at this moment, he seems somehow far away, concentrating on another universe. It doesn't take long, and it doesn't quite live up to the promise of the bath, but nevertheless, as I relax my forehead against his shoulder, I'm happy. My mission is complete and our intimacy has been re-established once more. I feel relaxed. Actually, a better word would be relieved, yes relieved. We've had sex now and that should last us for another two weeks. I have decided that two weeks is the maximum time I should allow to pass before having sex, assuming that some sudden grand office-related passion doesn't overtake me in between, and so far it hasn't. If Fergus has noticed the pattern he never mentions it and seems happy enough with the arrangement. Of course we have never actually discussed the change in our sex life, it's just happened like it's supposed to when you have kids.

'I love you, baby,' Fergus whispers in my ear and I feel guilty for thinking about him, my true love, with such objectivity.

'I love you too, darling,' I say, disengaging myself from his embrace and picking up the remote control to check the channels.

'Cup of tea?' I say, deciding I can't be bothered with any of it.

'Love one,' he says and, as I leave for the kitchen, he tucks himself discreetly back into his jeans.

As I drop two tea bags into the blue and yellow Italian mugs his mother gave us as a moving-in present, I catch sight of myself reflected in the dark glass of the kitchen window, translucent and ghostly.

After that first time we had lain naked on the white rug for what had seemed like hours, basking in the warmth of the sunlight that flooded in through the glass, we'd laughed and talked.

'I wonder how your pal Dora got along with Si,' he'd said.

'Poor bloke's probably dead in a ditch by now. Still, it should boost his record sales.'

I remember I'd leant back on my elbows, enjoying the feeling of my own hair, of my skin and the sun and for the first time in my life feeling every bit as beautiful as he told me I was. Another affirmation, I had thought, another sign of the perfection of our union, and I think that was the last time I ever thought to wonder if being with Fergus wasn't exactly the right thing for me to be doing for the rest of life.

Tea made, I return to living room, looking forward to curling up next to him for a few minutes' talk before bedtime. He's asleep, his head thrown back, snoring, his mouth open, a small silver trail of saliva tracking down his chin. I look at him for a moment and shrug, taking consolation in the fact that at least I'll have total command of the remote control and that I can enjoy my tea and watch that girls' film on Channel Four. I settle down on the carpet at his feet and lift the cup to my lips.

Without warning the monitor crackles into life and Ella's tinny wail fills the room. I look up at Fergus but he doesn't even flinch.

'Coming, darling,' I say to myself.

It's been a long night, or is it a short day, I wonder, looking at the cow clock and rocking in the stupid chair. My third visit to the nursery – it's five a.m. Apparently the six-hour night last night was a one-off special offer. After yet another feed, Ella's fist has loosened its grip of her ear and has fallen open-fingered to her side. Out of the window I see Doris Day mount the Deadwood stage and career it around the corner into George Street bound for the Windy City. I wonder if it's a sign; I've never had Doris before. Maybe a visit from her means that I should audition for the Players after all. Or maybe I am insanely tired and on the brink of being sectioned. 'Does she mean Hemel Hempstead?' I wonder before I snap my head up sharply and blink awake again. Only two hours until I have to get up. I have to go to bed.

Having gently lowered Ella into her cot, I look at her for a long time, searching for signs that this time she might stay asleep. I'm fairly sure she will. I creep out of her room and make for my bed, but just before I open the door I pause.

I've forgotten something.

Tomorrow, or rather today, Gareth Jerome is going to go over my plans with me, and I haven't even finished colouring them in. After making such a fuss about the whole thing, I don't want him to think I'm an amateur. I look at the bedroom door for a moment, picturing Fergus, his arm flung above his head, his mouth half open, and turn away, tiptoeing down the stairs instead. I set Fergus's coffee machine in motion, lifting my bare feet off the cold tiles like a cat on a hot tin roof as I reach for my book and carefully unfold my plan.

Right, well, I'm not sure what these plants over here are going to be, but I definitely think they should be pink.

Chapter Eight

As I sit over my untouched cup of coffee, I can feel the warmth of the May sun on my cheek, intensified by the glass of the kitchen window. I'm waiting for Gareth to arrive and this morning he's a little late. I have had my boots on for the last half-hour and now I'm worried I look too keen. Maybe I should take them off again, and go and sit in the living room watching *This Morning* as if I'd forgotten he was coming. But Mr Crawley was already here when I laced them up and he might notice, and think I was acting like a bit of an idiot, and he'd be right.

The thing is – and if you'd told me this a couple of years back I'd have said you were insane – that these last couple of weeks working on the garden with Gareth have been fantastic. It's as if I just needed something outside my domestic life to think about and focus on to get back on track, and learning about the garden and seeing it come to fruition is really helping me feel like me again.

Admittedly the first the couple of days were a bit awkward. The morning after I stayed up all night trying to finish my plan, I woke up with my head sticking to the marble effect kitchen worktop and my tongue glued to the top of my mouth.

Fergus had gently shaken me awake and removing my crumpled and drool-marked piece of grid paper, glanced at it and said, 'Is the grass meant to be pink?'

I'd thrown it in the bin in disgust and spent the following half-hour trying to work out how to be with the gardener. Haughty yet benevolent, I decided, and then I thought friendly but distant. I cursed this stupid house that needed so many tradesmen traipsing through day in day out when the only experience I had of dealing with help was making the gas man a cup of tea. I tried to think of Nan's allotment, of recreating the feeing of happiness I'd had there in the garden here. Then, I thought, I might just feel at home.

'So, what about these famous plans then?' Gareth had said to me the first morning he had arrived, the self-assured smile putting paid to all my plans to be aloof. I was still crumpled in my red pyjamas, my hair unbrushed and scraped off my face with an elastic band, and I was annoyed. It was all right for Mr Crawley to see me in all my morning glory, but for him, a person of more or less my own age and a bloke to boot, it wasn't really on. It meant I'd have to get up earlier and make more of an effort even if Ella was still asleep. He'd ignored my state of undress completely and had sat down on a stool next to Ella and started spooning the cereal she refused to take from me into her mouth, which she opened in eager readiness like a little bird, making me feel annoyed and jealous, possibly the two most dangerous emotions that can ever be combined in a woman.

'So, about my plans. The thing is . . .' I'd glanced at the bin where the screwed-up ball of paper now resided . . . 'that they are all sort of . . . up here, really . . .' I'd tapped my sleep-waxed forehead. 'So I thought we could discuss *your* plans and then see how they compare.'

Gareth had glanced at the bin as if he knew exactly what had happened to my famous plans, and looked out of the window.

'Oh yes, we could do wonders out there. Wonders.' He'd turned to look at me, his face illuminated with spring sunshine. 'How about down the bottom there we create an arbor, with roses all around it, and maybe a trailing Clematis along the back fence – like a real cottage garden feel, just right for an old house like this. We'll put in a bench and then in the summer you'll be able to go out there and relax, a special area for you, full of sensual smells and colours. A bit of living aromatherapy, like.'

I'd briefly wondered how I'd ever be likely to enjoy this sanctuary with Ella permanently in tow, but I let myself be carried along. There was something in the melodious tone of his voice that made it seem so possible.

'And then, for the little one here, a sand-pit, a nice bit of lawn to muck around in. A bed planted with non-toxic flowers she can eat, maybe down there in that left-hand corner. We could sort of fence it off with a low fence, maybe old railway sleepers, and you could put a slide in or a Wendy house?' Again that smile. 'I could build her one, special?'

I'd nodded at him enthusiastically. 'And then we could have a raised bed, like a herb garden or some veggies maybe. Organic for the little one and then, once this patio's down, we can plant out some containers. I tell you what, Mrs Kelly, it'll be fantastic!' He laughed with pure joy at the prospect, and for one terrifyingly electric moment I thought he might have hugged me with delight. Instead, though, he stuffed his hand into his pocket and grinned a little sheepishly. 'How does that match up with your plan?'

'Oh, well, call me Kitty, please,' I'd said, feeling the unfamiliar jar of my married name. 'And yes, that is more or less what I had in mind all along.'

So the next couple of weeks we worked together in precarious and precocious May weather, me harassed, grumpy, overtired and angry in turn, and Gareth bearing my mood swings with unfailing good humour and a visible belief that I would come to accept him eventually. We hacked, pruned, rooted out and dug up about two skips full of garden waste, fertilised, rotovated and fertilised again until, to be perfectly honest, it looked exactly as bad as it did in the first place. In fact, it looked worse. Whereas before it had had a kind of secret garden charm to it, now it looked like it had been napalmed, leaving only the burnt remains of the ancient lawn spread in ragged tatters.

Then one morning, when Mr Crawley and Tim were laying laminate flooring in the loft conversion and Gareth had got me picking rubble out of the mud, he'd dug his spade into the soil and leant on it, looking around him.

'I've got to say, Kitty, when I first came here I thought you were going to be a right stuck-up madam like most of the bored housewives round here, but you've really got stuck in. You're all right, you are.' He'd smiled at me then, me squatting up to my elbows in mud as if I were wearing silk and diamonds, and I can't pretend that it didn't feel nice. Gareth the *gardener* is actually kind of intense and really quite clever. At first glance you could have thought he was a bit of a cowboy maybe, a bit fly-by-night. You could have said that anybody who looks that heroic in combats couldn't seriously be interested in herbs, but he is, he really his.

He's focused and serious in a way that seems to evaporate the moment he comes in for coffee or a sandwich, which is twice a day usually, when Mr Crawley and Tim have gone off on some errand. He'll venture into the kitchen and I'll make him a coffee and we'll have a chat. I'd like to say that during these interludes his flashy good looks fade into the background and he is always Gareth the impassioned gardener, but I'd be lying. He flirts pathologically with the kind of relentless determination you imagine exists in the kind of people who climb Everest or walk across the Arctic, but instead with him it's not mountains he wants to conquer, it's pretty much every female that crosses his path.

I try not to take it personally; I've met his type before, dated most of them. They work very hard at making you feel special as they reel you in, then the moment you're hooked they chuck you back into the proverbial sea looking for the proverbial plenty of other fish swimming in it. He tells bad jokes and pulls faces at Ella and sometimes he brings out these books and shows me the pictures and names of the plants he has in mind for this border or that tub and listens to my half-baked ideas. But if you put all his attention into perspective, it's quite a laugh, really, a bit of a distraction.

So the last two weeks have gone quickly, when I thought that time was forever going to flow like treacle. I *feel* better and I'm fairly sure I look better. I think the sun and the air on my face have blown away some of the waxy pallor of my indoor skin, and I can feel the muscles in my thighs and arms aching at night as they get used to working again. I still look like a marshmallow man when I'm naked, but you know, every little helps.

Fergus has been home later and later, not until after ten for the last few days, so it's been good for me to have the garden to think about while he's got this rush on at work. It stops me from feeling all gloomy and abandoned, and each day I've made a mental list of things to tell him when he gets home. Except that for the last few days I've been asleep when he gets in, sometimes with Ella in my arms, and he always leaves so early, so our relationship has seemed almost like a dream – snatched kisses and words in those muddled moments just before or after heavy sleep. It's almost as if I've imagined it.

The front door slams and I tuck a stray strand of hair behind my ear and gaze with careful abstraction out of the window.

'All right, Kitty?' Gareth brings a breeze of warm air in with him, sharply scented with some kind of cheap aftershave.

I turn to him. 'Oh, hi, I was miles away,' I say vaguely, catching Ella's eye and winking at her.

Gareth sits across from me, leaning his bare forearms on to the table top, dipping his chin and levelling his eyes at me, the way he does when he thinks he's being charming.

'You're looking very ready and willing.' He smiles as he speaks, his eyes straying momentarily downward from my face.

I return his smile with a grin and push my freshly washed hair back off my shoulders with a flick.

'You should know by now that I'm always ready,' I laugh, playing his game. 'Do you want a coffee or shall we get on with it?'

Gareth leans back in his chair and tips his head to one side. 'We'd better get on with it,' he says slowly. 'Before I get distracted.'

I hold his gaze for a split second before jumping to my feet, sweeping Ella off her play mat and finding her sun hat.

'Come on, baby, time to make more mud cakes!' I tuck Ella under my arm and follow Gareth out into the garden. For a second I see Mr Crawley's face at an upstairs window, but then he's gone. He and Tim have been so thoroughly ensconced in the conversion that I've hardly seen him recently.

'So, what are we doing today, then?' I set Ella down on her rug and watch her as she reaches for a lump of earth, breaking it between her fingers with studied concentration.

'Today,' Gareth crouches gracefully and produces some orange string and metal spikes from his kit bag, 'I'm going to teach you about laying out beds, borders and pathways, so I expect your full attention and no slacking.'

I gaze round at the garden, bare except for the odd plant here and there, and wonder how he can possibly see anything existing here but this wasteland.

'You know, I'm sure I'm supposed to order you around,' I say casually, with a small smile. 'After all, it is me who pays your wages.'

Gareth straightens, metal stake in his hand, and narrows his eyes as he smiles.

'I think you'll find it's your better half that pays my wages, and anyhow,' he strides over to my side, dropping his voice a little as he steps just millimetres over the line into my personal space, 'I never let a woman tell me what to do. Usually I find they like to be told. A firm hand, that's what you ladies like.'

If I let it, this could be a moment when I could let a stupid, old-school Kitty crush win over my sensibly married recognition that Gareth is a rather vain and sometimes sexist kind of bloke, and I'd feel my knees buckle and bow under those wolfish eyes and that firm mouth that must make many a lesser woman crumble in his hands.

'Yeah, right,' I say instead, with considerable force of will. 'Has anyone told you this is the twenty-first century? Now what exactly do you want me to do?' I recognise the irony in my comment a second too late, and Gareth is already laughing when I catch up with him. 'Yeah, all right, all right. This is different. This is gardening.'

Gareth chucks me a ball of twine and starts heading off up the garden.

'Oh, that's all it is, is it?' he says over his shoulder.

I close the door on a mud-encrusted Ella and creep down the stairs to find Mr Crawley at the bottom. I raise my eyebrows at him by way of a greeting and enquiry.

'Mrs Kelly, I just wanted to check you were still on for the auditions next week?'

He speaks in a half-whisper. It must be the fresh air or maybe the ache in my legs and my back or perhaps the two cans of strong lager I had with Gareth over lunch, but whatever it is, all the half-baked excuses I've been toying with for the last couple of weeks have disappeared. I smile and nod.

'Yep, yep. Why not?' I glance at myself in the hall mirror. My face has caught the sun and my cheeks are flushed. Mr Crawley glances down the hallway towards the kitchen, where Gareth is washing up, and back at me.

'Well, time for me to be getting off,' he says, but for a moment he doesn't move. 'Everything going okay out there in the garden?' he says finally. 'Don't see many plants yet.'

'Oh, that's because preparation is everything,' I assure him breezily.

'Mrs Kelly, I hope I'm not speaking out of turn, but, well, are you sure it's not that he's trying to drag out the work and charge you more?'

I open my mouth slightly and close it again.

'No, Mr Crawley, I am certain that isn't the case. Gareth is serious about his gardening, he wouldn't do that.'

Mr Crawley presses his lips together and then smiles.

'I'm sure you're right. Well, I'll see you tomorrow and perhaps we might have tea in the afternoon? I've rather missed our little chats.'

I close the door on him, feeling guilty and disjointed. How have I got myself into a position where I feel bad about not paying the builder enough attention? I know what Fergus would say, he'd say I try too hard to be friends with everyone.

As I return to the kitchen I glance at the microwave. It's just after five. Ella will be out now for at least an hour until I wake her for tea and a bath. Fergus won't be home until God knows when – ten at the earliest going by recent times. That's five long hours watching TV, drinking tea or wine or both, waiting.

Gareth shuts the kitchen door behind him and stuffs his muddy overalls into a plastic bag, his wet hair plastered to his face.

'Could have done without that rain shower,' he says, a wry

smile on his face. It had come down out of nowhere. No spitting or darkened clouds to warn us. One moment the sky was bright with a few scattered white fluffy clouds and the ground was dry under our feet. The next moment it seemed as if someone had upturned a bucket on the garden and the mud had squelched and sucked under my feet as I ran inside with Ella. I'd expected Gareth to follow me, but instead he'd stood in the heavy rain, illuminated by the afternoon light, letting it drench him. Eventually I'd stopped looking at him and taken the now sleeping Ella to her cot.

'Won't get finished until tomorrow now, and look at the state of me!' he says now, pausing and looking up at the dark sky. 'Supposed to meet a lass later, too.'

'Oh really?' I say, with half a smile. 'What poor victim have you got lined up tonight then? Anyone I know?'

Gareth shakes his head and begins to fill the kettle. The fact that he doesn't ask permission to do so gives me some kind of pleasure.

'You don't know anyone, do you?' he says mildly, and I have to reflect that it's almost true, except for Clare from the One o'Clock Club, who I've now seen at two meetings and promised coffee to sometime soon.

'So, is it serious?' I enquire, taking my steaming cup of instant coffee. He's even remembered my one sugar.

Gareth sits astride a stool, his hand wrapped right around the mug, the tips of his fingers still red from the sudden drop in temperature.

'There's no need to get jealous, love.' He laughs.

'You wish,' I tell him, shaking my head in mock despair.

'Yeah, I do!' He smiles at me over the top of his coffee cup. 'No, it's not serious, she's nothing special. But what can I do? Women love me. It seems only fair that I give them all a chance to sample some of this good stuff!' He has a self-deprecating smile as he says it, but every other line of his posture shows that he believes every word he says.

'It must be hard,' I say breezily. 'All these women after you. Don't you ever get tired?'

Gareth grins and lowers his eyes and seems to look inwards as if remembering something or someone, some recent memory.

'Nope,' he says simply. 'Some things feel too good to get tired of.'

He stands suddenly and presses the palm of his hand into the small of his back, emptying his coffee cup and putting it the sink. 'I'd better be off.'

I look at the clock. It's still only five-thirty.

'Why don't you stay?' I say impulsively. 'For tea. There's this huge steak and red wine pie that's going to be past its sell-by date if I don't eat it tonight, and Fergus will probably eat in the office.' I assume that he will; he hasn't actually called me today at all, but for the last three nights that is exactly what he's done.

Gareth pauses, his bag on his shoulder.

'What about my date? Do you want me to stand her up?' he asks bluntly.

I feel the colour rise in my cheeks. I'd forgotten all about his date in the space of a few short seconds.

'Oh yeah, oh well, not to worry. I'll see you then.' I smile at him and get up, making myself look busy in the hope that it'll hide the fact that I feel foolish. Gareth drops his bag with a clatter and sits back down.

'All right then, you're on. Got any booze?' I hide my look of relief as I look into the fridge and reach for a bottle of wine. I wonder briefly about his nameless date – if she'll be waiting for him somewhere, wondering where he is – and then I open the wine.

I can't seem to catch my breath for laughing, and I pick up one of Fergus's brocade cushions and shove it into my mouth.

'Stop it!' I gasp. 'You'll make me wake up Ella!' And although it's just after seven and Ella should have had her bath and tea by now, I'm not ready just yet to start being a grown-up again. Gareth is sitting on the floor, his legs stretched out in front of him, his head resting on the seat of Fergus's chair.

'So I said to him, no matter which way you look at it, it's your pig in your bed, what do you expect me to do about it?' He grins and polishes off his glass of wine. 'I got fired, of course, but it's a good story.' At that point his mobile chirrups into life. He briefly scrutinises the display and rejects the call, slipping it back into his pocket and pulling himself into a kneeling position. He grabs the remnants of our second bottle of wine off Fergus's coffee table and begins to walk on his knees towards me.

'Want some of this . . .?' he asks, waggling his eyebrows.

'Ah, a man on his knees, just the way I like them.' I hold out my glass to him and tip back my head as the room swoons slightly around me.

'Hiya.' Fergus stands in the living-room doorway looking from Gareth to me. The room comes to an abrupt halt and I sit up, pushing my hair off my face. Gareth sits back on his heels, putting the bottle of wine on the floor.

'Hiya! You're home early,' I say, not sounding as delighted as I meant to, as I feel, after the initial shock. Instead, I feel like I used to when I called a sickie into work or when I was very little and got Mum's make-up out without her permission. I stand up rather unsteadily and go to him, putting my arms around his face and kissing his stubbled cheek. 'I thought you weren't going to be home for hours.'

Fergus shrugs and breaks free from our embrace. Looking into his eyes I'm relieved to see that he's exhausted, not jealous or angry with me. Relieved and a little disappointed.

'So, how's the garden going then?' Fergus extends his hand to the now standing Gareth.

'Getting there, mate, yeah. Start getting the plants in, lawn down and all that.' Gareth jams his hands into his pockets. I'm sure he'd like to get out of the room, but Fergus is still positioned in the doorway. 'Um, so, anyway, best be off.' Gareth nods at him to step aside, but instead Fergus turns around and walks out of the room to the kitchen, calling after him, 'Are we having that pie for dinner, it smells ni— Oh, you've eaten.'

'I'll see you later then,' Gareth says, winking at me as I open the door for him.

'Yeah, and thanks for staying, I mean, and missing your date,' I say, glancing over my shoulder.

'Oh, no worries.' He steps out into the rain-freshened air. 'I'm only about an hour late. I reckon she'll still be waiting.' And he's already pulling out his mobile as he opens his van door.

I look down the road, the promise of a warm spring evening sparkling on the damp pavements, and feel some kind of regret as I close the door and go back to the kitchen.

'I wish you'd told me you weren't going to be busy today. I could have got a sitter, we could have gone out maybe.' I go to lean on the fridge as Fergus examines the contents of the freezer with a scowl on his face.

'We are still busy, but I managed to get through a lot and I thought I'd come home on time for once.' He straightens his back with a beer in his hand, opens the can and takes a long drink straight from it. 'You sound like you'd rather I was late.' His tone is slightly defensive and I instantly climb down from my own slightly antagonised position. Fergus in one of his rare dark moods. I've learnt over the last year that with Fergus you can't make a direct reference to it; you can't, for example, ask him 'What's up?', because if you do you're nagging him or refusing to let him have his space. Instead you have to sort of

127

placate him on a general level and sometimes whatever it is that is bothering him will come out and sometimes it just won't.

'Don't be daft,' I say, going to him and putting my arms around him. 'I'm just surprised to see you early, that's all. It's great. I'll order you a Chinese and we can talk.' I kiss his tightly closed lips and open the freezer, looking for something to microwave for him, sensing that the very last thing he wants to do today is talk to me. 'Do you want another beer?'

Fergus shakes his head and looks at the work we've done on the garden closely for a moment before turning his back on the window dismissively.

'Where's my girl?' he says, a shadow of a smile on his lips. 'I think one of her smiles is just what I need right now!'

'Asleep,' I say, wondering if one of my smiles will do. 'She went to sleep after playing in the mud. One minute she was all thrashing about and shouting, the next snoring her head off.' I produce the smile. 'She's so funny.'

Fergus half laughs, but it doesn't look as if my smile has the right ingredients to lift his mood, at least not tonight. Right on cue, Ella's cries echo down the stairs as if the end of the world is imminent.

'Oh well,' I say. 'You order and I'll sort her out.'

Fergus glances at the menu I hand him, drops it back on the worktop and then disappears into the living room without another word.

It's taken me over an hour to get her back to sleep, and it's almost nine when I join Fergus, still clutching on to the faint hope that we might talk – I don't really mind about what, but just something that requires real words and proper sentences. He's staring blankly at the TV, not watching some cop drama. I pause for a moment in the door frame and decide what to do.

I sit beside him and lay my head on his shoulder. He doesn't acknowledge my presence. I know I should let him be from Mars and sit in his cave or whatever it is, but something about this mood seems different and, as a girl, I feel obliged to pester him about it until he either reveals what the problem is or accuses me of interfering and nagging.

'What's up?' I say casually, eternally optimistic that it might just be that easy. Fergus ignores me, his attention rapt in the plot of an advert he's seen at least a million times before.

'Fergus? I said, what's up,' I repeat, faintly annoyed. The talent he has for not acknowledging my existence these days is truly a remarkable one, one that makes me want to kill him, but a remarkable one nevertheless. Maybe on the planes of the Russian steppes early man had to develop this talent to cut out all surrounding distractions to hunt mammoths or something. Now, a few hundred thousand years later, there are no mammoths, just millions of really annoyed women contemplating murder. After deliberating over which to prioritise, the sofa arms or his wife, he turns to look at me, somewhat reluctantly.

'Ha, yeah, I know!' he says, hopeful that it will suffice.

'I *said*, what's up? Is there anything up?' My carefully constructed conciliatory tone has completely evaporated.

'Nothing, nothing's up. I'm fine. Just watching telly.' He puts his arm around me and stares at the screen again, clearly deciding that that will be enough to end my interrogation. I watch his profile for a moment, pursing my lips. Never go to bed on an argument, Camille always says, and I agree with her. It's just that sometimes you have to get the argument going before you can get over it and go to bed.

'You seem annoyed about something. Was it Gareth?' I finally voice my anxiety. I mean, I know and Gareth knows we only play flirt, but my tired and overworked husband might not.

'Who? Oh the gardener, why would he annoy me?' Fergus

shakes his head. 'I'm not annoyed,' he lies. 'Can I watch this now?' He gestures at a car ad.

I sigh and sit back in the chair. Unlike me, Fergus doesn't seem to see the cathartic benefits of airing his problems. I know that two train journeys, a day in an office and all the responsibility he has is tiring, and I know that sitting at home dandling a baby on my knee and turning on the dishwasher shouldn't be, even though it is. I just want some time to talk to him, some time to be listened to, some time to . . . exist for him.

'Well, I'll go and tidy the kitchen, okay?' I say, hoping he'll pick up on my rare offer to be domestic, a last ditch bid for attention, and come and sit with me. His gaze doesn't leave the TV and I'm fairly sure he hasn't heard me.

'Okay,' he says. As I stand up from the sofa, his arm flops heavily down as if he's forgotten I was there at all.

For a moment I stare at the kitchen wall as if I can see Fergus on the other side of it. It's not his fault, I tell myself. He's got a lot on his plate. He's too tired to realise that we never talk any more, or even just gossip and joke like we used to. I just have to give him some time to himself, and at the weekend we can be together properly, that's if the whole thing doesn't fly by in what seems like two hours, most of which he's asleep for. I tip the remains of the pie into the bin, decide that's enough cleaning for one night, and get out a packet of biscuits instead, eating two as I settle down to call Dora.

I listen to the ring tone for a very long time, waiting for her answer-machine to click on, not expecting her to be in. I am just about to hang up when she picks up the call, sounding a little breathless.

'Yes?' she sounds irritated.

'Dora, it's me,' I say apologetically. 'Were you asleep?' I can hear her sigh.

'No, not exactly. I was in bed though.' There's a short pause in which she is inevitably lighting a cigarette. 'I hope this is an emergency. I hope Fergus has fallen under a train and you need to borrow something black or something because I was halfway through a pretty good shag.' She sounds cross, but I know that she isn't. Besides, Dora once told me that she's never actually enjoyed sex, she just does it a lot because it seems polite. She was laughing when she said it, but I don't think she was lying.

'You should have just let it ring!' I say.

'I was letting it ring! But it kept on and on, putting me off my rhythm, and I thought it might be you and I didn't want to miss you.' I hear a muffled voice in the background.

'No, no. I have to take this call, it's an emergency. I'll be with you in a bit. Have another beer.'

I laugh.

'Not the love of your life then?' I ask her.

'Christ no. Nice shag and everything, but about as much personality as a block of wood. That's the trouble with these NA types, they think the fact that they've been stupid enough to get themselves addicted to something makes them fascinating, but really it's the only thing they've got to talk about and it's fucking boring.' I laugh again, picturing Dora, more than likely naked, taking a drag on her fag. And then something occurs to me.

'Hang on, if he's NA and you're NA, then you shouldn't be drinking beer, should you?'

There's a pause. 'I'm not. He is. And anyway beer doesn't really count, it's not mandatory you give it up, just recommended. It's like having a can of pop when you compare it with some of the things he's got up to.' She sounds sunny and self-assured, as if I'm worrying over nothing.

'Okay,' I say cautiously. 'If you say so.'

'I do, it's fine. So anyway, how are you? How's the kid and PC?'

'PC?' I can't think why Dora should be enquiring after our computer.

'Prince Charming! I can't be arsed to say the full-length version any more and I can't bring myself to use that fucking stupid name. I mean, who calls their kid Fergus?'

'Dora! Leave it out. I like it. Anyway Fergus is, he's . . . Well, he's pissed off actually and I don't know why. I tried to pick a fight with him but he wouldn't go for it.' I take a chocolate-chip biscuit out of the packet and stuff half of it into my mouth.

'Inconsiderate bastard,' Dora says. 'Mind you, I'm not surprised that he's pissed off, what with everything,' she says mildly. 'So how's the baby? I almost bought her . . .'

I interrupt her. 'Why aren't you surprised? What with everything what?' I say, wondering how my best friend seems to have a greater insight into my husband's moods than I do, and thinking of Fergus's forgotten encounter with her.

'Well, I.S.S, they're in a bit of trouble, aren't they? I heard my boss talking about it the other day. Something to do with spending millions on training their staff to sell and install this new generation software and no one's going for it. No one wants to make the investment at an uncertain economic time or something.' She says it as if she's reading a shopping list. 'He must have told you all this, surely?' she adds incredulously.

'No, no,' I say slowly, through a mouthful of crumbs. 'Do you think he might be in trouble then?'

The muffled voice of Dora's guest prevents her response.

'Okay, okay. I'm coming. Look, mate, I've got to go. Um, I don't know if he's in *real* trouble, that's just what I heard on the grapevine. I doubt it, though, I mean he's the CEO's blue-eyed boy, right?'

I listen hard for some nuances in Dora's voice, but I can tell that in her mind she's already off the phone and back in bed.

'Okay. Well, call me soon, okay? I miss you.' I hang up the

receiver and look at the phone. Fergus walks into the kitchen with his empty plate and looks at me, dark shadows draining the colour out of his eyes.

'That was fucking revolting. Dora or Camille?' he asks.

'Dora. I'm sorry I didn't cook – here, have a biscuit.' I hand him a cookie and wonder if I should ask him about work directly, or if I should skirt around to it. I look at the set of his chin as he washes up his plate despite the perfectly good dishwasher and decide to skirt around to it.

'Fergus, you know we don't really need a gardener. I know I've made a big fuss about wanting a lovely garden, but it could wait, it doesn't have to be right now, and maybe we don't even need to have the patio done either. I mean, we've got the kitchen and the bathroom sorted. That's all we need, really.' I look at his back, inwardly screaming at the thought of having this huge empty house to myself again. Fergus turns around, drying his hands, and sits down next to me.

'Why wouldn't we have that stuff done? Now that they've started?' He smiles his stock reassuring smile, which doesn't make it to his overcast eyes.

'Well, just in case you thought we had to tighten our belts a bit . . .' I begin.

'We don't. We don't have to tighten our belts. Don't worry about it. It'll be fine.'

I squirm in my seat and wonder exactly how far I should push this. If it hadn't been for my phone call with Dora I'd have believed him. I'd have been annoyed and frustrated that he brushed off my thoughts and suggestions with his usual paternal reassurance, but I'd have believed him and I'd have let it go. But if he refuses to tell me our real situation, if it happens to be something other than what I think it is, I can't let it go.

'Well, listen,' I say, 'I got a copy of the local paper today and guess what, they've got this part-time HR position up at the

Birchwood Business College, and there's a crèche. I though I could send in my CV and see how it goes. It's a really great place to work and it looks really interesting, they run all these different courses and do consulting and . . .'

Fergus leaves the room.

'Fergus!' I slide off my stool and follow him to the living room. 'Fergus! For God's sake don't just walk out on me! I am a person, you know, and do deserve a bit of recognition – just tell me what's wrong!'

Fergus sits on the sofa, his face closed down.

'There is nothing wrong. Okay? Everything is fine,' he says testily.

I stare at him, disbelief painted all over my face.

'Okay.' He relents. 'Things are a bit tight at work at the moment, there's a lot of competition and a limited number of contracts so I'm having to work my bollocks off to keep up my targets and . . .' Suddenly his forced reasonable tone erupts into anger. 'And I'd appreciate it if you could be just a little bit pleased to see me when I get home at night and maybe just once give me something to eat that hasn't been irradiated!'

My jaw drops open. 'You know I'm no good at cooking. And anyway I'm not your skivvy!' I whisper angrily, afraid that if I raise my voice I'll wake the baby again.

'No, you're not my skivvy, are you. Maybe you'd like me to get a chef and a cleaner to add to your fleet of domestic staff? Free up some more time for you to sit on your arse and get even fatter.' Fergus sits heavily on the sofa and begins to flick through the channels.

I swallow hard. I know he doesn't mean it, I know he's just worried and angry, but it takes a lot for me to swallow my hurt.

I kneel beside him and take his hand.

'Look, I'm sorry. I didn't know things were rough for you at work. If you'd tell me I could be more supportive. But please

134

don't have a go at me because you are angry with someone or something else. I'm on your side.' Fergus's eyes are fixed straight ahead. I try again, 'Listen, why don't I send my CV in to that job. It's only part-time. I could see Ella during my breaks and at lunchtime, and the walk up there every day'd be some exercise . . .'

Fergus turns off the TV and runs his fingers through his hair.

'No,' he says. 'You don't have to do that. You don't need to work. I can still support this family.'

'I know, and I'm so proud of you, but . . .' I falter, unable to think of the right thing to say. 'I am proud and I *love* you, you know how much I love you. But I don't care if we live in a one-bed flat with a leak in the roof, I'll still love you. I just want to feel that I'm contributing to this family too, it's just the way I am, and I think that if I had a job I'd start to feel a bit more like my old self . . .' I trail off as Fergus drops his shoulders, his anger falling suddenly away, making him look very tired.

He pulls me into an embrace.

'I'm sorry. It's just stress at work. It's nothing really, just a client I thought I'd landed pulled out at the last minute, but there are plenty more in the pipeline,' he says, more to himself than to me. I hold him close and think of what Dora told me. If I mention it he might think that I've been sort of spying on him, and I have the feeling that's the last thing we need right now. I decide not to mention it.

'It's okay,' I say to his chest. 'It's okay.'

'It means a lot to me that you don't care where or how we live, but I know how you grew up and I know more than anyone how things have been. I just want to take that burden away from you. I want you to feel secure, to know that you'll never have to struggle again, and you won't, you won't ever. I promise you,' he tells me, and I lean into his arms and think for a moment. I want to tell him that if I went back to work it wouldn't mean that he was failing, and that feeling secure in his love is the only security I need, but something tells me that to push him any more might hurt us both.

'I know,' I say at last. 'I know.'

I' m going to do without him. I concentrate on getting ready for a visit from Clare and try and push the thought out of my mind.

I look at myself in the mirror. Before Ella, hot weather like this – unseasonable or not – would have inspired me to wear as little as possible, a bootlace strappy top, maybe, and a flirty summer skirt. I'd have washed my hair and let it dry naturally wavy, and if it was a weekend I'd have flounced around Sainsbury's buying a picnic for the park, and if it was a work day, I'd have lounged languorously on the tube as if at any moment the heat might get too much for me and I'd be forced to rip off all my clothes. Before Ella *and* Fergus of course. Now eighteen months and two stone later I don't feel quite the same way. In fact, if there is an opposite way to feel, I feel it. None of my pre-E clothes fit me without new eruptions of lumps here or bulges there. I have discovered that now I have to think very carefully about the pros and cons of sleeveless tops. If I wear my jeans they hold the bottom of my tummy in but the top spills out over my belt. If I wear my denim skirt it gives me a waist but the bulge of my tummy makes me look like I'm still half pregnant. I laugh out loud and shake my head. Half drunk as I was with Gareth yesterday I'd forgotten I wasn't that Kitty any longer. I'd lounged on Fergus's sofa giggling and fluttering just like old Kitty would have, except that now I was wrapped in layers and layers of extra flesh. What a fool I must have looked.

I sigh and squint at my half-naked reflection. I think I can still see her there, the old me, Kitty with all her artifice, her coloured hair and eyes, her lipsticked cupid's bow and pencilled brows. When my love for Fergus had first stripped me bare of all that it had taken me so long to create, I had been grateful, light-headed and delirious; relieved and relaxed to be loved just for being, rather than for being me. Now, though, one wedding later, when I look at myself I see a stranger. A face a little heavier than mine ought to be, eyes bruised with shadows. Glorious red hair that I'd forgotten was out of a bottle faded to mid-range brown. Now, when I have a second to myself to think about myself, I sit au naturel in front of my bedroom mirror, looking for the insecure, longing-to-be-loved Kitty. The girl who prayed every day that that would be the day she would meet the right man, the woman who spent each empty hour wearing pretty clothes and doing exactly what she wanted whenever she wanted. The kind of girl who turned heads when she walked by.

You don't realise how important feeling sexy is until you don't any more.

'What shall Mummy wear, hey baby?' I ask Ella, but she's unresponsive, crashed out in the middle of playing on my bed, cinnamon spice lipstick still clasped in one hand, her cheeks pink with teething roses. She looks so helpless and vulnerable, and for a moment the sadness and horror left to me by my mum crowds the corners of the room in shadow.

'Mum,' I say out loud. 'I love you, and don't worry, I know. I know you wouldn't have left me if you'd had any choice. I know.' I watch the sunlight dapple the windowsill for a moment, waiting for some kind of sign, I suppose, but then the shadows are gone and the voices from the garden fade in again and the moment has passed.

'Kitty! Where are you?' Gareth shouts up the stairs. Ella twitches but doesn't wake up, only rolling over on to her side. I stand stock-still holding a T-shirt to my bra-only chest.

'Kitty? Are you up there?' For one moment longer I stand frozen in front of the mirror and then I hastily pull whatever item of clothing I'm holding over my head and go to the door; after all, it's only the gardener not the KGB.

'Coming!' I stage-whisper. I lean over the banister pressing a finger to my lips. 'Shhh, the baby's asleep.' Gareth smiles up at me, the improbable white of his teeth glinting in the shadows.

'You look nice,' he whispers back, his eyes running briefly over my torso.

'Oh . . . thanks,' I reply hesitantly, aware of my tangled hair and unwashed face and still feeling embarrassed about how I behaved, no, how I felt, yesterday. Gareth must have laughed all the way to the pub. When I look down at my hastily put-on top I see I picked one of my old-life T-shirts, far too tight for me now – pink glitter jersey with Las Vegas printed on the front. Back then it was ironic. Now I look like genuine white trash or a Vegas table dancer who's strayed into a not-so-flattering hall of mirrors. I hunch my shoulders over my chest and fold my arms, taking a couple of steps back as I realise that he's coming up the stairs.

'God, sorry. I look a fright,' I say nervously, pointlessly. 'I've just been deciding what to throw out.'

He appears unconcerned.

'Don't be stupid,' Gareth says as he reaches the top of the stairs. 'You look good, you should wear stuff like that more often. If you've got it, flaunt it, my mum used to say – is this a spare room? Can I go in here?' I look away from him wondering if he can really mean his compliments as he slides past me into the so-called guest bedroom at the back of the house. And anyway, what exactly does he want with me in the spare bedroom?

'Well, come on then,' he says, still in a whisper. I look at Ella sleeping peacefully on my bed. She looks as if she'll be out for a good while yet. I should really move her into her cot, but if I pick her up she's bound to wake up. A couple of minutes won't hurt. I push open the door.

'Well?' I say. Gareth is leaning on the windowsill looking at his handiwork.

'Well, I thought from up here you'd get a better view of the garden, like a bird's-eye view, see?' he smiles at me happily, clearly excited. An irresistible smile that it's impossible not to return. I go and stand by him at the window and look down at the garden.

'My Christ, it's carnage,' I say. Below me, what was once a wilderness of waist-high grass and weeds is now what looks like a muddy field at Glastonbury after a rainy weekend after two hundred thousand sales managers posing as hippies have trampled all over it. The cherry trees are still there, but other than that it's apocalyptic. It's not as if I didn't know what havoc we had wreaked, it's just that seeing it from up here makes it seem all the more total. I turn to look at Gareth open mouthed, but he only smiles, and his amber eyes alight with fire.

'Now you see, to the *untrained* eye, Kitty, yes it does looks like carnage, but to you and I, to gardeners of the heart, Kitty, of the heart and the soul and the mind, it looks like a blank canvas.' He reaches down and picks up a folder he had leant against the wall. 'A blank canvas on which we can paint . . . this!' With a proud flourish Gareth hands me his plan of our garden.

'It's beautiful,' I say with a gasp, noticing how pleased he is with the success of his theatrical unveiling. He nods, bouncing excitedly on the balls of his feet. He's handed me a bird's-eye plan of the garden painted in vibrant watercolour, showing each plant and where it will go, its name written alongside it in both Latin and English, and down in the bottom corner is a thumbnail sketch, a little painting of what it might look like when it's finished. I stare at the piece of paper and then at the expanse of mud and it's all I can do to stop myself from flinging my arms around him in gratitude. Somehow Gareth Jerome has come up with the perfect garden, the garden I have always dreamt of.

'Oh, Gareth, it's fantastic. I never knew you could do this – it's even better than Alan's; sorry Alan.'

Gareth shrugs with faux modesty and eyes me with obvious satisfaction.

'Oh well, you know. I always like this bit, the planning. It's more involved than you think, you know. You've got to plan a colour scheme, what'll be in flower when, how it's gonna look in winter . . .' He stops himself and smiles, lowering his eyes. 'Sorry, I just love it out there, you know? I get all *passionate* about it, all carried away.'

I smile back at him, swept up by his enthusiasm and self-assurance.

'Don't be sorry, I think its wonder—' I'm interrupted by an ominous thud from my room. I clap my hand over my mouth. 'Ella!' My worst fears are confirmed when after a second's silence my baby's high-pitched wail hits me in the gut and wrenches out my heart.

'Oh shit! She's fallen off the bed!' I race into my room to find Ella lying arms and legs akimbo in the middle of a pile of dirty laundry, her face red with shock and fury. Guilt-ridden I quickly pick her up and try to rock her.

'Oh darling, darling baby. Naughty Mummy left you and you fell off the bad, bad bed!' I soothe her, rocking her against my chest until her cries become resentful snuffles. Gareth watches me from the door frame.

'She all right? I'm sorry. It's my fault. I shouldn't have come up here.'

Ella's crying has stopped, and instead she stands up on my lap and begins to try and pick the bits of Lycra out of my top. I examine her closely.

'She looks okay. I think if she'd broken anything she'd be more upset, don't you?' I ask him anxiously, the way I would Mr Crawley. Gareth laughs.

'Oh, course she's okay! Apart from the fact that she fell on a big pile of pants! She's fine.' He looks at us for a moment longer, shaking his head, his reassuring lack of concern over my daughter's health somehow comforting and disconcerting all at once.

'Right, I'm off to stake out the lawn, are you helping today?'

Ella nuzzles her head into my neck, which I mistakenly take as a sign of affection until she starts to chew earnestly at the neckline of my top. I set her down on the bed again.

'Um, I, well, see, a friend of mine called me about coming round for coffee,' I lie. I'd called Clare as soon as I'd found out Mr Crawley wasn't coming and asked her to come over. I thought having someone else here would be the perfect way to keep my distance from Gareth. 'She's been on at me to have her over for ages, and what with one thing and another it's got delayed, so anyway, she's coming later. So no, I can't help.'

Gareth examines my face closely and I avert my eyes from his scrutiny, fearing that I'm an open book.

'You didn't get into trouble, did you? For having me round when he got home last night?'

I swallow and shake my head vigorously. No, I didn't get into to trouble I don't think: Fergus had far more to think about than wondering if his fat wife is shagging the gardener. 'Don't be stupid!' I manage a laugh.

'Cos I did,' he whispered conspiratorially. 'Bloody hell, nearly got my balls ripped off, thought I was never going to shut her up, but I did in the end. Wasn't worth all the effort as it turned out. I'd much rather've been having a laugh with you.' He turns on his heel and bounces down the stairs, leaving me standing stupidly in the door frame, collecting my wits one by one off the floor.

'Come on now, Kitty,' I say out loud. Somehow I've let this stupid crush turn into some ridiculous fantasy, and now it's dangerously close to getting totally out of hand. I'm sure Gareth isn't really interested in me, he can't be. But he must be able to see me acting like a stupid kid. He must be able to see it, and I bet he thinks it's a right laugh. Well, enough is enough, it's got to stop.

I'm just brushing my hair when Fergus's doorbell chimes, filling the hallway with what is apparently an exact replica of the bells of Canterbury Cathedral. Ella and I look at each other and she screws up her nose as she gives me a single-toothed grin.

'Exactly,' I say. 'I don't know what he was thinking.' As we reach the bottom of the stairs, the dying chimes of the bell have given way to rhythmic thuds against the front door.

'I'm only telling you once . . .' I hear Clare warn her son, and as I open the door Ted's legs flail against thin air as he struggles to be free of the constraints of his buggy. Clare grins at me.

'I swear he's whatsit. Hyperactivehyperattentiondeficit-annoyinglittlebugger-thing.'

I grin as I help her lift the buggy into the hallway.

'Or it's being nearly one, one or the other,' I tell her.

'Are you all right? Is this all your house or is it flats?' She looks around the high-ceiling hallway. 'It's bloody massive.'

I shuffle awkwardly. I still can't get used to the fact that I live in this house, and the thought that it is actually, technically at least, mine is something that seems so ridiculous I don't even consider it.

'Um . . . It's all mine, ours, I mean. But we couldn't have afforded it if Fergus hadn't bought it so cheap off an old lady.' Clare raises an eyebrow. 'Not that we cheated her or anything. I mean, she was dead and it needed a lot of work.'

Clare shrugs. 'It's lovely,' she says. 'I hope Ted doesn't totally wreck it before we leave.'

I laugh and show her into the kitchen.

'I shouldn't worry. I've been looking for an excuse to get the builder to stay on longer. He's like a male fairy godmother, I swear. Every time I get all of a dither about something, he goes and sprinkles his magic dust on it and it's all okay again. Do you want tea?'

'Yeah, cheers,' Clare says, and her eyes widen as Gareth opens the door.

'Need a glass of water – it's boiling out there!' He catches sight of Clare and I watch with interest as his eyes travel swiftly over her before he treats her to one of his rakish grins. 'Hello there, I'm Gareth.' He rubs the palm of his hand down his jeans and then holds it out to her. Momentarily Clare appears to have had both of her hands welded on to the handle of Ted's buggy, then she giggles and takes his hand.

'Oops, silly me. Hello, Clare. I'm Clare.' As she takes his hand I suppress a little smile as I see her cheeks flush. 'That's me, Crazy Clare to my friends!'

Gareth laughs at her and then, dropping her hand, drinks his water down in one.

'I'll get back to work then,' he says, looking at me. 'Seeing as I'm on my own today. Nice to have met you, Crazy Clare.' For a second his amber eyes appear almost luminous in the direct sunlight as he lets his gaze linger on Clare for just a fraction of a second more than is polite. As he walks back outside he takes another look at the sky and strips off his shirt. I try very hard not notice his stomach.

Clare looks at me open-mouthed.

'Fuck me, he's gorgeous. Cover your ears, Ted.' She bends and releases her son from his buggy, putting him on the floor next to a very reserved Ella. 'I wish you'd told me you had a fit bit of totty half naked in the garden – I'd have made a bit more effort.' She fans herself and sinks on to a stool in a mock swoon, tugging at the high neck of her loose cotton top.

'Do you really think he's fit?' I say casually. 'Not really my type.'

Clare gawps at me.

'You've got a pulse, haven't you? Trust me, if you're a bird and you're alive he's your type.'

I shrug, shake my head and put a cup of tea in front her, enjoying my pretence.

'Once, maybe, before I met Fergus and realised that having a boyfriend didn't have to mean night after night of angst-ridden waiting followed by messy and humiliating partings. No, I mean, objectively I can see he's quite fit, but he's a bit too obvious for me, and what's all that hair about? No one has long hair any more.' Today Gareth had tied up his hair with an elastic band, revealing the straight line of jaw and the shadows of his cheekbones. I blink and shake my head, returning my attention to Clare.

'I like it, something to grab hold of!' Clare giggles again. 'It must be because you're so happily married,' she says as she spoons in sugar. 'Your love for Fergus, it must blind you to his beauty.'

I like her reasoning, and even though I see his beauty as if it were a forty-foot billboard five inches from my face, I agree with her. In fact, it's his in-your-face beauty that's the trouble, that combined with the fact that he's clearly up for anything with anyone. It would have been all right, maybe at a pinch, to have a half-fantasy type crush on some other type of man, one not so good looking or . . . oh, I don't know, say, *real*? But with an actual person in your actual house while your actual husband is out most of the time, it's not on. It's childish and pointless and it's got to stop. And as I can't get Fergus to quit his job so that he can remind me how much I love him twenty-four-seven, I'll have to think of some other way of keeping Gareth off-limits.

'Yep, that must be it.' I glance at the children. Ella sits agog as Ted pulls himself up on a kitchen cupboard and begins to edge his way round the kitchen. Clare smiles at him.

146

'Don't drink any bleach,' she says cheerily before turning back to me and raising an eyebrow. 'So, it's your turn next to bring the cakes to the club. What are you baking? Something by McVities?'

I smile at her, half an idea forming in my mind.

'Ah well, I was down the town yesterday and did you know there's a café in the post office? They're Christians.'

Clare rolls her eyes at me. Of course she knows, she's lived here all her life and unlike me she goes out sometimes.

'Well, they have these chocolate brownies, home-made on the premises. So I bought them. All of them. Fifteen in total.' I take the tin out, lift the lid and tip it towards her, feeling pleased with myself. 'And look, there are still twelve left.' Clare stares at me.

'You're a genius,' she says with admiration and takes one out. 'Of course you don't really need to take more than ten.' I nod and take another one out.

'Ella fell off the bed today,' I say. 'I'm such a terrible mother. You know what I think it is? I think it's because my mum died when I was so young that I don't know what to do. Never had anyone to show me, you know?'

Clare shakes her head. 'Trust me, no one knows what to do at first. It's a total learning curve. In fact I don't think you ever stop learning, as far as I can tell.' She sips her tea. 'I'm sorry you lost your mum when you were a kid. What was it, cancer?'

I start at her frank enquiry. Most people are too polite to ask. Somehow her overt curiosity is refreshing.

'No, um, she was murdered actually.' I taste the bitterness of the word I hardly ever use on my tongue.

Clare's jaw drops.

'Bloody hell. I've never met anyone who knew anyone who was murdered before.' She takes my hand. 'You poor cow. It must have been hard on you as a kid?'

I gaze into my coffee for what seems like a long moment, wondering how much to tell her and deciding that I like her too much to tell her everything just yet.

'Oh well, you know, I was quite young so I didn't really know what was going on at the time.' Looking out of the window I see that Gareth's staking out is gradually coming into shape, and I feel a moment of regret that I'm not out there with him, the sun burning my shoulders and all thoughts of my life so far locked up tightly in this house. 'I missed having a mum, though. I still do.'

Clare squeezes my hand. 'Is he still behind bars, the bloke that did it?' she asks me.

I shift uncomfortably in my seat, I haven't discussed it at this length with anyone since meeting Fergus.

'No, well, not that I know of, anyway. They never arrested anyone.' A moment of silence hangs thickly in the air.

Clare studies her cup for a while and then, looking out of the window, diffuses any tension with a single stroke.

'Phwor, just *look* at his arse.' She admires Gareth as he bends over a stake. 'Nice and bony, just how I like arses to be!'

I sit back and laugh. 'Clare! The window's open, you know! He can probably hear you.'

Clare sighs and takes another brownie. 'I'm sorry, it's just that I haven't had sex in a while and I get all overcome with *urges*.'

I follow her lead and take another brownie too, deciding eight is more than enough for Ellie and her calorie-counting cronies.

'Lucky you, I've got the opposite problem – sporadic, in fact near-fatal, lack of *urges*. When was the last time you had sex then?' I lean on my hand, enjoying my first girly chat for ages.

Clare looks at the ceiling and begins to count on her fingers.

'Oh God, no use denying it. The last time I had sex was the

night Ted was conceived and that was shite.' I look at her, not exactly sure what to say. 'And, well, it's not as if you get out much when you're a single mum, and anyway, even if I did I'm not exactly Kate Moss.'

'No, thank God, you're lovely,' I say. 'What happened with Ted's dad then? Did you break up or what?' Clare looks at Ted. He and Ella sit side by side regarding each other seriously. Ted bashes a wooden spoon on the floor until Ella takes it out of his hand and bashes it herself. After a few minutes Ted takes back the spoon and the cycle begins again.

'The funny thing is Ted looks just like him.' Clare lets out a long sigh. 'Okay, I'll tell you, but it's not a pretty story, so be prepared.' She settles down, gazing out into the garden. 'I'm out with some mates, it's a Friday night. We all go to this club in Hemel. It's a total dive but everyone goes there so it's usually quite a laugh and you know everyone and everyone knows you. We're all dancing away when Jamie, that's his dad, comes up to me and starts dancing next to me. I mean, he'd come with his girlfriend, I could see her at the bar, so I didn't think anything about it, just him mucking about. Anyway, a few tracks in and he's right up against me giving it all that dirty dancing lark. I look about for Nikki but she's nowhere to be seen. I look around for my mates but I think they must have all copped off by then, 'cos it was just me. Me and Jamie and a few of his mates all dancing round us, like.

'Anyway, he leans against me and whispers in my ear that he wants to talk to me. 'Go on then,' I says, but he goes, no, he wants to talk somewhere a bit quieter and he takes me by the hand and leads me out into the foyer. I'm thinking, what's all this about. I mean, Nikki, she wasn't exactly classy, but she was thin, blonde, white halter-neck, you get the picture.' I nod, picturing Nikki in my mind's eye. 'And there I am, a big sweaty girl with running mascara.

'"Go on, then,"' I'd said to him again, feeling a bit embarrassed. But he said he fancied some fresh air and led me outside.

'"My coat's in there!" I said, but he told me not to worry, that he knew the bouncer and we'd get back in no trouble once we'd had our "talk". The brightness that Clare had begun her story with has faded slightly and her shoulders droop. 'So we're standing outside the club and I'm really quite pissed and he was fit, you know, tall and blond with the same eyes as Ted. Bright blue with those thick lashes.

'"Well?" I asked him.

'"Clare, I just wanted to say that I like you. I really really like you," I'd stared at him. I mean he's a fit bloke, with a pretty girlfriend just inside the club.

'"Cheers," I said. "I like you too."

'And then he sort of leant me against the wall and he went, "No, I mean I *really* like you." I couldn't believe what was happening.' Clare screws up her mouth. 'Stupid cow. Anyway . . .

'"But, what about Nikki?" I asked him, all wide-eyed. He looked me right in the eye and shrugged and said, "Nikki's all right. But she's the kind of bird you go out with 'cos your mates think she's fit." And I swear he actually said these words. He went, "You're the kind of bird a bloke could really fall in love with."'

'No!' I can't believe what she is telling me.

Clare shrugs. 'Yeah, and if I hadn't been so pissed, if I hadn't had a crush on him for ages and if I'd had a sniff of interest from anyone else, I'd have told him to piss off there and then. But I had and I hadn't so I didn't.'

'Oh mate,' I say, my voice warm with sympathy. No one knows better than me exactly what kinds of trouble that combination of circumstances can get you into.

'I know. So, there I am all pie-eyed, and he takes me down

this alley down the side of the club and the next thing I know he's all over me, going "Oh baby, oh yeah baby. I really want you baby, bleugh."' Clare takes a sip of her tea reflectively. 'It stunk of stale piss and vomit so it wasn't exactly romantic, but I was thrilled. I couldn't believe it. At last, I thought. It's happening to me! I should have known better.

'Anyway, it was over really quickly. He stopped moaning "Oh baby" and burped in my face and I wasn't even halfway there! But I thought, never mind, this is only the first time. It'll get better, the only way is up, if you know what I mean . . . He got off me and said, "Cheers, Clare, that was really special." So we're getting ourselves tidy and I realise my knickers are round one ankle so I'm just about to pull them up when he says, "No, let me have these. A memento." He gives me this gorgeous grin and looks all coy and sweet and sexy, so like a total dumb-assed bitch I say "okay".

'"I'll go back in first," he says. "Don't want to give anyone anything to talk about." And already he was backing off from me.

'"Not until you've told Nikki, you mean?" I say, and he says yeah, and tells me to wait ten minutes then go back in. And I wait. I'm standing there in the piss-filled alley and the booze and the heat of the nightclub's worn off and I'm cold and tired and I'm not really sure what I've done, but I keep thinking, well, Jamie likes me, he really likes me, he might even fall in love with me. *Stupid fucking cow*.

'So after ten minutes I try to go back in, but the bouncer stops me.

'"You ain't going in there unless you can pay," he says.

'"But I've already paid. I mean, I just came out with Jamie. He said you'd let me back in." I tried to tell him, explain that I was Jamie's friend and that my coat and purse were already inside, but he wasn't having any of it. Said he'd never heard of this Jamie bloke. But it was the way he said it, big smirk all over his face. He said I could wait until the club had finished and everyone was out and then I could go in and get my coat. I couldn't believe it. I'm stood there like a melon for the best part of an hour and then eventually people start filing out. Nikki comes out with all her mates, giggling and shit, and she sees me and gives me a right superior look and I think, "yeah, well, I've been fucking your boyfriend, love, pride before a fall and all that", and then Jamie and his mates come out, all laughing and pushing each other around. I'm just about to speak to him when I hear him go, "I'm telling you, you all owe me twenty quid each." He rubs his hands together. "I'm minted!" And his mates are going, "Oh yeah", and "Right mate". And he goes, "I've got proof," and he pulls my *knickers* out of his pocket and twirls them round his fingers! "You can tell they're hers by the size of them! Pitch camp in these, you could!" He looks right at me and laughs. "I won the bet," he said. And they're all laughing and joking and chanting, "Jamie pulled a pig, Jamie pulled a pig," and that was that. If I'd have been sober I'd have used a condom . . .' Clare's voice trails away to nothing.

'Oh mate,' I say to her, holding her hand. 'I can't believe it. What a . . . I can't believe that anybody would treat another person that way.'

Clare straightens her shoulders and lifts her chin.

'No, well, neither could I, but I thought, these things happen, just get on with it, you know. Then nine months later this little bloke popped out and my whole life changed. I was a mug then, thinking that I was going to find true love with someone else's boyfriend in the back alley of a dodgy club. Now I'm older and wiser and it's even less likely I'll find someone, with someone else's kid hanging off my skirts and stuck in a council flat.'

Ted, clearly fed up with playing pass the spoon, scrambles up his mum's legs until she lifts him on her lap and kisses his blond curls.

'I mean, I love him more than anything else in my life. But I don't want him to be the *only* thing in my life. Is that terrible?'

I look in the brownie tin, now there are only six left.

'Christ no! No! That's normal. That's right, and not everyone is like Jamie. I mean, look at Fergus, he's lovely, he's the loveliest bloke ever and there are others out there definitely,' I say with faint optimism, wondering, worrying, is 'lovely' enough.

'I hope you know how lucky you are,' Clare says with a small smile.

I hope I do too.

I look out into the garden and Gareth waves at me, and then, dropping his hand to his side, beckons me with a jerk of his head. 'Slacker!' he calls out with a chuckle, before turning back to his work. Clare gazes at him with open admiration, and the thought that's been occupying the back of my mind finds its way to my mouth.

'Well, what about him? He's nice and he definitely had a twinkle in his eye when he met you.' Which is not strictly true, but he definitely did check her out, the same way he'd looked at me on the landing in my Vegas T-shirt. And if he's looking at me that way then he's the kind of man who likes a bit of flesh on a woman and not just a skinny bit of totty hanging off his arm, I'm sure of it. Okay so he's a bit of ladies' man, a bit of a Jack the Lad, but that's just because he picks up these girls in bars and never bothers to get to know them. Probably thinks any girl who lets herself get picked up that way can't be 'relationship material'. Because most men think that way, even the nice ones, and you're a fool if you don't believe it. Maybe, maybe if he got to know Clare gradually through me, he'd treat her differently, see her for the sweet, pretty, funny girl she is. After all, any man who gets so soppy over petunias can't be totally shallow. And as for Clare, she needs some kind of lift far more than I do, moaning about my poor sad life in my huge house with my rich husband who adores me. What's more, if Gareth *did* get with Clare, that would put temptation firmly out of my way, and even if he doesn't it doesn't matter, because you don't fancy the bloke your mate actively fancies. It's just one of those unwritten laws.

Clare flushes a healthy pink.

'Me? Really? No he didn't. Did he? Really?' I watch her face fill with pleasure and decide that if he didn't, then he soon could do with a little bit of help from me.

'Oh yeah. I reckon all we have to do is arrange a few more meetings for you and you two could really hit it off.' Clare tries not to look at Gareth, his bare skin glistening with sweat in the sun, and fails.

'Blimey,' she whispers into Ted's hair and giggles.

Just as I am about to let her out of the door half an hour later, I stop her and hug her hard.

'Thanks!' she says looking mildly surprised.

'Look, Mr Crawley's taking me to these auditions tomorrow night – why don't you come with me? I'm dreading going on my own. It might be fun!'

Clare looks tempted but gestures to Ted. 'What about him?'

'Well, Fergus has got Ella, so I'm sure he can manage Ted too. It's only for a couple of hours, and you might bump into Gareth when you drop him off!'

'Well, I don't know . . .' Clare's face breaks into a grin. 'All right then, you're on.'

As I watch her retreat down the street, I smile to myself. Given Fergus's total lack of energy when he gets home and the fact that I suspect that he doesn't really know he has agreed to have Ella on his own (Me: 'Those auditions I told you about are this week.' Him: 'Mmmm?' Me: 'So you wouldn't mind having Ella that night?' Him: 'Ha, yeah, I know!' Me: 'That's agreed then'), maybe foisting another doubly boisterous child on him isn't quite fair, but I don't care. It will give him chance to see how he likes it, and anyhow, if he doesn't want me to work, and if my two best friends are thirty miles and a universe away, I'll have to do something else.

Chapter Ten

'You're sure you don't mind?' I kiss Fergus's chest and snuggle into the curve of his arm, hopeful that for once I have his undivided attention, which is usually stimulated by my nudity. Early morning light has crept into the room and this morning seems like the first morning in years that we've woken up together. Fergus grabs my arse optimistically.

'Mind what?' he says, sliding the palm of his hand up into the small of my back.

'Mind having Ted and Ella tonight while I'm out!' I say with exasperation. I wouldn't mind, but it's only been five minutes since I asked him. He rolls on to his elbow and kisses me deeply. We have reached a stage in our relationship where he only kisses me like this as a precursor to sex. I wriggle away from him.

'Well, do you?'

His arm reaches around my waist and pulls me back flush against his body.

'No, of course it's all right.' He kisses my ear. 'I mean, how hard can it be to sit with a couple of babies for a few hours? I only wish I got to sit at home all day playing with Ella. It'll be a piece of cake!' He nuzzles my neck and runs the tips of his hand over my nipple. I close my fingers around his wrist and push his hand firmly away. At last the excuse I've been looking for to halt his advances has arisen, and just in time judging by the other early riser I can feel pressing into my belly.

'Hang on a minute – what do you mean how hard can it be? Are you saying that I don't work hard?' I say, sitting up and pulling the duvet protectively over my chin.

The playfully lazy smile Fergus has been wearing evaporates abruptly. He sits up in bed, pushing his tangle of black hair out of his eyes. For a moment I look at him as if for the first time, and my heartbeat races and I want him, want him as much as I ever have, but then I blink and it's only Fergus again and I'm glad my ploy to crowbar him out of his mood has worked, glad that the distance between us, which I hate, has been firmly bridged.

'I didn't say that! I said that I don't mind looking after another baby too. I didn't say I thought motherhood was easy!' He pushes back the bedclothes and walks to the wardrobe. 'Is there a shirt ironed?'

I pull the covers completely over my head. I forgot to re-iron his shirt after I borrowed it. Basically, if I'm not willing to fuck him then he can't be arsed to talk to me. I lie in the half-light of the duvet still smarting from his previous comment. If he knew, if he had even the faintest idea what it's been like here alone day after day, week after week, feeling as if my real life is still on hold, then . . .

'I said, is there a shirt ironed?'

I ball my hands into fists and resist the urge to scream.

'No. But it's dress-down Friday, isn't it?' I listen to a pause from the other side of the duvet, and Fergus's body weight thuds on to the bed and he pulls the covers away, noticing my frown with mild amusement.

'It's just that we don't seem to spend any time together, you and me any more. I see you for half an hour in the morning and then by the time I get home we're both knackered.' He looks uncomfortably past my face and at the headboard. 'I *need* you, Kitty.' I look at the ceiling, and notice the shadow of dust that highlights the plaster ceiling rose.

'I need you too,' I respond cautiously, trying to temper my instant fury. 'But I need you to see me and hear and notice me at times other than when you want to . . . to have sex,' I finish lamely.

'I love you, you know that.' Fergus lies beside me in only his smart–casual shirt and his boxers. 'I do notice you, if you only knew. I think about you, about being like this all the time. I need it, I need our . . . physical relationship. I need . . . that.'

I roll on my side and look into his eyes, taking his hand in mine.

'I know, I need you too, like that I mean.' I'm aware that no matter how much I try and sound as if I mean it I sound empty and hollow. 'Really I do, it's just that since the baby . . . It's just, I don't know, it takes a bit more to get me in the mood these days, that's all.'

I put my arms around his neck and he holds me quietly for a long time, both of us feeling the small spaces between our bodies as if they were acres of loneliness.

'I'm sorry, but I'm sure it will come back, and I love you and don't have an affair,' I say into his chest, feeling guilty since pretty much all of my fantasies and dreams over the past few weeks have been about doing exactly that.

'Don't be stupid,' he says, breaking the embrace with a platonic kiss on the side of my nose. 'I'd better get ready so I can make sure I can leave on time tonight. Don't want you missing out on your stage debut.'

I watch him dress and wonder how much he understands and how much he pretends to understand, hiding his real worries away under his laid–back façade. Wondering how much, really, either one of us knows about the other.

'All set for later then?' Mr Crawley leans on the kitchen counter and drinks his coffee. It's just him today; Tim's gone somewhere to price some materials. Today is his last day.

'Well, I'm sort of all set. I mean, I'm not really.' I am stupidly excited about the whole audition thing – I think it's a hangover from TV talent hunts. Maybe someone in the audience will discover that there's a niche for a gravelly voiced thirty-something singer who wears loose tops and can't act.

'But what shall I sing? Do you think "Windy City" or "The Dead Wood Stage"?' I ask him.

Mr Crawley smiles at me.

'How well can you sing?' he says.

'Well, I can carry a tune if it's not *too* demanding, nothing higher than "la" or lower than "do" if we're going to be Julie Andrews about it. Strictly chorus material, I'd say.' I shrug off my fantasy of running about in yellow gingham holding a bunch of daffodils just like Doris.

'Well, that is a slightly limited range,' he says kindly, and hums a few bars of each tune to himself.

' "Windy City",' he says after a moment's deliberation. 'Gives you more scope to act the song instead of sing it. Sort of like a lady Rex Harrison.'

I nod and tap my fingers on the worktop as I hum it through. 'Oh yes, that'll be fine. Of course, I can't act either, but what the hey . . .'

Mr Crawley watches me intently as I wipe down a work surface.

'Mrs Kelly. There was something I wanted to ask you?'

I snap up my head and look at him with my recently acquired certainty that all news is bad news.

'Have we gone over budget? How much? Is it more than £500?'

Mr Crawley shakes his head.

'No, no. In fact we've come in just a bit under . . .' He runs a hand over his thinning hair. 'It's, um, well, my children don't live locally now. My son Christian and his lovely wife Naomi live in Holland, and Lucia and her husband are down in Dorset, run a hotel, charming place. I could move to be with them but the business is here, and I've made a good deal of friends over the years . . . What I'm trying to say is that I have come to enjoy your company a great deal over the weeks that I've been working here, and that I hope that our friendship will extend past the termination of my contract.' As he speaks he turns his back on me and examines the garden. 'He *has* got a good eye that lad, I'll say that for him. A bit fly-by-night maybe, but a good eye all the same.'

I hold back the urge to hug him from behind.

'Oh, Mr Crawley, I'd *love* us to still be friends. In fact, I've been thinking about telling Fergus that I wanted this wall knocked down just so you would stay a bit longer!'

Mr Crawley turns back to face me, smiling.

'Well then, Kitty, you must call me Ian and that's that. I've sent the bill to your husband and I'll pick you up tonight at seven for the auditions?' He holds out his hand to me and I take it, finding myself on the edge of tears, because despite everything that he has just said it feels as if my guardian angel is leaving me.

'Thank you for everything, I mean *everything*: the kitchen, the bathroom, the damp coursing in the dining room, the loft conversion, the child care, the parenting tips – everything. You've been so good to me.'

Mr Crawley squeezes my hand and, putting his other hand on my shoulder, kisses me lightly on the cheek.

'I'll see you later on,' he says quietly, and then he is gone.

'I reckon he fancies you, the dirty old bastard.' I jump and find Gareth poised in the door frame, laughing. I am horrified as I feel the heat rise in my cheeks. That is not the way Mr Crawley and I feel about each other. I know that, but somehow Gareth's uniquely levelling gaze makes me feel uncomfortable and guilty.

'Don't be mad,' I say awkwardly, avoiding meeting his eye. 'He's not like that, he's . . . he's a very good friend.' Suddenly I remember why it is that Gareth has been out all morning and my moment of disconcertion evaporates. 'Oh, have you got it, have you got my turf?' I jiggle up and down on my toes and Gareth laughs, scooping his length of chestnut hair back into a ponytail.

'Yeah, I've got it. I tried to work out if I could bring it round without going through the house, but it's too tricky and I don't think your neighbours'd be too happy about me climbing their fence every few minutes with a couple of rolls of turf balanced on each hand. I'm gonna put some matting down in the hall and bring it through that way, okay?' He grins at me. 'Feel like getting off your lovely arse and helping me today?'

I hesitate, trying to ignore his reference to my arse, and dither.

'All right then, I've got an hour or two.' I pick up Ella, who has so far been absorbed in eating the cord of her pull-along frog on the grounds that she can't pull it along yet anyway, and plonk her in her playpen. She sits and blinks for a moment, observing her confinement as if she is wondering what the words 'play' and 'pen' are doing being so closely associated with each other. She bursts into angry tears, complaining bitterly to me about it and probably threatening to phone ChildLine.

'Oh,' I say, turning to Gareth. 'Maybe not then.'

He tuts and crosses his arms.

'Don't mind her, leave her for a few minutes.' He leans into the pen and ruffles her hair, which does precisely nothing to improve her mood. 'She'll be all right, won't you, you little minx. You've got to remind them who's boss, you know, otherwise she'll have you at her beck and call all of your life.'

I look at baby Ella, who has clamped her teeth over the nose of her frog and is biting down hard as if she knows that it will make her sensitive gums even more sore, and her cries even harder to ignore.

'Darling.' I lean over her and she grabs the neck of my shirt, pulling it dangerously low.' I hastily detach her fingers. 'Don't do it if it hurts!' I say to her. I look at Gareth, who's regarding me as if I have about as much backbone as a limp rag, and steel myself to be firm with her.

'I'd better get her out,' I say instead. He shrugs and trots down the hallway.

'Fine, it's up to you. But I warn you, it'll take me twice as long and I might not get it all laid today and it'll go all yellow!'

I look at Ella, whose face has reached the kind of purple-pink reserved for when she is especially unhappy, and for the first time in my life decide to take a leaf out of Scary Poppins' book.

'Now come on, baby, Mama won't be long. Look at all your *lovely* toys, look!' I hand her her pull-along frog but she bats it away and flings herself on the floor of the pen. I feel terrible, but for some reason I don't want Gareth to see that I've given in to her. 'Okay, well, I'll be back in five minutes, all right?'

Outside, I hold the wheelbarrow for Gareth while he loads it up with rolls of green turf and listen to Ella's cries turns to sobs and sniffs and then finally into her usual happy gobbledygook. Gareth hefts the last roll into my barrow and rests another on each shoulder.

'See, I told you. Happy as Larry now. She's got you under her thumb, that one.' He grins, and I shrug, conceding that he is probably right, and attempt to wield the barrow with some difficulty.

'No, no, lovely,' Gareth says mildly. 'You don't push the

barrow, I'll push the barrow. If you can help me get it over the front step and bring these couple of rolls that'd be great. That is, if you don't mind getting a bit dirty with me.' He laughs the kind of laugh I'd expect to hear after sex and just before a fag. Thoroughly disconcerted for the third time since he appeared from nowhere this morning, I pull myself together and follow him into the hallway and through the kitchen, stopping briefly to find Ella earnestly but more or less cheerfully chewing her frog, and then out into the garden. Gareth's jeans slip down a little over his hips as he unloads the wheelbarrow, and I remember my mission.

'So, um, what did you think of Clare then, the other day?' I say casually.

'Clare?' Gareth straightens, looking genuinely mystified.

'Clare who you met here? My friend Clare? Blonde with lovely eyes?'

Gareth thinks for a moment.

'Oh, you mean "Crazy Clare", the hefty girl with a kid. Yeah, she seemed all right.' He smiles pleasantly at me and turns the unloaded wheelbarrow around. 'Right, at least four or five more trips, I reckon. Great for your abs and your upper-body strength.'

I trot after him.

'I haven't got any abs any more, and if I develop any more upper-arm strength I'll qualify for Miss Universe.'

Gareth chuckles to himself.

'I wouldn't say Clare was hefty,' I follow up. 'I mean, she's not long ago had a baby. All of us are a bit "hefty" after childbirth. Well, except for Posh Spice and those bastards with a personal trainer and a husband who does liposuction. Oh, and all those people who didn't eat for two during pregnancy.'

Gareth has started humming to himself but I persist. 'I mean, she's very attractive really. Didn't you notice her eyes?'

Gareth stops dead in front of me and I walk into his back. He turns abruptly and looks into my eyes.

'*You* aren't hefty.' His eyes travel over my face. 'You're all curvy and soft. When I say hefty I mean sort of solid and square.' He regards my face for a moment longer and then begins to reload the barrow. 'And I'm sure she has lovely eyes, but she is a *bit* hefty.'

I stand where I am and breathe in and then breathe out. Curvy and soft, that's what he said, but he said it as if it was a sexy thing to be, not as if I were a well-upholstered sofa. I smile to myself, feeling momentarily girlish and coy, and forget that I'm supposed to be helping only and not flirting or succumbing to any of his tricks. I'm sure that given the chance Gareth might really like Clare, but maybe what happens in the end doesn't really matter. I mean, there's no reason really to tell her that he thought she was 'hefty'. In fact, I think it would do Clare the world of good just to have someone or something to dream about for a while, boost her confidence, give her hope. And maybe when Gareth does get to know her he'll see what a fantastic girl she is and fall for her anyway, and if he doesn't . . . well, we'll think about that when we get to it.

We repeat our journey four or five times in a pleasant silence broken only by Gareth's sporadic whistling, and on our final leg I stop and whirl Ella out of the pen and on to my hip. Half an hour later we're finished, and it occurs to me that Gareth's claim that it would take all day to do it on his own was slightly exaggerated. But no matter how much I tell myself his opinion shouldn't matter to me, I don't mind because I'm soft and curvy and after all that lifting a slight tug around my midriff suggests there might still be some abdominal muscle there after all.

'Right now.' Gareth wipes the heel of his hand across his forehead, having unloaded the last roll of turf on to a sort of pyramid on Mr Crawley's patio. 'Time for our next lesson. See, what I've done here is rake over the ground until it's level, taken out any big bits of stone and roots, shit like that. Then I've fertilised it, trodden it down and raked it over again, while you were lounging around all lady-of-leisure-style.' He lays a warm palm on my shoulder, his fingers squeezing me slightly. 'Preparation is everything, Kitty; you can never spend too much time on preparation. You've got to look after your lawn and your lawn will look after you. Neglect it and it will run to weed, go bald and die.' He picks up a roll and, sinking on to his haunches, unfurls it and then, with a disarming lack of embarrassment, rests his cheek gently against the grass. 'Soft as velvet, just right for you and the little one.'

Ella and I look happily at each other, imagining twelve months of summer and endless fun and outdoor games. Well, at least I am. I think Ella is quite possibly hoping she'll be able to eat the lawn rather than frolic on it.

'Oooh, it's like a carpet,' I say happily. 'A thick green carpet!'

'Yep,' Gareth nods, 'and it's not much cheaper either, except I know this bloke who got me something off, so even though you've got your sugar daddy hard at work you don't have to worry about it too much.'

I half laugh at his bad joke, feeling suddenly guilty that I'm standing here in the sunshine with another man while Fergus is slaving away under the strip lighting of his office. A trickle of sweat shivers down my back and I shake off the feeling, telling myself that, after all, this is exactly what Fergus wants, although maybe without the soft and curvy comments.

I watch, mesmerised, as Gareth begins to lay the piece down, resting his knees on a plank of wood and tapping it gently into place.

'It's fabulous,' I say. 'I never thought I'd see the day when I got all excited about grass. Especially the kind of grass that you walk on!'

Gareth laughs.

'I've got some of the other kind if you fancy a smoke?' he says mildly. I blink obscurely, affronted at the suggestion and surprised by my reaction. I haven't smoked in years, but I've never been bothered by other people doing it. Yet somehow Gareth's suggestion seems unseemly. Maybe since Dora no drug seems harmless to me any more.

'Um, no, not for me, breastfeeding.' I smile, feeling prudish.

'Oh yeah, I forgot about that.' Gareth's smile is slow and sweet and not for the first time today perfectly ambiguous. 'Right, well, it's best I get this laid this afternoon or else it'll spoil if I leave it overnight. You going to get down here with me?' he enquires.

I shake my head. 'Oh no, I've got stuff to do in the house . . . Clare's coming over. You should come in and say hello.'

He nods, turns back to his work and begins to whistle again. I turn back to the kitchen feeling sort of . . . dismissed.

Once I'm back inside, the cool of the kitchen helps me put everything back into perspective. Gareth sort of jangles me; for starters he's good looking in an irresponsible way. The kind of handsome that shouldn't really be allowed outside of movies and books. He's a bit flirty, true – in his native habitat probably a smooth operator, and he enjoys saying what he thinks – stuff like that curvy and soft comment. He also enjoys getting a reaction, I can see that. But you just have to see him out there laying his cheeks on grass to know what kind of person he really is. Sometimes a bit too bold, a bit of a lad, but a gentle person and kind. I mean, he has to be, otherwise he wouldn't have faffed around potting up the few shrubs left in the garden, and building them a makeshift shelter where they can recuperate as he regularly feeds them up with plant food. It's as if he imagines that his charges might one day climb as high as the sky and open a door to a land full of giants.

I pick Ella up and take her upstairs to feed her. Settling Ella on my lap, I lean back into the pillows. I am shocked by how bereft I felt when Mr Crawley left, an emotion which I haven't been able to think about until now. I suppose I don't need a degree in psychology to rationalise how attached I've become to him. He reminds me so much of my dad – not my dad now but my dad back then, before Mum was murdered.

Back then he was a kind of TV dad: big and handsome. The sort who takes you to the park and teaches you to ride your bike. The kind who reads you a story even if he's really tired and even if you want it halfway through his favourite TV show. He'd take me to the pictures, and pick me up when I was supposed to be running in the father and daughter peg-leg race just because he knew how much I wanted to break the coloured tape that stretched across the finishing line. I wanted that more than I wanted to win fair and square. But now that Dad's disappeared behind the depression and the drinking and the years and years on disability benefit. That dad was murdered along with my mum and now I can hardly bear to see him. He's only seen the baby once since she was born, and it's my fault – I *should* ring him, I know. I *should* take her to see him. I *should* invite him down here to stay, but I can't. I can't because wherever he goes he brings the cloud of the past with him as if it's attached permanently above his head, and sometimes it seems he won't be satisfied until he can suffocate me with it as well as himself.

It wasn't an instant transformation. For a few weeks he was the proverbial tower of strength – everyone around him admired him and leant on him. Everyone said how well he was coping under the circumstances, how strong he was being for me. All of it: the funeral arrangements, the move to a new flat, the grief. For a long time it all went on above my head until one day I said to my nan, 'Nan, when's Mum coming back from being dead?' I mean, I knew that she was dead. I'd been told that she was dead, I'd seen it myself with my very own eyes, but I don't think I understood what dead meant. I think I thought it was like going on holiday feeling poorly and coming back all better. My nan didn't answer me for a long time, and I watched her bury her face in her hands, her salt and pepper roller-set curls creeping over her bony fingers. If she cried then, she never let me see those tears.

Instead, after what seemed like for ever, she pulled me on to her lap and held me close to her chest, and told me, 'Mummy's *never* coming back, darling, she's gone for ever. A bad person hurt her and she can't come back . . . not because she doesn't love you or doesn't want to – she just can't. She's gone to be with her dad, Grampy. They'll have a rare old time together, won't they? Laughing and joking all day long, I shouldn't wonder, and looking down on you to make sure you're all right.' She took my chin between the rough skin of her thumb and forefinger and looked me in the eyes.

'It's just you and Daddy now, love, and you've got to be a good girl for Daddy. A good, big, grown-up girl for Daddy, and look after him like your mum would if she was here, okay?'

That moment when I realised that Mum wasn't coming back, that she really wasn't ever coming back, was the first time that I knew I should cry. I cried for a long time. I cried for my mummy and I cried for myself.

'But Nan, who will look after *me*?' I sobbed into her shoulder.

'I'll look after you, darling,' Nan told me. 'I'll always look after you, never you fret.' But losing her daughter had broken my nanna's heart, and she was dead by Christmas.

It was after that that Dad stopped being a TV dad and started being my dependent. For the next nine years we lived on whatever I could conjure up out of tins, or eventually a second-hand microwave, and although I did all his washing and ironing, all of my best efforts couldn't keep him in his job and he was on disability after only a few years. I washed the floors and windows, took the neighbours hand-me-downs and when, at the age of eleven, my period started I asked the lady in the chemist's if she would tell me what to do. She'd taken me in the back and given me a cup of tea and talked it through with me. I didn't feel sorry for myself because by then I'd forgotten what it was like to have my mum. It wasn't until the day I left my dad's flat for good that I felt free again. Free at last to miss her.

I draw Ella's curtains and creep out of her nursery, adeptly jumping the creaking floorboard with a new professionalism that I am quietly proud of, and retreat back into my room, picking up the phone.

'Starbrite Records, Human Resources Department, Camille speaking, how may I help you?'

I laugh at the way Camille rattles off this unwieldy greeting with cheery sing-song efficiency. I affect a terrible accent.

'Oh hi, it's Madonna here, I'm ringing to see where my pay cheque is – I have to buy Rocco some new diapers!'

'Oh hi, Kits, what's up?' Camille has never been fooled by me, and for five of the most nerve-wracking moments of my life she once had me believe I was discussing UK tax law with Jennifer Lopez, and she's not even signed to Starbrite.

'Not bad, quite good actually. You'll never guess what I'm doing tonight!' I tell her, and I'm still listening to her hysteria five minutes later.

'Oh my God, I can't wait to see this! I can't wait! Book me my ticket now, front and centre!'

I roll my eyes. 'Well, don't get too excited, I haven't even auditioned yet, and I'm only going to be in the chorus and maybe help sweep up a bit.'

Camille giggles. 'Oh, bless you and your efforts to get involved in small-town life!'

Her city slicker comment smarts, but I hide it well.

'Well, it's not so bad here. I've got a new friend called Clare. She's lovely, you'd like her and, well, it's not so bad.' I think of the surfeit of street cafés and estate agents that the high street bristles with. 'Almost cosmopolitan, and if Fergus and I could spend a bit of time together it might even be perfect. Pros and cons, I suppose,' I sigh.

'Well, speaking as one who only ever sees her boyfriend when he's on a London stopover, I think absence makes the heart grow fonder.'

I consider her relationship with Alex: in the four years they've been together it's been a non-stop whirlwind of romance and sex, so why isn't it like that with Fergus and me? Why is it that pretty much every time he walks in the front door my libido picks up its briefcase and hops on the love train to London? For a heartbeat I feel the hot panic that rises in my chest whenever I allow myself to consider the possibility that I may never feel that way about Fergus again.

'Yeah, well, that's because you're not so knackered you can't even muster the energy to sleep,' I say. 'Do you think I should get done up in sexy underwear and flounce about on the bed or something?'

Camille snorts laughter down the phone. 'Look, this is you and Fergus we're talking about here. One of the world's definitive romantic couples – like Rome and Juliet! Anthony and Cleopatra. Cathy and Heathcliff. You don't need sex tips already, do you?'

I open and close my mouth.

'Didn't pretty much all of those couples end horribly, usually in a violent death?' I ask her, perturbed.

'Oh yeah, but you know what I mean. You and Fergus, you're solid.'

'Yeah, of course we are. We just need some time together.' I'm not sure that that's all we need, but it's pretty near the truth.

'Well then, get the old bag to sit for you.' I can hear Camille begin to tap at her keyboard. My old boss must be within reach of her radar.

'I suppose I could, it's just that after last time . . . listen, how's Dora? I spoke to her a few days ago and she had some bloke in the sack. Have you seen her?'

'Ahhhhhh. That makes a lot of sense. No, no I haven't. She's got all pally with those NA birds, and she wouldn't say but I guessed she was seeing some bloke.'

'Well, she told me it was as boring as watching paint dry, so he must have done something pretty good to impress her. That's good then, I guess she's getting herself together. Maybe her NA friends are the people she needs to be around at the moment.' I look at myself in the wardrobe mirror, hoping to see the soft and curvy person Gareth described, but his vision of me has lost its magic and all I can see is that I've burnt the bridge of my nose and look indelibly embarrassed.

'Maybe, maybe.' Camille sounds dubious. 'It's just not like Dora to ditch her friends for a man. I miss her.'

I turn away from my unsatisfactory reflection, look out of the bedroom window and see the entirely satisfactory expanse of lawn that is spreading over my garden. Gareth sees me and waves, beckoning for me to come down.

'Camille, I've got to go. Come and see me. Come and see me soon! I've got grass we can lie on!' I say. Hanging up the phone, I lean out of the window.

'It looks great!' I call out.

Gareth shades his eyes and regards me. 'Yeah, it does, doesn't it!' He laughs with boyish delight. 'See where I've created the beds — gorgeous, all curvy and soft, just like a good garden should be.' I smile lamely. Somehow, now he's applied that term to a flowerbed it's lost its charm. Oh well. 'And tomorrow we'll need to water it if it hasn't rained by tonight. In the meantime don't you walk on it, okay?'

I shake my head. 'Are you off then?' I look at my watch, it's not quite five.

'Yeah, stuff to do, but I'll see you later!' I watch him disappear into the house and then a few minutes later hear the front door close. At least he's learnt not to slam it.

I don't mind him going early, but I feel sorry that he won't be here when Clare gets here. I'd half sort of promised her he would be, and now I've let her down. I'll just have to find another way to get them together.

Chapter Eleven

I'm spinning Ella around and around and around.

'Clever girl!' I tell her, kissing her much more than she thinks is appropriate, which is not at all. She screws up her face and bats my affection away with her fists. I laugh and plonk her down on the floor.

'Go on then – do it again for Daddy.' Fergus crouches over the other side of the room and reaches out his hands.

'Come on then, come on, clever!' Ella grins at her daddy and then begins to crawl – forward! She looks a bit clumsy, her arms and legs aren't exactly co-ordinated, but yes, she is defiantly going forward.

'I'm so glad she isn't a lost cause,' I say to Fergus. 'I mean, of course, I'd still love it if she never crawled forward, it's just that bloody Calista is about to sit her GCSEs and she's only two and a half.'

'Is she really?' Fergus looks impressed.

'No.' I say. 'But whenever I go down there it's "Calista was doing handstands by three months, blah blah blah blah".' I stick my fingers down my throat and mimic vomiting.

'Careful, Kits, you want to be holding on to that anger and resentment, it'll help you get into character.' Fergus grins and Ella finally reaches him; he lifts her high above his head, pretending to drop her until she's hysterical. I laugh with delight;

he seems more like his old self this evening, light-hearted and actually here in spirit as well as body. It's a shame it happens to be the evening I'm going out.

'What, as a cowgirl? Will you give her her tea?' I ask him. Fergus nods and carries her away to the kitchen just as Canterbury Cathedral rings out its tinny bells.

'Are you ready then?' Clare says as I open the door to her. She has blow-dried her hair and put on just enough make-up to intensify the green of her eyes.

'Wow! You look fabulous,' I say as I take in the cut of her top and skirt. Gareth was wrong – Clare is not solid and square at all. In fact, when she's not covered from head to foot in a man's outsize roll-neck jumper she's got a lovely figure, the sort of figure that Gareth would compare to the contours of a newly created flowerbed.

'Hefty, my arse,' I mumble as I lead Clare and Ted to Fergus and Ella.

'Pardon?' she says.

'I mean, hefty, my arse, isn't it?' I say stupidly. 'In these trousers. I wish was all got-up like you now.'

As we enter the kitchen, Fergus is gingerly dabbing carrot and wholewheat pasta from around Ella's mouth as if it is radioactive material.

'She's not very keen on lumps,' I tell Clare, 'but I'm not too worried because for about three months she wasn't very keen on food, so it's progress at least.'

Clare smiles shyly at Fergus.

'Hi,' she says like a schoolgirl, making me feel the seven years older than her that I am.

'Sorry, Clare, how rude. Fergus, Clare. Clare, Fergus.'

Fergus reaches out a hand to her and drops a kiss on her cheek. He's the sort of man to kiss anyone in passing, but Clare's cheeks grow rosy and she lowers her eyes as she composes herself.

'Um, this is Ted. He looks like a right terror, but he's not so bad. Oh, who am I kidding, he's terrible, he was born with all that hair so I haven't been able to tell if he's got 666 tattooed behind one ear or not!' She laughs but Fergus looks uneasy. 'He's had his tea and he had a poo this afternoon, so hopefully you shouldn't have to worry about that.'

I can see from the look on Fergus's face that the thought hadn't even occurred to him until that moment.

Clare continues, 'He's not slept all day so he should go down to sleep and hopefully stay that way, but I must warn you that he has the superhuman ability to go for twenty-four hours without sleep if he thinks there's something more interesting to do, and he's not really used to men, so you might qualify.' By the time she's finished her speech, all her school-girl bashfulness has gone and instead she's the smart and sassy single mum that I have begun to know and like. In that one moment, though, I can see exactly how Clare was led up the alley by Jamie – she's just like I used to be. The kind of person whose years of toughly constructed defences can be swept away by some pretty eyes and the promise of some longed-for romance.

She hands Ted over to Fergus, who smiles at him matily and ruffles his blond curls.

'All right there, mate? We'll be all right, won't we, eh? Blokes together, we can watch the footy.' Ted pokes Fergus's chin curiously but generally seems quite happy. Meanwhile a highchair-bound Ella bangs her still full bowl jealously against the table, sending orange lumpy mush everywhere. Just as I reach for a cloth the doorbell chimes.

'Ah, that'll be Mr Crawley. I'd better go.' A brief look of panic passes over Fergus's face.

'You will be all right, won't you?' I say anxiously. 'Because if you think it's too much, then I won't go . . .'

'I'll be fine.' Fergus puts Ted down in a patch of mush. 'Oh. Bugger.'

'He's got his jammys in his bag,' Clare says helpfully. The doorbell chimes again. Fergus reaches across the mayhem and kisses me.

'Just go! I'll be fine, I promise!'

I gingerly kiss my sticky baby and we head out into the refreshingly cool air of the night.

The moment we close the door Clare grabs my arms a little too tightly.

'He's fucking gorgeous, you lucky cow!' she giggles. 'You are married to a fucking gorgeous man. You have a fucking gorgeous gardener. You bastard, how did you do it?' I smile and try to look modest, but the combination of her appreciation of my husband and his determination to manage with those babies has started a small warm glow in my tummy. Maybe when I get back home tonight my libido will have taken up residence again.

'Yeah, well, I was five years older than you are now when I met him, so don't write yourself off yet, okay?'

Clare smiles but seems a bit downhearted. 'He wasn't there then, Gareth? I thought it'd be too late for him to be hanging about, but I did my make-up and everything. I feel a bit stupid now.'

Mr Crawley opens the rear passenger door to his four-wheel drive as if he is our chauffeur.

'Ladies, your carriage awaits. Ready for an evening of music, song and Mrs Ponsenby's wailing, I hope?' he enquires pleasantly.

'Yes!' we chorus with a giggle.

'Good, I'm going to put on some opera and warm up the old tonsils a bit. I hope you don't mind.'

'Not a bit,' I say, and as Mr Crawley begins to join in with an Italian opera in a home counties accent I lean closer to Clare.

'You're not stupid,' I whisper as I slide next to her. 'Anyway, he mentioned you today, specifically, without any prompting, I might add.'

Clare twists in her seat and stares at me. 'Never! Did he? What did he say?'

I catch the reflected light from her shining eyes and wonder if my little white lie was entirely wise.

'He said he thought you had lovely eyes,' my mouth says before my brain kicks in.

Clare deflates a little. 'Oh, that's what everyone says to fat people. Lovely eyes, nice hair, 'cos it's the only part of your body that can't put on weight.'

I stand at the crossroads of honesty and deceit and decide to take the more trodden path. If anyone needs some shiny-eyed moments in her life, it's Clare, even if they're not entirely based on fact.

'Yeah, but then he said he thought you were really pretty!' I nudge her with my shoulder and nod in affirmation. Clare's face is a picture of delight, and for the rest of the journey she stares out of the window lost in dreams.

We enter the town hall and the murmur of the Berkhamsted Players gradually grows louder as we approach the hall the auditions are to be held in. Clare and I follow Mr Crawley in, feeling like it's our first day at school.

The conversation in the hall may dip slightly as we enter, or the implicit lull might be in my imagination, but whether it is or not I feel like I have about fifty pairs of eyes trained right on me, going, 'That top with those trousers and those hips?'

'Right, ladies, first things first.' Mr Crawley looks around the hall. 'Let's get you down on the list now, both of you, for singing and any other . . .'

'Clare! Clare Brown as I live and breathe.' A booming voice

cuts through the air and seems to knock Clare physically off balance. 'What are you doing here, my love? I thought you'd be treading the boards by now? West End, Broadway, that was your plan, wasn't it?' In the time it takes for this man to finish his sentence Clare regresses by about, I'd say, approximately ten years.

'Hello, sir,' she says with weary resignation, avoiding his eyes and turning the toe of her boot in a little. 'How are you?' I fully expect her to produce an excuse as to why her homework is late any second.

'Ah, Bill, glad you could come on board again,' Mr Crawley says a little cautiously as he stretches his hand out and shakes Bill's enormous hands. 'Kitty, this is Bill Edwards, retired music teacher and sometime musical director of the Players, though I must say, Bill, I rather thought that after last year's "episode" you wouldn't be showing your face again?'

Bill Edwards laughs thunderously and tosses a long, steely grey ponytail, yellowing at the ends with nicotine and slicked back with some kind of gel that may be grease, over his shoulder. It's the kind of capricious gesture that I had hitherto only ever attributed to supermodels and ponies. He must be well over six foot in height, and possibly as many feet around the middle. His booming laugh descends, and he gives a low, gravelly chuckle as he remembers the 'episode' in question.

'Ah yes, Ian, a woman scorned and all that, but never let it be said that Bill Edwards has not stood in the face of a woman's wrath and lived to tell the tale!' He finishes with an Olivier-style flourish and then bends his head towards mine. 'Anyway, her husband forgave her and last time I saw him in the pub he told me he was glad I'd taught her a new trick or two!'

I smile anxiously and take a discreet step back out of the haze of whisky. Unabashed, Bill blunders merrily on.

'So, Clare, what happened then? Changed your mind about

what you wanted to do?'

Clare looks perfectly dismayed as her buried teenage dreams are cruelly exhumed and flung in her face. 'Something like that, sir,' she says with a small empty smile.

Bill Edwards lays his heavy, fat-fingered hand heavily on her shoulder.

'This girl, this girl here gave me hope in the midst of chaos and despair. She was my only shining light during two decades, *two decades*, of Kylie Minogue cover versions. God help me.'

Clare looks as if she might be about to sink under the weight of his hand.

'Right, well then.' Somehow Mr Crawley manages to disengage Bill's grip on Clare with zero fuss. 'Let's get you two down on the list then, shall we, before our esteemed director, Ms Caroline Thames, frightens you off? See you a bit later on, Bill,' Mr Crawley says, deliberately leading us away through the mêlée.

'So you can sing then, can you, you dark horse?' I say to Clare as we thread our way through the crowd.

'Oh, a bit, not as good as he was saying.' Clare sighs. 'It's *his* fault, kept going on and on about what a great talent I was and how I should work at it, had me round his house for extra lessons after school, really built me up until I believed it. Stupid fool that I was I thought I really could be someone, but that sort of thing doesn't happen in real life, does it? Not to real people. Not to me, anyway.'

I push my hands into my pockets and try to think of something positive to say.

'Well, I mean, look at all those TV talent searches. You could go on one of them.'

Clare snorts. 'I could have about two years and three stone ago.' She shrugs. 'Anyway, he was exaggerating. I was never that good – I was just a bit better than the rest of my class.'

'Colin.' Mr Crawley leans over a trestle table and shakes the hand of a tall man in his mid-forties with a thick shock of greying black hair that has been styled in the manner of a breakfast TV presenter. 'This is Kitty Kelly and Clare Brown, I bring you new talent!' he says in full am dram mode.

'Kitty, Clare.' Colin shakes both our hands and I try to catch his eye and fail. 'Colin Davies, Assistant Director in charge of casting.' He looks us both squarely in the chest. 'I must say it's nice to have some fresh talent in the house, most people your age think this is all too dull for words.' His gaze remains exactly one foot beneath Clare's eye line. 'Very refreshing indeed. So I'll put you both down for the singing audition for a part and any other talents I might be able to make use of?'

Clare and I exchange an alarmed look.

'I've got a sewing machine, so I could help with costumes?' Clare says hesitantly.

'Marvellous. Mrs Crosby's had to give it up this year – arthritis, terrible shame, hems all over the place.' He tears his eyes away from Clare's chest and returns his attention to my torso.

'And Kitty?' He ogles me openly and I really can't believe that a man can be so lecherous without any hint of embarrassment. Maybe he's used to the female members flinging themselves at him in the hope they get a walk on part with a line.

'Do you mind?' I say tartly, feeling unusually compelled to make a fuss. My sharp tone regains Mr Crawley's attention and he quickly appraises the situation.

'I beg your pardon?' Colin asks my left breast.

'Oh, ah, Kitty . . .' Mr Crawley tries to intercede but for once I decide to make a stand.

'If you are going to engage me in conversation, do you think you could look me in the face occasionally in between ogling my tits?' In my anger, the remnants of my Hackney accent creep into my voice. Colin's breakfast smile freezes on his face and then falls. Mr Crawley's face is a picture of dismay, and even before Colin speaks I suspect I've let him down somehow.

'Ah yes, Kitty, you see Colin has a . . .' he begins.

'Severe sight disability,' Colin finishes with his swiftly reinstated stellar smile. 'Terribly sorry, should probably have mentioned it, but everyone here is so used to me by now that I'd almost forgotten about it. I have some sight but I am registered blind, I was born with a congenital defect. Although I look like I'm staring at your, um, middle, I'm really "seeing" your face, although admittedly a very fuzzy one. Odd, isn't it?' he says kindly.

I bite my lip hard as the only immediately available means of punishment and wonder if, when I've stopped picking on a blind person, I could maybe kick over a sick child or something?

'Oh, oh, I'm sorry. I'm really, really sorry . . .' I begin.

Colin shakes his head and his perfect hair doesn't move.

'No need to be, it's quite refreshing actually. Some people are too embarrassed to ask and many are more likely to accept that I'm an old pervert rather than ask any questions, so at least you've cleared the air – but just for the record, even if I could see your bosoms they would hold little allure for me. I bat for the other side. Now you're both on the list, so . . .'

I exchange a puzzled glance with Clare.

'Colin, if you don't mind me asking, if you can't see very well then how do you know who to cast?' I ask him in the spirit of refreshment.

He laughs and momentarily sucks on the end of his pen.

'Well, Caroline does all the visual stuff. My sense of hearing is more acute and also, kooky though it may sound, I seem to be able to sense when we have exactly the right person, which is why over the last decade the Berkhamsted Players have consistently outperformed that band of amateurs in Tring, at least in my humble opinion.'

'Don't you and Caroline ever disagree?' Clare asks him, and his smile wanes a little.

'No one ever disagrees with Caroline . . .' he begins before the woman herself confirms his statement.

'Right, everyone, quiet please!' Caroline, a tall, red-haired woman with a paisley printed pashmina flung round her shoulders silences the room instantly.

'Caroline Thames, Director, Dictator and Despot,' Mr Crawley whispers in my ear, with the merest hint of affection. 'Screeching old harridan and control freak, but she certainly seems to get results.'

'First of all, thank you for coming,' Caroline tells us with brisk insincerity. 'I'm glad to see a few new faces in the crowd,' she carries on with the tone of a permanently slightly angry person. 'Lots to get through. Let's get the auditions over first, and then we can get back to having a drink and a chat. Take your seats please and be quiet. Andrew! Lights, please! Bill, put that glass of wine down and get to the piano while you can still remember how to play. Colin, who's first?'

Clare, Mr Crawley and I shuffle into the middle of one of the rows of plastic chairs that have been set out before the stage area.

'Barbara Ainsley!' Colin calls out, and a slender woman with a neat brown bob and calf-length print dress walks into the spotlight.

'Barbara,' Caroline Thames's voice booms out of nowhere. 'Nice to see you – how are the children? Good.' She doesn't bother to wait for a response. 'What number have you chosen to entertain us with?'

'Um, the kids are fine and, um, I thought I'd do "Secret Love", if that's okay?' An audible groan can be heard from the area of the piano, and Barbara's cheeks pinken as the first bar of the song is played.

Caroline Thames lets her sing one verse before stopping her and shouting, 'Who's up next, Colin?'

And the parade continues. Clare and I count six 'Secret Loves' four 'Windy Cities' and three 'Deadwood Stages'. Oh, and one husband and wife act do a sort of barber-shop version of the 'Black Hills of Dakota'.

'Don't reckon you've got too much to worry about,' Gareth Jerome says in my ear. I blink and spin round in my seat. He really is there. Somehow he has managed to occupy the middle seat of the aisle behind us without us noticing. I glance at Clare, who is frozen rigid and sunk as low as possible into her chair. Mr Crawley eyes him with a hint of disapproval and returns his gaze to the stage.

'What are *you* doing here?' I whisper. 'Didn't think this was your kind of thing.' Gareth shrugs and smiles.

'I didn't think it was yours either, until tonight.' He stretches his arms along the backs of our chairs until he encompasses both Clare and me within his long-limbed reach. 'No, I heard Mr Crawley tell you about it and you and Clare talking about it and I, well, I thought I'm still quite new in town so I might as well come along and volunteer for some scenery painting or something, meet a few new people, charm a few old ladies, pick up some work. Can't hurt, can it?' The breath of his whisper tickles the back of my neck. 'Besides, I thought it might be a laugh.'

Mr Crawley twists in his seat. 'Gareth, can I suggest you keep it down?' he says as if admonishing a small boy.

Gareth catches Clare's eye and winks at her before sinking back into the shadows. In the dark I reach for her hand and judge her reaction by the fierce grip with which she squeezes my fingers. If she's happy he's here, then so am I.

Mr Crawley takes his turn with all the aplomb I have come to expect from him. Within seconds he's transformed himself before our very eyes from the tall and faintly aristocratic epitome of old-school Englishness into a rotund, bawdy, over-the-hill cowboy singing for all he's worth.

'He's good, isn't he?' I whisper to Clare.

'Yeah, it's like magic. I mean, you can see it's Mr Crawley, but it's like it's another person entirely!'

We are both still congratulating him on a virtuoso performance when the crunch comes.

'Clare Brown!' Colin shouts, and Clare jumps in her seat.

'Oh, bloody bugger,' she says, immediately frozen to the spot, the terrified whites of her eyes luminescent in the gloom.

'CLARE BROWN!' Caroline Thames breaks the sound barrier.

'Go on, you'll knock the socks off this lot!' Gareth says encouragingly, squeezing Clare's shoulders.

She smiles over her shoulder at him and squeezes along the row of chairs before climbing up on to the stage with about as much grace as one can muster when it involves clambering via a plastic chair.

'At last, someone who won't contribute to my early death. What are you going to sing, Clare?' Bill asks, his voice warm with genuine affection.

'Um, well, I thought . . .' Clare clearly hadn't thought about it until this moment.

'"Secret Love" of course! Show all these silly women how it's done!'

Clare's sensitive cheeks pinken immediately and a ripple of consternation runs through the hall, but before it can gather pace Bill has played the opening bars and Clare has begun to sing.

In seconds the hall falls totally silent. Coughs cease, whispers abate and sniffs dry up.

Clare has a beautiful voice, an incredible voice. Rich and

pure, each word she sings carries to the back of the hall, ringing in the air like a perfectly tuned bell.

'She's amazing,' Gareth breathes in my ear, and I turn to look at his profile. He's spellbound. I smile to myself: at last, a genuine development to report to Clare.

'Tricky last verse coming up,' Mr Crawley says quietly. 'A real test of her mettle.'

Clare's voice soars to the challenge and then re-enforces the melody with breathtaking power before letting her tone drop to a gentle whisper. She lives each word of the lyric, her face a shining picture, and as the last note echoes in the rafters she folds her hands over her heart and closes her eyes.

I glance at Gareth again and think, 'No wonder she sings it with such meaning – she has her own secret love, one I've created for her out of thin air.'

A second's silence follows her performance before the hall erupts into applause. Clare puts her hand over her mouth and giggles before climbing down from the stage and returning to her seat.

'You were fabulous. Fabulous!' Mr Crawley tells her and kisses her on the cheek.

'Bloody hell, Clare, I thought you said Mr Edwards was exaggerating!' I say warmly.

Gareth puts a hand on each of her shoulders. 'You were amazing, really amazing,' he says, his amber eyes focusing on her.

Clare glows, her eyes sparkle and her smile lifts her whole face. She looks beautiful.

'Kitty Kelly!' Colin calls and my blood runs cold.

'Kitty Kelly? Is that a stage name or an unfortunate coincidence?' I hear Caroline ask Colin as I head for the stage. Now that it's come to it, I can't think what on earth I thought I was doing.

'Um, "Windy City",' I mumble miserably. Somehow, as Bill

kicks in the opening um-pa-pa, I find Mr Crawley's face shining in the gloom of the auditorium as if it has somehow been illuminated just for me. He smiles at me and nods his encouragement, and although he must only be mouthing the words, I'm sure that I hear him say in my ear as clear as day, 'Just enjoy yourself – have fun and enjoy the moment.'

I fix my gaze on him and pretend we're at home in the kitchen. I know that my voice alone isn't going to get me anywhere, so I throw caution to the wind, jut out my chin, bow my legs and lower my voice, imagine that I *am* Calamity Jane and slap my thigh. Five minutes later I find that everyone in the room is laughing, two minutes after that I realise they're laughing because they think I'm funny and not because they think I'm crap. My spirits lift and I throw any remnant of reserve to the crowds and clown it right through to the bitter end. There's no rapt applause like there was for Clare, but as I make my way off the stage there are many friendly comments. 'Very good!', 'What fun!' and 'Well done' follow me as I return to my seat. Caroline Thames strides out on to the stage.

'Well done, everyone,' she says briskly, without the slightest hint of sincerity. 'As you know, we believe in working on instinct in this company and making gut decisions, so *we* won't be keeping you waiting for a week while we wait for someone to type the cast list – we're not the Tring Troubadors after all!' For reasons that I'm just beginning to understand, that comment rouses a competitive cheer. 'Colin and I will nip into the office now and discuss our findings and be back in half an hour with a decision! In the meantime there's more wine and biscuits, so enjoy, because this is where the fun ends and the hard work begins!'

'Yeah,' Gareth says as we ease our way out of the chairs, 'right here is where you start paying!' Clare and I giggle and exchange delighted glances as he invites Clare to go with him to fetch us some wine.

Mr Crawley watches him as he goes, a slight frown on his face.

'Mr Crawley, um, *Ian*, is there a problem? Where's Tim tonight, anyhow?' I ask him.

For a second his eyes remain fixed on Gareth's back, and then he returns his attention to me with his usual charming smile.

'Flu, his mother tells me. To be honest with you, I think it's far more likely that he's got a girlfriend. It was bound to happen sooner or later. I just hope it doesn't distract him from his grouting.'

I can't tell if he's joking or not, so I smile at him and remember my sudden vision of his face just as I was about to sing.

'Do you know, the strangest thing happened up there . . .' I begin, gesturing at the stage. 'I sort of heard your voice in my head and . . .'

Mr Crawley tips his head to one side and looks at me.

'Did you? Must have been nerves or something,' he says, displaying the kind of attention he usually reserves for Ella. 'Oh Lord, there's Mrs Ponsenby, I'll go and say hello to her now before she finds out she hasn't got the lead this year and goes into full-on diva mode.' He disappears instantly into the throng; like me he must think that Clare's bound to have got the lead.

As I wait for Clare and Gareth to return, I scan the faces of the Berkhamsted Players as they chat, laugh, gossip and bicker. They are somehow different from what I had imagined. I suppose I thought they would all be caricature versions of Fergus's mum, or stout and angry women sporting tiaras and minks. Although Mr Crawley said they needed fresh talent, Clare and I are not the only people under thirty-five here, even if we are heavily outweighed by older members. There are more women than men, it's true, but rather than the stiffly desperate and sad brigade of divorcees that I had expected, they are all different, all rather beautiful in a way I hadn't imagined. And the male members seem terribly brave to me, almost heroic for carving out this place for themselves in a world where it is far easier to be alone and bored. For no particular reason that I can think of, this collection of ordinary people are oddly touching, and for a brief moment the threat of tears stings my eyes. I sniff and swallow hard, and put my sentiment down to my good old hormones.

'I must say – Kitty, is it? You were fab.' I blink hard and smile at the woman next to me. It's Barbara Ainsley. 'And your friend, Clare, well, makes me realise my pretensions to anything grander than the chorus were somewhat unfounded. Amazing!'

'Thanks,' I say.

Barbara leans in a little closer to me. 'I hope you don't mind me asking, but I couldn't help but notice that you came with Mr Crawley. Are you very good friends? It's just that he's a terribly good catch, you know, and half of Berkhamsted's single ladies are here tonight, so if there's no hope we'd all like to know.' She gives me a sweet little smile and a wink indicating that either way there would be no hard feelings, even if he was my . . . um . . . 'lover'.

'Oh God, no!' I say quickly, feeling my face burn. 'No, he is my friend, yes, but strictly platonic. More of a . . . good fairy, really!' I say, thinking of his shining face in the crowd when I auditioned. 'Oh, but not a fairy, not in the Colin, oh fuck. I mean, oh dear. Oh sorry, Barbara.'

Barbara laughs uproariously. 'You're very amusing,' she says, and just in case she thinks I meant to be, I leave it at that, firmly buttoning my lip.

'I said to Harriet, that'll be it, he'll be being kind. If he's not flung himself about since his wife passed all those years ago, he's hardly about to start now with a floozy half his age . . .' She claps her small hands over her mouth before saying, 'I *do* beg your pardon, of course I didn't mean you . . .' She looks at me for one second more. 'Well, I did mean you, but obviously I was totally wrong, and anyway we should have known better. Mr Crawley is always helping someone. It just seems to be in his nature!' She bobs her head, almost as if she is taking a bow, and then excuses herself, no doubt to impart the good news to her friends.

My friends return en masse and I take a warm glass of white wine from Clare. It tastes of cardboard.

'You two took your time,' I say. 'I've had a delegate from the Mr Crawley appreciation club over here interrogating me as to the nature of our relationship.'

'Told you he was a dirty old man,' Gareth jokes, his golden eyes half closed. Clare giggles and flutters her lashes, flirting without any trace of subtlety. I leap to Mr Crawley's defence, deciding not to take Gareth's comment with a pinch of salt.

'He *is* not . . . Oh look, here she comes. Get ready for local celebrity, Clare!' I say.

The conversation dies instantly the moment Caroline Thames takes the stage, and I must say that considering she only rules the am dram club in a small home-counties town, she does cut a fairly impressive figure.

'QUIET!' she shouts at a hushed congregation. 'Right, well, Colin and I have discussed this at some considerable length and I won't beat about the bush – the role of Calamity Jane came down to two new members . . .' Clare and I exchange glances. 'Now, I'm sure we all agree that Clare gave us an exquisite performance earlier on, one that moved us all . . .' I nudge Clare and she bites her lip. 'However, in musical theatre it is not merely the quality of the singing but the overall performance that's important, and, to be frank, that the character looks the part. So we're going to give the female lead to Kitty Kelly, with understudy and a chorus part to Clare. Oh, and Clare, I understand you have a sewing machine, so I'm putting you down for costumes, okay?' A murmur of dissent rumbles in the crowd.

'Bloody fucking ridiculous!' Bill Edwards's voice booms out of the crowd. 'What the fuck do you think you're doing, woman? The person with the best voice should get it, not the one who can ape about like an idiot. Fucking ridiculous!' He points at me. 'If she gets it I'm quitting, no offence, Kitty.'

Caroline rolls her eyes and folds her arms over her chest.

'Fine, there is more than one person who can play the piano in the town, Bill. Have you forgotten one former sixties rock star who's been longing to step into your shoes for some time now?'

Bill tosses his ponytail and mumbles, 'I don't think one top fifty novelty hit about a talking flower qualifies you as a rock star,' but his stand clearly crumbles when he thinks of his rival taking over his place.

'Um, excuse me?' I pipe up. 'I don't want it. I mean I don't want the lead, you should give it to Clare, I mean, she'd be much better and . . .'

Clare pushes in front of me. 'Look, stop all this fuss. Kitty will be better for the part. Of course she's more believable. I don't mind, really, all right? So let's leave it at that then.' She finishes and, turning on her heel, walks out of the hall.

'At last a voice of reason. Right, so first rehearsal is next Wednesday and . . .'

I look at Mr Crawley and Gareth and head out of the hall after her. The night has taken on a chill and as I walk out on to the high street I find myself folding my arms against the cold. I know she can't have gone far – her coat's inside and I've got her son at home. I look around me and see that in fact she hasn't gone anywhere at all. Instead she's sitting on a bench right outside the town hall door, her face in her hands.

'Oh mate.' I sit next to her and put my arm around her

shoulders. She looks up, and, although her face is wet with tears, she smiles at me.

'I'm fine, I'm fine. I mean, of course they're not going to want a fat Calamity Jane, are they? I mean, whoever heard of such thing!' She laughs without joy and looks away from me. 'I blame Mr Edwards, he was always doing that to me at school, making me think I could be more that I am.'

I take her hands.

'Clare, for one thing, if they want me then they've got a fat Calamity Jane, and for another, it's a stupid am dram musical, its not exactly a sensible way to judge the success of your life. Anyway, I won't take the part. I just won't turn up next week. I don't even want it, for God's sake. Imagine what Fergus is going to say when I tell him he's got to come in from a hard day at work and look after the baby every Wednesday for weeks! It's stupid.'

Clare returns her gaze to me and smiles.

'Don't give up the part. I want you to do it. If you leave, then I'll have to, and, well, at least now I know I'll see Gareth once a week if I'm coming here, and it's a night out after all.' A small smile curls around her mouth. 'I'm sure Fergus will want to help out with Ella, and don't mind me, I'm just overreacting, that's all.' She lifts her face to the cooling balm of the night and I search her face, wondering how much unhappiness she manages to hide there.

'Well, okay,' I say hesitantly before I remember what I have been dying to tell her ever since she gave her performance. 'Gareth was blown away, by the way, when you were singing. He said, and I quote, that you were "amazing".'

Clare wipes the heels of her hands across her face, leaving small smudges of mascara in brown crescents under her eyes.

'Really?' she says, cautiously pleased.

'Really,' Gareth says, leaning on the wall by the steps, now

191

wearing a long sheepskin coat that looks undeniably sexy.

'Did you used to be in the SAS?' I say, slightly flustered. 'You are always popping up out of nowhere!'

He laughs. 'Territorials for a while back in Wales, but I think I'm just naturally a quiet person. Light on my feet, you know, like an animal?' He performs a faux tap dance, finishing with a low bow. He crouches down next to Clare. 'You *were* amazing,' he says softly, holding her gaze in the liquid amber of his eyes. 'So, who fancies a quick drink?'

'Oh no, I'd better get back,' I say quickly. Gareth's sudden display of intimacy with Clare has sent a sudden jolt through my system that I am not very pleased to note seems like jealousy. I think of Fergus for the first time this evening, and long to be with him, but Clare's eyes bore into me, willing me to accept Gareth's invite. After all, if I go home, then so must she.

'Oh, well, maybe just a very quick half . . .' I say reluctantly.

'Kitty! You left this!' Mr Crawley comes out of the hall and hands Clare her coat and me my red zip-up tracksuit top. I smile gratefully and put it on, drawing the hood up over my ears against the chill of the breeze. Mr Crawley helps Clare into her coat. 'With all the fuss, I haven't been able to say well done. I'm sorry, Clare, because you were wonderful, but I think Kitty will do us all proud, don't you?'

Clare shrugs and stands up. 'Yeah, I'm sure she will. Are you coming for a drink?' she asks him.

Mr Crawley looks surprised and disconcerted in turn before rearranging his face into his normal amiable demeanour and shaking his head.

'Ah no, better get back home. I'll see you soon.' He kisses me lightly on the cheek and then Clare, and eyes Gareth. 'Make sure they get home safely, there's all sorts hanging around this time of night,' he says, and with one last look over his shoulder he heads for the car park.

'Bloody old fogey,' Gareth says with a mischievous chuckle, linking arms with both Clare and me. 'Who does he think he is, your granny?'

For fifteen minutes I look at my watch and feel anxious while Gareth tells Clare about his home town and how he got involved in the territorial army before he chucked it all in to be a gardener.

'When it came down to it,' he says, leaning on the bar, 'I'm not the sort of bloke who wants to kill things, not even in principle. I'm the sort of bloke who likes to nurture stuff, make it grow.' He flicks his hair off his shoulders. 'I think that's what gives me a greater understanding of motherhood, because I'm quite maternal myself.'

Clare watches him, transfixed with admiration. I hate to break the moment, but I'm starting to feel like a gooseberry and I think I've done my bit for the night. What's more, seeing Gareth's pulling technique in the third person is far less entertaining than I had imagined.

'Look, guys, I'm sorry, I think we'd better go, Clare,' I say apologetically. 'God knows what condition Fergus will be in after four hours with two babies.' As I say it I realise that I am rather hoping that he *is* frazzled and despairing when I turn up because then I'll be the hero for once, and he'll realise exactly what it's been like for the last few weeks and maybe *then* he'll understand.

Gareth raises an all too perceptive eyebrow.

'Well, surely it must be your turn for a break by now, isn't it?' he says with an affable shrug. 'I'm just saying, it won't hurt him to help you out a bit, that's all.'

Clare sighs and finishes her drink.

'Yeah, I wish I had someone on call to help me like Fergus.

193

Ted'll think he's been adopted.' She smiles at Gareth. 'He's probably celebrating! Thanks for the drink, though.'

'No worries,' Gareth says warmly. 'I've not got many friends round here yet and it's nice to meet someone I can really talk to.'

Clare looks as if she might float a couple of inches off the floor.

'Right, I'll just nip to the loo and we can be off,' she says, and as she heads to the back of the pub there is a visible bounce in her step.

'Are you all right?' Gareth asks, pre-empting my attempt to quiz him on how much he likes Clare. I'm taken aback, surprised by the speed with which he refocuses his undivided attention.

'Me? Yeah, I'm fine,' I say. 'Why wouldn't I be?'

He leans a little closer to me and grins, showing just the tips of his immaculately kept white teeth.

'You shouldn't feel guilty about being out for a couple of hours, you know. I know I'm not that experienced in serious relationships, but I do know that sometimes a bit of a break from them can actually improve them, if you want it to.' He grins at me, and I find myself smiling back at him in agreement.

'I know, I know. A drink can't do any harm, can it?' I sip the last of my drink, tasting the acrid sharpness of the lemon in the bottom of the glass. 'So, Clare was fantastic tonight, don't you think?'

Gareth studies me for a moment before curling up one side of his mouth in a lazy half smile. 'She's a good singer,' he says. 'She's not my type, though, so don't get any ideas, okay, Cilla?'

I feign a look of shock and hide my disappointment. Maybe he doesn't really know what his type is. I didn't really know what my type was until I met Fergus. Until I met Fergus I thought men like Gareth were my type.

'I'm not!' I protest too loudly. 'But she's really lovely, you know, you should get to know her.' And then. 'Anyway, you were flirting with her like there was no tomorrow back there!'

He fixes me with his intense eyes, and for what seems like an eternity we regard each other.

'Was I flirting? See, I never think of it as flirting. I think of it as being a good listener and having empathy with the person I'm talking to. It's you women that get it all mixed up. The trouble is you're so surprised when a man actually listens to you that you come over all funny.'

He smiles, and I shrug in acknowledgement.

'You have great teeth,' I say out of nowhere, and he laughs, clearly pleased by the compliment.

'Well, my ma always told me, keep your teeth nice and clean and girls are more likely to want to kiss you.' He drops his gaze to his feet and looks back up at me through a fringe of thick lashes. 'I'm still hoping,' he says with a shrug, and I find myself smiling back at him, drawn in by his strange combination of naive insouciance and artifice. He reminds me of a much younger man, a schoolboy testing his sexuality, rather than a practised womaniser. And yet I get the feeling that he is far more of the latter than the former.

'All set then,' he says to Clare over my shoulder as if the conversation we've just had never took place.

'Yep, back to the grindstone,' she smiles up at him. 'I'll see you around then?'

'I expect so,' Gareth says warmly. 'See you, Kitty.'

One of the first things I learnt to like about living in this town was the sky, especially at night when the weather is clear and the stars are visible with a crystal clarity I never experienced in London. As we begin our walk home, I link my arm though Clare's and crane my neck, looking for Orion's belt.

'That went quite well, didn't it?' Clare says anxiously. 'I mean, I didn't seem too needy or anything? Did I?' I think of

Gareth's claim of empathy.

'No!' I say. 'No. I think he understood you very well.'

'It seemed as if he did like me, didn't it? You know, I mean I think in time he might really like me.' Clare bobs on my arm. 'What do you think?'

'Ummmm.' I spot the three bright stars of the belt and make a wish. 'Yeah! For sure!' I tell her in my best upbeat tone. Somehow I feel I've started the ball rolling on something that I'm going to find very hard to stop, and when the fall-out comes I'm going to be smack in the middle of it.

From outside the house the glow of soft lighting in the living room is the only visible sign of life, and the wailing I had expected to hear echoing down the street is not evident.

'Ominously quiet,' I say to Clare as I let us in. 'Maybe they've gagged and bound him and are penning a ransom note in crayon even as we speak.'

'Nah,' Clare says. 'They'll have eaten the crayons first.'

I push open the living room door. Fergus is sitting on the floor, his long legs stretched out in front of him, his back leaning against the sofa. On either side of him are the large red sofa cushions, and arranged on each of them in angelic repose is one sleeping baby. I can't help but smile.

'How'd it go?' Fergus and I whisper to each other at the same time.

'Fine – I got the lead!' I reply.

'Fine – no trouble at all! Really? The lead! That's fantastic,' Fergus says, his eyes full of pleasure. I can't decide which revelation is more surprising: my theatrical success or his miracle touch with the children.

He gets up awkwardly and steps over Ella. From the doorway I can feel Clare watching us as we embrace. I break away self-consciously.

'I can't believe you managed all this on your own,' I say. 'I'm

196

really impressed.'

'Ah, well, it wasn't quite . . .' Before Fergus can finish Georgina bustles in with two mugs of tea.

'Excuse me, dear. Oh, you're back, I didn't hear you come in!'

I look from her to Fergus and back again. 'You called your mum in?' For some reason it seems to me akin to cheating at a maths exam. Georgina hands one mug of tea to Fergus and another one to Clare – men and guests first, that's her rule. 'I'll make some more for us girls, shall I?' The babies stir at her voice and Clare sets down the tea and goes to Ted, picking him up and rocking him back off to sleep before settling on the cushionless sofa.

'Yes, I'll help you,' I say pertly, and as I follow Georgina out of the room I scrutinise Fergus, who's standing with hands on his hips, smiling stupidly.

'And I will too,' Fergus says, and we all file out together leaving Clare with her son in her arms staring into the real-effect gas fire.

'So when did you arrive then?' I ask, unable to keep the slightly accusatory note from my voice.

'Oh, hours ago,' Georgina beams. 'He was in a *terrible* state, I can tell you. Trying to change the little boy's nappy, he'd done a number two, and then Ella thought it might be fun to climb in all the mess and crawled off with the nappy stuck to her knees. When I arrived, all three of them needed a good bath and a scrub. I put his clothes in the wash.'

She is clearly very proud of herself for being useful, and I am grudgingly impressed that she was prepared to compromise her Jasper Conran trousers over baby poo. I smile as I visualise the scenario.

'Is that really how it happened?' I turn to ask Fergus, who stuffs his hands into his pockets and shrugs.

'Sort of. Well, yeah, pretty much exactly as it goes. Mum saved my life.'

Georgina smiles to herself as she refills the kettle, delighted to be able to do something to redress the balance of opinion after her last stint with her grandchild.

'Thanks, Georgina, it was good of you to drop everything and come over,' I say formally.

'Delighted to, dear, any time, you know that,' she says, deliberating ignoring my thinned lips and stiff shoulders.

I look at Fergus, and seeing that he is desperate for me to smile, I oblige.

'So, a bit harder than you imagined, then?'

He looks around him as if for distraction then takes his arms out of his pockets and hugs me tight.

'Christ, darling, I don't know how you do it all day. You're superhuman.'

I smile into his chest, delighted to hear the affirmation I hadn't known I'd wanted so badly.

'Not superhuman, dear,' Georgina says as she takes two more cups of tea next door. 'Just a typical woman.'

For a second longer I stand in Fergus's embrace and wonder that, for the first time since I've known her, I am actually agreeing with my mother-in-law. Maybe she's not such a wicked old witch after all.

When I walk back into the living room, Ella is still fast asleep and Clare has Ted's bag packed and her coat on.

'I'll get off,' she says.

'Well, hang on a sec, Clare,' Fergus says. 'I'll give you a lift home along with Mum. Can't have you and Ted wandering about in the middle of the night.'

Clare's smile of gratitude at Fergus's suggestion is transparent. I wonder how long it's been since anyone has been really kind to her. She seems to have been all alone for a very long time, without even family for support. If I was in her situation, I would have gone crazy by now, I'm sure.

Georgina stands by the mantelpiece and gazes down at her granddaughter.

'She looks *just* like you, darling,' she says to Fergus. 'Same hair, same nose, even the way she curls her little fingers round her ear. You were *exactly* the same. A carbon copy.'

As she smiles indulgently, my hackles rise instantly. Ever since the day my daughter was born, my mother-in-law has insisted that she is a replica of her son as if I didn't carry her everywhere for nine months, as if I didn't contribute an egg and presumably at least some of her DNA. I know grandmothers are supposed to be proud, and I know, really I know, that she doesn't mean to totally exclude me from the creation of my own child, but if she tells me one more time that holding Ella is like holding the daughter she was never able to have, I'll . . . I'll . . . I'll nod politely and say 'Really? That's nice.' Fergus knows how much this rankles with me.

'Do you think so, Mum?' he says sweetly, catching my eye. 'I've read babies have to look like their dads when they're born so that the father knows his missus hasn't been playing away – a throwback to caveman days or something. But now she's getting bigger I think she looks more and more like Kitty. She certainly has her spirit – and her beautiful smile.' As he speaks he looks me in the eyes, the corner of his mouth just curled up.

Georgina scrutinises the baby for a moment longer. 'Mmmm, maybe a little. Around the ears.' It's a small concession but a significant one, even if she has no idea that she's made it.

'It's just occurred to me,' she continues, 'that she hasn't seen her Grandpa Simpson in months. When's he coming down, Kitty? We should have a little do for her, or something. I mean, we've never had a christening and it'd be nice. All of us could get together and you could put on a little spread?'

I stare at Fergus, my smile frozen in horror, and although he knows exactly what I think about that idea, he chooses to drop me right in it with an ever so slightly gleeful glint in his eye.

'That's a really good idea, Mum. Kits, why don't call your dad in the morning and see if he can come down next weekend? Clare, you and Ted can come over too, and Mr Crawley and even the gardener, wossisname – Gareth, is it?' He spreads his arms expansively. 'I mean, the house is finished and it won't be long until the garden is, so why don't we celebrate – our new life as a family in Berkhamsted.'

Somehow the intensity in Fergus's voice, the robustly optimistic note, tells me that for some reason he *really* wants this to happen, and as I don't seem to have given him anything he wants recently, I lose heart in the protest I was planning. For some reason it is really important to Fergus that we show everyone how happy we are and how successful. Not for the first time, but maybe with new clarity, I can see that I'm not the only one of us struggling with this new life we've made for ourselves.

'Well, I suppose I could make some sandwiches,' I say cautiously.

Fergus eagerly jumps on my half-hearted assent. 'Great, that's settled then. You call your dad in the morning, and get Dora and Camille down. It'll be great!'

On his last word Ella startles and wakens with wide eyes full of alarm. She takes one look at her grandmother and bursts into hysterical tears, probably coincidental but still a small victory. I scoop her up and instantly she's wide awake, looking around her with wide, bush-baby eyes.

'Aye dee!' she says as if her evening is just about to begin. I look at Fergus.

'You'd better get this lot home and I'll work on trying to get her off again.'

As Fergus bustles everyone out of the door he stops and drops a kiss on my cheek.

'I'm sorry to land that on you, love, but you won't have to do anything. We'll just buy stuff from M&S.' He pauses as Georgina helps Clare down the front step with the buggy and whispers, 'I just want everyone to see how happy we are, to see how well we're doing.'

'Okay,' I say with a half smile. 'Okay.'

Fergus catches my fingers and squeezes my hand hard. 'Because we are, aren't we?' he asks me, watching me closely with anxious eyes.

I press the palm of my hand briefly against his cheek.

'Of course we are,' I say.

Chapter Twelve

For most of last night, Doris Day sat on the end of my bed. She looked really lovely in a turquoise blue chiffon number that brought out her eyes.

'Listen, Doris,' I'd told her sternly. 'When I've gone half mad sitting up in that chair, fair enough, I expect the musical hallucinations, but when I'm in bed asleep? It's not really fair, is it?'

Doris had pressed her lips together and given me a slightly stern look.

'All I'm saying, darlin',' she'd said in her soft husky voice, 'is that you've got a lot to deal with right now, the baby and Fergus. Are you sure you can take on something as demanding as Calamity Jane on top of everything – it's not an easy role, you know.'

She'd crossed her shapely legs, showing off a gorgeous pair of silver sequined evening slippers. 'You know, I've had a lot of experience of this kind of thing, trying to strike out on your own and have a career. You've seen all those films I did with Cary, James and Rock, haven't you? Even when I was playing Calamity it turned out the same. In the end I always realised that love and family are really the only important things, and all this gadding about playing at independence is just a sham.' She'd leant in a little closer to me, a tiny smile on her shell-pink lips.

'We're women, honey – we're meant for marriage and motherhood.'

'But Doris,' I'd protested, 'you might have played all those parts, but in real life you were an internationally renowned film star, probably with as least as much power and money as all the men you ever knew! You played the part of the housewife – but that wasn't you!'

Doris had pursed her lips and set her hands firmly on her lap, crossing her ankles under her many skirts.

'And in the end I left all of it behind for my family,' she'd said sternly, standing up and going to the window. 'Well, darlin', if there's one thing I've learnt, it's that the heroine never sees sense until the final roll of the film. I just hope that you see sense in time, but after all, what will be, will be.' She'd vanished into a haze of her own light, and I'd found myself sitting up in bed, blinking the dream away.

'All right?' Fergus had mumbled in the dark. 'Talking, you were, in your sleep.'

'I'm fine, go back to sleep,' I'd said, wide awake now, my head full of Doris. Maybe she did have a point about one thing, maybe joining the Players was a bit too much to take on. But I couldn't back out of it now, and anyway it was the *only* thing that I was doing in addition to my life as a mother, and many women had to work and parent, and a lot of them did it alone. It might have been different in Doris's day, but things had changed now, things had moved on.

'Sod off, Doris,' I'd silently told the empty part of the bed where she'd been sitting. 'I might not be able to have it all, but at least I can have some of it, whatever it is – so there!'

'Right, we're off.' Fergus finds me still languishing in bed pondering last night's dream. Saturday mornings have become the only few precious hours that I spend alone every week whilst he takes Ella out to do the weekly shop. I used to come with him, but now that he's worked out that he can buy anything as long as it's pre-prepared and microwaveable, he doesn't need my input any more. He looks every inch the perfect and proud father as he stands with Ella perched on one hip, dressed up to the nines with her frilly hat on.

'I thought you were going to Waitrose, not the Ritz,' I say, suppressing a smile. Whenever Fergus takes her out he dresses her in her finest apparel.

'We are, but she likes to look nice, and besides, there's this shelf-stacker in the nappies aisle she's got her eye on, flirts with him every week.'

'Yeah, well, I'm sure she can do a bit better than a shelf-stacker,' I say absently, stretching out my arms and sitting up.

'It doesn't matter what he does, surely, if she loves him?'

I blink and look at Fergus. He seems to be genuinely defending our baby's friendly overtures to a sixteen-year-old Saturday boy shelf-stacker.

'She doesn't love him, she's a baby. Don't be mad.' I reach for my dressing gown and get out of bed.

'I know that.' Fergus pursues his entirely pointless point. 'But say if she was older and she really did want to go out with a shelf-stacker, it wouldn't matter if he loved and cared for her because surely his feelings for her are more important than anything. Money or possessions or anything.'

I frown at him, and hug both of them in one go.

'Of course,' I say. 'But shall we worry about it in, oh, I don't know, sixteen years?' Ella gnaws happily on the end of a length of my hair, regarding me with her father's intensely blue eyes. 'I know, baby, we can take you out tomorrow – we could go up the common or to the Chilterns, couldn't we, now that it's practically June, up the beacon everyone keeps telling me about, and Ella can roll down some hills!'

One of the things that had occurred to me as I was trying to get back to sleep last night was that the three of us hardly ever did anything as a family. So far this year we hadn't gone anywhere together, let alone had a holiday. When I thought of it I was rather surprised that Fergus hadn't come home one day and told me he'd booked a family cruise round the Med, but that was probably my fault for expecting him to organise everything and maybe he thought that would be one expense too many after the house and the garden. I might not be Nigella, I told myself, but at least I can get us doing stuff together, stuff which doesn't involve sitting in front of the TV or taking it in turns to get the baby to sleep.

Fergus looks surprised, pleased, guilty and miserable in turn until his face settles into morose.

'That's a lovely idea, darling but, well, I was about to tell you, I, um, I got a call on my mobile while you were still asleep,' he says. 'I'm really sorry, but there's this big deal hanging in the balance and someone's fucked up and, well . . . I'm going to have to go into the office tomorrow. I'm sorry, love.'

My shoulders sink and my heart plummets, and suddenly my own beacon – the two shining days that get me through the grey monotony of the week – blinks out and dies. I can't face the thought of a lonely Sunday.

'Not on Sunday, Fergus, please! I hardly ever see you as it is, and now you're going in on a Sunday?' I feel as if he's just told me that he's leaving me for good, as if he's never coming back. No, wait, I feel as if he left me weeks ago and only now is it sinking in.

Fergus avoids my eye, disengaging Ella's finger from my hair as I struggle and fail to rationalise my anger and put another brave face on it yet again.

'I know, but there's a *really* good contract up for grabs and we really need it, we really do. You know what we were talking about the other day? Well, this is my chance to iron out those worries and get everything back on track.' Ella bucks in his arms but Fergus holds on to her tightly, keeping his eyes on me. 'But some sodding graduate trainee was running the presentation through and there was a problem with the software and it's been lost, a whole week's worth of my work lost! The presentation's on Monday so I have no choice but to go in and set it all up again. It's lucky I've got it backed up on my PC otherwise I'd really be up shit creek.' He briefly squeezes my shoulder. 'I'm sorry, but at least now it's just a matter of setting it up again, and Tiff's volunteered to come in and help me do it, so I should only be gone for half a day or so?' Ella pulls off her hat and drops it on the floor.

'Tiffany's helping you?' I say, instantly jealous. All this time I've been worrying about hanging out with the gardener a little bit, and he's off to spend our one family day with his secretary without so much as a second thought. 'Look I don't care! I don't care about your presentation or the graduate or anything. I just care about us being together, we *need* to spend time together, Fergus, surely you can see that?' Fergus rolls his eyes, not really hearing me, or if he's hearing me choosing not to understand. 'You are never here, you get up so early, get home so late, and if you are here I end up handing Ella over to you just so I can have a fraction of a life outside these four bloody walls! When do we get time to be together, all of us, properly? Never! Please, Fergus, please don't go, find someone else to do it. Please.'

Fergus bows his head and then shakes it.

'I can't get someone else to do it, I have to do it, okay? Not for laughs, I just have to.' He looks at me pleadingly. 'Come on, darling, don't be mad with me. You know that the last thing I want is to have to go into work again on my day off, but I don't have any choice. I have to go.' His voice rises sharply with exasperation. 'And anyway, if you're so worried about me running

206

off with another woman why don't you, why don't . . .' he falters to a stop. 'Oh, let's talk about it when I get back.' He turns on his heels and marches out of the bedroom door, Ella's head bobbing cheerfully over his shoulder.

'Why don't I what?' I shout, following him on to the landing as he walks down the stairs. Ella waves right at me as if to distract me. I'm not sure if it's accidental or purposeful, but right now I ignore it. As he reaches the bottom, Fergus stops and thinks for a moment before looking back up at me.

'Why don't you ever want to make love to me any more?' he says softly. 'And before you say we do, yes, I know we do, at least once every two weeks when you've gritted your teeth and thought of England or whatever. And then you make it pretty clear that you just want it to be over.' He looks away from me and kisses Ella's curls before facing me again. 'I haven't felt close to you since that time in my office, and then, I don't know, I think it was the situation that turned you on and not me.'

We look at each other for a beat, separated by a flight of stairs.

'Are you saying that if I don't sleep with you any more you're going elsewhere?' I say, able only to go on the defensive. 'Have you forgotten that I gave birth to your daughter a few months ago? That it hurt me badly, that I got ripped pretty much from top to bottom. You don't just get over something like that.' My voice trembles but the more upset I become the harder Fergus's face sets.

'No, I haven't forgotten that, and no, I'm not saying I want an affair, don't make this about me . . . I'm trying to say that I miss you, Kitty. I've been trying to say it for weeks, but you're always tired or you change the subject or something. I know marriage is about more than sex, but I'm working so hard at the moment and there's so much I've got to deal with and even more than sex, it's the intimacy I miss. When I come home I need you to be there for me, to be the person that loves me. But if I try to get close to you you shut off. You don't let me in any more. For God's sake, Kitty. I'm lonely.'

For a moment I see how ridiculous we must look, talking this way two floors apart, Ella bouncing patiently in her dad's arms, utterly unaware of the maelstrom she has created in our lives.

'I'm sorry,' I say, feeling injured and guilty. 'I thought I'd explained. I thought you understood.' I feel my stomach twist and contract, it seems as if no matter how often I try to tell him how I'm feeling, his blind refusal to acknowledge any kind of problem rebuffs all of my attempts. Fergus looks at me and I can see tears intensifying the colour of his eyes.

'Don't forget to call your dad,' he says softly, and he walks out of the front door.

I stand for a long time on the landing until, despite the sun, the chill of the morning raises goosebumps on my flesh and I make my way along the corridor to the bathroom, somehow too numb to cry. Fergus and I have been half discussing our individual problems for a long time now, but have never once revealed our true feelings. Instead we've just skirted around each other with hints and half-truths, or in my case avoided it altogether. Steam begins to rise as I run the bath, filling it with water as hot as I will be able to bear, and then, dropping my dressing gown around my ankles, I force myself to look at my reflection in the full-length mirror. I conjure up mental images of the person I was when I first met Fergus until she is standing behind me.

Well, to begin with, the hair that I used to pay to have cut, coloured and styled every three months, even though I couldn't afford the phone bill more often than not, has grown far too long. It straggles in tangled curls to where my waist once was, heavy and dull, feathered with broken and dry discoloured ends. The oval face and pointed chin that Fergus used to love to kiss is now supplemented by a small pouch of fat that has appeared just underneath my jaw. The first time I caught sight of my profile in a mirror after this new arrival, I felt that I was looking at a stranger, or worse still, a version of myself who I had assumed was at least another ten years away, a version whose face was heavy and thick. Maybe if I'd seen my mum grow old it would be less of shock, but as Dad has always told me, I look just like her, except that now I'm older than she ever was, sailing into dark waters uncharted by memory or experience.

Before Ella I'd always wished that my breasts were a bit bigger and firmer. Now they are at least three cup sizes bigger than they used to be, with stretch marks that have gradually faded into silver lines along the top of them. They are softer now than they used to be, and less rounded. They used to be a symbol of my sexual power; now they are the ultimate symbol of maternity. Once they used be alluring and mysterious, now I have them out every five minutes and everyone in Berkhamsted from the milkman to the checkout girl at Smiths has seen them. The old me turns sideways so that I can better dwell on my body's lost profile. Once I used to loathe the slight curve of my belly, which was never concave or even flat despite my sporadic bursts of various fitness regimes. Now it too is covered in a road map of stretch marks and it seems to hang from my hips in a white fatty wedge. I can hold it between my finger and thumb and it feels like I've had a cushion surgically implanted to keep me at bay from Fergus's embrace.

The tops of my legs, the legs that Fergus used to love kissing, have grown thick and round and my feet, which swelled in size during the last stages of pregnancy, have never returned to their normal size. I tip my head back and squint, looking at the blurred image of the woman opposite me as objectively as possible. I'm not obese, I'm not revolting to look at. I just have the body of a woman who's gone through something remark-able – but somehow none of that comforts me. Whenever

Chapter Thirteen

The Sunday that Fergus had to go into the office was sunny but blustery with swooping gusts of wind whipping the trees back and forth. When he'd gone I took Ella to the local park, more a square of grass, really, with some swings and a slide boxed into one corner, and as we swung back and forth together I thought of my old local park with its ponds and fountains and its birds and baby deer and I thought that not everything in this town is better than home, not everything by a long shot. I whiled away an hour window shopping and staring in estate agents' windows, trying to guess how much our house might be worth now, and then with Ella fast asleep I went back to Fergus's dark house, echoing with emptiness, where I watched TV until I fell asleep. Anything to avoid making those party phone calls. The very last thing I felt like doing was partying.

Fergus was in before six, but I couldn't bring myself to be pleased to see him. I'd watched the clock tick the precious hours away until he'd be back on that train again, hours I knew we should be spending talking, laughing, maybe even making love, and I stayed as far away from him as I could, leaving him alone, tired of trying to make it up to me and angry at my refusal to relent. Now it's Monday, and neither Mr Crawley nor Gareth is here to avoid, so I relent finally to the inevitable and pick up the phone. I try Camille first but find she's got a week's leave, so I phone her place.

'Hullo?' A deep American accent greets me after I dial Camille's number.

'Alex! Hi! How are you? Back in London, obviously?' I laugh nervously.

'Hi, Kitty, really good to speak to you!' Somehow Alex manages to sound sincere. 'Yep, I'm here for a whole week, so Camille's taken some time off work and we plan to just hang out and enjoy our time together. How's your little one?'

'Fine,' I say breezily. 'Listen, is Camille around? I just want a quick word. I won't keep her too long, I promise.' I picture Alex, an improbably handsome airline pilot who looks rather like Denzel Washington and Will Smith rolled into one, and I feel guilty for intruding on their precious time together. From experience I know that a week for them to spend together is a rarity, and here I am about to unload at least two hours of my worries on to Camille. I can't do it to her, it's just not fair.

'Hi honey, what's up?' Camille says cheerily.

'Oh, nothing at all really,' I lie. 'Actually, bloody Fergus's bloody mother has talked me into having a sort of party next weekend. I can't think why I agreed except it was a serious case of emotional blackmail over my failure to plan a christening, and I was sort of hoping you could come down. It'd really make things easier for me if you were going to be there?' I ask, trying and failing not to sound too needy.

'Oh yeah, love to. Is that all?' Camille says brightly, obviously keen to be off the phone. 'Of course I'll be there. Alex goes back to the States on Friday so sure I'll be there, only I can't really talk now, Kits. You understand, don't you?'

I know that if I pushed the point, Camille would shut the bedroom door and sit on the end of the phone talking things over with me for as long as I needed her to, but I don't even bother to tell her about my part in the musical because I know how much she wants to be off the phone.

'Okay, well, have a lovely week! I'll call you Friday,' I say, and we say our goodbyes. Putting off the inevitable, I dial Dora's work number. A slightly tetchy sounding colleague picks up and informs me that if she knew where Dora was, she'd be having words with her herself, and that if I did speak to her could I remind her about her verbal warning? I choke her off in full throw and quickly dial Dora's flat, glancing at the clock as I wait for it to ring. It's almost eleven; she must surely be up by now. If she's not, what does it mean, where could she be? I blink away an unwelcome image of her cold and sprawled across her kitchen floor. I'm just about to hang up when she picks up.

'Mmm?' she says, sounding groggy.

'Dora, it's me. Did I wake you? Did you forget the weekend's over? I just spoke to your work, they're not best pleased.'

There's a long pause and I can hear extensive rustling going on.

'All right, Kits, yeah, you did wake me, but never mind. I feel like shit. I've got a . . . a hangover like you wouldn't believe! Can't make work today, no chance,' she says as if the last few months have never happened.

'Hangover?' I say, trying to sound casually breezy. 'Are you drinking again? On a school night?'

Dora belches in my ear.

'Oh, well, yeah, but only lager. It doesn't really count, honest, and, well, I don't know, it's not as hard as I thought it would be to stay clean, so I figure a little drink and a spliff now and then can't hurt, can it? It can only help me relax, actually.'

I listen intently to the tone of her voice, trying to pick up on anything that might give me a clue as to what she's really thinking. When it comes right down to it, I don't know enough to know if what she's doing is okay or not. I don't know if she's just getting back to the normal life that most of are allowed to enjoy, or if she's beginning to find her way back into smack again.

'So, what do NA say about it? It's normal, is it, to do this?' I get the feeling that Dora isn't listening to me and for a moment I wonder if she's passed out. 'Dora,' I say loudly, my voice tinged with panic. 'Listen to me, are you okay, are you really okay?'

'Yes! I'm fine!' Dora laughs. 'Look, I'm not going back there again. Not ever. I'm fine, I promise. In fact, you know that bloke I was shagging? The really dumb one? Well, he's next door right now with a stonking morning hard-on just waiting for me to sit on it!'

I laugh with her, but frankly the last thing I need right now is such a vivid picture of her sex life.

'Well, I'm glad he's got something going on that will keep you amused. I won't keep you, I just wanted to tell you that we're having a sort of party next weekend. Camille's coming down; will you? I mean, it's only for the baby, it's not a real party or anything. Frankly I'd rather wait until she's one, or at least christened, but it sort of got taken out of my hands. Fergus's mum will be there and I'm inviting Dad. You can bring thingy, stonking hard-on, if you like.'

There's a pause during which I'm not exactly sure if Dora is still on the line.

'Dora?' I say impatiently.

'Sorry. Bruce is tempting me. Yep, next weekend. I'll be there.' Suddenly the old Dora phases back in. 'So you're asking your dad? How do you feel about that?' she asks bluntly.

I briefly consider if she really wants me to tell her right now, or if she really just wants me to get off the phone but is trying her muddled best to be a best friend. I decide on the latter.

'Oh, God knows,' I say. 'Look, call me in the week for a

proper chat, okay? I really need to talk to you.' I feel my estrangement, both physical and emotional, from my oldest friend keenly.

'Okay, love, I'll call you, I will,' Dora says. 'We'll talk, I promise.'

I hang up the receiver and stare at the phone. I'm not really sure that I should be organising a family party when Fergus and I are in the middle of, well, whatever it is, but I can't really think of anything else to do and now there's just one person left to call. My dad.

I count the number of rings as I wait because I know from experience that my dad won't pick up the phone unless it's rung at least sixteen times, on the grounds that if someone really wants to talk to him they will wait. On the fourteenth ring I fight hard against the impulse to hang up, and again on the seventeenth and eighteenth ring. On the nineteenth he picks up.

'Eight-eight-oh-nine-nine-four-seven-oh?' he says as if he's asking a question he doesn't know the answer to.

'Daddy, it's me,' I tell him as brightly as I'm able.

'Kitty! Well, my.' There's a long pause. 'Well. It's so nice to hear from you.' I just know that even now he's dabbing at his eyes with a hanky. 'And how is everything? How's that little girl?'

A peculiar mixture of guilt and anger wells in my chest. I feel terrible for not seeing him for so long, and furious that our relationship is so fragile.

'She's wonderful. She wants to see her grandpa?' I say questioningly, taking a deep breath. 'Listen, Dad, we're having a bit of a get-together next weekend, a few friends and family. You can come if you want to?'

I know that he would never countenance going on public transport on his own, so as an afterthought I say, 'Fergus could

215

pick you up and you could stay over and he could take you back the next day.' There, I've done everything I can. When he turns me down now it won't be because I haven't really, really tried, it'll be because he's too much of a coward to come and I won't have to feel bad about it.

'Oh no, dear . . .' he begins.

'Right, well, never mind,' I say quickly, hiding my relief and disappointment, but my dad jumps in before I can say any more.

'No, I mean yes. I'd like to come, but don't worry about Fergus coming to get me, I'll come on the train.'

I stand stock-still in disbelief.

'But Dad, you haven't been on a train on your own in . . . I can't remember when. Are you sure you'll be okay?' Maybe he's on some new kind of pill. Ecstasy, maybe.

'Yes, Kitty, I'm fairly sure I'll be fine. I've been going to a club, a sort of bereavement group.' Mum died twenty-three years ago! I want to scream at him, but I bite my lip until it hurts. 'And I've met someone there who lost someone violently, like we did. She's opened my eyes a bit, made me see how much I was missing out on. What with all these pills, how much I've let you down, and myself. She said maybe that was why you never really bothered with me. Anyway, I've spoken to the doctor and he agrees with me – I've started to cut down my dose . . .'

The stark reality of his words hits me in the chest.

'Dad! That's not true, it's just I . . .' The sentence hangs in the air. I can't find a way to finish it.

'Look, not to worry. The main thing is I'm fairly sure I can make it to you on the train. It must be your mum, getting you to phone. I've been wanting to talk something over with you but was finding it hard to get up the courage to call you. But it's all arranged. Must be your mum.'

I hold on to the receiver silently. When I should be feeling

216

joyous and happy at his attempts to change his life, I find that his words fill me with a futile sense of dread.

'And maybe Fergus'll meet me at the station?' My dad fills the silence and I snap out of my reverie.

'Yes, yes, sure,' I say, and then on impulse, 'why don't you bring your friend?' I really have to see this woman, I have to see in person anyone who in the space of a few short weeks has got my dad out of his flat and even contemplating coming off the pills. And maybe if she's there he won't want to do this talking to me thing.

'Well, that'd be lovely. I'll ask her. I'll find out some times and call you back, okay?'

'Okay, Dad, bye then,' I say quietly.

'Bye then, love,' he says cheerfully.

I sit and stare at the phone for a while.

'What do you think, Mum? Do you think he means it?' I say out loud. Mum never answers and leaves me to ponder the question on my own.

With all of my phone calls made and all of them different from the way I imagined them to be, I go back to the bedroom and sit on the bed. In the last few days I've begun to realise that I'm not the person I thought I was any more, and I don't know yet just exactly who it is I'm supposed to be.

Last night, after Fergus and I went to bed without exchanging more than two words, I tried to remember Mum and Dad arguing, or if they had had a long period of spring frostiness like Fergus and I have begun to experience. I can't ever remember them raising their voices to each other. That doesn't mean they didn't talk in angry whispers behind closed doors, or that maybe, like Fergus and I going to bed last night, they sometimes didn't talk at all.

For the first few years after Mum had gone, Dad and I didn't argue, not once. So many people had told me I had to be 'a very good girl for Daddy' that I'd taken it totally to heart. I never played up, not with him. They'd offered us a new place then, a house in Essex, but Dad hadn't wanted to go, he'd wanted as much as possible about our lives to stay the same. Although nothing ever could.

I'd walked to school with the kids from two doors down, with my own key on a multi-coloured shoelace round my neck, and when I got in I'd do that day's tasks against a background of cartoons, *Grange Hill* and then *Nationwide* till my dad came home, and it was like that day after day, week after week. And then, I remembered, when I was eight Dad got us a colour TV for Christmas, as a surprise. They were expensive then, and he must have been saving for months in secret, he must have been thinking for weeks about how excited and delighted I'd be to finally get a TV like the neighbours. Christmas morning I got out of bed as usual, and as usual we prepared our cereal, and as it was a holiday and because we always gave presents after lunch, we went to switch the TV on straight away, to watch the Christmas service. Dad sat smiling at me and nodding at the TV, raising his eyebrows in anticipation until eventually I asked him, 'What? Do you want your present now?'

His face had fallen and he'd shaken his head. 'It's in colour, it's a colour TV!' he'd sighed and slumped back in his chair. 'I thought you'd be so pleased!'

I'd frowned at him and then looked back at the screen, seeing the unadjusted orange-tinted colours for the first time.

'Oh, Daddy, it's great! It's better than Gary Anderton's.' I'd gone to him and climbed in his lap. 'It's because I always imagine the programme in colour, Daddy, that's why. I just thought I was imagining it,' I'd said to him. 'It's great not having to imagine it any more.' And I'd put my arms around his neck and kissed his cheek. It was too late; I'd disappointed him and the rest of the day was spent in silence. That was the nearest we came to arguing, perhaps because he became gradually more withdrawn and silent, less of a father and more of a flatmate. It wasn't until I hit my thirteenth birthday that we really started to argue, and then it was all one-sided. Suddenly angry and scared, I started shouting at him, screaming at him, over every little thing until eventually he didn't even bother to respond, because by that time he was gone.

Gareth hefts his kitbag on to the kitchen counter and looks at me.

'Where's Ella, then? Never tell me she's in bed already and its not even seven?' I smile wanly and pull myself up on to a chair.

'She's been asleep since five,' I tell him with a sigh. 'This means she'll be up by ten and then up all night. I thought babies were supposed to just fall into a routine. I mean, I'm trying, but it never seems to happen . . .' I sigh again and look at the clock. Fergus had told me he wouldn't be leaving work until gone nine. Mr Crawley had been round for a cup of tea, but he'd left an hour ago and I had sat idly listening to the radio, watching Gareth build my gazebo, not able to muster the energy to actually go and talk to him, feeling that I was so out of practice that I might actually have forgotten how to.

'Working late today?' I say at last as he washes his hands and face in the sink. He flicks his hair off his damp face and wipes the water away with his fingers.

'Don't worry, I won't charge you extra.' He looks at me and reflexively I brush my hair off my face and straighten my back a little. 'Are you okay?' he says with a smile. 'You seem a little down?'

I wonder what he sees when he looks at me now, what he thinks. I wonder if he really cares, or if it's his famous empathy, aimed at a woman who might be vulnerable, may be open to suggestion. And then I decide that I don't care. I'm not as naive or as hopeful as Clare, and right now I don't care why he is listening to me, just that he is.

'No. No, I'm okay really,' I say before contradicting myself. 'I mean, I'm fed up with being alone. I know that I have Ella, and that you and Mr Crawley are usually around, but it's not the same as having a proper adult companion even so, and I feel alone. I don't think married people should feel that way, should they?' I glance at the clock. At least three more hours until Fergus gets in. I've been here before not so long ago, and not so long ago I decided definitively that I shouldn't go here again. But I also decided then to make the most of my life with Fergus, to put energy and effort into 'us' – except that Fergus is never here and that seems to be impossible.

'Do you want a beer?' I ask Gareth, ignoring the remaining part of me that is counselling caution against telling this stranger what's going on in my heart or my head. It's a concern that never touches my thin-skinned surface. I'm just sick of being on my own.

Four crushed cans rock back and forth on their axes as Gareth slams his hand down on the worktop and I laugh again, tears pricking at my eyes this time. I'm not entirely sure how all my good intentions added up to me getting drunk with the gardener again, but right now I don't care. One drink led to another and I'm having a very rare laugh.

Flicking the hair back from my shoulder, I tip back my head until I can feel my neck stretch and the floor swoon beneath me. If I was the old, young Kitty Kelly, this would be my second date with Gareth, maybe even a sex date. I giggle at the entertainingly dangerous thought, but Gareth doesn't even raise an eyebrow, he's in full raconteur mode and any reaction from me is bound to be because of him.

'So I said to him, I'm sorry, Woody mate, but rules are rules and you can't be one of us until you've been initiated. Winter it was, mind, February, and the sea was *freezing*, but he so wanted to be in with us that in he went, not a stitch on, and stood there up to his waist for five minutes like we said . . .'

I wipe my hand across my face, focusing on his story. 'I don't know why I'm laughing, it's not funny. It's horrible. Poor Woody! I can't believe you made him do it!'

Gareth giggles helplessly, his eyes bright at the memory.

'I know, I know, it's just some people are so gullible you can't help yourself. So anyway, five minutes go by and out he comes, shivering all over he was. He was *so* cold you couldn't hardly even see his dick, like a shrivelled up little acorn it was!' He laughs uproariously. 'Poor bloke. We did him give half a bottle of whisky after that and he was okay in the end. Off work for two weeks with pneumonia, but no harm done. He was a good bloke, Woody. Do anything for anyone, one of those types. The twat.' He smiles at me. 'You look a bit better. You've got a bit of your sparkle back.'

I shake my head, conscious of my clean hair rippling around my shoulders.

'What sparkle?' I giggle, pursuing the compliment, forcing myself to draw back as Gareth fixes me with his predator eyes. He leans a little closer to me over the counter and cocks his head to one side as he regards me.

'I mean you have a glow, a sparkle about you. I can see it in there burning brightly, just waiting for a bit of passion to ignite it, to burst back into glorious flames.'

For two, maybe three, heartbeats I allow myself to float a little closer to his lips before pulling myself up in my seat.

'Sounds like a health hazard,' I say, and then, 'You're funny, with all your charm and chat-up lines. I bet you get any woman you want with all your la-de-da fancy lines. Never taking no for

221

an answer. What happened to that girl you saw after me the other day? Still on, is she?' As I speak I realise that the two cans of lager have gone to my head and that I sound maybe a little more challenging that I had intended.

Gareth smiles to himself and seems to box away his cut-price charm before my very eyes. 'I do all right,' he says affably. 'And what about you? Do you do all right?'

I giggle. 'Of course I do all right! I've got it on tap, I'm married!' I insist loudly, losing my balance a little on the kitchen stool. I should have eaten, but eating on your own turns out to be boring. Gareth is still smiling to himself as he stands and begins to gather up his belongings and pack them away.

'Yeah, well, that must be what's given you back your sparkle then, except if it were, you would never had lost it, would you,' he says quietly. 'Still, thanks for the drinks, but I'd better get going, don't want the gardener here half cut *again* when your husband gets in, do you?'

I toy absently with a crushed can, my beer-lagged brain just catching up with his previous comment.

'It's just because I'm not tired any more. That's why I look better. I used to look like this before Fergus, you know, and Ella. It's got nothing to do with Fergus, or you!' I say defensively.

Gareth smirks and leans across the counter towards me.

'*I* never said it did.'

His fume-filled breath warms my face momentarily, and then I watch him as he zips up his jacket, and decide, despite his half-baked attempts to conquer anything in a skirt (or in my case a pair of jeans), that I wish that he did want me. I wish that he did make a play for me, because then, just for one fantastic moment, I would feel alive, I would feel free of everything stacked up on top of me. At least he's here. At least he listens. At least even the thought of a man like him seriously thinking sexually about a woman like me does make me sparkle, just a little bit.

'Thank you,' I say suddenly. 'For talking to me tonight when you could have been out with one of your flunkies. Thanks. You've been a friend?' I phrase the statement as a question just so that I can reaffirm the exact nature of our relationship for us both.

'No worries,' Gareth says, and suddenly he stoops to kiss me on the cheek and I feel the slightest graze of his stubble. 'See you tomorrow, pal,' he says, and he heads for the door.

After he's gone the house seems suddenly cold and grey again, and I feel the weight of the two dark floors above me, empty except for my tiny baby. I resist the urge to rush up the stairs and bring her out of her cot to sit in front of the fire with me. Instead I go to the kitchen to make a cup of tea. I look at the clock. It's ten to ten.

And Fergus still isn't home.

Chapter Fourteen

I'm staring at a tray of miniature chicken supreme vol-au-vents that Georgina has just unveiled before me with the kind of flourish that is usually warranted by turning water into wine or something.

'I knew you'd be struggling with the catering, dear, so I thought I'd contribute a little bit.'

I try not to look at the twelve round turrets of flaky pastry and greyish mush, but somehow their lure is magnetic.

'Well, thanks,' I say lamely. In fact, my fridge and oven are both full right now of dozens of party-style buffet foods all bought courtesy of Marks & Spencer's, all ready in under fifteen minutes, and all requiring no more of a struggle than removing the packaging before placing in a preheated oven, and these are just whatever the French word for a nibble is – after that I have a main course. I'm hugely proud of it. I had no idea you could get whole roasts prepackaged. Of course Georgina knows nothing about my chicken and my duck, so she's still preening over her efforts.

'I mean, I'd have done more, but I didn't want you to accuse me of interfering *again*,' she says pointedly through her fuchsia lipstick-framed teeth, and I wince. I was rather hoping she'd forgotten about that.

After Gareth left on Monday evening, everything else went

downhill. To say it's been a difficult week would be an under-statement. In fact it's been exactly the kind of week you don't need to have in the run-up to an event where all the most important people in your life will be under one roof judging you.

When Fergus finally came home on Monday night it was almost eleven, and true to form Ella was up again and bright as a button, screeching for her daddy as soon as he got in through the door as if I'd been beating and starving her all day.

Fergus kissed me on the cheek and flopped on to the sofa with Ella.

'Do you want anything?' I asked him awkwardly, still a little fuzzy from the lager. Fergus had begun to heroically row the boat with Ella, pulling her back and forth on his knee.

'No, I had a pizza at work. A cup of tea would be nice, or a beer if you haven't already drunk it all.' He smiled as he said it, and I wondered how I could explain that there wasn't any left without having to mention that Gareth was here too.

'Have a glass of wine instead,' I said. 'Lager'll give you nightmares.'

When I returned a few minutes later, Ella reached out and grabbed the edge of my jumper, pulling me down to sit beside her and Fergus, smiling at us each in turn.

'She knows, you know,' I said to Fergus after a while, feeling strung out and tired.

'She knows what,' he said without looking at me.

'That we're fighting. She knows and she doesn't like it. She hates it.' I watched his profile in the hope that the best thing between us right now might help us find a way back into what was good about our relationship.

He put his palm on the top of her head, before blowing a raspberry on her cheek, making her giggle and shudder all at once.

'I know she knows,' he said. His face looked full and heavy with sadness. 'My mum and dad were at it hammer and tongs for most of my childhood, and I knew about it, even when I was really little. I knew about it and I hated it.'

'Were they?' I asked him. I sounded rather more intrigued than was appropriate under the circumstances, but it was just that Daniel was such a self-possessed and quiet man that I couldn't imagine him engaging in any kind of unseemly dialogue with his wife.

'Oh yeah, they hated each other for years, for as long as I can remember until I was about ten, and then Dad left home for about two weeks. I don't know where he went or who with to this day. But Mum went to pieces, guzzling the whisky and popping tranqs, the works.' He half smiled. 'It was like living on the set of *Sunset Boulevard*. I was left wandering about that big house making beans on toast for tea and telling the lads at school everything was fine and that my rugby kit was still dirty because our washing machine was broken. Eventually I had to tell a teacher, who phoned my mum, and then some aunt turned up from somewhere, and then the whole Irish family mafia kind of thing was set in motion and someone's cousin found Dad and talked to him and about a week later Dad came home. They never talked about what happened, not in front of me, at least, and they were just different with each other from then on, as if they'd both realised how easily everything they had could have fallen apart. They really loved each other, still do, but back then they let everything else get on top of them and they forgot it.'

As he spoke he loosened his tie before pulling it off and dropping it into Ella's delighted hands. 'I don't want that to happen to us, Kitty. I mean, I know I'm not very good at explaining how I feel, but I don't mean to go on about sex all the time. I don't know how to explain it. I don't care if we never have sex again, just as long as you remember that you love me.'

I leant into the curve of his arm and breathed in his scent in a few deep breaths. Ella pulled my hair companionably.

'I'll never forget that I love you,' I said, smiling up at him, my head tipped at an acute angle dictated by Ella's none-too-gentle attentions, and I made a silent promise to make that statement true. 'Ouch! Or you, pickle.' She lay her head on my shoulder and we all held each other very tightly for a moment before watching TV and drinking red wine long into the night until Ella eventually slept again.

When Fergus returned from putting her into her cot, he took me in his arms and held me quietly. I held my breath until I could muster up the courage and energy to speak again.

'Would you really not care?' I said suddenly into the companionable silence.

'Not care about what?' Fergus said into my hair.

'If we never did it again?' I wriggled in his arms so that I could look at him.

'Would you care?' he replied cautiously.

I nodded heartily. 'Yes, yes of course I'd care. I love making love with you. I just seem to have fallen off the horse and I'm having a bit of trouble getting back in the saddle, sort of thing. But I know I will eventually . . . get back on the horse, and what's more *love* getting on the horse and riding the horse – hard.'

Fergus laughed and held me tightly for a second.

'Great analogy from Kitty Kelly, there. Was that in one of your magazines?' I shrugged, glad to have made him laugh. 'Listen, when I was banging on about intimacy earlier, this is what I meant. You and me together, talking and not talking, but together, close. I'd rather have this and no sex than emotionless sex neither one of us enjoys.'

I took his glass out of his hand.

'Oh well, if you like all this sitting about staring into the gas fire nonsense, then you won't be interested in taking me for a riding lesson right now,' I said with my best sexy face. The sweetest smile that I'd fallen for in the beginning spread slowly over Fergus's face and I drew him into my arms. In perfect silence and the darkness of our bedroom, we made love, half drunk and half asleep, companions and friends more than passionate lovers, but at least we were close and at least we had talked. It felt like a beginning.

When I woke up the next day he'd already gone, leaving a note by his side of the bed.

'My mobile's gone flat, call Tiffs if you need me,' and he'd scribbled her number down quickly. Which meant he knew it, and probably off by heart. Despite hours of rationalisation, for the rest of that day until he came home I felt jealous and angry, and as soon as he got in we had another fight. Not about us, not about sex, this time, but about the washing machine. It's a long story.

In the meantime I waited around for Gareth to turn up that morning but he never came. It was only after a call to Fergus and then a hunt through the *Yellow Pages* that I realised I didn't have any kind of contact number for him. I couldn't even remember seeing one on the side of his van. I remembered Daniel had recommended him to Fergus and I phoned him to ask for a number, but he said he'd heard of him through a friend and had never actually had the number.

'It's rather strange really,' he said to me. 'I can't remember where I heard about him or how I got in touch with him in the first place, now I come to think about it.'

Gareth turned up on Wednesday as if nothing had happened, the heroic glaze I'd given him whilst whiling away many hours in his company considerably tarnished.

'All right?' He breezed in through the door with a quick glance up at a sky patched with clouds as he entered. 'Looks like it might be a nice day.'

'Where were you yesterday?' I demanded, by way of a hello. 'For a whole day I waited in for you and you never turned up. I do have a life outside this house, you know. If I'd known you weren't going to bother turning up, I could have gone somewhere, done . . . something.'

He smiled at me a smile that said, 'Yeah – like what?'

'Listen, I'm your gardener, love, not your . . . not your bloody boyfriend.' He didn't respond with the abject apology or even the friendliness I'd been expecting after Monday evening, after everything. 'And besides, I *did* tell you. I *told* you I was going away for the day to price up another job for after this one. I *told* you I wouldn't get back from Luton until Monday afternoon. I *told* you last week.'

'No you didn't,' I protested weakly, before remembering. 'And when I saw you on Monday you said see you tomorrow, I remember!'

Gareth sighed and gritted his teeth. I was almost certain that he'd never said anything about having Tuesday off, but he was so self-assured and I was so all over the place that I couldn't be sure if he did or not.

'I don't remember saying that. If I did, it was just a reflex, just because I always say it, it's not a bloody promise!' he told me angrily, and I found myself backing away from him, shocked by his sudden, sharp, aggressive edge. He caught my reaction and his face instantly softened.

'Look, I'm sorry. It's just that I had a hell of a trip, shit loads of traffic, and I didn't get back till late and then the neighbours' bloody baby kept me up all night, and I keep thinking about . . . Well, sometimes you can't get everything you want and it pisses me off. I shouldn't take it out on you, though.' He dropped a long-fingered hand on to my shoulder. 'I did tell you, honest, but you're so busy and all, what with running this place all on your own, you must have forgotten.' He smiled then with the kind of delight little boys reserve for train sets and spiders. 'I've got a van full of plants out there. If the weather's going to be as good as I think, we can spend all day planting out? I'll teach you Latin names.'

'Really?' I cried, almost forgetting my anger with him. Before I could even finish the cheer, a clap of thunder had shaken the sky until it opened, letting out a torrent of rain.

'Just our luck, right?' Gareth said with a complicit grin, and I let us be friends again. A friend, after all, doesn't break any promises.

Five minutes later I'd made him a coffee and we both sat in the kitchen watching the rain.

'It looks like someone picked up the Channel and just dumped it all in one go,' he said bleakly.

'I thought you country blokes were supposed to know about weather.' I eyed him speculatively. 'All that rain in Wales. I'd have thought you'd be able to sense it or something. Nice day my arse.'

Gareth lifted his chin and shrugged.

'I grew up on the nastiest council estate in Cardiff,' he said. 'Not exactly what you'd call rural, but anyway, I'll give it another go.' He examined the thick low covering of angry cloud closely. 'I reckon it's going to rain for a bit yet,' he said, returning his gaze to me with a wry smile.

'So, if you grew up in a city, why are you a gardener?' I asked him. It was a stupid question, but it was chucking it down with rain, and since his disappearing act yesterday I'd realised that while I'd let him into my home, my life and to a certain extent my head, I knew practically nothing about him.

Before answering me, Gareth looked at his reflection in the

day-dark window for a moment longer, and I could see him weighing up his options. It was a look I'd seen before, but only ever in the mirror. It was the way I'd looked when I'd debated whether or not to tell everyone the whole truth about my mum.

'Well, I always thought I'd join the army right from being a little lad, but when it came to it I failed the entrance exam.'

I kept my mouth shut and tried my best to look just half interested, but I honestly thought all you had to be able to do to get in the army was add two and two together and prove you weren't psychotic. Or maybe you had to prove you were. One or the other.

'I was gutted,' Gareth continued. 'Never thought of doing anything else, never bothered with school. I was just waiting to be old enough to enlist. So anyways, I knocked about on the dole for a while, did a bit of labouring and then a mate of mine got me into the TA and I loved it. For a while it became my life. I went on all the manoeuvres, playing soldier and all that, packed in my girlfriend Lauren because she was sick of me going away every weekend. I just hung out with the lads. It was good. I suppose I thought they were sort of my family.' He sighed, pulling himself back from the memory and changing the subject. 'Have you ever noticed that everyone, everyone you ever meet in the world, has a story to tell, a tragedy. All of us. Six billion people wandering around the planet bumping into each other, desperate to tell each other about the fucked-up things that have happened to us, not one of us really giving a shit about anyone else's problems.'

I thought about the fucked-up things that had happened to me and decided that so far in life the only 'good' thing to come out of it is that I instantly trump everyone else with my own tragedy. It's a story that instantly makes a 'my boyfriend's chucked me' or a 'my parents are divorced' story look a bit lame.

'Go on,' I said, wanting to know if Gareth could trump me.

'Anyway, my dad used to knock my mum around when I was kid, sometimes me, but mainly her.' He said it casually as if he were describing cartoon violence. 'And then he ran off with the local barmaid. Big fat bottle blonde, knocked her around for a couple of weeks and when she came running back he took off. I didn't see him for years until one day I got home from a weekend's orienteering and there he was, sitting in the front room eating chips. The first thing I said to him was, "Where's my mum?" He nodded to the kitchen. I went in and there she was, sitting at the table, a black eye and a broken nose, two teeth out, trying to peel some sodding spuds to make him more chips. I don't know, she must have been in shock, sitting there peeling spuds, bleeding all over the table.'

'What did you do?' I asked, my eyes widening at the look on his face as he remembered the image. He looked like a hawk about to pounce on a mouse.

'I broke his nose for him. And his arm.' He looked directly at me then and mimed out what happened next. 'I got my hands round his neck and I bashed his head on the radiator, I kept on bashing it until my mum dragged me off. I gave him "severe head injuries",' he said, his tone just the other side of proud. He settled back on his stool and looked back into the rainy afternoon. 'So anyway, I got eight months for assault and GBH because even though it was only a first offence, and I was trying to protect my mum, I really, really battered him,' he said matter-of-factly. 'At least I know he won't be beating anyone else now. He lives in a halfway house in Cardiff, can't do very much for himself any more, something to do with severe trauma to the cerebral cortex or whatever, I dunno. They did tell me, but I always forget.' His smile was one of pure satisfaction.

'Fuck me,' I said. 'You were inside? For almost killing some-one?' My stomach lurched. Gareth caught the apprehension in my tone and his face had fallen.

'Oh fuck, I knew I shouldn't have told you. I try not to tell anyone. They find out you've done a bit of time and that's it, no one wants to know you. I was only in for five months in the end, not long enough to get any qualifications or nothing, but long enough to help in the prison garden. I learnt a lot there, it helped relax me and chill me out. For the first time I realised that I'd been angry all my life, ever since I was big enough to know what he was doing to my mum. I'd been angry, been waiting for that day, even when I thought I'd never see him again, because I wanted to show him a taste of his own medicine. When he'd gone away I'd almost forgotten about it, then the moment I saw him, the moment I saw my mum, I knew what I had to do. I had to finish it right then and there, and I did. And now I hardly ever get angry any more. I'm just a chilled-out bloke who makes things grow.' He looked at me and smiled. 'Beautiful things.'

The sound of the rain thundered down on the patio and we smiled at each other. If anyone knew what it meant to overcome a violent past it was me, and for some reason he didn't scare me. If I had a sixth sense or an intuition like the magazines were always telling me I did, then Gareth didn't make it ring any bells, at least not in that way.

'So, tell me about what happened to you?' he said bluntly, and my stomach clenched.

'Me? Nothing really. I'm one of those average people you were talking about. Moaning because my husband's home a bit late from work.' I smiled at him. 'Well, you know that, I bend your ear about it often enough.' I gave a half-laugh, hoping to end the conversation, and I did, but not the way I wanted to. Gareth looked suddenly sullen, his eyes shadowed and dark.

'For God's sake, don't be so apologetic. If I were you I'd be moaning. I mean, I don't know the bloke or anything, but from what I can see you're on your own practically all the time dealing with that baby while he's up in the City till all hours. For one thing, if I were you I'd be wondering what he was doing all that time . . .' He'd got into full flow and suddenly I wished for the other Gareth back, the up-front, casually flirtatious Gareth. I was afraid I'd let him in too far.

'He's working hard for Ella and me!' I jumped in anxiously, dismayed that he should pick up on my throwaway comment and begin to dissect it so brutally.

'Well, I wouldn't be so sure about that, and for another thing, if I was married to someone like you, if you were my wife . . .' he held my gaze, his amber eyes bright with intensity . . . 'if you were *mine*, I'd treat you right, I'd make damn sure you were never out of my sight.'

The wind hurled hard clouds of rain against the window and I jumped in my seat, wondering if he had really said what I thought he had.

'Well, that's not practical. You can't go around work with your husband all day long can you?' I said awkwardly, choosing to ignore the moment. To smother the moment and beat it to a silent, bloody pulp. I stood up and headed into the hallway. Somewhere in the last ten minutes my imaginary flirtation had tipped over into something else, something that had scared and exhilarated me all at once and felt terrifyingly free. For this moment, in this hour, I was a different person, lost in a new world full of different possibilities, and it scared me. I remembered my promise to Fergus, to never forget that I loved him, and I knew then that it *was* true. All the problems that had been conspiring against us, they were bad, yes, and serious too, but they weren't enough, never enough, to make me forget that Fergus and Ella were my life. The loves of my life. I needed to get the distance back between Gareth and me as quickly as I could. My dangerous game had strayed too far beyond the boundaries of fantasy.

'This rain's not going to let up. You should just go.' I stood there waiting for him in the gloomy daylight until he joined me, feeling the passing moments draw out a space between us.

'Kitty, I'm sorry, I . . .' he began with a casual insouciance, the suggestion implicit in his face that nothing had happened. I brushed the doubt away and began again. 'I might have got a bit carried away, but if you just knew how . . .'

'Actually, maybe we should leave the garden for a bit. I really feel like having my house to myself. I'm sorry if that means you have to take the plants back, but I think it's best. I'll call you,' I said brightly, not forgetting that I had no number to call him on. As I opened the door, Clare was wheeling Ted up the path, soaked through to her skin. Gareth and I exchanged glances. I'm not sure what his meant, but mine screamed, 'Please just go!'

'Oh God!' she said as I helped her in with Ted, who was snugly warm and dry under his rain cover, kicking at the plastic in greeting. 'Fucking spring, eh! Oh, hi!' Her robust greeting morphed into girly sing-song as soon as she saw Gareth.

'I must look like a bomb site, a wet one. Fuck.' Gareth took the buggy off her and wheeled it into the kitchen, studiously ignoring me.

'Come on, little mate,' he said as he went. 'Let's get you out of there.'

Clare gave me a wide-eyed smile.

'He's a natural with kids, isn't he?' she whispered. 'You don't mind me just turning up on the off-chance do you? It's just that they don't need the set people at this week's rehearsals, and I thought I won't see him until Saturday otherwise, and I'd like to get to know him a bit better before we meet at a social gathering, if you know what I mean?'

I stared at her for a second trying to work out what she was talking about, and then I remembered. Ever since the casting, Clare had been hearts and flowers about Gareth. She had banged on about nothing else at the One O'Clock Club until even Calista's nineteenth recital of 'Twinkle Twinkle Little Star' had seemed more alluring. On the way home I had promised I would ask Gareth along to the party on Saturday.

'Oh, um, he can't come,' I said, grateful for once that since giving birth my memory had deteriorated. Clare's face had fallen. 'Yeah, I know. Never mind though, hey. I'll pop upstairs and get you a towel and you go and talk to him before he goes.'

Once upstairs I checked on Ella, who was still sound asleep on her tummy, her head pressed right up against the bars of her cot. Then I went back into my room and sat on the bed, practising my breathing. For a moment down there I'd thought, actually I was sure, that Gareth had been coming on to me, that really he'd meant what he said about all that 'if you were mine' business. My heart was beating hard and my mind was racing, rewinding and replaying the scene over and over again. He was out of order, bang out of order, and I should have known, I should have seen it coming, I'd practically invited it in. He didn't have to tell me he was a womaniser, you just had to look at him to see he'd be the type to go after the unobtainable, to keep going after it until he'd caught it and used it and finished with it. I knew him exactly, he was like about four of my ex-boyfriends, all of my boyfriends up until Fergus. You see them as a challenge, you imagine you might be the one to tame them, but you never are. They take control of your life, fatherly at first, and then gradually they suffocate you until you see nothing else, until you are nothing else but part of them. That was Gareth, that was exactly Gareth, and sitting there on the end of my bed, trembling, I couldn't help longing, almost, to feel that engulfed by something again, so lost in another person that it didn't matter if I disappeared after all. I clutched on to the edge of the bed and waited for the floor to right itself. Fergus was my way out from all of that, it was with Fergus I became my own person again. I may have let that feeling of confidence slip a little, but I wouldn't let it slip away.

As I walked back down the stairs, Clare's boisterous laughter was filling the kitchen. I pushed open the door and saw Gareth with Ted balanced high on his shoulders, twirling him around and making him scream with delight.

'Where's my towel?' Clare asked me brightly.

'Oh Christ, I knew there was something I went upstairs for!' I said with hysterically edged brightness. 'Sorry, blame the baby brain.' I handed Clare a wad of kitchen roll. 'Will that do the trick?'

She took it happily and I could tell that at that moment it wouldn't matter if it rained putrid maggots down her neck, she'd still be glowing like a fresh spring flower.

As Gareth swung Ted down, Clare said, 'Gareth can come, by the way, that thing he told you he had on wasn't this Saturday after all, it's the one after. He got it wrong. Brilliant, isn't it?' I looked from Clare to Gareth. Yes, it was brilliant, considering that I hadn't even told him about the party.

'Oh good,' I said flatly, avoiding Gareth's eye, feeling the beginning of something inevitable. 'Gareth, I can't pay you to sit around all day, you might as well have the day off,' I said carefully, pleading with him to leave with every syllable I spoke.

Gareth smiled at Clare.

'No charge for the pleasure of my company,' he said to her, his voice warm and low. She almost disintegrated with joy.

'You don't want to hang around listening to baby talk, though, do you? Go home.' I said again, more pointedly this time. Gareth redirected his gaze to me.

'I'm all right,' he said, with a touch of determination that only he and I could hear.

'Gareth, I want you to go. Do you know what, I've just heard the forecast and it's going to be like this all week. Have the week off, go on.' He held my gaze for a beat longer, and his eyes told me that it wasn't over yet.

'Fine,' he said. 'I'll see you Saturday.' He bent down and kissed Clare on the cheek. 'Sorry I couldn't see you for longer, Clare,' he said before picking up his jacket and going. I waited for the slam of the front door but there was none.

'What did you do that for?' Clare said with dismay. 'I really think he likes me!'

I'd sat down opposite her. 'I know, but there's something I wanted you to know, that's all,' I said, desperately trying to think of a way to extricate her from her daydreams without hurting her.

Clare's face fell back into its habitual expression, which was one void of any expectation.

'He's got a girlfriend,' she sighed.

'Um, no.'

I stared at her blankly, trying to find a way to explain the shift in my perception of Gareth, wondering if I wanted to warn her off for her sake or for mine.

'He's gay, is he gay?' she asked, a touch more brightly. 'I've always said you can't argue with someone fancying Ricky Martin.'

'No, Clare, he's not gay. Look, we were talking before and . . .'

Clare had raced ahead of me.

'Oh my God, don't tell me he fancies you! Please don't tell me that he fancies you! I couldn't stand it! The first decent bloke I've had a sniff of in months and he fancies my happily married best friend!'

Whatever I had been about to say to her, I was halted in my tracks; after only a few weeks Clare thought of me as her best friend.

'No!' I said. 'He's been inside. I'm not supposed to tell

anyone, but I thought you should know. He's been inside for GBH. There, I've said it now. Don't tell him I told you, will you?' I decided not to tell her the circumstances; after all, I was hoping she'd lose interest in him.

'GBH?' she said.

'Yeah, that's why I wanted him to go. He freaked me out,' I half lied. It was only half a lie.

'Well, well thanks for telling me, but I mean, look at him! He grows flowers for a living! He must have had a good reason. Someone like Gareth just wouldn't lash out for the sake of it.' She filed the information in the dark recesses of her mind and dismissed it as circumstantial. 'So what should I wear on Saturday?'

At the rehearsal that evening I'd been really glad that Gareth wasn't there, and it *had* been fun. The leads all read through the script and we did a few warm-up songs together. It turned out that Colin was really funny and that Bill was a great musician who probably should never have been a teacher. Clare measured people's inner leg, Mr Crawley and I laughed hysterically as we tried to follow the choreographer's simple enough dance moves, and I got to know Jim, a forty-something mechanic who played Wild Bill Hickock, Calamity's love interest. Apparently there's a kiss, but he'd promised to brush his teeth and no tongues. Afterwards, as I was sipping a sherry, waiting for Clare to get back from the loo, I found Caroline suddenly at my side, peering at me intently as if she was about to peck me with her finely pointed roman nose.

'Now, Kitty, how are you finding it?' she said without preamble. I blinked and raised my brows.

'Fine, it's fun. Really fun,' I said with my best interview smile, all ready to list my three worst points as if they were positives. Caroline tucked her chin back into her neck and pursed her lips, her jet earrings trembling slightly as her jowls settled.

'Ah, yes, *fun*,' she said thoughtfully. 'You don't really know about the Berkhamsted Summer Festival, do you? I mean, of course, yes, it *is* meant to be fun, it *is* meant to be an occasion of laughter and splendour, but is not meant to be fun for *you*, Kitty, do you see?' I opened my mouth and closed it again. I did not see.

'Of course, I don't mean just you, heavens no. I mean all of the Players, every one. It is each Player's responsibility to take this honour very seriously, or at least they should do. It's not just the quality of the production I'm thinking of, or my reputation, though God knows I've spent years building it up. It's the Tring Troubadours. I'd never say this on record, but last year they were better than us, more focused, better sets – more in tune. This year we absolutely have to better them, we have to. For the honour of the town!' She took a swift shallow breath. 'And, well, your arrival seems to have brought a kind of levity to the proceedings that is proving rather distracting . . .'

I smiled inwardly with delight. Me? Frumpy Kitty? Distracting? Levity?

Caroline continued, her voice a hoarse stage whisper, 'I mean, since you've joined, even Ian, er, Mr Crawley, acts like a teenager half the time, and he is usually such a dignified man!' She stared at me with her black eyes and I gathered that I'd missed my cue to respond.

'So you're saying you want me to have less fun?' I said slowly, trying not to smile.

'Yes, exactly,' she replied with a tight little smile. 'More focus, less fun, let it be your motto!' She waved her hand as if casting a spell and I shrugged compliantly, swallowing my bubbling hysteria.

'I'll certainly try,' I promised sincerely.

Caroline bobbed her head in a quick nod before flying off to bully Barbara next. At last Clare bounced up behind me and linked her arm through mine.

'Well, that was fun,' she said.

But it wasn't until we got back home that things *really* went wrong.

'Hi!' I called as Clare and I went in through the door.

'Hello, dear.' This time I was expecting Georgina, I had even arranged it, as I knew Fergus wouldn't be back before I had to leave and that when he did get in he couldn't cope on his own, not after a day at work.

'Everything okay?' I said, still feeling friendly towards her. She was in high spirits.

'Yes, dear, everything's fine, we've had a gay old time. Fergus got in about eight and I made him shepherd's pie, it's his favourite, you know. He gave Ella her bath and then I put her to bed.'

'She just went down?' I said, surprised.

'Well, she made a bit of a fuss for a while, but she soon learnt that when *Grandma* puts her to bed she stays in bed.' I bit my lip as I followed her into the living room, trying to remember that I liked her now. Fergus was just polishing off what looked like the remains of a home-made apple pie right out of the dish.

'Mmmmm, Mum, that was delicious, no one cooks like you,' he said. 'Hi, darling, come and give me a kiss.'

I bent over and kissed his forehead, trying not to be resentful; after all, it was hardly fair. If you don't cook, you can't complain if someone else does. You can feel slightly narked when your husband so obviously enjoys one of the domestic pleasures you've been denying him recently, though.

'Hi, Clare,' he said over my shoulder. I had forgotten that Clare was even there. 'Did you have a good time?'

'Yeah, I'm making Kitty this huge pink ballgown, it's going to be fab,' she said with a giggle. Fergus wolf-whistled sarcastically, if such a thing were possible.

'What about you, Kits? Did you do some lassoing or something?' he asked me, his face beaming with contentment.

I smiled. 'It was so cool, I'm really enjoying it. I mean, it's totally not hip or anything, but that's half the fun. Except I'm not allowed to have fun any more, Caroline told me.' Clare and I grinned at each other.

Georgina appeared from the kitchen with a cup of tea, clearly delighted to be mothering my husband again. She handed me the tea, presented in the 'best' china, a flowery Doulton number which was part of a ludicrously expensive service she and Daniel had bought us, even though we had begged for something simple and microwave-proof.

'While I was making Fergus some dinner, dear, I couldn't help but notice you were a bit low on basic supplies so I've made you a list. I've left it on the counter.' I took the tea and gritted my teeth through a polite smile. 'You know, herbs, all that store-cupboard stuff Delia recommends, vital to spruce up any basic dish.'

I raised a mildly aggravated eyebrow. 'Thanks then,' I said, hoping she'd leave before the other eyebrow got all irritable too.

'Oh, and I hope you don't mind me saying this, dear, but, well, Fergus has bought you such a lovely kitchen, it seems a shame not to use it properly. I know how busy you are, so I've rearranged your cupboards for you, I hope you don't mind.'

I looked at Fergus and his eyes pleaded with me, 'Just say you don't mind.'

'No, no, I don't mind,' I said awkwardly, spitting the words out of my mouth. 'Thanks, that's lovely.'

Fergus got up and stretched with a theatrical flourish that would have gone down well with the Players. He looked at where his watch would have been if he hadn't taken it off for Ella's bath.

'Wow, is that the time? Right, Mum, I'll just grab my coat and I'll take you and Clare home.' Before World War Three breaks out, he might as well have added. As he went outside, Georgina beckoned me closer to her. I went, mesmerised by the thought of what new atrocity she could commit in my living room.

'Now, I hope you don't take this the wrong way,' she told me, priming me to do exactly that, 'but it seems to me that Fergus is under a lot of pressure at the moment, working hard for you and the baby . . .' I waited patiently for the final straw . . . 'and really, darling, I know it's the twenty-first century and all that, but I do think that if you cooked him a few decent meals a week it wouldn't mean that you were tied to the kitchen sink, and . . .'

'Oh, shut up you interfering old bag,' I thought, but out loud as it happened. Out very loud in a shouty, angry tone. Clare clapped her hand over her mouth and backed hastily out of the door.

'I beg your pardon?' she said predictably, and I thought, 'in for a penny . . .'

'I said, shut up you interfering old bag! How *dare* you, how *dare* you come in here and rearrange my cupboards and judge me on my housewifery skills! I don't want to be a housewife, I'm *not* a housewife. Your bloody son has forced me into being a housewife, I'm not allowed to do any bloody thing but *be* a housewife, and now you, *you* are having a go too. Is there a mark on the back of your neck that reads Stepford?'

Fergus ran into the room. I think it was at that moment that I realised the true meaning of what it meant to have said too much.

'Kitty!' Fergus looked from Georgina to me. 'Mum, what have you . . . Kitty!'

'You ungrateful little tramp,' Georgina said. 'He picked you up from the gutter . . .'

'The gutter?' I couldn't believe what I was hearing. 'What, you mean Hackney?'

'*Yes*, the gutter, are you deaf as well as ignorant?' Georgina spat, her face transformed by fury. 'He takes on you and your baby . . .'

'*His* baby! The baby that looks so much like him I might as well be a test tube!' I yelled at her, staring at Fergus, waiting for him to step in and defend me. He just stood there, mouth open, arms outstretched.

'Yes, that's right, and if you had been, at least she would have a decent mother!' Georgina had hissed.

At last Fergus moved between us, pushing us apart.

'Mum, Kitty, please . . .' he said. 'You'll wake up the baby.' It wasn't the display of marital unity I'd been hoping for, so I waded back into the breech on my own account.

'Ha! You wouldn't know what it meant to be a decent mother if the bloody Virgin Mary came down from heaven to give you lessons!' I told her, waving my stupid tea cup at her. 'At least *I* don't think it's fine to leave my baby crying all alone, at least *I* won't leave her to make her own tea and do her own washing whilst I get pissed and stoned because my husband is so bloody sick of me going on at him all day that's he left just to get a bit of peace and quiet!'

Georgina stopped dead, mid–riposte, clearly stunned.

'What do you mean by that?' she said, her voice wobbly.

'Fergus told me,' I said, holding her gaze, avoiding Fergus's look. 'He told me about when Daniel left you. And I'll tell you something else, I bet he wishes he'd never come back!' I hit her so far below the belt it still makes me wince. All of her anger drained from her face in a second, and for once she looked every one of her sixty-two years. She turned away from me and Fergus then and made her way to the door.

'Yes, well, do you know why he went?' she said quietly over her shoulder. 'He went because I was too hard to be with, because I was too proud, I never showed him that I cared and he felt unloved.' She straightened her back and lifted her chin. 'Yes, he did go, and yes, it did nearly break my heart, but in those days people didn't run out of marriages the way they do now, and he came back, he gave me a chance to see what I might have lost. So you'd better take care, young lady, because if Fergus walks out on *you*, he might find it easier *not* to come back.' She walked out of the door.

'Mum!' Fergus called, rushing after her, stopping briefly at the door. 'Darling, I'll have to go after her, explain why I told you about it, all right?' I nodded dumbly, it was not all right. 'I'll be back in a bit, all right?' I nodded again, not trusting myself to say anything more, and when I'd shut the world out I curled up on the sofa and wept. Georgina was wrong, she had to be, it wasn't going to be cooking that would heal my relationship. It couldn't be.

'Kitty?' Clare touched me on the shoulder. 'I've made you some tea with some whisky in?' She held out a steaming mug. 'Blimey, you really laid into her, didn't you?'

'Oh God, Clare, I thought you'd gone! I'm sorry you had to get caught in the middle of all that.' I thought about just a few of the things that had been said. 'Sorry, mate, what a fucking bitch.' I said, wiping my eyes with the heel of my hand.

'Yeah, she was like the queen of bitches,' Clare agreed heartily. 'The *Trisha Show* level of bitchiness.'

I took a deep gulp of tea, glad to feel it burning my throat.

'No, not her, me. What a fucking bitch.'

Chapter Fifteen

So we are British and, despite Fergus's tenuous links with a Celtic past, we are English, and more than that we are southern English, and even more than that we are Home Counties (via Hackney) English and, in the true and proud tradition of that breed, up until this moment we have been pretending that the whole thing never happened. She never called me a guttersnipe or implied that my baby was illegitimate, and I never accused her of being a vicious evil android.

I don't know what I expected to happen – World War Three, the whole of the Berkhamsted WI sending me to Coventry, a front-page splash on the gazette maybe – but as it was, Georgina had phoned me the very next day and offered to make vol-au-vents. Fergus had picked up the phone and, after a brief and wary chat with her, he'd handed me the receiver saying out loud, 'Darling, Mum wants a quick word!' and mouthing 'PLEASE BE NICE TO HER!' I'd braced myself for the full force of her anger and felt somehow let down by the offer of diminutive pastries, but Fergus had assured me that that was her way of making peace and I should accept it.

Now, with my father, my ex-addict best friend and out-of-order gardener about to turn up I feel that I have to have at least one thing sorted out before the meal begins. I close my eyes and pretend I'm from California.

'Listen, Georgina, I just wanted to talk to you before the others arrive . . .' I begin.

Georgina presses her lips together, no doubt anticipating a reprise of last week's folly.

'Yes, dear, what can I do for you?' she asks me, clearly demonstrating with every line of her body that she does not want to talk about what happened. Well, she's just going to have to.

'I wanted to say that I'm sorry, I'm sorry about all that stuff I said,' I tell her, rushing out the words before her gimlet eyes and perilously high hair freak me out so much that I lose the power of speech. In fact, my straightforward and what I imagine to be California-style apology freaks her out instead, and for one delicious moment I enjoy the power it gives me over her before I remember I am supposed to be healing the rift not exacerbating it.

'The thing is,' I continue before she can regain her composure, 'it's that, well, part of me was a bit pissed off with you for rooting about in my house as if you owned it like that, and telling me how I should look after my baby and my husband, but also . . .' I struggle to find the right words . . . 'sometimes I think I might feel a bit jealous of the way you love Fergus. Not jealous of you, but jealous of him. I mean, no one ever loved me in that way, or at least not for very long.' It's not until I finish the last word that I know what I am going to say, and I surprise myself with the truth. Rather reassuringly, Georgina lays down the knife she has been holding and leans against the counter.

'I am sorry too,' she says with visible relief. 'It's ridiculous, isn't it? Here we are, both grown women, and yet I haven't felt that way since I was a little girl on the playing field. Oh, and, well, that business with Daniel . . .' She shakes her head slightly and her red up-do trembles.

247

'I'm so sorry I brought that up . . .' I try to tell her, but she waves my apology away.

'Now listen to me for a change. The thing is, I do know how I'm behaving when I talk to you like that.' She makes a futile gesture. 'It's like I'm on some runaway train for stereotypical mothers-in-law and I can't get off it, *but*, having said that, my reasons behind what was said are that I do care about you, whatever you might think. I care about you and Fergus.' She crosses her arms and looks out at the half-finished garden.

'When he first picked you I *was* disappointed, I can't deny it. I'd always pictured him with the Masterson girl from Chesham, lovely girl, terribly nice family and immaculate manners. But *anyway* love is love and you can't deny it. So I made a fist of it, and maybe it would have helped if we'd got to know you before the wedding, but anyway, as I came to know you I came to like you and I could see, *can* see, how much my son adores you. When I said about making him dinner once in a while I did mean it. I wasn't trying to tie you to the kitchen or turn you into a robotic wife – I was trying to show you how important it is to show someone that you care for them, that you cherish them. That baby of yours is a wonderful, beautiful little person, but a baby can rip a couple apart, especially a couple who really hardly know each other. Now, I've said this to Fergus and I'm saying it to you. If you don't want to cook for him, then run him a bath; if you know he's going to be in late, video one of the dinosaur documentaries he likes so much. Little things like that connect you to one another.' She touches her hair with her hand, looking into the middle distance and some memory. 'Otherwise you'll drift so far apart you may not be able to find your way back.' She takes a deep breath and presses her pink lips together. 'I'm parched now, shall we open a bottle of wine?'

I laugh incredulously and take one from the fridge.

'I had absolutely no idea you felt that way,' I tell her as I search for the corkscrew, our new intimacy emboldening me. 'In fact I had no idea you had feelings.'

Georgina laughs and raises an eyebrow as I look fruitlessly for my bottle opener.

'You'll find your corkscrew in the drawer under the sink by the dishwasher, dear,' she says lightly, and we exchange a smile as I retrieve it.

'Well, it's true that expression of emotion has never really been my thing, it's something Daniel has taught me over the years. At St Mary's School for Girls they taught you deportment, arithmetic and geography but not how to communicate properly. Actually, I've learnt an awful lot from watching Oprah Winfrey. Sometimes one just has to lie back and pretend one is American.'

We laugh together as I pour out the wine and clink glasses.

Fergus and Daniel enter the kitchen with a wary trepidation that Ella has managed to mimic in miniature, her big eyes round and anxious. When they see us smiling and sharing a glass of wine, all of them, even my baby, seem to give a collective sigh of relief. Daniel and Fergus exchange a glance.

'I told you I heard laughing,' Daniel says with a smile. 'He thought it was screaming and that you two were after murdering each other in here.'

Oh God, I could die listening to Daniel talk. I'm sure it's not the done thing to fancy your father-in-law, but even after forty years of living in Hertfordshire he still has a little twinge of Dublin in his voice.

'No, we've made up, in fact,' Georgina says lightly. 'Now, Daniel, have you brought all the chairs down? Fergus, have you made the beds? You know you can never trust your guests not to go in bedrooms?'

I sip my wine as my mother-in-law takes over my party, and walk over to Fergus, winding my arms around his waist.

'I love you,' I whisper into his ear, just loud enough for him to hear, fuelled by an urgent imperative to let him know. He looks down, almost surprised, and smiles a tiny smile that tells me he loves me too.

Cathedral bells ring out through the house and Ella almost leaps from her father's arms in excitement as she seems to have recently learnt that the bells signify some kind of change from her usual routine.

'Come on then, baby, visitors!' Fergus says to her as they go to answer the door, and I wish for a moment that I could call that peaceful moment back and live it for one second longer.

'Hello! Hello! Hello!' Camille greets Fergus in triplicate.

'I didn't know what to bring so I brought some jerk chicken. I'd like to say I made it to my Aunty June's recipe, but I bought it from Tesco on the way up!' As her one woman cacophony enters the room she flings her arms around me in a fragrant hug, dumping her Tesco's bag on the counter.

'Let me look at you!' she all but shouts, and I catch Georgina rolling her eyes. 'You look bloody great!'

'Thanks. So do you,' I tell her, just as I see Dora. Camille's entrance was so ebullient that for a moment I wondered if Dora had even come, but there she is standing almost translucent, almost absorbed into shadow.

'Hello,' I say, kissing her lightly on the cheek, sweeping my eyes over her, trying to make out if she's lost more weight from her naturally slim frame, or if it's just that her skirt and clingy top make it look like she has.

'All right?' She half smiles at me and looks around the collection of people. 'Got a beer in the fridge?'

I want to be able tell her that it's too early to start drinking, but as I'm holding a glass of wine in one hand, and as it is almost twelve o'clock, I suppose I can't. I watch her drink deeply, straight from the can that Fergus hands her. Her fine hair has grown a little, and that might be accentuating the hollows of her cheeks. She has some shadows under her eyes, but Dora has always been the sort of girl with paper-thin skin that looks as if it might tear or bruise under the slightest pressure, and if the mythical Kev has been keeping her up then she's bound to look a little fatigued. The waistband of her skirt gapes a good inch from her hips, but for the first time in my life I'm not jealous of her natural thinness. She looks fragile and brittle. I know enough now to know that weight loss does not necessarily add up to drug abuse. In fact, during our phone calls Dora delights in telling me which of the perfectly healthy-looking and sometimes even chubby celebrities she's seen at her last meeting – confidentiality never being her strong point where gossip is involved. But even as I feel the heft of my own hips push at the material of my trousers, I know when someone is too thin, and Dora is too thin. Something's going on and I need to find out what.

'So, little bird,' she says, taking Ella from Camille's arms. 'How are you? Yeah? You look a lot less scary than the last time I saw you. The last time I saw you, you were like this big lump with mad staring eyes and you never really had much to say for yourself.'

Ella grins at her happily. 'Goy de goy de goy!' she intones in a sing-song voice, and I worry that Dora's thin arms might drop her but I manage not to say it out loud.

'I've always said that,' Dora tells her as if she was a thirty-year-old herself. Before I can say any more the doorbell goes again, and as I head up the hallway I think of appropriate responses for whoever it might be. To be honest, even before I open the door I know it's Gareth, and an unexpected rush of anticipation gathers rosily in my cheeks. It's not as if I welcome the tension he's bound to bring into my home, it's more like the . . . novelty of being at the centre of something again, even if it is the centre of something so dangerous.

After almost a week of dreading this moment, I find I'm looking forward to seeing him. Maybe after he's had time to think about it he'll realise he made a bit of a prick of himself, and we can go back to being gardening friends again. The drama will be over for sure, but at least I'll be able to relax again.

I swing open the door and grin at him, which on reflection might be why he looks so disconcerted. I'm trying to show him that I have no hard feelings, but he looks as though he thinks I might have overdone the sherry, or just possibly he was looking forward to seeing discomfort and anxiety in my face. I push that thought away and beckon him in.

'All right?' he says at last. The bright sun gives his hair a reddish tint and somehow seems to intensify the gold of his eyes, and noticing that makes my mouth dry and I swallow hard.

'Hi,' I say awkwardly and back away from the door, clearing his entrance into my home. He steps through the doorway until we are just a few breaths apart and I can see him even now adjusting his game plan. It is clearly not over for him, despite all my half-hopes that it might be.

'I'm sorry about what I said the other day, all that macho stuff about "if you were mine" and all that. It was well out of order.' He shuffles and hangs his head, and for a moment I feel as if he might be genuine, except for that look on his face when I first opened the door and the way his body is slowly drifting closer to mine.

I take a step back and examine the door frame, unable to reconcile a growing sense of disappointment.

'I really like you,' he continues. 'I think I got carried away with other feelings, feelings I shouldn't have. I know you're really happy with Fergus. I won't try or say anything like that again, all right? Do you forgive me?' He dips his chin a little and smiles up through his lashes.

For a second longer I look at the door frame before dragging my gaze to meet his.

'Okay, make sure you don't,' I say with perfect composure, trying to let him know that I know exactly what he is doing, even if I'm letting him. Trying to let him know that I'm in control. 'Everyone is in the kitchen.'

I take a few deep breaths of spring air before closing the door again. As Gareth reaches the end of the hallway I hear him say, 'All right? I'm Gareth.' I look up abruptly and see Dora standing looking after him. For a moment I'm certain she couldn't have seen or heard anything, but as she looks back at me she raises an overplucked eyebrow.

'You're a bit of a dark horse, aren't you?' she says with the very edge of a smile. 'Must tell me all about it later . . .'

Before I can reply the doorbell chimes again, and I think that should I ever happen to be in Canterbury and should the cathedral bells sound anything like these ones, then I will probably be compelled to go around opening stranger's doors and thrusting mini-sausage rolls in their faces. The bright sunlight makes me blink after the gloom of my hallway assignation, and for a moment I'm not really sure what I'm seeing.

Mr Crawley and my father and my father's friend have arrived together.

'Mr Crawley?' I greet him with delight. 'Dad!' I say to my father. 'You made it. Well done!'

I look at his friend, who is entirely the opposite of what I imagined she might be, and hold out my hand. 'Hello, I'm Kitty.'

The curvaceous black woman squeezes my fingers very tightly. 'Pleased to meet you,' she tells me. 'I'm Joy Parsons, I met your dad at a social I run.'

I smile and nod – Dad never mentioned anything about it being at a social, but whatever it is I must admit he looks good on it.

Sort of . . . well, almost kind of vibrant. I show the threesome into the living room, calculating that there must be no room left in the kitchen by now, and if I'm honest I'm keen to keep my dad from the group until I've fully assessed his mental health. After all, he may look vibrant, but he still might be a raving loony.

'So, I thought you were going to call and Fergus was going to get you from the station?' I say to Dad, testing him for some deranged response. He looks, well, sort of polished.

'Well, yes dear, but you know my memory. I left the number at home and as we came out of the station, Joy and I, we asked this gentleman here for directions and it turned out that he is a friend of yours and he gave us a lift! What a coincidence, eh?'

I smile gratefully at Mr Crawley and wonder how it is that he manages to be in exactly the right place at exactly the right time whenever I need him to be.

'Wine.' Mr Crawley hands me a bottle and kisses me on the cheek. 'Nothing too fancy, I'm afraid, but not too bad. Where's the little one?'

'Oh, she's starring as the main attraction in a game of human pass-the-parcel in the kitchen. Take a seat and I'll get you a drink, then get everyone to come in here.' I look hard at my dad. He looks okay, and if somehow he got from Hackney to here on public transport with Joy then he must *be* okay, at least for now. As I leave the room, trying to keep the drinks order in my head, he follows me into the hallway.

'Don't worry,' he tells me earnestly.

I look at him enquiringly. 'Worry about what?' I say breezily.

'Worry about me. I . . . I need to talk to you later about a few things? Okay?' He grips my wrist tightly until it hurts, and the familiar sensation of claustrophobia I have always felt when he's around begins to creep up on me.

'Yes, yes, okay. Of course,' I say, releasing his grip with my fingers. 'Of course. Now I must go and sort out the food.

Fergus!' I call out as I back away from him. 'Dad is here! And Mr Crawley! Oh, and Joy!'

I look over my shoulder to find my dad still watching me. 'Go back in the living room, Dad, and sit down. I'll be back in a sec.'

As I enter the kitchen I see that between them Camille and Georgina have laid out all the finery M&S had to offer *and* the vol-au-vents on the flowery china. Daniel is folding serviettes under the close observation of his wife, and Dora is standing in the door frame of the open back door, intermittently waving the smoke from her cigarette into the back garden.

Fergus and Gareth are standing on the lawn, with Ella sitting happily at Fergus's feet ripping up pieces of grass and eating them. My irritation at Fergus letting his daughter snack like a calf is soon eclipsed by the fact that they look as if they are arguing. They are standing only inches from each other's faces, eyeball to eyeball, mouths and chins set in anger.

'What's going on?' I say to the room at large, and as I push past Dora she breathes a stream of smoke into my face.

'They're having a bit of a disagreement, I think,' she says with half a smile. 'Over some English rose I reckon.'

I shoot her the most venomous look I can muster in a state of high anxiety as I head towards them.

'I'm sorry,' I hear Fergus say, 'but that's a deceitful and underhand way to behave. And entirely unprofessional.'

Gareth shakes his head angrily. 'If you would just let me finish,' he says, his eyes burning, 'I discussed it with Kitty and *she* agreed to it. Or does she need your say-so for everything . . .'

I almost trip over my baby in a rush to get between them.

'Agreed what? What's the problem?' I sweep Ella up off the ground to her angry protest, and use my finger to fish a pulpy mass of grass out of her mouth.

Gareth looks pleased to see me.

'I agreed with you that the original budget wouldn't stretch to everything you wanted in here,' he says, his eyes still fixed on my husband. 'I told you the new costs and you agreed them. It's up to you. If you want me to complete with the price we first agreed then we drop the gazebo, or the big plants, the trees and the Wendy house . . .'

'Oh not the trees,' I say with dismay.

Fergus looks at me in disbelief.

'Did you seriously not think of checking all this with me before you spent another thousand pounds?'

I feel his anger like a slap in the face, a slap I can hardly endure in front of a triumphant Gareth.

'Well, usually when I ask you about cash, you say not to worry and that everything is fine. I meant to ask you, but . . .' I desperately don't want to fight. Not here, not now and not in front of Gareth – the last thing I want is for him to think I'm put upon by an overbearing husband.

I turn to Gareth, avoiding his eye. 'Look, let's just drop the gazebo, okay? It's not that big a deal, and the trees – we don't need the trees.'

Gareth shrugs, but before he can reply Fergus interrupts.

'Yes we do, if you *want* the gazebo, if you *want* the trees, then you will *have* them,' he tells me angrily. 'I just wish that when I discussed this with our gardener I'd been prepared for what he was about to say!'

I open my mouth and close it again, wondering if there is any way I can make this better, and quickly. The last thing I need right now is for Gareth to see so clearly for himself the cracks in our relationship.

'Fergus, I . . .' I begin, but before I can say anything he walks back to the house.

'Are you okay?' Gareth asks me gently, any hint of smugness carefully removed from his expression.

'I'm fine,' I tell him shortly. 'Absolutely fine. He's just under a lot of pressure at work, that's all. It's my fault.' I hold his gaze for a moment longer and turn on my heel, feeling Gareth's gaze on my back.

'I'm saying nothing!' he calls after me. 'Nothing at all.'

As I enter the kitchen Fergus seems to be back to his usual self, pouring drinks for our guests, who all seem to have congregated there now. My poor dad and everyone must have thought I'd abandoned them.

'Can't we go into the living room?' I plead. 'That fireplace cost us a fortune, didn't it, Mr Crawley?'

Mr Crawley laughs and we both say together, 'Though considerably less than it might have done.'

Georgina leads everyone out of the kitchen until just Fergus and I are left. I sense Gareth's presence in the garden and turn my back on his watchful eyes as I try to explain myself.

'I'm sorry I didn't tell you about the quote, but every time I ever ask you about money you tell me it'll be fine, you tell me not to worry.'

Fergus shrugs, pouring a large glass of red wine. I remember Georgina's words earlier and I swallow my anger.

'This thing is,' I continue in a studiously even tone, 'that I'm not used to having to check every little financial detail with someone else. I'm used to being my own person, I always have been. I know that . . .'

'Another thousand quid is not exactly a little detail,' Fergus interrupts me, refilling his already empty glass. 'And do you know how much I spent on all this crap today?' He gestures at the empty packages and trays of food. 'One hundred and twenty quid, for some sausage rolls!'

I hold on to my voice tightly. 'As I was saying, I know you want to look after Ella and me, and I want you to, but that doesn't mean that you have to carry the entire financial burden yourself. Let me help, let me work too.'

Fergus studies his empty glass for a moment. 'You'd just be working to pay for child care,' he says in a slightly less confrontational tone.

I take heart and press on.

'Well, not if I had that job up at the management college. They pay well and there's a crèche there, and anyway, once Clare's registered as a childminder we could use her. Ella loves her, and childminders are cheaper than nurseries.'

'Yeah, but that job will have gone by now,' Fergus says, stuffing one of his mum's vol-au-vents into his mouth.

'Well, maybe it has, but I could give them a ring, and anyway, in principle you don't object to me looking for a job?' I ask, my hopeful heart in my mouth.

He shakes his head and runs his fingers through his hair, leaving flakes of pastry in his fringe.

'Kitty, I need to talk about something with you . . .' he begins just as the sodding bells chime again.

'Is it that you want to install a knocker?' I say with a smile. 'Tell me. I'm sure your mother will answer the door.' I hear voices at the door that confirm my suspicions. Clare has arrived.

'Now's not the time. Later, when everyone is gone, okay?' Fergus says, taking my hand. 'We'll discuss everything then, all right?'

I nod, and as Fergus leads me down the hallway to join the others I look over my shoulder and take one last look at Gareth, staring at the sky as if it's about to fall in.

Clare and Ted stand on the periphery of the group, both looking terrified and shy.

'Hiya!' I say to her, touched by her vulnerability and shocked by Ted's. I kiss her on the cheek and lift Ted from her arms, setting him on the floor.

'Have you met everyone?' I do a round of introductions.

'Right, I'll just check on the food. Does anyone need a drink?'

'I'll help you,' Clare says quickly and follows me out of the room.

'Smells nice in here,' she says, looking incredulous.

'M&S paprika-roasted chicken and whole Peking duck, preroasted potatoes and preprepared vegetables. Now all I have to do is heat up these fresh sauces in the microwave and I have a meal. I love modern life.'

Clare looks out into the garden.

'Oh, so he is here then. I had wondered. What's he doing out there? It looks like he's praying for rain!'

I watch Gareth, his head still tipped back, his eyes fixed on the heavens.

'I have no idea, maybe he is.' I pause. 'He had a bit of a tiff with Fergus about money. They got all blokey. You know, squared up to each other. He probably should leave.'

Clare taps on the window and waves at him. He starts when he hears the noise but quickly refocuses his gaze on her, breaking into a swift sweet smile and walking back towards the house.

'Maybe he was praying for rain,' Clare says as he approaches, pulling at the ends of her hair. 'It's started to spit.' She admires him openly. 'He's all Daniel Day Lewis in *The Last of the Mohicans*, isn't he?' She giggles, and as Gareth approaches the house in his tatty jeans and his worn brown leather jacket, I can kind of see what she means.

'Clare!' he says as he enters, the first mist of a light drizzle clinging to his hair and skin in bright droplets. He kisses Clare on the cheeks and squeezes her shoulder. 'How's it going?'

'Fine! I'm glad you're here. I hardly know anyone out there. Can I sit next to you at lunch?' she rushes eagerly.

I studiously pour out the last of my drinks order.

'Are you staying?' I ask him briskly.

'No. Look, Clare, I'm sorry. I think I'll be in the way if I stay. I don't know if she told you, but I had a bit of a disagreement with Mr Kelly and, after all,' Gareth looks right at me, 'you don't want the hired help at your lunch party, do you?' Clare's dismay is palpable.

'But I thought we could get to know each other a bit more, you know . . .' She catches my look and closes her mouth. 'Well, all right, I'll see you on Wednesday then?' she finishes instead.

I hand Clare the drinks tray.

'Will you take these in, Clare? I just need to check the food.' Clare reluctantly takes the tray and heads back to the living room.

'Don't mess around with her,' I say to him. 'She really likes you.'

Gareth shrugs. 'I really like her,' he says. 'Do you want me back on Monday or not?'

I stare at him, and find that I don't.

'No. I really think that after everything that's happened it would be best to leave it as it is. You've done the basic, really good work, but I'll finish it myself.' I knot the oven glove I'm holding awkwardly in my hands. 'I just think it would be best.'

Gareth sighs, pulling his hair back from his face and holding it at the nape of his neck.

'Listen, Kitty, all that stuff I said, all right? I *do* like you. I like you a lot, it's pointless pretending that I don't. You're a big girl, you can see it for yourself. But I'd never make a move on someone already in a relationship, not unless they wanted me to. I care about what happens to you, that's all. I want to be your friend.'

I shake my head, taken aback by his sudden frankness. 'I don't think we can be friends,' I say. 'It won't work, we'd still be . . .' I can't think of a word to describe what I'm thinking. I don't want to.

'Why not?' Gareth persists, standing a little closer to me. 'Why couldn't we be friends? We get on. We have a laugh, don't we? Why couldn't we be friends at least? We are both grown-ups.'

He keeps moving forward until the air is squeezed out between us, his voice low and insistent. I turn my head away from him but he bends his face ever nearer to mine.

'Because you want more than that and . . .' I falter, biting my tongue on what I was about to say.

'Oh, come on, Kitty.' Gareth's temper flares briefly. 'I'm tired of fucking around this! Just say what you mean, for once. And what?' He persists, ignoring, no, revelling in, my discomfort. 'And you do too? And you want more than just friends too?' He runs his forefinger down the length of my face and gently turns me to face him.

'Is that it? Say it.' I look into his yellow eyes, and in that moment I don't know what I want except that I want him to be gone.

'And I do too,' I say.

In an instant he breaks the spell between us and laughs.

'I knew it,' he says. 'I'm never wrong. I'll see you Monday.' He heads for the hallway.

'No, Gareth! No. Don't come back here any more! I said no!'

By the time I've caught up with where he should be he's gone. I didn't even hear the door shut.

'Oh fuck, oh fuck, oh fuck, oh fuck,' I whisper, wondering exactly what I've done as I head back to my guests. My cheeks are flushed, my heart is pounding, but despite my discomfort I feel awake and aroused in a way I haven't felt with Fergus in a long time. It feels terrible.

'Lunch is ready!' I say, feeling the shakiness in my voice.

Fergus looks at me carefully. 'You look like you've been slaving over a hot stove,' he says lightly.

'Well, I have!' I answer defensively. 'In a way. The stove is hot and I have been over it.'

'I know,' he says with a smile. 'It's just I've never seen what that looks like before.'

Everyone laughs and I smile. I smile really, really hard.

As Fergus is fiddling about with his coffee machine trying to make cappuccinos when all anyone really wants is instant, I count how many people I'm supposed to be having a chat with in the next couple of hours.

Chat one: my dad, probably concerning my mum's death, although for the first time in years I've seen him actually take part in a social event instead of sitting on the sidelines drugged up on diazepam waiting to be taken home. I mean, he's not suddenly transformed himself into a fatherly Oscar Wilde when it comes to conversation or witty repartee, but he's been involved and engaged, even discussing old London buses with Mr Crawley, who seems to know something about everything. As for Joy, she seems to be a master of making people feel at ease. Within a few minutes of entering the house she had Camille and Clare involved in a conversation that had them both in hysterics until they turned naturally to conversation with each other. So chat one with my dad. With any luck he's having too much of a good time to remember it.

Chat two: with Camille about Dora. Dora has been fine. She's stayed with her one can of lager, sipping it almost regally throughout lunch, persistently refusing a glass despite Georgina's attempts to foist one upon her. As the meal progressed she seemed to relax a little, and if it wasn't for the fact she only had one can of low-alcohol lager I'd say she was a little tipsy. She even played pee-bo behind a tea towel with Ella, something unprecedented in our times. Maybe having seen her for a good couple of hours this afternoon, Camille and I don't need to talk about her after all.

Chat three: with Dora. She saw Gareth and me talking and I don't know what she saw or what she thinks she saw, but she's known me the longest and she only has to look at my face to see exactly what's going on. I'd like to keep that chat with Dora, I'd like to know what she thinks is exactly going on, because I'm not entirely sure myself.

And finally chat four: scheduled with Fergus after everyone has gone home. Chat four about money and about me getting a job, I hope, and I suppose I'd better tell him that I've sacked Gareth. At least I think I've sacked him. And then after we've got that out of the way, I'm going to make him feel cherished and loved just like Georgina said I should. I'm going to seduce him.

The heat of the kitchen has steamed up the rain-cold windows, the dark afternoon throwing them into a silvery relief, as if the whole house is covered in ice. The conversation around the kitchen table seems to be going on without me and I let myself drift far away from the hum of guests, trying to keep all sharp edges firmly out of focus. Even though it's only four o'clock, I've already had a large brandy and then another one, so that the events of this morning seem far away now and ever so slightly unreal, as if they'd happened to someone who looks a bit like me and isn't me at all. Oh no, hang on, that *is* me.

'Kitty, love.' My dad appears at my shoulder like a ghost, making me jump.

'Shit, Dad,' I say, sitting up in my chair. 'Sorry, I was miles away.' Miles and miles away, which is exactly where'd I'd like to stay right now.

'I thought maybe I could have a word?' Oh, chat number one, then.

'Sure.' I nod encouragingly, hoping it's not the sort of chat that's going to involve me leaving the table.

'Maybe next door?' Dad asks me cautiously.

'Of course, Dad,' I say, unable to mask my reluctance. 'Um, Fergus, get those chocolates out. I'm just going to have a word with my dad.'

'Lovely cornicework,' Dad tells me as we make our way to the living room.

'Mmmmm, Mr Crawley. He's fantastic,' I tell him, and I settle down on the sofa. I feel a little drunk and sleepy. I'd really like to be asleep right now in the half light of a wet summer evening, curled up on my sofa, and to forget about everything.

'So?' I say brightly, blinking myself awake. 'What do you want to talk about?'

'You,' Dad says, out of the blue. Dad hasn't talked about me in, well, since Mum. He's talked about Mum a lot, himself frequently, the injustice, futility and unfairness of it all often – but never about me specifically.

'Me?' I say, feeling uneasy.

'Yes you.' He sits by my side and takes my hand. 'I've been a terrible father to you . . .' he begins.

'No, Dad, you haven't,' I say, but I don't mean it.

'After your mum, I don't know what happened to me. You must understand, Kitty, that I meant to be strong for you. I promised her. I promised your mother that I'd never let you miss having a mum, that I'd be your mum and your dad, but I failed so badly, I know I let you down.'

I run my fingers across my forehead. It looks like this might be about him and my mum after all.

'Dad,' I say almost impatiently, 'even if you had tried, no one could have stopped me missing Mum, not even you. Not even Nan, if she'd still been around.'

Dad pats the back of my hand.

'I'm not explaining myself very well. Joy says that the only way I'm going to rebuild our relationship is to clear it all up once and for all.'

I shake my head, not understanding him.

'Dad, nothing happened between us. I mean, obviously something did happen, but nothing specifically between us,' I say again, hoping that Fergus or someone, anyone, will interrupt us.

'Yes it did, something did happen,' Dad says insistently. 'It's just that you didn't know about it.'

I look at him. In the ever-decreasing half-light, his face looks grey and ashen. A shiver runs up and down my spine.

'I tried to put it out of my head, forget about it. I'd look at you and see how hard you were trying, just a little dot, you were trying so hard to be all grown-up. I tried, Kitty, not to feel the way I did, but I couldn't make it go away. I loved your mum. I loved her so much, and God forgive me I wished it hadn't been her . . .' He trails off, staring at me as if seeing me for the first time.

'What do you mean?' I say uneasily.

'The ambulance men, they said that if she'd been found sooner, even just a few minutes sooner, they might have saved her.' He is clasping my fingers in his dry hands and I pull my hand from his, feeling instinctively ill at ease.

'Yes, I know that. Of course I do,' I say, even though I'm not actually sure if I have ever known that on a conscious level. 'But what's this got to do with me?'

'I blamed you,' Dad says simply. Shockingly. 'I blamed you for not finding her sooner. In a funny sort of way I blamed you more than I blamed him.'

I shrink back from him as if I were only seven again.

'You blamed me?' I repeat.

'I know. I know it was wrong, you were only a child. How

could you know she was there waiting to be found, waiting for you to save her? How could you? But all I could think about was how much pain she must have been in and how she must have been hoping, waiting for help, waiting for someone to find her, and that when you did find her it was too late.' His face is cold, angry and hard. For the first time ever it is as if his mask has slipped and for a second I can see that he's hated me, *hated* me, for all of these years.

I only know that I'm crying when I taste the tears on my lips.

'I can't believe you came here today to tell me this, to blame me for my mother's murder?' I pull myself off the sofa. 'Don't you think I know that it's my fault? Don't you think I blame myself, have done every day since it happened?' I stumble to the door and punch on the light switch, filling every corner of the room with artificial yellow light. Dad stands, clasping his hands together.

'I'm not trying to hurt you, sweetheart, I'm trying to help you. I do know, yes I do know that. After it happened I tried to love you, no I *did* love you, but I just couldn't show it. I didn't treat you like a daughter. I left you to it until the grief and the anger became so much part of me I couldn't remember what it was like to live without it. I was weak, I wasn't the man you needed me to be.'

He reaches out his hand to me.

'Kitty, I'm trying to tell you I was wrong. I've been wrong all these years, and so have you. I know it wasn't your fault, I know that. I've hurt you maybe more than you'll ever get over, and I'm sorry. I've hurt your mother and I'm sorry. I feel like I've been asleep for a hundred years, asleep trapped in a nightmare, and only now am I beginning to wake up. I wake up and see you shining so brightly, with your own home and your own family, everything you've created and achieved on your own despite me, and I'm proud of you, so proud of you, Kitty.'

He touches his hand softly to my cheek.

'I'm so proud of you, Kitty. I've never told you before. That's all I wanted to say.'

I back away from him as far as I can.

'You're lying,' I say angrily, furious. 'You're lying because you want that back, all that pretence of the father and daughter team. I saw what you really thought of me, Dad, I saw it just now in your face and I've always known, even back then, even as a child; it's only now that I realise what it was. I thought you were, I don't know . . . isolated by grief or something.' I struggle to express myself, my words rushing out in a jumble. 'That you were still mourning, that you were too sad to love me. But you didn't want me because you hated me, you hated me, your little girl!' My voice rises sharply and I'm aware of a lull in the hum of conversation from next door.

'Kitty.' Dad comes towards me and I find myself raising my hands over my face. 'Please, Kitty, that's not true. It was true once, yes, and if you saw that, I'm sorry. It's not true now, Kitty. All I want is for us to begin again. It's late, I know, terribly late to begin to make it up to you, but not too late, I hope . . . Kitty?' His words wash over me and all I can see is that look on his face, that terrible angry look.

'Everything all right?' Fergus's voice dilutes the atmosphere in an instant as his head appears around the door, and I rush into his arms.

'I want Dad to go,' I say quietly. 'I want him to go now.'

Fergus looks at me in puzzlement. 'What's happened, Kitty, what's he said?'

My dad's face seems to crumple and age before me. 'Fergus, I think I've upset her. I didn't mean to . . . I was trying to explain things . . . make things right . . . and . . .'

I shake myself loose of Fergus's grip.

'And you said that it was my fault that Mum had died, and you said that you hated me, that you'd always hated me.' Even now I can't remember if that was what he said, but it is all that I can hear. I feel Fergus's presence behind me and his hand on my shoulder.

'You can't come into my home and speak to my wife that way,' he says, his voice dangerously low. 'For years the only thing you've ever done is drag her down, and I've watched her drag herself out of the life you gave her and become a wonderful woman and a perfect parent, despite having no support from you at all. I won't have you try and drag her back down again. I won't let anyone do that to her ever again, do you understand? You'd better go.'

Suddenly I see him for the old man he is, his shoulders bent, his skin papery and dry, and I wish with all my heart that our lives could have been different, that we could have just been a father and daughter having lunch every weekend like we always did.

'Fergus, please. Don't make me leave like this,' my dad pleads, but my shoulders stiffen stubbornly under Fergus's hands and he reads my resolve.

'Just go. Just go. You can wait in the hall. I'll get Joy's and your coats and drive you to the station myself.'

My fingers find Fergus's and I squeeze them hard before leaving the room and hurrying up the stairs to the cool quiet of the bathroom to splash myself with water. I want to cry. I want to cry until I am dry as a desert, but I can't. Maybe it's the shock, or the brandy, or Gareth, but now that Dad's gone I can't seem to feel it any more, at the moment at least. Dora pushes the door open.

'What happened?' she asks me blankly.

'My dad, as usual, fucking me up.' I glance up at her sweat-sheened face. 'Look, let's not get into this now, I need time to . . . I just don't want to think about it now. It's too hard.'

Dora shrugs, experienced after years of understanding how I

cope with difficult feelings, and sits on the edge of the bath.

'I quite like your kid,' she says, languishing against the door she has shut behind her, still nursing her one can of lager. 'I think it's because she's more human and less like the thing out of *Eraserhead*.'

I muster a smile and sit down on the loo.

'Hasn't that gone disgustingly flat?' I say, nodding at the lager, hoping not to be interrogated about my red-and-white-streaked face, but Dora doesn't seem to notice it, or if she does she says nothing.

'Oh yeah, I finished it ages ago.' She fishes a half-vodka bottle out of her bag and pours a good measure into the can. 'But the good thing about vodka is it never goes flat. And before you ask why the can, it's because Camille kept going on at me on the way up here and she's bound to think I'm using again just because I like a little drink every now and then. Jesus.'

I open my mouth to reproach her, and find that I just don't have the energy.

'By the way, your dad was wrong, really wrong back then, but from what I overheard I think maybe when you've had a chance to think you'll see he's trying to do the right thing. Either that or I'm so bollocked I'm hallucinating.' She burps fragrantly into her hand.

I decide on the latter and change the subject, knowing how capable Dora is of hurting people without knowing the reason why. Especially when she's drunk.

'Camille will know, you know. She'll just be more pissed at you for trying to hide it from her.'

Dora shrugs and slides down the side of the bath to repose on Fergus's New England-style white floorboards.

'So, how long have you been doing the dirty on the Prince, Cinders?' she sniggers.

'Dora!' Please, Universe, God even, give me a break, just one.

'Don't be ridiculous!' And even though I'm telling the truth, my voice carries a high false note.

'I saw you canoodling with him. Don't blame you, he's fucking dishy. I'd shag him.' Her voice bounces loud and clear off the tiles.

'Dora!' I hiss, crouching down to her level. 'I am *not* shagging Gareth. If you must know, he sort of made a pass at me, and he didn't even do that really, and anyway I told him to get lost. I sacked him, for fuck's sake!' Dora's eyes regard me, empty of expression.

'Oh, okay. Why did you look like such a quivering wreck, then, when I caught you at it?'

I turn my head away abruptly and stand up.

'Dora, you might think you're funny, but you're not. You're fucking with my marriage, okay? What if Fergus heard you saying all this bullshit? Just shut the fuck up.'

'Ohhhhhhh.' Dora pretends to shake. 'That's me told, then.' She struggles to her feet. 'I might go to bed, where is it? In there?' She wobbles out of the bathroom and into the guest room. 'Night!' she says before closing the door on me.

It's just six o'clock. Now is the time when everyone is supposed to be leaving, not inviting themselves to stay the night. I look at the closed door feeling utterly exhausted, and wondering what everyone down there must think of me.

'Darling!' Fergus calls up the stairs. He must not have gone to the station after all. 'Come and look at Ella!'

I shake Dad and Dora out of my hair, put my happy face on and hurry down the stairs, hoping it's nothing that will require a trip to casualty. As I rush into the room, I see that my baby has pulled herself up on the sofa and is standing there clinging on to the edge, wobbling back and forth.

'My baby!' I say, and her proud smile eclipses every other moment of the day.

'She'll be walking soon, you mark my words,' Daniel says softly.

'And then you'll be more tired than you are now!' Mr Crawley laughs gently, taking my arm and squeezing it softly, and in an instant I know that he's telling me he's there if I need him.

'And you can buy her shoes!' Camille claps her hands with glee.

'Might as well leave her there,' I say to Camille as she puts her coat and hat on.

'She was drunk on vodka!' she repeats in disbelief. 'I don't know about this. What do you think?'

I shake my head and shrug. 'I don't know either, but look, I'm pretty sure she'll be there until the morning so I'll catch her when she's sober and try to talk it over with her properly. I'll call you, okay?'

Camille pulls her hat on. 'Are you okay, or are you at the not-talking-about-it stage? I mean, I don't want to butt in, but, well, we all pretty much heard everything.'

I smile at her levelly.

'I'm at the not-talking-about-it stage. I just need to adjust again, I'll be okay. He's not really been my dad for years, so it makes no difference really. Nothing to talk about right now.'

Camille nods and kisses me on the cheek.

'Okay, we'll save it for the next girly drunken night,' she says. 'I'm on the end of a phone if you need me.'

I nod and hug her tightly.

Mr Crawley has agreed to take Camille down to the station and to drop Clare back home. Georgina and Daniel have loaded the dishwasher and thrown all the packaging away and are leaving too.

'That was a lovely day,' Georgina says, kissing me on the

cheek. 'I'm sorry that things didn't go so well with your father,' she understates with fully reinstated Englishness, but I know that even by mentioning it she is offering me her support.

'Thanks,' I say, and I surprise her with a kiss on the cheek.

'Ah yes, really great food. Compliments to the chef,' Daniel says, winking at me.

'I'll let M&S know,' I say, wondering if I have the energy to speak even one more word. I close the door on them and sink back against its solid surface.

'Bloody Mary,' I say, managing two.

'Yeah, I know. I'm knackered too,' Fergus says, pulling my limp body towards him.

'No, I mean I want a Bloody Mary. Have we got any Tabasco?'

He laughs and leads me up the stairs.

'No, we don't have any Tabasco or tomato juice or vodka, but your daughter is in bed and your best friend is out for the count and we do have a little bit of time to ourselves.'

As we enter the bedroom I flop on to the bed and Fergus leans over me scrutinising my face.

'Are we having our chat now?' I say, sleepily abstracted.

Fergus takes my fingers in his.

'To be honest, Kitty, we all heard most of what your dad said to you . . . I mean, now that he's gone, considering what he said and how you feel about it you seem weird, a bit too okay. Don't you want to talk about it, cry or something?'

I manage a smile and wind my arm around his neck.

'No. No. I never talk much about anything, Fergus, except to you and sometimes to Dora. I'm not a talker, I don't want to talk about what happened. I'm angry and I'm hurt, but I want it to go away now. I don't want to think about it or him ever again. Especially not tonight, especially not now. If I ever change my mind I'll let you know.'

Fergus lies flat on the bed and looks at the ceiling.

'It's just, I totally understand how you feel but I'd hate you to turn what might have been the beginning of something, even if it was a difficult beginning, into an end . . . Because you've been carrying this around with you for so long. Don't you think it would be marvellous if you could work things out and let it go?'

'I'll let you know,' I repeat, closing my eyes and feeling the length of Fergus's body lock in the contours of mine.

'You are a wonderful woman, do you know that?' Fergus whispers into my ear. 'When I think of all that you've had to deal with, everything you've been through and are still going through, I'm amazed that you've managed to be such a warm, funny, compassionate person. And a wonderful mum, the best mum you could ever be, and the best wife. I'm sorry if sometimes I'm too tired or stressed to remember to tell you that, but I never stop thinking it, not for one second. Don't ever let anything stop you believing that either, will you?' He finishes by kissing my hair.

'Thank you,' I tell him, sinking into the warmth of his body. 'I'm okay, I'm too tired to cry, even if I could.'

'Don't cry, my love. Just sleep, I'll be here when you wake up.'

Chapter Sixteen

I love these kinds of Sundays. The kind when the hazy blue of the morning sky is light with the promise of a warm day, casting sharp black shadows into cut-glass relief. I especially like Sunday mornings like this one, a morning of pure bliss after a night when Fergus and I found each other again amongst the avalanche of complications that has become our lives. Or a few hours at least when we were just ourselves again, pure and simple. Even after Dad, even after accidentally telling my gardener in the middle of a family party that I wanted him sexually, and even when my best friend is sitting opposite me still dressed in the previous day's clothes looking as if she's been reconstituted in papier mâché whilst my baby and husband still slumber, it's impossible not to feel tranquil. Fergus has made it impossible.

I'm practically living a reality version of the Waltons.

Dora moans faintly as she gently bangs her head on the counter, her long white arms folded over her tousled head.

'Christ,' she mumbles in an uncharacteristically gravelly voice. 'Did you spike my vodka with something?'

I smile to myself, thinking of the countless Sunday mornings that she and I have huddled shivering over endless cups of tea, regarding each other warily with mascara-smudged eyes and tentatively dissecting the events of the previous evening with the uneasy caution customary for those with a fatally lapsed memory. Except that those Sunday post-mortems usually began after midday and not at 6.30 a.m. like today. I place a cup of thick black coffee within reach of Dora's immobile hand.

'Why don't you go back to bed?' I ask her. 'I have to get up at this time even when Ella is sleeping – it's some fucked-up motherhood thing. But you don't. Go on, I'll even lend you some pyjamas and stick that lot in the washer-dryer.'

Dora's long fingers snake around the mug, and she raises her head as if she is drawing strength from its warmth and the aroma of caffeine. One dark eye regards me over the rim of the mug, squinting through the steam.

'You must be in a good mood to offer to do washing for me, or has the prince finally brainwashed you into being his lackey?'

The effort of talking is clearly too much for her and she leans her cheek flat on the counter, which gives her an out-of-kilter look that seems oddly suitable.

'That sort of layabout behaviour was only possible when my body was still young enough to knock back the toxins and elasticised enough to snap back into shape,' she explains. 'Now that I'm thirty I'm too old to sleep hangovers off any more. My age demands that I feel every terrible moment as penance for still behaving like a teenager when I should know better.'

As she finishes her speech she straightens up in her chair, the bones of her spine clicking back into place with an audible crack, and a red smudge appears on her alabaster skin where it met with the work surface. Evidence, at least, that she still has blood in her veins.

I covertly examine her arms for track marks, although I'm not altogether sure what track marks look like. All I can see is that she's got a small bruise on the inside of her forearm, one that looks like a sex bruise, but that seems to be about all. The sun creeps across Gareth's lawn as I wait for her to take a good few gulps of the scalding hot coffee. Discussing Dora's life choices with her has never been easy, even at the best of times. Attempting to discuss them now when she's still desiccated could be a fatal error, but the chances of me having her in front of me again in the near future are slim, and I have to make the most of the opportunity.

'So . . . seen any more celebs lately?' I ask casually.

Dora sighs, clearly forcing herself into conversational mode, and thinks for a minute.

'No one good. Oh, hang on, I did see that geezer from breakfast telly. The quite cute one who looks like he should be gay but isn't?'

I smile encouragingly. 'Oh yeah? Whereabouts?' I try not to sound like I'm quizzing her, but covert operations have never been my forte.

'Oh, at that place, um, you know. Whatsits, supposed to be "the reincarnation of the world's greatest ever rock venue" – more like a post-modern granny's tea room. Total shite actually. I went there thinking "yeah I'm hard core" and I came out close to losing the will to . . . got it, the Marquee. I saw him there. Which just proves he's not gay 'cos he's got no taste.' She offers me a weak smile which I return as I sit opposite her, my own cup of coffee in hand.

'At least you still go to clubs,' I say, sipping my drink, tasting its bitterness on my tongue.

'You still go to clubs,' Dora tells me happily. 'It's just that they're populated by fat people with kids, that's all.'

I purse my lips and refuse to rise to her bait. 'Talking of exclusive membership – what about at NA? Seen any more celebs there?'

It has taken me an age to get around to the point, which is to find out if she is still going to meetings. Dora looks absently out of the window for a while, her semi-glazed eyes following the flight of a crow across the sky.

'I thought you'd get more country birds out here, like, you know, pheasants. Or peasants. One or the other. Or maybe both,' she tells me earnestly. I back up my pursed lips with a schoolmarmish squint and she rolls her eyes. 'I haven't been for a bit, all right? It doesn't mean the world's going to stop turning. And anyway there's no point. I mean, I practically have my own NA group what with the girls, even if they are a right pair of idiots, and, well, Bruce's been in the same boat, so we just, you know, we keep each other within the right boundaries.' She shrugs and rolls her stiff and crackling neck.

'Okay. So what are the right boundaries?' I ask her, trying and failing not to sound judgemental. 'What does this "Bruce" think is acceptable behaviour?'

'Oh fuck off, Kits,' Dora says mildly, just a hint of agitation seeping into her voice. 'I gave up smack, not my whole fucking life. We help each other not to overdo it, not to be stupid, that sort of thing . . .'

Her voice trails off, and she avoids meeting my eye. Nothing she says rings true and I'm not sure if it's a legacy from the past or the present that's thrown her out of kilter.

'Are you using again?' I ask her at last.

Dora slumps down on her stool and tips her head right back so that I can see the faintly blue throbbing pulse in her neck.

'I can't believe you're asking me that,' she says to the ceiling.

'Well, Dora, the last time you were I didn't ask you outright and you nearly died. I love you. I don't want you to die. I know you're smoking again, and I know you're lacing your lager with vodka . . .'

Dora laughs suddenly, shaking her head like a rag doll.

'Fuck! This from the girl I did two grams of coke with in two hours. Have you totally forgotten what it's like to have a good time! I had some vodka – big deal. Don't get into acting out your mum fantasy on me, you've got you own poor little kid to fuck up now,' she laughs. She's not angry or aggressive, she just seems exhausted.

She's right, of course. The first time Dora took an amphetamine we were together. We had some speed we'd bought off this kid from the sixth form. I'm fairly sure it was eighty per cent baking soda, but in any case we'd rubbed it into our gums and giggled all the way through double maths until the last bell rang. We were fifteen: half of our lives ago. And it wasn't so long ago that in the heat of a club or a party Dora and I would exchange 'I dare you' looks before taking another pill or another line, both seeking the same kind of oblivion. The only difference is that when I started to get bored with the three-day come-downs and the empty wasted nights talking about fuck-all to strangers, Dora had started to need it. At some point when I was getting less and less interested in that whole scene, she was unable to define herself without it any more. She was no one unless she was high. In some ways, whatever is happening to her now is happening to me too. I just need to know what it is.

'Dora, how long have you known me? We've always told each other everything, right? I told you about how my CDT teacher felt up my tits in the stockroom cupboard, and you were the one who told him to lay off me. God only knows what you said to him. You told me about when you shagged both Martin Kennedy and John Coombes at Beccy Archer's sixteenth, and I was the one who beat the shit out of Beccy for calling you a whore, although you were, actually.'

Dora shakes her head and smiles.

'Just look at you now, who'd ever have thought you used to be hard,' she muses. I sigh with exasperation. 'And if you tell me everything, why won't you talk about your dad? You know it's fucking you up. You should go and see him. I think in his own fucked-up way he was trying to sort things out between you . . .'

'Dora! Don't make this about me. What I'm trying to say is that we have both done some stupid things in our time, sometimes because we didn't think about things and sometimes because things just happened. But you took the biscuit, all right, because *you* nearly killed yourself. Now tell me, what are you into right now? I won't judge you, I just don't want you to keep anything from me, okay?' I say as convincingly as I am able to in front of the friend who has been my mirror over the years.

Dora looks me right in the eyes.

'I am not using any Class A drugs,' she says, with half a smile. We watch each other for a moment longer. 'Now, can I get a shower, and what time is the first train out of this dump anyhow?'

I've offended her, pushed her too far, but with someone like Dora sometimes that's the only approach to take. I don't know if she is telling the truth. I do know there is nothing more I can do right now, but I need Dora alive and I'm not going to let her kill herself. Not again.

'Talking of doing stupid things,' Dora says as she stops in the door frame. 'If you fuck up what you've got with Fergus for some scraggy bit of pretty-boy stuff then you are more stupid than all of us, all right?'

I open my mouth, but before I can think of anything to say she is gone.

279

Chapter Seventeen

My Nan always said time waits for no man, and that a watched pot never boils and that a stitch in time saves nine. My mum always used to say 'cobblers' and roll her eyes at me behind Nana's back, and I always used to wonder exactly how it was that a person could put a stitch into time? Would it be someone like Doctor Who, who would somehow be able to loop space around to make things happen faster? And save nine of what, I wondered. Light years? I asked my mum and nan this very question once, but the pair of them just laughed, and kept laughing until the tears sparkled in their eyes.

'Oh Ellie,' my nan had said, 'she's a proper one, your girl.' It wasn't until very recently that I understood that the domestic practicality of the saying had nothing to do with the space–time continuum at all. Shame really.

Nan probably would have something to say about me sitting watching the microwave clock, too, waiting for it to be 10.30. I've chosen it as my official deadline. If Gareth's not here by ten thirty then he's not coming and I have sacked him. I have officially put that whole kitchen moment behind me and I am moving my life on.

It's 10.27 and I've been willing and dreading each minute that has gone by for the last half an hour.

If he had turned up at say nineish, I was prepared for that.

After all, in the rush and the heat of the moment I'd forgotten to tell Fergus that I'd sacked him, not to mention engaged in extramarital intense staring at him. With the distance of two days between us, that moment in the kitchen seems oddly unreal and dreamlike now, as if I watched it happening to someone else on the evening news. The frisson of excitement wore quickly away, and the lingering sense of unease merged seamlessly into refusal to think about everything Dad had said, or even to acknowledge it.

At 09.01 this morning I could have handled Gareth turning up. I would have simply told him straight out that if he wanted to finish the job in the way we originally agreed then he could, but that I was categorically not interested in anything else from him. Otherwise he could send the bill for the work to date to my husband. And I would have stressed the word husband.

He still wasn't here when the microwave clock read 10.00, and I found that I was feeling rather low as I realised that I'd actually been looking forward to seeing him, to laying down the ground rules with a friendly but firm smile. He has never come later than ten before, except for that day when he didn't show up, and so when the microwave clock read 10.01 and I was certain that he wasn't coming and I hadn't felt the relief I had expected, I decided to take my mind off of myself for a change and engage in some actual housework. Then I decided to take Ella out into the garden and sat with her on the grass Gareth and I had laid together, letting her pick at the dew-damp blades until her leggings were soaked and I had to bring her in to change her.

Finally, at 10:21 I ran out of excuses and vacuumed the parquet hallway floor while Ella sat on the doormat chewing at the corners of the telephone bill. For a few trance-like moments I found myself actively enjoying the rhythmless drone as I kept one eye on Ella and one eye on the frosted glass in the door. I let the mundane task lull me away from that strung-out kind of tense feeling that I haven't experienced since the night after I first slept with Fergus. Waiting and *waiting* the whole day for him to call me, hoping it would be soon and not a predictable Wednesday later. He'd called at eight o'clock that evening.

'Is it too early?' was the first thing he'd said to me.

'No? Not at all – what do you mean early?' I'd asked, nonplussed.

'Well, I wanted to call you about five minutes after you left and I've been making myself wait so that I could look cool. I think it's usually supposed to be three days, but six hours is all I could manage.'

I'd laughed and twirled the phone cord in celebration of meeting a normal man for the first time in my life, a man who seemed to experience emotion in the same way I did and who didn't feel the need to play out the same old games.

At 10.25 I couldn't justify vacuuming any longer and took Ella back to the kitchen. We sat down, looking at the clock. Well, I'm looking at it. Ella is chewing her toe.

10.32. I scoop Ella up off the floor and begin the first part of my plan to move my life and my family's life on. On the second floor of the house, the part of the house we haven't got around to renovating yet, is Fergus's study. I don't know why Fergus needs a study, he just has one, and in it is his old PC and a black leather office chair that I imagined he thought was quite sexy and possibly a bit James Bond-like. I sit Ella on my lap at the desk and contemplate the ancient and clunky PC. It's dusty, and the cream keyboard looks grey and dirty. I haven't used it since the day we moved into the house. I'm not even sure I remember what to do, especially not with this relic of the last century. Ella bashes the keyboard enthusiastically and babbles excitedly.

I switch it on and wait for something to happen. Nothing does. I plug it in and repeat the process and sit back in the old office chair as it whirs and beeps into life, enchanting Ella. I look at my watch.

Well if he's not coming now I'm going to write a letter of application to that management college just in case there is the slightest chance that they still have that job open, or maybe even put my CV on file. I'm going to move my life forward, wrench it out of the suspended animation it's been subsisting in these past few months and change things. If I really have sacked Gareth, then it must be for the best, it's a sign. It's like Doris saying it's time now to put all your half-baked daydreams behind you and get back in the game. It's time to throw yourself one hundred per cent into your marriage and your family. And your career as a musical artiste.

And that's what I'm going to do.

Fifteen minutes later I'm struggling to fill in the gaps in my CV with something more compelling than 'Had baby, got fat' when I hear something downstairs. The doorbell has not peeled, there's been no knock at the back door, and yet there was definitely a noise. I pick Ella up and settle her on my hip.

'Shush a minute,' I whisper into her ear, a command which she cheerfully ignores. Standing at the top of the stairs I tilt my head and listen. There is someone in the kitchen. In films, when the heroine goes into the basement armed only with a torch, you want to save the psychopath a job and kill her yourself, don't you? No one knows better than I, though, how situations that are both horrific and terrible never seem so until viewed in the cold harsh light of retrospect. In this case, as I edge down the stairs and creep quietly along the hallway, I know it's not Freddy Krueger who's making himself a coffee in my kitchen, it's Gareth. What I really want to know is how he got in.

'How did you get in?' I ask him, pleased to have simul-taneously foiled his own plan to surprise me and made him jump. He spills a little boiling liquid on his hand, he swears and shakes it before sucking his finger, his eyes full of mirth.

'Shit, you should join the SAS,' he says, grinning. We smile at each other and I set Ella on the floor. I should be furious at his easy arrogance, but somehow, despite everything, I find it dangerously appealing. He shrugs and casts his eyes about the room before focusing them on me, and holding up a key.

'Spare key. You gave it to me, remember?'

I remember meaning to give him one the way I did Mr Crawley, but I don't remember actually giving it to him, although I suppose I must have done.

'I also remember sacking you,' I said, remembering to be cool. 'If you're going to ignore me the least you could do is ignore me punctually.'

Gareth rolls his eyes.

'Well, this morning I was thinking about everything and I thought, okay, so she's officially sacked me, but somehow after what she said I wasn't too convinced that she really meant it, all right?' He rolls his eyes theatrically before locking them on to my face. 'Can't think why, it must be something you said, and so I'm just back to check.'

He holds my gaze and I wonder at being referred to in the third person that way, as if he's come to discuss me with myself as a separate entity. In some ways I wish that there were two of me: one Kitty Kelly and one just Kitty, free to fuck herself up anyway she chooses. Gareth takes a step closer.

'Did you really mean what you said?' he asks me, and I wonder desperately which part of what I said in those few minutes he's talking about. The 'yes I want you' or the 'no you're fired' bit.

'I don't know,' I hear myself say out loud, as if the mythical other me has taken over this conversation without my permission. I stutter, struggling to wrest the conversation back from this rebellious doppelgänger. 'I mean, I don't know if I wanted you . . . to finish work on the garden or not.' My voice levels out as it returns to me. 'I think we both got a bit silly, didn't we? Said things we didn't mean to and it got out of hand. You know that I'm in a relationship, a happy one, and you embarrassed me.'

I pause for a moment and picture a string of empty days, me with Ella at my feet as I work on the garden waiting for Fergus to come in. Me alone and peaceful without having to worry about whether Gareth might show up or not, about what he's going to say or do or what might happen. Just me and Ella and sometimes Fergus, normal and settled and sometimes happy.

My stomach makes a lurch for the centre of the earth and I say the very thing I know that I shouldn't. 'If you can promise not to try anything like that again, then yes, I'd like you to finish the garden,' I say, sounding weak and uncertain, deliberately oblique and as obscure as I can about the one issue that burns fiercely between us. God knows I shouldn't have said it, and certainly not like that. Even then I couldn't bear the thought of all those days alone with nothing to think about except when Fergus might be home. Like a stupid, terrified little girl I wait anxiously to see what the consequences of my folly might be.

Gareth thinks for a moment, his mouth twisted into an approximation of a smile as he turns his head away, his eyes lingering on the embryonic garden, surveying his handiwork and, I guess, imagining its completed splendour, planning his next move.

I'm not prepared for what he says next.

'I can't do that, Kitty,' he tells me, his eyes fixed on the bright horizon. 'That's not how I feel about you and you know it. I've tried not to feel the way I do, but I do. I can't be here and not want you, or not tell you how much I want you. You know that, and that's why you asked me to stay on. You don't give a fuck about the garden, you just like the idea of stringing me along, leading me on. Turns you on in a way your little husband can't, doesn't it?'

He turns to face me, pinning me with his angry eyes.

'Doesn't it?'

I shake my head dumbly and hold Ella close against my body, shielding her from his quiet anger.

'You think that I'm playing a game. I can't stop thinking about it, about what it'd be like to . . .' He shakes his head. 'You can finish the garden yourself, I've got better things to do.'

He picks up his jacket from the counter and brushes past me as he heads for the front door. I stand rooted to the spot, waiting for the sound of the door closing firmly shut. It never comes. After few moments my heartbeat slows again. I breathe, loosening my grip on an entirely oblivious Ella.

'Well,' I say out loud, testing that I'm in full possession of myself again. 'That's that sorted.'

I wait all day for the feeling of loss and disappointment to fade away into relief. For the sense of empty peace I had anticipated to settle over me, leaving me free and easy to concentrate on what really matters, not some half-baked fantasy about someone I barely even like, let alone love. But instead I let myself imagine Gareth driving his van a little too fast down the country lanes, frustrated and angry because he can't have the one woman, the only woman, that he might have loved. The only woman who might have changed him.

It's rubbish, of course. If he's angry it's because he won't be able to notch me up on his bedpost, won't be able to boast about shagging a married woman down the pub. I know that on a conscious level, but now that the real danger has abated and I'm left with this quiet peace deal, I let the whole mundane and sordid business drift into yet another complicated romantic fantasy culminating in Fergus and Gareth fighting it out for my hand. I wonder how Fergus would feel if he knew that another man wanted me.

'Ella asleep?' is the first thing Fergus asks as he comes in, and I wonder why he doesn't sense the vibration of what might have happened in the air.

'Yeah, we spent the afternoon digging again. She's exhausted. You should have seen her covered from head to toe in mud.'

Fergus smiles as if he can see her, and I feel a spilt second of jealously.

'Why were you digging? Why wasn't that over-priced shyster out there digging? God knows he should be earning his money.'

I hand him a takeaway menu and he laughs. 'What's up, can't be bothered to programme the microwave?'

I smile, but his comments smart.

'No, I just fancied a change, that's all,' I say, sounding hurt. The small thought that surfaced in the garden this afternoon keeps nagging away at the back of my mind. 'I sacked him.'

Fergus scans the menu without even a twitch.

'Good,' is all he says. 'I didn't want to say anything to you, I know how much you wanted it. But to be honest, Kitty, spending all that money on turning our backyard into Kew Gardens was a bit rich.' Without looking up he reaches for my hand. 'I'm glad you saw sense in the end. I might have crispy duck, do you want to share?'

I withdraw my hand from his.

'That not why I sacked him, although I would have done if you'd ever been straight with me about money.'

At last he looks up, puzzled at my irritation. 'What do you mean?' he asks.

'I mean that one minute you're all largesse and "buy yourself something nice, darling", and the next you're like an out-ofseason Scrooge. Am I supposed to be able to spend our money, or should I be waiting for a weekly hand-out?'

I am surprised to see Fergus's face crumple and age so abruptly.

'I'm sorry, I know it's hard for you. It's hard for me too. It's this sodding job. One minute you think you might have cracked it, and the next the flying carpet's been pulled out from under your feet and it's a long way down.' He pushes the menu to me across the table. 'Maybe we should sit down and work out a budget. That's a good idea.'

I suppress a silent scream. This isn't turning out the way I'd pictured it – it's gone from jealous and passionate rage to domestic accountancy in three easy steps.

'So aren't you going to ask me why I sacked him?' I crowbar my way back in.

Fergus looks mildly intrigued. 'Why?' he says amiably.

'Because he came on to me,' I say. 'Tried it on. He wanted an affair. He wouldn't stop going on about it and I had to sack him.'

I watch Fergus's face carefully, waiting for that split-second reaction that will tell me how he really feels.

He laughs. Uproariously, hugely, loud enough to wake up Ella if she wasn't so tired. He slams his hand down hard on the table and wipes tears from his eyes.

'He never!' he asks me, grinning from ear to ear.

I nod my head. 'Yes, he did. And I don't know why you find it so hard to believe.' I can't help sounding hurt. I'd expected to have to drag him back into the house after he'd stormed off looking for satisfaction.

'Cheeky bastard!' he exclaims instead. 'So what does it feel like, Mrs Kelly, having to fight off your first tradesman?'

I stare at him angrily.

'You don't care, do you?' I say incredulously. 'Another man

tries to fuck your wife and you don't care?' I shake my head.
'I don't get it. Maybe it's because you don't really believe me,
or maybe it's because you think he can't have meant it
seriously. After all, who would seriously want to fuck poor fat
old Kitty?'

Fergus's smile shuts off and it dawns on him all too late that
he's failed his stealth exam.

'Kitty, of course I care, I do, it's just that . . .'

I cut across him in a swathe of fury.

'It's just that there you are up there living life on the edge,
being yourself, being alive, and here I am installed in my very
own little birdcage waiting for you to come home and feed me
little bits of your time, and it's just that I'm too boring or too
staid for anything like that to happen to me. Isn't it?'

In the second's silence before he responds, we hear Ella's cry
echo down the hallway. Fergus gets up.

'It's not that, Kitty,' he says softly, looking hurt and confused.
'It's because I trust you. Surely you see that? I don't care if, I
don't know, Russell bloody Crowe came down here and tried
it on with you. I'd laugh, all right? I'd laugh because I'd know
he'd made a fool of himself. Because I trust you. In the same way
that you should trust me. Okay?'

I nod bitterly.

'Let me get her back to sleep and we can talk a bit more, but
don't be angry, Kitty. I trust you because I love you, and
because I know you love me.'

When I look down I find I have screwed the takeaway menu
into a tight little ball.

'He trusts me,' I say out loud. 'And why wouldn't he? He
loves me.'

After half an hour of waiting it becomes clear that Ella isn't
about to just go back off to sleep, and I pad up the stairs to find
Fergus playing with her and her bricks on the nursery floor.

'I thought we were going to talk?' I say, hating myself for sounding petulant.

Fergus grins at me. 'I know, love, but, well, it's just that it's something and nothing, isn't it? It's not *really* a big deal, is it? Why don't you have a nice bath and relax. I'll make us some cheese on toast.'

I smile at him wanly and lean over to kiss the top of his head.

He's right, of course – only a madwoman would want to bring jealousy and disharmony into her perfect, happy little family. It's only that for just one moment I wanted him to be fierce and passionate about me, the way he used to be before, before everything became so wonderfully normal.

Chapter Eighteen

One day I'd come home from school with one sock missing and a rip in my gingham summer uniform. When Mum had seen me she'd sat me on her knee and wrapped her arms tightly around me.

'What happened, pickle pie?' she'd said softly into my ear. I'd leant my head back against her shoulder and sighed. Maybe then had she noticed that one of my hair bobbles had been ripped out and that I had a long scratch across the bridge of my nose.

'Mummy, I can't go to school any more,' I'd told her sadly. 'Abby Morgan doesn't like me. She beat me up for showing off, she said.' I remember quite clearly the feeling of horror and shock I had felt to find that not everyone loved me, that not everyone wanted to hear everything I had to say, not everyone thought that I was the lovely girl my mummy always said I was. Even more shocking was that Abby Morgan's dislike of me spilt over into a physical attack of pure anger. She was furious with me for being myself. No one had ever felt that way about me before, and faced with that strength of feeling I'd decided that the best thing to do about it would be to stay at home from now on and just have Mum as my best friend, which I told my mum in no uncertain terms, very proud of myself for not wailing like a baby.

Mum had listened to me tell her about my first-ever fight

with a quiet calm and, although I didn't know it, I imagine she was half smiling to herself as I spoke.

'Darling,' she'd told me, kissing my ear. 'When I was a little girl I used to think of every day as if I were sailing my own little ship at sea. Sometimes the sea is clear blue and calm and everything is easy and happy. Sometimes, though, there's a storm and the sky grows dark and the water's rough and choppy, throwing your little boat all around so that you have to hold on very tight, and remember that sooner or later the storm will pass and it will be calm again, easy and happy once more.' She'd squeezed me tightly before setting me back down and going to the cupboard to find the Robinson's juice. 'You've had a rough time of it today, but I don't think too much damage has been done. Just hold on and soon things will be calm again. As for this Abby Morgan, I think that tomorrow you should go and find her and ask what it is that makes her so angry. She sounds like she needs a friend, to me. Oh, and if she touches you again, you tell me and I'll go and have words with her mother.'

Of course it didn't end there; I'd burst into angry tears and argued about my enforced return to school for the rest of that night and all of the next morning. I'd clutched my Muppets sandwich box close to my chest as I'd entered the school the next day, feeling seasick through and through. I needn't have worried though because the moment Abby Morgan had seen me she'd run up to me and asked if we could make up, make up, never ever break up, and we became skipping buddies for the rest of the week. In those days the calm and the rough ebbed and flowed from hour to hour and day to day until it just became the routine rhythm of my life.

After Mum's funeral I'd remembered her telling me that story, and I hung on, hung on as tightly as I was able, waiting for the calm weather again. When I met Fergus, for the first time in *all* of the time that had passed since, I thought I'd found my safe harbour, I thought I'd never have to brave those angry dreams again. But here I am in the middle of the deep blue sea on a home-made leaky raft in a force ten gale, and what's more, I think I'm sinking.

I knew that married life would have its moments of stormy weather, but I'd never imagined they would be like this.

I never imagined that I'd be sitting alone over a bottle of red wine waiting, still waiting, for Fergus to come home at 9.30 p.m., while the smell of his ever-so-slowly-burning dinner thickens the air.

I never dreamt, after months and months of trying to get my baby off to sleep, that once she'd been in bed for two whole hours I'd want to wake her up again just so I wouldn't be alone.

After I met Fergus, I never expected to think about or feel about another man in a sexual or romantic way again, but somehow or other I have been, sexually at least, for the last half a bottle since it's become clear that Fergus isn't going to be in in time for his first marital home-cooked meal after all. I've let myself think about Gareth's hands all over me. It's just a harmless kind of revenge, that's all. As Fergus put it, its 'something and nothing'.

The meal burning in the oven is all my fault. I should have known not to break my rule of fifteen years never to be domestic again, but after Gareth had left this morning, and after the world had returned itself to an even keel, I thought of everything that Georgina had said to me and Doris's advice on matrimony, and the only way I could think of overcoming the restlessness I felt was to embrace my status as a housewife. To make the word manifest and to cook. Perhaps to the average person on the street it might not seem like a terribly grand gesture, but to a certified expert on me like Fergus it would look exactly like what I meant it to. A towering gift of love, an affirmation of my commitment to him. Christ, I was practically renewing my marriage vows.

Fergus had been out of the house maybe only twenty minutes this morning when I bundled Ella into her buggy, stuffed my hastily completed CV into an envelope and headed for the door. I was going to make shepherd's pie; I was going to show Fergus that my cooking, even though I had chosen not to display my prowess so far, was better than Georgina's any day of the week.

As I wheeled Ella around Tesco's selecting the best ingredients, I pictured Fergus's face as he walked in through the door and sat down to a steaming home-cooked meal. Okay it's June and the promise of a sweltering summer is already lingering stickily in the air, but in my imagination it was a cold dark evening and he was thrilled to be presented with my nurturing sustenance. On the way home I posted my now rather dogeared CV to the management college, and when I got home I spent almost an hour preparing my pie whilst Ella slept face-down in her playpen. That afternoon I picked up all her toys from the living room floor and even dusted, pausing only to wonder if the spirit of Doris had seeped out of my dreams and off the stage into my head: 'A Woman's Touch'. Once I was done, I sat Ella on the rug and we played with all of her toys until the room was covered once again. At five I called Fergus, but it was Tiffany who picked up the phone.

'Hi, Tiff,' I said breezily. I pictured Tiff raising her eyebrows as I had never addressed her by her nickname before, but so confident was I in my home-cooked bliss that I felt expansive and generous. 'Listen, can you ask Fergus to call me if he's going to be in any later than seven?'

Tiff told me she would and so when, after feeding Ella and bathing her and putting her to bed just like Scary Poppins said, Fergus hadn't phoned, I'd put my pie in the oven and changed into a low-cut top. I'd brushed my hair and even put on a bit of mascara, enjoying my 1950s fantasy act. I'd found his favourite wine and opened it to breathe and laid the kitchen table. Then I'd sat down and I'd waited for him to walk through the door.

Only it's almost ten and he's still not home. Of course he isn't, why would he be? Have you *ever* read a book or seen a film or a soap when one character tries to improve relations with another and everything goes according to plan? Don't you wish that just *once* there wouldn't be that mishap or misunderstanding, or that *one* person would tell the truth whilst the other kept the deep dark destructive secret to themselves? I know that personally, after two-thirds of a bottle of Fergus's favourite wine, I do. I would have thought that he could have called, but I suppose if my life is to be ruled by the gods of pointless drama, what probably happened is that the usually efficient Tiffany fell down two flights of stairs, which caused her to suffer from temporary amnesia, meaning she was unable to pass on the message and now needed an urgent brain transplant. Either that or he just forgot. Either that or she's hoping that I'll think he's forgotten and we'll fight and then she'll nab him on the rebound, bitch. Or he just forgot.

In any case, I pour the last two inches of wine into my glass, giving the bottle a good shake, and peer into the wine rack looking for something else Fergus has been saving for a so-called special occasion. I find a bottle of port that his father gave us on our wedding day and crack the seal, drawing a smiley face in the dust that films its dark surface. Doris watches me, leaning against the fridge in a crisp gingham dress, replete with sparkling apron over her full skirt.

'The important thing is to give him a chance to explain, honey,' she tells me. 'Don't just go leaping down his throat the moment he walks in the door. If you let him explain, then he'll appreciate everything you've done here today and you'll have the moral high ground.' She watches me top up my wine with port and wrinkles her nose in disgust. 'A lady is never seen to be inebriated,' she sniffs before vanishing just as the phone begins to ring.

'Fergus,' I mumble to myself, and I lurch towards the phone. I try to remember Doris's words and keep my voice sweetly calm as I answer. 'Where the fuck are you?' I demand by way of greeting.

'Kitty?' Mr Crawley enquires sounding rather alarmed. I sink on to the hallway chair and rub my fingers over my eyes, catching the wreck of my appearance in the mirror opposite.

'Oh, hi, Mr Crawley, sorry about that. I've, um, got flu and Fergus said he'd be home hours ago with the Lemsip, but he seems to have been delayed. Soz—' I hiccup audibly and slouch low enough in the chair so that I don't have to look at my dishevelled reflection. 'So, um, whatcanIdoforyou?' I rush the sentence out hoping that the absence of pauses will cover up any slurs.

'Nothing really, I just called for a chat. Is everything quite all right? Would you like me to come over?'

I pause for a moment, confronted with the fact that my evasive slouch has resulted in me jamming one of my legs behind the telephone table and extending the other at an obtuse angle, which probably means that I won't get off this chair without actually falling off it.

'Kitty?' Mr Crawley speaks into my ear.

'Um, no, I'm fine, really, just this flu, and to be honest probably a bit too much medicinal whisky. Fergus'll be home soon and then everything'll be fine,' I tell him with as much assurance as I am able to muster.

'Well . . . all right.' He sounds dubious. 'I'll see you tomorrow then, at the rehearsals?'

I nod, and then remember he can't see me.

'Yep-a-doodee,' I tell him confidently. 'Oh, and Mr

Crawley?' I've just remembered something I want to tell him. 'I love you.'

It takes me some time to replace the receiver on the phone, which turns out to be the fruit bowl after all, and then some considerable time more to ease myself out of the chair. It's not that I'm afraid of falling off – in fact the notion somehow appeals to me – but that if I do fall off the clatter might wake up Ella, and the thought of trying to handle her whilst being unable to even walk makes me want to phone ChildLine, not to mention the fact that if I fed her right now, both of us would fail a breathalyser test. Once off the chair I look at the hall floor and find it rather appealing, so in the absence of anyone to tell me to do otherwise, I lie down on it, my head pointing towards the front door.

As I gaze up at the ceiling rose, following the pattern of plaster roses and ribbons that have been dulled by dust and time, I imagine that Gareth has appeared just like magic, in that way that he sometimes did, and he's standing over me in the hallway, looking down at me and smiling. It's a sweet smile, an innocent one, a smile that shows that deep down he's a gentle man, a kind man who just needs rescuing from his wanton ways. He doesn't speak, he just crouches next to me, brushes the hair from my face and strokes my cheek with his forefinger before lying along side of me, tilting my face to meet his. He kisses my forehead and each one of my closed eyes before pressing his lips gently against mine, softly at first and then a little firmer, each kiss a declaration of love. His hands gently disrobe me, laying me bare beneath his gaze and his tender touch, so sweet and gentle and loving and . . . then I hear a key in the lock. I blink at the ceiling rose and banish the imaginary Gareth back to the shadows with more than a little regret.

'Hi, I'm . . . fuck, Kitty, Kitty!' Fergus rushes to my side, picking up my hand and peering into my face. I think of Doris.

'Where the fuck have you been?' I ask him, and then as an afterthought, 'Dear?'

Fergus studies my face, his own a picture of confusion before he catches the scent of my breath and it all becomes clear.

'Christ, you're drunk! Where's Ella?'

I snort and roll on to my stomach. 'I dropped her down the bog. Where do you think she is? She's in bed, has been for hours.' I scramble on to my knees and then Fergus pulls me to my feet.

'Come on, I'll make you a coffee,' he says, and even distanced from the world as I am behind this red wine warmth I can hear the weary tone in his voice. Like he's got a sodding leg to stand on.

'It stinks in here, what have you done?' he asks me, sniffing the charred air. I flip open the oven with theatrical finesse to release a billow of black smoke.

Fergus quickly shuts the hallway door to cut off the clouds escaping towards the smoke alarm. Without pausing to find the oven glove I reach inside and pull out a baking tray, resplendent with the burnt remains of his dinner, feeling my fingertips burning from miles away.

'I cooked. For you, a proper actual meal,' I try to explain. 'It was all special, I did all this stuff and I cleaned and everything and told that fucking bitch to tell you, but she only wants you to shag her and actually, if you knew everything that had been going on in *my* life, you might make a bit more of an effort instead of just turning up when you please. I mean you might appreciate me a bit more. But anyway I wanted to do something to help and then you didn't come home . . .' I trail off and tip the remains of the shepherd's pie into the bin.

Fergus stares at me and then claps his hand to his forehead.

'Oh God, you mean Tiff, you told Tiff to tell me to call you – and she did, honey. I just had to go straight into this meeting and

I . . .' He raises his hand in a gesture of exasperation and then drops it to his side. 'It just went out of my head, and then once I got there it became clear it was going to go on for hours and I . . . I just forgot. I'm sorry. Tiff didn't tell me you were cooking!' he added, as if he might be able to blame it on poor old Tiff after all.

'I was rather hoping she'd had a near-fatal accident,' I tell him, disappointed in his mundane excuse. I watch him for signs of anger as he picks up the opened bottle of port, but instead he only shrugs and pours himself a glass.

'I love it that you cooked. Why don't you do it again tomorrow?' he asks me lightly, with a terrifying lack of intuition. 'So what stuff should I know that would make me appreciate you more?' he smiles. 'Is it even possible for me to appreciate you more?'

I stare at him, muddled and angry and, not quite understanding why, remembering the touch of excitement I felt when I last saw Gareth. The flutter of feeling in what's been an otherwise numb and half-dead body, mummified flesh.

'I'm going to bed,' I say out loud. 'I'm going to sleep in the spare room.' Fergus laughs and catches my hand, pulling me tight against his body. I struggle to break free but he winds his arms around me, pinning my arms to my side.

'Let me go!' I tell him angrily, but he only laughs again and squeezes all the tighter.

'No, no, I won't let you go. Not until you've told me why you've got this silly notion in your head. I've said I'm sorry, haven't I? You should have told Tiff you were planning a surprise!' He tells me as if I were Ella. I writhe furiously.

'I swear if you don't let me go . . .' I threaten, but Fergus's serene smile seems set in stone.

'What? What will you do? Just tell me, Kitty. What's up?' His laugh is cut brutally short as I kick him hard in the shins and stumble back out of his grasp against the door.

'I'll tell you what's up,' I challenge him, feeling on the very edge of my life with my toes tightly curled. 'You're so *sure* aren't you? So bloody smug and *sure*. Sure you can trust me, sure that I will always be here waiting for you, sure that I love you.' I grip hard on to the edges of the door to support myself and feel the words tumbling out. 'I'll tell you what's wrong. I don't know if I *love* you any more. Or even if I ever did.' Fergus becomes perfectly still as my words sink in. 'So you can fuck off and be *sure* about that then, all right?' I say stupidly.

'But Kitty, I . . .' he begins.

'I'm going to bed,' I repeat, and I walk as quickly away from him as I'm able, ricocheting off the walls as I fall in to the spare bedroom. I sprawl on the bare mattress and blink at the light bulb, which still shines like a bright beacon even after I shut my eyes.

Chapter Ninteen

I open my eyes, certain that something has happened but not quite able to work out what. The morning light streams in through open curtains, almost obliterating the weak yellow light of the bulb but not extinguishing my final memories of before I closed my eyes.

I haul myself off the bed and rush to Ella's room. Quietly pushing open the door I see her still sleeping, her small body pressed into one corner of her cot, her face half hidden in the mattress. Fergus can't have gone without waking me up, I'm sure of it, so I pad down the hallway to our bedroom. The bed is empty and unmade, the house is quiet. He's gone.

Faintly panicking I pick up the bedroom extension and dial his mobile number, hoping that he's still on the train and that I can get hold of him. Empty seconds tick by as I wait for a connection to reach across the static, and when I finally do hear a distant ring I hold my breath. He'll know that it's me calling – his display will show 'Home' so he'll know that it's me and that I'm calling to apologise. That's why, when the connection is cut dead mid-ring, I know that he doesn't want to talk to me. I know that somehow, for the first time ever in our relationship, I've hurt him more than he can bear to talk about.

When we first met, we were like, God, I don't know, Laurel and Hardy or Morecambe and Wise. We were hilarious – when we were together we pissed ourselves laughing on an hourly basis. Dora used to say that we looked like we'd been welded together because our bodies were always touching somewhere. Some part of each of us was always melded to some part of the other like two fatally attracted magnets. We couldn't let each other go, not even for a second, because it felt like letting go of your own hand. I didn't expect those feelings to last for ever, but I didn't expect them to swing so visciously into a bleak negative. One thing is still the same, though. Maybe we don't tell each other jokes about nothing every few seconds, or cling to each other remorselessly any more, but I *do* still love Fergus, of course I do, and always have. I think I loved him even before I met him. And I love him more than I ever did then. I love him so much that some small part of me wants to be free of it, free of the responsibility of being his. I think that small part was the only bit left sober last night and that's why I said what I did. Somehow I have to get hold of Fergus and explain. As I sit on the edge of bed contemplating what to do next, a small sound finds it way down the hallway and under the bedroom door. I smile to myself. Ella is singing.

Afraid of disturbing her, I creep back along the hallway to her room. Through the crack in the door I can see her standing up in her cot, her pointed chin tipped up, singing to her cow-jumping-over-the-moon clock. There's no tune, exactly, but she's tuneful, content to be listening to the sound of her own voice. She must get that from me.

'Hello,' I say to her, and the singing is abandoned for peels of embarrassed laughter.

After Ella has had her breakfast, I sit on the bottom stair with the phone in my lap as she tugs hard on the cord and then my trouser leg in turn.

'Hang on, pickle,' I say to her. 'Mummy's just got to

apologise abjectly to Daddy, hope that her self-destruct button has misfired for once, and then we can go out and see your friends.'

Today should be the One O'Clock Club but frankly I don't really know if I can face it. Maybe Clare and I could have our own One O'Clock Club round her house. Or even down the pub. I run through my rehearsed apology again and dial Fergus's office number.

'Fergus Kelly's office, can I help you?' Tiffany picks up.

'Hello, Tiffany, it's Mrs Kelly here. Can I have a quick word with my husband, please?' I say, careful to sound happily married.

'No,' Tiffany tells me bluntly. 'I mean, Fergus told me to tell *you* that he'd be in meetings all day long and that he would not be able to return your calls all day.' I listen to her prim efficiency. Has Fergus told her about our argument or has she just guessed? I refuse to be kept out of his life by this firewall – it's ridiculous. I need to speak to him in person to know, to be sure, that everything's all right.

'Well, you'll have to get him out of a meeting, it's urgent,' I say firmly, wondering if being the boss's wife holds any sway whatsoever.

'I'm sorry, Mrs Kelly, I can't do that,' Tiffany says through tight-sounding lips. 'Fergus said that the only reason he was to be brought out of this meeting was if there was an emergency concerning his daughter.' Tiffany paused like a well-practised barrister. '*Is* there an emergency concerning his daughter, Mrs Kelly?'

Exasperated and deflated I conceded defeat. Fergus knows that I would never use Ella in that way to get his attention.

'No, no,' I say. 'Listen, Tiffany, will you ask him to call me and tell me when he's coming home, and will you make sure that he does?'

I hang up the phone and take the cord away from between Ella's teeth, who seems to be intent on cutting the telephone off for good. What else can I do? The PC is sitting upstairs but we've never got around to getting it connected to the Internet, so I can't email him, and I can't just bundle Ella on to a train and take a day-trip to London; that would be ridiculous. Finally I hunt through my bag until I find my all-but-redundant mobile, and sigh with relief as I see that it still has some battery power left. I'm rubbish at texting. I never get it right, but it's the only thing I can think of doing, so I fiddle about until finally I have something approaching a coherent message.

'I do love U. Please, so sorry. Wrong.' I press 'send', and imagine Fergus in his meeting, if that's really where he is. I imagine him jumping a little as he hears his phone beep at him. I see him picking it up, his face grave and serious, and reading the display. And then I see his face break into a sweet smile and relief flood over his face. In my imagination he quickly excuses himself from this meeting, *if* that's where he is, and he goes straight away to the nearest quiet corner and calls me.

And he calls me.

Now. He calls me *now*.

Now.

Well – maybe he really is in a meeting and he just can't get out of it. For a few minutes longer Ella and I sit looking at the house phone and my mobile phone, willing either of them to ring, or in Ella's case willing just one of them to land in her lap so that she can chew it. Neither does.

I look at Ella eyeing my mobile hopefully and consider the alternatives. Well, obviously I hurt him pretty badly. I mean, you come in after a hard day at the office and your wife tells you she's never loved you and moves into the spare room. That would hurt anyone, let alone someone who works a twenty-hour day. He's confused, probably, and angry with me. It's just that Fergus isn't the kind of person who stays angry very long, unless this time I've driven him so far into his cave that he might never come out.

When the phone does ring a few seconds later it isn't Fergus.

'Hello!' Clare sounds excited.

'Oh, hi.' I sound disappointed.

'You'll never guess what.' Clare's voice drops to a not very convincing stage whisper. Ted must be asleep because I can't think of any other reason why she's whispering in her own house.

'Um, you've been picked to star in *Chicago*?' I say lamely.

'No! Dope. I'm officially a registered childminder as of today. I'm on the list and everything. Brilliant, isn't it?'

I smile wanly, trying hard to muster the enthusiasm Clare needs to hear.

'That's fantastic, Clare, you'll be able to wow the One O'Clock Club gang,' I say as brightly as I am able to.

'Oh bollocks, can't be arsed with that lot of stuck-up cows today, and anyway they've all got nannies called Candida or something. A childminder would be much too low-rent for them. No, listen, I was thinking why don't you drop Ella round here and leave her with me for the afternoon, and I can practise. I mean, what if it turns out I can't cope with more than one kid, then I'd be up shit creek, and also it'll give you a break.'

My mind races and I wonder if it would be stupid of me, really stupid, to do exactly that and then jump on a train to London?

'Well, I could,' I say, trying not to sound too eager to be rid of my daughter. But before Clare can agree I add, 'I must admit I could use the afternoon to myself. I've had the mother of all fights with Fergus and I really need to see him.'

There is silence on the end of the phone.

'Clare?' I say into the receiver.

'Oh God, sorry, I was just talking to Ted.' Clare can hardly repress a giggle, and it dawns on me that she is not alone.

'Clare, have you got someone there? A man?'

Another short silence follows.

'No!' Clare says, clearly meaning yes, and then in a real whisper, 'I can't talk now, it's supposed to be a secret. I'll tell you later, all right?' She resumes her normal voice. 'No, no, there's no one here. No one at all. So what have you and Fergus rowed about, tap fittings in the en suite?'

I wince at the brief insight Clare gives me into her view of my married life and wonder who, how and where she suddenly found a boyfriend without me knowing, and what happened to my half-baked plans to fix her up with Gareth. Oh yes, his insistence that he wanted an extramarital affair with me, that's it. Well, it's a relief that he's out of both of our lives at last.

'Not exactly. I cooked him dinner and then I told him I didn't love him any more. Of course I didn't mean it, but, well, it's really pissed him off, surprisingly,' I say, managing to trivialise my relationship problem with reliable flippancy.

Clare whistles though her teeth.

'You told Fergus you didn't love him any more!' she repeats, scandalised. 'Well, I suppose you do need the afternoon off to fix things up. You stupid mare, honestly, you stupid fucking mare. That man worships you.'

I sigh audibly. 'I know. So listen, will the man who isn't there be there when I come round?' I ask.

'There's no one here,' Clare repeats with staged assurance, and I giggle.

'You are a dark horse,' I tell her gravely. 'I'll see you in about an hour. And Clare, thanks, you're saving my life here – and my marriage, I hope,' I tell her grimly.

'Oh, go on with you,' Clare laughs. 'It's not that bad.'

★

Ella didn't even notice me leave, she was too busy playing with Ted's toy phone, playing with it so sweetly that I can guarantee she will have her own model the next time I walk past a toy shop. Which she will look at for five minutes before disregarding in favour of a piece of string. I should have learnt by now that she only plays with other people's toys, but then again I should have learnt by now not to tell my husband that I don't love him when I do. Really I do. As I shut the communal door of Clare's flat behind me, I realise I was so wrapped up in my own worries that I didn't even ask her about the secret boyfriend, even though she was moon-eyed and obviously dying to talk about it. I mentally promise to make it up to her as soon as I have spoken to Fergus.

As I turn out of Clare's road, a train rattles by, heading for Milton Keynes. From this side of the valley it's about a ten-minute walk down to the station, and I take a short cut down through the playing fields to walk along the side of the canal that will actually take me about ten minutes longer. Maybe the fresh air will give me a chance to think things over, or maybe decide not to go. Dora would say that by rushing to his side to subjugate myself I would be appearing too needy and needy is a turn-off. But when you're married, do those rules still apply? Do you really have to go through life pretending that you're not all that bothered? Surely it should be the opposite. But then if that's the case, Fergus shouldn't have barred all of my incoming calls, he should see that I'm trying to make amends and he should talk to me. For the first time ever in our relationship, Fergus is behaving like a normal man, and I don't like it.

As the Victorian train station looms nearer I find myself slowing down until eventually I stand stock-still by the canal lock situated across the road from its doors. The water has been let out of the lock and now there's a deep, maybe twenty-foot, drop down into damp darkness. I move closer to the edge and peer down into the gloom. Really I should be racing to that train that's just pulling in, I should be running. That's why, after all, I've found my best underwear, even an underwired bra, and poured myself into it. That's why I've washed and brushed my hair and put on a bit of make-up and my best top. Because all through the preparations I have pictured Fergus's face when he sees me standing there in his office, when he sees for himself how much I love him and want him, and then maybe we can have sex on his desk again and everything can get back to normal and before I knew it there would be weeds in the garden and the plants would all have died.

But there's something that's stopping my feet in my tracks on the wrong side of the road and at the far side of the canal just looking at the station instead of going to it.

'Want to go somewhere?' The intrusion makes me jump and I stumble forward and am forced to fling out my arms to steady myself. Gareth's fingers circle the top of my arm and he pulls me away from the lock's edge.

'Fuck, Gareth! I'm really sick of you creeping up on me,' I say angrily, my heart thundering in my chest. I pull my arm out of his grip and rub away the red fingermarks.

'Didn't you hear anything I said to you?' I ask him, trying desperately to slow my breathing down. Now that he's here suddenly in front of me, I'm finding it hard to decide if he's the real Gareth or the fantasy version or both.

'Yeah, I heard what you said, but, well, I'm not the sort of person to give up easily, and I don't think you really want me to give up. Haven't you been thinking about me?'

I look away from him and into the sun. 'No,' I lie. 'Not in the least.'

'Do you want to go somewhere?' he says, his voice suddenly urgent. 'It's a lovely day?' He smiles at me, tipping his head to one side, and the sun ignites the amber of his eyes into a molten gold. 'Why don't you let yourself just be free for once?'

I blink and shake my head.

'What do you mean, Be Free? I am free.'

I think of all my obligations stacking up behind me like dominos ready to push me flat on my face, of my intended trip to London, and for a moment I wonder what if, when Fergus sees me standing in his office looking like mutton, he doesn't laugh and fling his arms around me. What if his distaste is as clear as day and he turns his face away from me. Walks away from me.

As if he can read my thoughts one by one, Gareth's smile stretches out and relaxes.

'It means whatever you want me to mean. Come on, Kitty, for once give yourself a break from the treadmill of life and let yourself be free.'

The heat of the day seems to be emanating from the core of the earth and radiating up through my feet until it reaches my cheeks. Once, before I met Fergus, after the end of another affair, I walked to the edge of Tottenham Court Road, closed my eyes and stepped off the curb. I wasn't suicidal, I wanted nothing more than to be alive, I just wanted to make sure that I should be. I wanted to let fate decide my future.

'Okay,' I say with the same kind of rush of fatalistic excitement. 'Where are we going?'

If I closed my eyes right now I'd swear I was falling into the pitch-black bottom of the empty lock.

Gareth drives fast, and he doesn't wear a seatbelt, and in the spirit of adventure neither do I. He's wound down the window so that the blast of hot air and the rattle of the engine drown out any possibility of conversation as he drives me out of Berkhamsted and into the countryside. I lean back in the high seat of the van and enjoy the moment, enjoy the feeling of being somewhere in the world that only I know about. Not Fergus or Georgina or even Mr Crawley could find me now. For once I'm out of the tomb of that house with the wind in my hair and the sun on my skin. I'm free, free from thinking, free from caring, free from responsibility, if even just for an hour or so – free from the life that I love and that terrifies me. Just for an hour or so I can be a no one, an invisible being who doesn't mean anything to anyone.

It doesn't take long before we're free of the main roads and speeding along the winding and largely empty single-track roads that weave in and out of the Chilterns. I lean out of the window as the view of the valley opens up before me. It's beautiful, and even from here in the passenger seat of a stinking old van I feel as if I could be flying, dipping and hovering over the vast expanse of fields. In a year of living in Berkhamsted I have never been here, never had the chance. I've been either too tired or too sore or too busy catching up with all the things that spending every single day at home demands, and which take up too much time for me to have the weekends free. For the first time in almost half an hour Gareth rolls up his window, nodding at me to do the same, so that the radio phases gradually back in. He leans over and turns it down, sitting back in his seat and running his tongue over his dry lips. He seems as exhilarated as I am, and excited.

'We're going up the beacon. Have you heard of it?' he asks me as he corners a bend, fear embracing aplomb. I laugh and grip hold of the dashboard. For some reason, right now the thought of just a slight thickness of glass between me and the world hurtling headlong into my face is appealing.

'Oh yeah, I've wanted to come up for ages, bring E—' I stop myself. I don't want to think about Ella right now. I just want to think about me, be that nobody.

I catch Gareth smiling to himself, and he swings into an

empty grass car park cut into the side of a hill, killing the ignition and leaping out of his seat in one easy movement. He's leaning against the side waiting for me as I struggle to jump out gracefully.

'It's going to be a hot day, the first really hot one of the year.' He looks at my pale skin with eyes almost as bright as the sun. 'You'll probably burn.' He turns on his heel and I begin to follow him across a small road and then up to the top of the beacon.

'What were you doing hanging round the canal anyhow?' I ask him, for the first time wondering at the coincidence of bumping into him.

He laughs as he walks on ahead.

'Well, the girl I was working for fired me and I've not got much on right now. I was going for a walk, and, before you say it, yes, it was a bit of a coincidence, wasn't it? But only if you think coincidence is unusual. In fact coincidence is pretty much the governing law of the universe. If it wasn't for a huge great big fucking coincidence we wouldn't exist at all. None of us, I mean. I really don't know why people get worked up over the idea, frankly. And anyway, I've always believed you can make things happen if you want them to. The power of positive thinking.'

He stops on a small chalk ridge ahead of me and holds out his hand. 'Come on. Of course these are nothing compared to hills back home, those are real hills and mountains. When I was in the TA we climbed right up into the fog and the clouds until we had to feel our way down again with our fingertips. Fucking scary, but great too.'

He grips my fingers a little more tightly and I find myself returning the squeeze. Fucking scary, but great too.

We make the rest of the incline in silence until we reach the very top of the beacon. The hot wind whips my hair from my face and steals my breath as I look out at the vast flat plane of the valley beneath.

'It's beautiful,' I say to Gareth, who is standing by my side with his hand on his hips.

'Oh yeah, I knew you'd like it. This is what you've been needing, Kitty. Time to yourself, time to think about yourself.' He pauses and seems to collect his thoughts. 'I know you say you don't want me, but I do wonder if you know what it is you do want? I mean, how can you, with your whole life piled on top of you like that. How can you even see past the end of your own nose.' He smiles. 'Even if it is a very nice and slightly sunburnt one.'

I laugh and shake my hair off my shoulders, feeling youthful and coquettish for a moment, like the person I used to be before Fergus, even if that person was lonely, scared and angry too.

'There's a dip in the hillside over there, it'll shelter us from the wind and sun. We can sit and watch the view,' Gareth says, leading me roughly over the turf until I'm half running over the peak of the beacon and a little way down the hillside to the dip he's talking about.

'Blimey, Julie Andrews eat your heart out!' I collapse in breathless laughter. 'Is this where you bring all your women?' I hold my breath, only half teasing.

He shrugs and reclines into the stiff and bristling long-stemmed grass.

'It's where I come to think, work things out. It's where I've brought you.'

I sit on the grass beside him and look out at the fields below, strung together in irregular patches of colour.

'It's hard to believe that real people live down there,' I say, wondering at my own life, the life that I have left down there somewhere around the sharp curve of a country road. Silence drifts between us for a moment and I steal a sidelong glance at him. If he hadn't turned up just when he did I'd be on that train by now. Actually I'd be on the tube. Maybe it's like he said, maybe it's the law of the universe. I steal a sideways glance at him. Maybe he knew where to find me, somehow maybe he'd planned it. I find the thought peculiarly chilling and I push it to the back of mind, preferring the empty optimism of happenstance.

'Tell me your story,' Gareth says, as if he wants me to stop thinking about where I could be and what he could be.

I turn my head sharply to examine him.

'You know it: married, baby, house.' I say the three words with an edge of guilt. Not one of them can possibly describe what my life means to me, but at this moment I don't want that feeling, Gareth is right. The love I have for Fergus and Ella smothers me, obliterates me.

Gareth shakes his head and rolls on to his elbow to examine me.

'No, that's not your story. When I told you about my dad, you looked like you knew, like you had a story too. Like I said, everyone has a story, but you looked like yours was something important, something difficult and hard. I could see it in your eyes.'

He pauses and I consider his face, wondering if I should let him into my life. On that day he talked about beating up his dad I had wanted to be Kitty Kelly, happy wife and mother. Today I just want to be me, and this story is me, and if he can take this story then he can take me.

'Okay, I'll tell you, but listen. I have hardly told anyone this story and, well, it's just for you, you're not to tell anyone, okay?'

Gareth nods and sits up attentively, drawing his long legs up under his chin and crossing his arms over his knees. He looks at me and waits.

I look back then and I wait. I wait to see myself walking

round the corner of Bethune Road on my way home from school. I've got my spring term uniform on, a pink gingham dress, and my satchel slaps against my hip as I avoid the cracks in the pavement, worried about breaking my mother's back. It seems strange that back then I was allowed to walk home from school on my own, but we all did it, stopping at the lights on Stamford Hill, waiting for the rush of traffic to stop so we could cross. Sometimes, when I was on my own like on this afternoon, I'd feel like a queen, a special girl with the power to halt four lanes of traffic just for me. All over London things slowed down for my safe passage. Of course I remember the date exactly, but even if I couldn't I would have known that it was late spring, early summer, because on the way down the tree-lined avenue I stop at each tree and jump as high as I can to snatch blossom from the low branches, making my mum a pink lace bouquet of flowers which she'll put in a milk bottle and stand on the windowsill alongside the posies from yesterday and the day before. Rushing is something I don't do, and I dawdle on the stairs, watching the kids from 22b playing hopscotch in the car park.

'You want a game?' Kelly Simms calls out to me.

'Nah, better get back,' I tell her, but I'm slow up the steps, letting my satchel slip gradually off my shoulder and down my arm until it bumps along after me, smacking against each concrete step. I am hoping the builder will be gone when I get in, because he's been there both of the previous days and I haven't liked him and his stupid jokes and impressions. He wanted to make Mum laugh all the time and he teased me about the flowers I brought her. Only me and Dad should be making my mum laugh, and I know that Mum loved the flowers because when she took each bunch from me she smiled and kissed my hair, saying, 'I'm the luckiest mum in the world to have such a thoughtful girl.'

When I finally reached our door it was open a little, resting quietly on the latch. I pushed it open and stood in the hallway. The radio was on somewhere, playing Brotherhood of Man, 'Save All Your Kisses For Me'.

'Mum,' I shout out much louder than the small flat merits. 'Mum!'

I push open the bedroom door and stick my head round. Maybe she's gone to sleep with the radio on again. Mum can do that. She can sleep through a herd of elephants, Dad says; it drives him mad. But the room is empty; the turquoise bedspread is still rumpled from this morning and the radio sits on it. An older child might have thought to turn it off, but I just turn on my heel and walk back out, still clutching my rapidly wilting spray of blossom. Mum's not in the kitchen or the living room, the bathroom or my room. She must have gone next door to Mrs Anderton's and left the door on the latch so I can get in. I have my own keys, but maybe she's forgotten. I go to the kitchen, set the flowers on the counter and find the biscuit jar, take one biscuit out and replace the lid. Then I stand there for a moment and, shrugging, lift the whole jar down and take it with me into the living room. I switch on the TV; it's *Scooby Doo*. I watch it for a while, kicking my feet restlessly against the base of the armchair and eating four biscuits in a continuous, mesmerised row. It turns out it was the caretaker in a mask – *again*. I sigh and switch the TV off, faintly angry with Mum for not being here to make me a drink and ask me how my day was. I jump out of the chair with the biscuit tin under my arm. If I put it back now she'll never know and I can go and play hopscotch after all. It's then that I hear a thud from Mum and Dad's bedroom, followed by silence. I listen for a moment before I realise: the radio has stopped playing. I pad back to the bedroom door.

'Mum?' I call out again. 'Are you back?'

I push open the door, wondering if I can get the biscuit jar back on to the shelf without her noticing. But the room is empty. I frown and look around, and then I see it: the rumpled bedspread has somehow fallen off the far side of the bed, taking the radio with it. I breathe a sigh of relief. Mum won't catch me stuffing my face before tea after all. I jump on the bed, diving across its expanse to retrieve the radio, and there she is.

Her eyes are wide with panic; both her hands are closed over her throat. She's bleeding through her fingers, her chest is heaving, her mouth is moving, but she can't seem to speak. I stare at her. It is my mum, lying on the floor between the bed and the window with a hole in her neck, a dense black cloud gathering beneath her. I am frozen to the spot, can't move. Mum presses her lips together and, maybe with her last ounce of strength, raises herself up a little and smiles. She smiles because she knows that I am afraid.

'Get. Help,' she whispers, her dry lips still twisted into a smile.

'Mummy?' I clutch the bedclothes close to my chest. I can see she is afraid too.

I leap off of the bed and run next door. As soon as I'm outside it's like I wake up – the noise of reality pollutes my ears. I bang on Mrs Anderton's door again and again, I slam my body against it screaming, I'm screaming.

They didn't let me see her again. I knew she was afraid and that she needed me, but Mrs Anderton made her teenage daughter hold me on her lap until the ambulance had gone. I begged her to let me go, let me go to Mum and put my arms around her and tell her it was going to be all right. She died before she got to hospital. It was probably the builder, but they never caught him.

It's always the same. For a few minutes after I've said it out loud, I feel numbed, as if each of the few times I've recounted that

316

moment has pulverised what remains of my nerve endings until I almost don't feel it any more. I watch a gust of wind racing up the hillside, knocking the tall grass flat in its wake until finally it steals my breath from out of my mouth. How strange that I should be retelling this again almost on the anniversary of her death, almost twenty-four years exactly since she was killed, almost all her 'lifetime', almost all of mine lived again without her.

Gareth says nothing and I'm glad of it. Instead, as if from a distance, I feel his arm circle around my shoulder and pull my stiff body forcibly into his embrace. His cold lips brush my temple.

'I knew you were like me,' he says eventually. 'We are the same kind of people. I knew it from the first moment I saw you. I thought, what's a girl like that doing with a life like this?'

I listen mutely, watching the clouds chase over our heads as we fall back on to the prickly grass with a thud. For one terrifying moment I can feel the earth turning.

'Some people,' Gareth says into my ear, his fingers still gripping my shoulder, 'are survivors, and others are victims – they can't help it, it's just the way they are born.' He rolls on to his side, closing any of the remaining distance between us, watching me closely. 'Take Clare, for instance. Victim. It wouldn't matter if she won the lottery tomorrow – she'd still let *anyone* do *anything* to her. Not like you and me, though. I know what it's like to be fucked up, and now I don't let anyone treat me like that twice.'

His words catch my attention on their returning ebb after the first flow has washed over my head. I turn my neck stiffly to face him.

'What do you mean?' I say, forcing myself to focus on him. This is not the reaction I had expected. I'd expected a sweet gesture of empathy from him, the kind of care he shows to his plants or his watercolours. Not a declaration of war.

'I mean you and me like this. In each other's arms. *This* is what you need.'

It occurs to me at exactly the same moment that his mouth closes over mine, and his tongue forces my lips apart, that nothing he's said so far makes any sense, but still I can't seem to move in response. His kiss fills my mouth, his fingers pull at my hair, and his pelvis grinds against my hips, and I let it happen, my eyes wide open, letting the summer speed by. Here on the highest point of this hilltop I feel a thousand feet under water, drowning, painless and numb.

Then he breaks his embrace and I feel my damp lips chapping in the hot breeze as he leans back, his eyes hot gold.

'I've wanted to do this to you since day one,' he says, his cold dry fingers finding their way under my T-shirt and pushing the material into a bunch under my neck. I shake my head as if I'm trying to lose an angry wasp, but still I'm only rising towards reality.

It's when I see his fingers squeezing and pinching my skin that I truly realise what I'm allowing to happen, and I gasp for air, jerking in shock and anger. Prising my arms from between our bodies I close my fingers over his wrist and stop his hand, digging my nails in hard.

'Just wait,' I say, pulling his fingers away from me with a small smile, forming an escape strategy even as I disengage him. 'I don't think this is the right thing to do right now. I'm not ready for this, I'm sorry.'

From the moment he turned up in the van to the moment he asked me to talk about my mum, he was playing me, still doggedly going after his prey, refusing to admit defeat. I've pushed this whole charade as far as it can go only to find I don't want this feeling any more. I don't want to be cut loose and floating with the tide. I smile and hope he won't take it as an out-and-out rejection. I hope he'll just let it go.

Gareth half laughs, shaking his head as if puzzled or embarrassed maybe, and sits up, still astride me. I breathe out gratefully as he lifts his weight off me and begins to pull my T-shirt back down.

'Thanks. I know you must think I've been sending mixed messages, but . . .'

Still laughing, he catches both my wrists in one hand and presses them into the ground above my head. He's not exactly rough, and his smile is fixed in an expression of tenderness, but somehow it's almost like autopilot. His mind seems switched off behind those eyes, as if he's seeing only my body and not me at all.

'Great tits,' he says bluntly, and with his free hand he pushes my bra up painfully over my breasts until they are bare, the too-tight wire cutting and pinching. I pull my hands free, but then he uses both hands to stop me and lowers his head. I squeal as I feel his teeth grate on my skin.

'Gareth!' I say over his head. 'Please just wait a minute, please. I don't like this. You're hurting me!'

He moans softly in reply but he doesn't stop, he doesn't ease the pressure on my arms, and when I try to move he presses his weight ever more firmly against me.

'Gareth!'

My angry shout echoes in the empty air loud enough to shock him and at last I buck free of him, breaking his attention, and roll away from him. I sit up and pull my T-shirt over my sore and saliva-damp torso. I want to cry for a moment, but I hold my breath until it passes. It's just Gareth, it's just us.

'Christ, didn't you even hear me then?' I slide back away from him across the grass, desperate to put a physical space between us. 'I don't want this, all right? Just friends, we said.'

I've been in situations like this before in the past, when a man really doesn't understand you're not interested, and sometimes I wonder why should they? I've climbed half naked into bed with some men I've no intention of sleeping with, winding them up and up, certain of my right to say no when I want to, and sometimes when I haven't felt so strong-minded I've had sex with them just so I could go home without a fuss. But all of that was before Fergus. I'm not that person any more. I don't use my body in that way any longer. I shouldn't even be here, I should never have put either Gareth or me into this situation, just using him to test how I felt about Fergus and my fantasies and dreams.

And now I know one thing for sure: maybe Fergus and I were fools to rush into our life together so quickly, but even if we can't make it work I don't want this. I don't want to betray Fergus this way with a man I don't love or care about.

'Why don't we just forget about it and go back?' I say with bravado. 'I'll be late otherwise.' I hope he won't ask what exactly it is I'm going to be late for. I have no excuse ready.

Gareth sits back on his heels and watches me for a moment, takes a deep breath, and then smiles, the same sweet smile he had the day he showed me his painting of the garden plan.

'Of course, but look, I know what you're going through. You're not sure if this is what you want, you feel responsible and guilty. That's okay, I understand.'

I try to keep the edge of gratitude out of my returning voice and allow myself a small sigh of relief, hoping the wind will sweep away any sign that he has frightened me. Seemingly oblivious he sits with his back to me, his head bent as if he's intently studying the grass between his legs. 'Look, you've been through a lot of stuff, I understand all of that and you don't have to worry. Sometimes we make the wrong choices, say the wrong things, but it doesn't matter.'

I hear a sudden snap like the dull twang of an elastic band. 'All you have to do is relax. I'll do all the hard stuff.'

Gareth turns back to me still smiling, his flies open, his penis full and hard and sheathed with a condom. The fear, anger and anxiety dissolve in seconds; I have never seen a more ridiculous sight in my whole life.

'Gareth!' I squeal, clapping my hands over my mouth, unable to suppress a giggle that spurts between my closed fingers. 'What the . . . what the hell do you think you're doing?'

Tears prick at the corners of my eyes. I've seen some pretty appalling attempts at seduction in my time, but this has to be the worst. If it wasn't for the total impropriety of the situation in the first place, I just know that it would make Dora and Camille scream with laughter if only I could tell them.

Gareth's smile freezes on his face.

'What? I'm being safe, aren't I? You don't know what's about these days.' He waddles on his knees towards me, his dick bobbing gently as he approaches, and I laugh all the harder, hysterical now with disbelief.

'Come on, Kitty, I'll lose it if you keep this up,' Gareth says impatiently, grabbing hold of my ankle.

I bite my lip and smile at him. 'Listen, this isn't going to happen, all right? Just . . .' I try not to look at his crotch, fearful that I won't be able to control myself. 'Just take it off and let's go home and forget all about it, okay?'

I can't help but sound patronising, and in that instant I know I've made a terrible mistake. Even the fake smile has fallen from his face like a shadow evaporating in the sun. I've made him angry. He pulls on my leg hard, tipping me on to my back, and my head bounces off the hard turf. I laugh again and try to wriggle free, but his fingers dig sharply into my calf as he drags me across the grass towards him, lunging forward and throwing his body hard on to mine. He knocks the breath out of me and I can hardly speak.

'Gareth,' I gasp. 'I said stop it.' My breath is heavy and laboured and I worry he'll think I'm enjoying it – worrying now when it's too late. I gasp for air. 'I'm sorry I laughed, this isn't funny now so just stop it.' He does not look at me as one hand goes to my jeans, loosening the button fly in one jerking movement and pulling hard at the material until it's midway over my thighs, biting into my flesh. I open my mouth again but before I speak he gags me with his tongue. This time it's nothing like a kiss, and I begin to retch as he forces himself in my mouth. I feel his fingers dig their way between my thighs, prising them apart, and I try to struggle but I can't move.

I try to close myself up but it's impossible, and then he's there inside me and that's the only place, he is the only place there is in the world. I stop moving then, I stop struggling, sensing that he wants me to, and I wait, feeling the sharp ends of the rough grass graze my cheek, a small outcrop of rock bite into my back.

It isn't long, just a few seconds, less than a minute, and he shudders to a halt, withdrawing from me at almost the same moment and rolling on to his back. I'm afraid to move, to say anything that might provoke him again. I overstepped the mark, I took it too far. I've let another man have sex with me. I've betrayed Fergus. I've betrayed myself. I've let this happen.

'I told you if I didn't get a move on I'd lose it,' he says mildly after a minute. 'I'm sorry it was over so quick. It's your fault. You turned me on too fucking much with all that protesting! I'll try to hold on to it next time.'

I carefully pull my jeans up, sitting up and pushing my hair out of my eyes, wiping the back of my hand across my mouth, fighting with whatever is left of my free will the urge to weep. If he wants to be conversational that's fine, anything's fine as long as he doesn't touch me again and I get home. The skin around my mouth and neck tingles; he must have grazed me with his stubble. I'll need to moisturise.

'Will you take me home now please?' I say, surprised at how even my voice sounds and appalled at how cowed.

'Don't you want a cuddle?' Gareth sits up, pulling off the condom and throwing it into the grass. 'Most girls want a cuddle after a shag.' He smiles at me with luminous, delighted eyes, his genuine nonchalance making me doubt everything that has happened in the last few minutes all the more.

'No. I want to go home. Just take me home, okay?' I manage a weak smile. 'I'm tired,' I add, hoping he'll take that as a compliment.

Gareth shrugs and climbs to his feet, holding out a hand for me. I force myself to take it and let him pull me up, although I'm certain my legs will collapse from underneath me the moment I'm vertical.

I swallow hard and concentrate on putting one foot in front of the other as he leads me down the hill, waiting for the exact moment when I can drop his hand without him taking it the wrong way. My mind races. It's clear by the way he's swinging his arms and humming to himself that he wants us both to pretend this was consensual. That I never told him I didn't want it, or not until it was too late, anyway. I feel my skin still shrinking over my flesh at the thought of his touch, and I swallow hard.

If that's what I let him believe, what do I tell myself? Or Fergus? What do I call it? Gravity pulls me faster down the steep incline until I break free from his hold and run the last few steps to the van, slamming against its doors.

'Blimey, someone's feeling perky,' Gareth smirks as he unlocks the passenger door. I scramble in and wind down the window, desperate to let some oxygen into the airless vacuum. The plastic seat covering is hot to the touch and sticks against the bare skin of my arms.

Before he turns on the ignition, Gareth looks at me and leans over to plant a kiss on my cheek.

'Come on,' I say carefully. 'Clare'll be bringing Ella back soon.'

Gareth shrugs and pulls the van out on to the road.

'I thought you were going to pick her up?' he says, and I realise that he's right. This time it's as if he senses my desperation, and he drives all the more slowly, almost leisurely, with his elbow resting on the open window as he hums along to the radio. The urgency of this morning's bone-rattling trip is all but gone. Of course, that's why he asked me about Mum; he couldn't have known what my story was, but he must have guessed it would be something that would make me vulnerable, emotionally ripe for comforting and eventually more. Except he'd skipped the platitudes and gone straight for the physical. He must have planned his 'seduction' before meeting me at the canal. He must have been following me, just waiting for the right moment. I suppress the urge to scream at him to go faster or to jump out of the van door, knowing that I have no idea where I am or how to get home. And gradually, eventually, the empty roads turn into villages and then towns and then the first houses of Berkhamsted open up in cul-de-sacs and avenues until the buildings bristle and thicken into the high street.

'I'll drop you at the end of the road, all right? Don't want anyone asking questions, after all.' He pulls into the curb. 'So, how about tomorrow for a rematch. It's supposed to be fine again.'

I find myself laughing.

'What?' Gareth smiles awkwardly. 'Not that bloody laughing again. I don't know what's so funny. You're lucky I didn't find it a turn-off.'

I shake my head, my hand firmly gripping the escape route of the door handle.

'The funny thing is that at no point today have you listened to me.' I tell him. 'You want to start an *affair* with someone who DOES. NOT. WANT. YOU. I didn't want you to kiss me Gareth. I *didn't* want you to grope me and I DIDN'T, I DID

NOT, want you to have sex with me. You raped me, Gareth. Do you understand what that word means? None of this is okay. You raped me.' My breath runs out before I can finish and the last three words become a whisper.

Gareth just smiles.

'I knew you'd be like this, all stuck up about it. Don't worry, I understand. You feel guilty for having a bit of fun, and now you're trying to twist it.' He nods at the house. 'You should relax and admit you're just a married, middle-class whore. You're like me.'

Fury then erupts, wiping out my fear and disgust in a single moment.

'Don't you ever say that!' I scream in his face, loud enough to fill the empty street with my anger. 'I am *nothing* like you, and I swear if you come near me again, *ever* again, I'll report you to the police and you'll be back inside before you know it. You've had what you wanted, now just leave me alone.'

Gareth lunges across me grabbing hold of my fingers, which are latched on to the door handle, and squeezing them tightly.

'Well you're right about one thing,' he says, spitting into my face. 'I did get what I wanted and it wasn't that good – sex with some slack-cunted bitch never could be, so maybe I'll just give my attentions to people who appreciate me. But I can't promise to stay out of your way, Kitty. I mean, there's the Players tonight and Berkhamsted's a small town. You never know when I might bump into you. Or your husband.'

I elbow him in the ribs and push open the door, stumbling out on to the street, gasping for air that he hasn't breathed.

As I scramble for my front door, I grip my own wrist to keep my fingers steady and jam the key into the lock, slamming its solid weight hard behind me and turning the deadlock. I run down the hallway and through the kitchen, fumbling through the cutlery draw until at last I find the seldom-used back door key. I lock it and, remembering Gareth's copy, bolt it too and back away into the hallway, the only place I feel safe, and sit huddled on the stairs.

'Just breathe, Kitty, just breathe,' I say out loud. 'After all it wasn't so bad, not really. I mean it was nothing, hardly anything at all, it was . . .' I run out of words and stare blankly ahead. Did that count as infidelity? I think of Fergus and the train I should have been on to see him and I wish with all my heart that I'd just taken the train, that I'd just said no right then and there. We'd have made up by now, Fergus and I, and maybe we'd have come home together and picked up Ella and maybe spent the evening with her and her Sticklebricks when she should have been in bed. All of those predictable, mundane, wonderful things could have happened if only I'd done what I should have in the first place.

'God, he'll know, he'll know the moment he sees me,' I say out loud. I look at the answerphone blinking cheerfully, showing three messages, and before I press play I know exactly what they will say.

'Hey, darling, look, I'm sorry about before. I should never have told Tiff to hold your calls, I was just angry and . . . well, listen, it's just gone two and I'm on my way home so I'll see you in a bit, yeah?'

I look at my watch. Ten to three. Before the message has even finished I am up the top of stairs and in the bathroom, filling the bath with the hot tap. The rush of the water and the clanking of the ancient pipes almost disguises the sweetly hopeful sound of Fergus's voice in the following two messages. What have I done?

I've ruined us.

Chapter Twenty

I'm still sitting on the toilet looking at the steaming calm surface of the untouched bath when I hear Fergus close the front door behind him, sending the faintest ripple shivering across the surface of the water. It had seemed to me a defeat to get into the bath, an admission of failure. After all, what happened with . . . him . . . it was nothing, so why should I feel the need to wash it away, as if a bath could do that anyway?

'Kits?' Fergus calls up the stairs. 'Where's my two best girls?'

I test my dry lips with my tongue and splash a little of the water over my tear-stained, rash-reddened face.

'Ella's at Clare's and I'm up here,' I call out at last, listening to each note of my voice for any nuances that would give away anything that had happened in the vacuum of this morning.

Fergus takes the stairs two at a time, pausing to knock before pushing open the bathroom door.

'Oops, sorry,' he says. 'Were you just getting in?' He catches my swollen eyes and reddened nose then sinks to his knees beside me – he thinks that he's done this to me.

'Oh God, darling, I'm sorry, I'm sorry for behaving like such a shit, you've been beating yourself up over nothing and I didn't even have the good grace to talk to you when you tried to make up. I'm so sorry.' He closes his arms around my neck and I rest my head on his shoulder, inhaling his presence as if it's a drug, a tranquilliser.

'Don't apologise,' I say, finding my voice cracked and strained. 'Everything, *everything* that happened was my fault.'

Fergus moves away from me, his hand still resting on my shoulder, and examines my face.

'No, you're wrong. It's not your fault, not all of it. It's not mine either, really. If it's anything, you can blame it on how much we love each other.' He drops his hands and settles back against the closed bathroom door, and for the first time I notice he looks exhausted.

'There have been redundancies at work, Kits. Not today, I mean – about two months ago the first wave went and last week another twenty. Voluntary, most of them, and a few new people, but the time is coming when it might be me. It's stupid really. I mean, if anyone should know what a precarious business I'm in it's me. If the markets are suffering, so are my clients. If my clients are suffering, they don't want to spend thousands on new IT systems that might not pay off for months or even years. I've been working all these hours trying to pick up the business that's going to keep my name on the pay roll, and my salary packet up to what we're used to.'

Fergus's shoulders slump and in front of my eyes he seems to deflate, as if months of private worry and stress-fuelled adrenalin have been the only thing maintaining his three dimensions.

'But it hasn't worked,' he continues, almost languorously. 'I've been running to stand still, to go backwards even. If I keep earning at the rate I am today, we'll be twenty thousand worse off at the end of this year than last. And I'm not even sure I can keep that up.' He lifts his head, holding his hair off of his forehead, and I can see the wash of tears brightening the blue of his eyes. 'When I met you I wanted everything that was you, all of you, all to myself, all at once. I thought that was how it was supposed to be. I thought that was all that we needed, to be together. I don't know, Kitty, maybe we *did* get married too soon, maybe it would have been better if Ella had come along two or three years later. But one thing I do know, Kitty, is that I still love you. It doesn't matter what may come, you and Ella are still everything to me. It's just that by trying to rescue you I've pushed you to the brink. I realise that now, and I'm sorry, and, oh God, Kitty . . . please don't leave me.'

I sink on to the floor and hold him close, pinching my eyes tight shut. I should tell him now, if I'm going to. I should tell him while we're alone in this moment, when for the first time in our relationship it is okay to be wrong or have doubts, where everything doesn't have to be a textbook fairy tale to be acceptable. I should tell him that I think I've been raped and why I let it happen. But I can't, because if I do it will sweep away all the bridges he's just begun to build for ever. I don't want to lie to him, but I can't tell him, I can't. Not now. It would kill him.

'I'm not going anywhere,' I say, sniffing loudly. 'I mean, what would be the point of going anywhere without you?'

Fergus half smiles and tips his head back to look at me. 'We can sort out money,' I say. 'We've still got a lot more than most people, and if we cut back on loads of things it'll be fine. I can begin to work, and I should make up the shortfall even if I work locally and, well,' I take his hands in mine, 'maybe we could sell the house? It's not as if the three of us need all this . . . emptiness?' I say hopefully.

Fergus cups my face in his hands.

'Darling, whatever happens we won't have to sell your house, not your home.'

I hold his eye for a moment and make the decision to be honest with him about one thing at least.

'I hate this house,' I say, avoiding his eye.

Fergus's hand drops away from me like a dead weight.

'But I thought . . .?' he begins, and I press the tips of my fingers to his lips.

'I know you did. That day you brought me down here and *told* me we were buying it I tried to believe it when you said it was perfect for us, a dream house – the perfect setting for our family. But it's your dream, Fergus, and everything in it is yours, your choice, your taste. To be perfectly honest, I've always felt as if I've been intruding here. And anyway, it's far too big and it's too grand. Even with all the work Mr Crawley's done to it and, and the garden, I still don't love it – I actually hate it.' I glance over at the bath, now full of tepid water. 'When I was sitting waiting for you to come home, I realised that during the year I've been here I've lived practically my whole life in this house – it's become like a mausoleum. I know that sounds dramatic, but I'd like somewhere smaller, just three bedrooms and a small garden that I can make nice for Ella on my own and, well, all the renovation work should have put thousands on the price. We could decrease the mortgage, ease things a little bit.'

Fergus just shakes his head, his face confused and hurt.

'I know you wanted this to be perfect. We both wanted that,' I say, mirroring his earlier gesture by taking his face in my hands. 'Not just the house, but our marriage, our lives together, our baby, us. But life isn't perfect, Fergus, not even when you're lucky enough to love the person you're married too. And I *do* love you, more now than ever.'

Our arms close around each other and our bodies interlock on the blue and white tiled floor of the Victorian bathroom and both of us weep – for different reasons, perhaps, but together. Together, as a partnership, at last.

My nan always used to say that every cloud has a silver lining. I used to lie on the windowsill of her living room staring up at the passing clouds and wonder where it was, this silver lining, and what it was made of. Was it like the purple lining in my duffle coat, for example? One rainy day I asked Nan to show me the lining and she laughed and led me to the window. The sky was heavy and grey, brushing the tops of the surrounding high-rises with their cumbersome girths, but no silver lining was to be seen. Nan sat me on her knee and told me about when she and Granddad used to run a pub in Tottenham and the cat they used to have that was as big as a dog and twice as fierce. Then we played I Spy, and then, just as Nan told me I had to get down to save her legs, it happened. The sun blossomed through the rain and for a second gilded the sky with its silver light.

'There you go,' Nan said. 'Silver lining. What did I tell you – look, you can almost see enough blue sky to make a sailor a pair of trousers!'

She'd bustled off to the kitchen then, leaving me to puzzle over how you could possibly make trousers out of the sky?

After a while, Fergus and I settle in each other's arms on the bathroom floor.

'They never tell you about this bit, do they?' Fergus says. I feel his smile against my forehead.

'They? Who do you mean?' I ask him.

'You know – they, the people who have constructed this whole myth about fairy-tale endings and say that the getting to the wedding bit is the bit that's hard and that everything else is plain sailing. There's no version of *Cinderella* where a few weeks later Prince Charming gets deposed and they have to go and live in a council house in never-never land is there?'

I manage a smile and sit up.

'I think you're getting your fairy tales mixed up. But you're right, and I sort of think it's a good thing in a way.' Fergus raises an eyebrow, clearly too tired to question me verbally. 'Well, I mean, yes, you're right, we all need to believe we should be a certain way – thin, successful in a career, excellent at fellatio – and we all suspect that if we are going to be happy things have to turn out a certain way. Married, house, kids, etc. Well, I know that our journey together isn't a walk in the park, but I do still believe in our happy ending, because it's now and tomorrow and . . . for ever and a day. The trick is to make sure it's every day and not to keep waiting for it to arrive when it might never come.'

I reach over the bath and pull out the plug.

'I want Ella to be optimistic about life – realistic, yes, but optimistic too. I'm going to read her *Cinderella* when she's big enough, but with a short paragraph on after ever after appended.'

As the last of the cold water glugs noisily down the drain I restop the plug and turn the hot water back on again.

'I think I will have a bath after all, if you don't mind.' I smile at Fergus. 'After all, Clare's got Ella for another hour or so, so if you like you could join me?' I'm shaking at the thought of him touching me, but I know that I need it. I know that I need this to wipe out the memory of the morning, even if only for a short time.

Fergus's eyes light up as steam begins to cloud the mirror and the windows, frosting them with a silver mist. Smiling and silent, we undress each other, our eyes fixed on each other until Fergus pulls me hard into the length of his body and kisses me, so sweetly that just the faintest touch of his lips washes me cleaner than an ocean full of water ever could.

Chapter Twenty-one

The hum of the Players buzzes in the wood-panelled hallway of the town hall before I even push open the double door into what our esteemed director calls the auditorium and most of the rest of us would call a rather large hall with a makeshift stage. I scan the crowd for Mr Crawley as I enter, and then Clare, who didn't need Fergus to baby sit after all tonight, but at first glance I can't see either one of them. At the back of the hall, though, through the literally vibrating throng of the cast, I can see the freshly painted scenery stacked neatly against the wall. My mouth feels suddenly dry and my heart races, but I take a glass of red wine from the trestle table in the corner and take a long draught, despite the protest of my nauseous empty stomach. Before the image can materialise I pinch it forcibly out of my mind's eye.

'It was nothing,' I say quietly to myself. '*He* is nothing. I'm just going to forget it ever happened. Nothing happened.'

I wait until my heart gradually begins to slow to a normal beat and until I breathe again. The bruises, the shock, the anger are all still there just below the surface of my skin, but I know that if I am to have any chance of escaping Gareth once and for all, no one can know what really happened to me. I have to make it go away, pretend that it never happened. At last, something that I know I'm good at.

I've tried, I really have tried not to come tonight, but Fergus was determined that I should.

'You love it, why wouldn't you go?' he'd said as he'd dried my hair gently with a towel. 'It's the one thing I've seen you do that makes you laugh – besides Ella, that is – and what's more it's free! I demand you go. I'll pick up Ella from Clare's and tell her she can meet you there. Okay, Calamity?'

He was so sweetly pleased with himself that I could hardly refuse him, so I came. And on the short walk into town I kept repeating to myself, 'He's nothing. What happened was nothing. Nothing happened,' until I was certain that my head knew the truth as well as my heart did.

Intuitively I knew that Gareth would not come here tonight. It would be too obvious, not his style at all really, but even so just the thought of him swaggering into the room to the eager ministration of a dozen or so lonely ladies with long-untended gardens makes my heart lurch and stomach contract until my mantra doesn't work any more.

'Are you okay?' Mr Crawley's hand on my shoulder seems to instantly steady me and I lean into it, just slightly.

'Me? I'm fine, much better, I mean, after my cold.' I remember slightly too late my drunken excuses to him on the phone. He scrutinises me closely and I resist the temptation to close my eyes against his examination.

'Kitty,' he begins quietly. 'If there's anything I can do . . .'

I laugh heartily. 'You know me too well!' I giggle stupidly. 'A glass of wine would be lovely. Thanks ever so.' Mr Crawley presses his lips together but seems to decide to let the moment pass and disappears instantly into the crowd.

Eager to attach myself to a group I see Barbara talking animatedly to Bill, her shiny bob jiggling with agitation as she rises repeatedly on to her toes in an excited discussion.

'It's true, Bill!' she protests, stamping her heel ever so

slightly as she says it. 'I heard it on Radio Four, for goodness sakes!'

Bill snorts derisively as I approach the group.

'What's true?' I ask, praying the answer won't be that 'Kitty Kelly shagged her gardener up on the beacon this morning'. Gratifyingly Barbara looks at me as if I'm the cavalry.

'*Calamity Jane* has recently been discovered to be a lesbian musical,' she tells me seriously. 'In fact, and don't take this the wrong way, Kitty, but actually the main role is the one I'm playing – Katie. It's about her sexual awakening in the Wild West, which is a metaphor for vagina.'

I open and close my mouth.

'Right,' I say, turning to the mountainous quivering human that is Bill. 'What do you think, Bill – Wild West as vagina?'

'Total bollocks!' Bill proclaims with his least conversational shout. 'There used to be a time when lesbianism was an elegantly discreet way of fucking, and now it's bloody every-where. If you ask me, lesbians have prostituted themselves as a culture to men's pathetic egocentric fantasies. I mean, you can't turn on the TV without two women fiddling with each other's bits these days. And now Calamity Jane was a lesbian. What next? Juliet shagging her nurse over the balcony? Jane Eyre having it away with the housekeeper? Total rubbish.' The rest of the cast has fallen into a somewhat shocked but mostly confused silence.

'I think it's got more to do with a modern society that's happy to be culturally diverse and accept its many faceted aspects, which has room for all kinds of people, even in prime-time TV slots, Bill,' I say calmly. Bill murmurs bollocks a decibel lower than an Oasis gig.

'I must say, Barbara,' I say, 'I can't really see it with Calamity Jane. I mean, she's madly in love with Wild Bill?' It seems faintly ridiculous for me to be discussing the motivation of my version of Calamity, but I'm intrigued and relieved to have something else to think about for a moment.

Barbara tips her head to one side, giving me a curiously birdlike look.

'Well it's obvious when you start to think about it. Calamity loves to dress as a man; lesbians dress like men, although I've never understood why, really, but anyway – she hates all things girlish and despises Wild Bill . . .'

'Have you never heard of sexual tension!' Bill bellows, causing another momentary hush in the chatter. 'It's what we had last Christmas just before the panto and what dissipated rapidly half an hour later in the props cupboard!'

I give up, looking aghast, and instead marvel at Barbara's determination to ignore her tormentor.

'*And,*' Barbara continues as if he wasn't there, 'and when she goes to Chicago to find Adelaide Adams it's plain she finds her sexually attractive, it's in the script.' Sensing Bill's next interruption Barbara rushes on, 'When her and Katie are in the cabin they sing "A Woman's Touch" – it's clearly about lesbian masturbation . . .'

'I thought all female masturbation was lesbian,' Bill says, pushing Barbara over the limit at last.

'Bill, I slept with you two days after my husband walked out on me for a teenager. There was no sexual tension. I was a pitiful confused woman on the rebound, not to mention diazepam, and I needed some comfort. All I can say is, thank God we did it standing up as at least I made it out of that cupboard with my life if not my dignity intact, and it is you that insists upon attaching more significance to what happened than I. It was a sordid pointless encounter that I didn't want to engage in and which I used to regret. Now I can't even be bothered to regret it any more.' Barbara spits at him like a small sleek harrier in full attack.

'Exactly!' I shout, knocking her sideways out of the air.

She blinks at me and smiles. 'Thank you for understanding, Kitty.'

I smile back at her. 'No, Barbara – thank you.'

Barbara gives Bill one last long scathing look. 'Secret love,' she says coldly. 'A love so secret she can't speak its name. Lesbians.' She crosses her arms under her small bust, pivots on her heels and marches backstage.

'Well, Bill,' I say with a wry smile, 'there's one woman you haven't quite managed to work your charm on.'

'Majestic,' Bill sighs. 'Like Diana the huntress. Ah, Kitty, unrequited love, it's a terrible thing.'

The house lights dim before I can respond, and a spot illuminates Caroline on stage.

'Right, let's get a move on, shall we!' Caroline's dulcet tones instantly hush the chatter and gossip.

'As you know, tonight was to be our penultimate rehearsal, Friday the dress rehearsal and our first performance next Wednesday. However, there's been a change of plan. Today is the dress rehearsal, Friday's slot has been cancelled due to double-booking with the sixth form summer ball, and our first performance is on Monday, now running for *five* shows, okay?' A stunned silence flattens the atmosphere.

'Um, but,' I hear Clare's voice pipe up. She must have arrived late. 'Some of the costumes aren't quite finished yet, Caroline. I've arranged to fit Calamity's ballgown tomorrow so it'd be ready for Friday's rehearsal and . . .'

Caroline taps her heel vigorously.

'Yes, yes, I'm perfectly aware of the constraints, but I had hoped that I was working with a team of professionals here, a group of people who when asked to can rise to a challenge and above it!' She flings her unseasonable red velvet scarf over her tightly veined neck. 'Now, as you well know, the Tiny Tot Tap

337

and Tango Troupe were supposed to be performing for the festival here on Monday and Tuesday evening, but there's been an outbreak of chickenpox that's sweeping through the primary schools of Berkhamsted and the troupe's dwindled from forty-seven to six, a huge disappointment for the camcorder-bearing parents of our community. Our mayor called upon me to save the day. "Caroline," he asked of me, "are you the one to save us from looking bad in the *Gazette* when they compare the Berkhamsted Festival to the Tring one?" And I said unto him, "Yes, I am the one, Kenneth."' She fixes us with a steely eye. 'Are you going to make me a liar or are you going to prove that we *can* do it and, what's more, increase the door takings by as much as seventy pounds!' Caroline raises her fist and rattles her bracelets fiercely like an am dram Amazonian queen, and a strangely bloodthirsty cheer rumbles through the crowd.

'I'm sorry,' Bill mumbles miserably in my ear. 'Did someone just say we declared war on the French?'

I smile to myself. 'More like the Tring Victorian Street Festival,' I reply, wondering not for the first time what ancient grudge means that the two towns, barely five miles apart, couldn't schedule their respective festivals on different weeks.

'Same thing,' Bill sniffs, before edging through the crowd towards the piano.

Wild Bill snogs me with stoic diligence as the final curtain falls, and I bear it stiffly, counting the seconds until it is over. I thought the dress rehearsal went pretty well, all things considered – things like Barbara's state of high-coloured coquettishness ever since her encounter with Bill, which makes me wonder if she's been wonderfully Shakespearian about pretending not to like him. And the fact that Wild Bill, bless him, can't seem to get much wilder than a mildly agitated elderly house dog, and that the only person in the whole ensemble who's got a voice worth listening to has been sitting in the wings fringing a fake suede jacket from Mark One with curtain trimmings. But at least for an hour or so I haven't thought about anything else. I haven't thought about where Fergus and I go from here and I haven't thought about . . . anything else.

'Do you fancy a quick drink before we go?' Clare asks me as she packs away her handiwork. 'I don't feel much like going home right now, I'm all overexcited.' She tries to bite her smile back but it seems irrepressible.

I look at her sideways, noticing the flush in her cheeks, and remember that she had a man round at her flat when I spoke to her this morning, a morning which seems light years away.

'I wish that an afternoon with two babies would give me that kind of glow,' I tell her, raising an eyebrow. 'What's going on?'

'I've been dying to tell you.' Clare laughs, her eyes dancing and her resolve to keep a secret crumbling instantly. 'Oh, I'm not supposed to tell, but . . .'

Just as she opens her mouth Dora appears over her shoulder. I shake my head and pinch myself that it really is Dora, and for some reason my first thought is that she's come to tell me she's dead, and my second thought is that she knows about Gareth and she's come to help me.

'Dora! Oh, thank God!' I exclaim, holding my arms out to her. Dora smiles, looking vaguely surprised at my reaction, and hugs me, confirming that she is real, and at least currently alive. She's really here with a real overnight bag. And a very real suitcase.

'Oh hiya.' Clare deflates, seeing her opportunity for indiscretion fade away.

'All right, mate, all right, Kits.' Dora's arm clings around my neck. She's not drunk, at least not with any substance I can smell; instead she seems to be holding on to me almost for protection.

'How did you know?' I ask her. 'Oh God, I'm so glad to see you.' I glance over her shoulder fully expecting to see an ex in full sail heading towards us after her blood, usually because Dora's moved into their flat, turned their lives upside down and left with their favourite CD. Has she chucked Bruce or Wayne or whoever it was who sounded like a hero in a western?

'Know what?' Dora looks at Clare. 'I just thought I'd pop down for a few days . . .'

I eye Dora's large suitcase on wheels and laugh hysterically, feeling my façade slip dangerously low.

'What were you planning we should do, our very own fashion parade? Open a shop called Dora's Entire Wardrobe?'

'Oh, it looks like more than it is, you know. Tampons.'

I shake my head and pick up her overnight bag. 'Come on, you can tell me at home,' I say, whispering to Clare, 'you can tell me all about "him" tomorrow at the dress fitting.'

Clare raises a hopeful eyebrow and the three of us head for the door.

'Ah, Kitty.' Mr Crawley grabs my arm. 'You never did get your wine. I apologise.'

I shrug; I had forgotten it. 'Don't worry,' I say, but he holds on to my arm, still searching my face for something. 'About anything, really. I'm all right.'

In that moment that I say it I believe it, and Mr Crawley seems to also as he lets go of me. In that moment everything is fine, back to normal. Fergus and I have finally let go of our fantasy marriage in favour of a real one, Dora is here like the proverbial good fairy/bad penny, and whatever predicament she's arrived with is bound to keep my mind off things. Even Clare seems to have replaced her permanently forlorn air with a smile.

And what happened with Gareth was nothing. Nothing happened, it was nothing. He is nothing.

★

The moment Fergus sees Dora standing behind me in the door frame his face goes from shock to irritation to relief in about five seconds flat. Maybe, like me, he's secretly pleased that there's a third adult in the house to diffuse what's left of weeks of accumulated tension.

'Dora! What a nice surprise,' he says, kissing her, and I almost believe him.

'Where's Ella?' I ask. Usually she has either crashed out mid-play or is still up pulling Fergus's hair or enthusiastically engaging in some repetitive game that Fergus lost interest in about a minute after he initiated it.

'In bed, has been since eight-thirty.' He looks at my incredulous face. 'I know, it's a miracle! I read her a story, sang her a song and she went to sleep instantly, possibly to escape the dreadfulness of my voice. Tea?'

As Fergus heads off to the kitchen, Dora falls headlong on to the sofa, picks up a cushion and stuffs it over her head.

'Ooooh, this is a nice sofa,' she moans. 'This isn't any of your DFS rubbish, you can tell. Gorgeous. I'll sleep here.'

I perch on the few square inches of sofa remaining and look at her. In the warmth of the lamplight she looks almost translucent, as if the light in the room is coming from within her paper-thin façade.

'What's happened, Dora?' I ask her quietly.

'Oh, fucking Thingy, I split up with him, only the fucker is still in my flat, can't get him out, the wanker. I don't know why I ever let him in in the first place. It's never my policy to let men into my house. Must have had an embolism or something.' She delivers this speech with her customary hard-bastard indifference, but etched across the planes of her face is another story.

'Sorry, Dora, do you have sugar?' Fergus sticks his head round the door, nods at the recumbent Dora and makes a quizzical expression, which I return with a 'blowed if I know' shrug.

'Shit loads,' she replies into the pillow, and Fergus and I smile at each other for a moment longer before he softly closes the door behind him.

'So, what about you?' Dora examines my face. 'What's happened to you?'

I sit on the floor by her head and try to gauge if now is the right time to talk to her. I decide that it isn't.

'Listen, I know you. You wouldn't leave a man you didn't want any more in your flat. You'd throw him out and kick him in the nuts, and then you'd stamp on his head a bit. This is out of character. There's more to this than an ex that won't go away, otherwise you wouldn't be here, you'd be at Camille's. I know I'm the last resort friend, and there's no point in denying it.'

Dora smiles and hauls herself up into a seated position. 'You're not a last resort friend, you're just the best one. No offence to Camille, but you have a more special bond with the person you broke into the boys' changing rooms with. It's history.'

I smile at the memory of eleven-year-old Dora and I huddled behind the less than fragrant coats and duffle bags on sports day determined to find out once and for all what a willy looked liked. When the boys filed in after a cross-country marathon and duly stripped off for a communal shower, we couldn't believe our eyes.

'That surely can't be what all the fuss is about,' Dora squealed. 'Its revolting!'

We were caught, of course. Suspended for two days and reviled for the rest of that term as pervy sluts.

'Don't give me all that pally reminiscence crap.' I force myself to snap out of my reverie. 'You always do that, always. What happened?'

Dora blows the air out of her cheeks and tips her head back to examine the ceiling.

'Well, you and Camille were right, I guess. About the booze leading me on the rocky road to ruin and all that jazz. As soon as Bruce and I started boozing we started smoking and then doing the odd line until it got to be a regular thing, and then . . . the thing I can't believe is how little time it took, Kits. After years of building up to smack and months of getting off of it, in less than two months I was right back where I started.'

I don't let the faintest hint of what's raging in my heart show on my face as I ask her the inevitable question.

'Have you taken heroin again?'

Dora closes her eyes for a moment before opening them to look me in the face.

'Yes.' Her eyes are perfectly unreflective black pools. 'I got in from work yesterday and he had a fix all ready and waiting for me. Said it was to celebrate our anniversary. I didn't even hesitate, Kits, I just went to it, and, and I wanted it. And for a while there it felt fucking fantastic, just like coming home. I woke this morning, realised it was ten a.m., and every part of me was hurting, begging for more of it. I knew he'd have some more gear on him, I knew I could have it if I wanted it . . .' Her thin white fingers reach for my hand and grip it tightly. 'But I don't want to die, Kits, not yet. So I left him to it and I packed my bag and I came here to you because you know me the best and you'll sit on my head to stop me going back out there, I know you will. I can't go back there, Kitty, it'll kill me.'

In a second the anger and fear dissipate and Dora and I hold each other, each one of our years of knowing each other etched into the ease with which we are able to hold each other.

'Oh God, Dors, you've done the right thing. You'll be all right here,' I say, holding her close.

'I know, I know I will. Sodding Bruce. What kind of a twat is called Bruce anyway.' Dora hastily wipes her tears away. 'Listen, I'll need to find a meeting locally, starting tomorrow.

Will you help me? And can I stay here until I'm all right again?'

I nod yes and yes to both questions.

'What about Bruce? How are you going to get him out of your place?'

Dora looks stricken for a moment. 'I dunno, I could get him whacked, I suppose. I know people. Look, I don't want to talk about Bruce any more. I want to talk about you. Something's happened to you. Did you fuck the gardener?' My face must have revealed the truth before I dissemble, and Dora's eyes widen. 'You did!' she whispers. 'You fucked the gardener! Fuck me!' She looks at me with disbelief. 'I've got to tell you, mate, I disapprove. I mean, Fergus – he adores you . . .'

'Shhhh.' I look hastily around. 'Look, it's not like that, it just sort of . . .' I find that I can't speak and just at that moment we hear Fergus in the hallway. I just press my lips together and silently plead with Dora to do the same. She squeezes my hand, frowning with concern as Fergus carefully places his tray of teas on the table.

'So, Dora, what's new?' he says amid a luxurious yawn.

Dora shrugs nonchalantly. 'Oh you know, escaping to the peaceful refuge of the country to avoid a life of crime and degradation in the big city. I expect Kitty'll fill you in. Oh, and I missed you, Fergus, so much.'

Her tone is the gently sarcastic one she always uses with Fergus, and his returning smile is the same one of weary tolerance that it has always been. I breathe out in relief. Dora won't let me down, not even if she disapproves.

Chapter Twenty-two

Fergus looks at his coffee with a grim determination.

'Have I made it too strong again?' I ask him, wondering at his expression.

'Nope, it's fine.' He smiles and then, as if he's remembered something, says, 'It's just that you never know if today's the day you'll get the chop, you know.'

I lean against him, my arm about his shoulder.

'Well, if it is, it is. We'll be fine. You'll get a bit of redundancy, won't you?'

Fergus shrugs and nods. 'A bit, yeah. And I've been looking about for something else, but pretty much the whole industry is in the same situation right now. No one's hiring. I could always do some support work somewhere I suppose.'

Dora strolls into the kitchen with my honeymoon dressing gown on reading a letter printed on thick cream paper.

'Your post came,' she tells me, nodding at the letter. '"Dear Katherine, thank you for your recent application. I regret to inform that you that the post you applied for has already been filled . . ."' Disappointment overtakes the violent urges her habitual intrusion of my privacy has always evoked in me. '"However, due to your skills and experience we would like to meet you for an informal lunch in the near future to asses your eligibility for any future positions that may arise, Yours

Sincerely blah blah blah blah."' Dora drops the letter on to the counter. 'Well, hold the front page,' she says dryly as she pours herself a coffee.

I look at Fergus and smile.

'There is a god,' he says, and we hug, before kissing each other deeply.

'Well, I'd better get off. See you, Dora.' He kisses me on the cheek. 'Tell that baby I hope she enjoyed her lie-in after her two-hour playing session with Daddy at three o'clock this morning. Do you know that after about an hour I kept hallucinating . . .?'

I follow him to the door and watch him disappear over the bend of the hill. It's a beautiful morning, already warm and bright, with the smell of suburban hedges and flowers heavy in the air. The sort of place where nothing bad ever happens.

With a sudden impulse I step out barefoot on to the warm paving stone and walk lightly on to the street. Glancing quickly around, I reach up to the lowest branches of the tree outside our house and pull off some blossom, enough to make a posy.

'What *are* you doing? Dora questions me from the door frame.

I smile at her and run full tilt back into the hall, wiping my bare feet on the dormat.

'These are for Mum, for her anniversary. I want to put them next to that photo of us, the one where we're wearing matching head scarves. I need to find a milk bottle . . . Do you even get milk bottles these days?'

Dora follows me into the kitchen shaking her head and hands me a small vase.

'Your mum would love that. Here, try this.' She appraises me carefully. 'You don't look like you're about to leave him for the gardener,' Dora says as I return to the kitchen. 'You *look* like you're about to do a photo shoot with *Hello!* magazine.

"Cinderella reveals all – My perfect life with royal hubby".'

I sigh and sit on a stool at the table, burying my head in my hands.

'I'm not! I'm not about to leave him,' I protest. 'I love him, I . . . God, I'm not leaving him,' I say, suddenly exhausted and desperate to go back to bed again and just sleep. If only I hadn't seen Gareth that morning, if only I'd got on that train and gone to see Fergus. Then we'd have all of this new communication and happiness and I'd have none of the . . . guilt.

Dora raises an eyebrow at me. 'Oh yeah? Well then why? Why did you shag . . . Gareth, is it? Cute, yes, marriage-wrecking material no, and I know you, Kits you're not the type to do it just for kicks.'

I look out into the garden. The lawn that we laid together has started to grow out of control, inching thickly above the soft velvet surface I had imagined into a haven for angry cats.

'I don't know why it happened. I . . . Fergus and I had a big fight, just one of many over the last few weeks. We've both been tired, both had our own problems, both too scared to tell the other one because neither one of us wanted to admit things weren't perfect . . . You know, when everyone tells you how right you are together it's scary to think that they might be wrong, do you know what I mean?'

Dora nods. 'Well, yeah, but if it isn't you two then it's no one and we all might as well go home,' she says mildly. 'And?'

I told her about the dinner and the port and me telling him I'd never loved him and she winced and grimaced in all the right places.

'So the next day he flounced out without speaking, refused my calls and I was all set to go up to London and see him, to apologise and . . . well, Gareth just . . . appeared out of nowhere. He said did I fancy a ride out to the country, and he asked me about Mum and, well, I don't know, he seemed like he might understand, so I told him. And then he sort of lunged at me and . . .' I struggle to keep a hold of my voice. 'It just happened. It was horrible. It was nothing.'

Dora examines me closely. 'Then why did you let him do it? You could have just said "thanks but no thanks".'

I bite my lip hard hoping for the metallic taste of blood in my mouth.

'I didn't let him do it. I asked him not to do it but he did it anyway.'

It takes a moment for Dora's face to clear with the realisation of what I'm saying.

'Dora, please, don't say anything, please. It was horrible – horrible – and I just want to forget about it, that's all,' I say, tears streaming down my face.

Dora winds her arms around my neck and leans her forehead against mine.

'Kitty, shhh. Kitty.' She takes my face between her hands. 'You're telling me that he . . . that he raped you, aren't you?'

I nod, tasting the warmth of silent tears on my lips, desperately holding on to the scream in my heart.

'You can't forget about it, Kitty,' Dora whispers. 'You can't, you have to tell . . . people. You have to tell Fergus, and the police. People. You can't let him get away with it. It'll kill you!'

I shake my head and begin trembling at the very thought of it.

'No, Dora, please, please,' I plead with her. 'I can't tell anyone. Fergus will kill him, it will tear us apart, he won't ever be able to understand. Please, Dora. If Fergus finds out then Gareth has won. I was foolish enough to think that he wanted me, that he might even care about me, but he didn't want me at all, he just wanted to destroy someone else's happiness. He wanted to make me into nothing. If Fergus finds out then he'll have succeeded.'

Dora shakes her head, her eyes bright with fierce anger. 'You're wrong, Kitty. Fergus would never judge you like that, he loves you. He'd be devastated, but . . .'

'*No!*' My voice rises. 'You know me, Dora, better than anyone. You know I can do this. You know that if I try very hard I can just make it go away. Help me, okay, please just help me.'

Dora watches me silently for a moment.

'If that's what you want,' she says at last. 'But if that bastard does the same thing to another woman, what then? How will you feel then?'

I turn my head away from her. 'I can't think about anything else now, I just need to know if you'll help me?'

Dora turns my face back to look at her. 'Of course I'll help you,' she says. 'And if I ever see him, I'll fucking kill him.'

I know that she means it. The tension shatters as Ella's shouts reverberate through the house.

'I'll go,' Dora says quickly. 'Can I go?'

I stare at her, wiping away useless tears. 'Are you sure?' I say, nonplussed, numbed.

'Yeah, unless you think I'll scare her or drop her or something?' She seems to consider it a real possibility.

'No, no. Go for it. She'll need a change, though . . .' I call after her, but she is already out of the door and taking the stairs two at a time. I take a deep breath and begin to make a list of everything I have to do today, just a normal, happy day like any other.

Dora hangs up the receiver and hastily scribbles an address on the back of an envelope with Ella sitting on her knee, attempting to chew the very same pen Dora is writing with.

'My God, no wonder your mum's gone fruit loops,' Dora says to her as if she were conversing with a twenty-year-old.

'You're a mentalist. When do you grow out of this chewing thing and progress to, I don't know, being interested in shopping?'

I watch them getting on like a house on fire in pure disbelief. I mean, I know Dora's been through a lot recently, and I know she's found the strength to pull herself back from the edge after taking smack again, but unless the road to Damascus cut across the Euston to Milton Keynes line somewhere between Harrow and Wealdstone and Kings Langley, I can't see why she has suddenly decided to like, even appear to love, my child. Or any child for that matter. Must be some kind of genetic imperative.

'Are you all right?' I ask her as she sings Ella her own particular brand of nursery rhyme.

'Me? Yeah, I'm fine. I've just realised that the whole godmother thing is coming round and I thought I'd better start campaigning, you know how it is. Don't want that bloody Camille to get all the glory.' She exchanges a frown with Ella. 'Right now, how about . . . *Ride a cockhorse to dum de-dah dooo! La de da dee something da, flipperty floo . . .*' she sings and Ella laughs her head off.

'So, where is Hemel Hempstead? Sounds like the third ring of hell. There's an NA meeting there today at eleven.' She turns back to Ella. '*She shall have doooby-do something she stuuuufff!* Why isn't there one in Berkhamsted? I mean, I have to get a sodding bus to get to this place and I bet they don't even have proper shops. Honestly, the country.'

I smile apologetically. 'It's not far on the bus, the stop is on the high street. Will you be all right on your own because I'm supposed to be having a costume fitting at Clare's, but I could postpone it and come with you . . .?'

Dora shakes her head. 'No, don't want some frumpy old mother and her kid cramping my style, do we Ells. I've yet to explore the sexual proclivities of the Home Counties. It could be a rich new vein . . . couldn't it? Yes, it could, yes it could!' She smiles stupidly at Ella.

'Dora, please don't get involved with another NA person. Don't take it personally, but the ones I've met seem to be really shocking losers, or maybe that's just your taste in friends. Find someone who's, you know, normal, or at least bordering on it.'

Dora shrugs, looking momentarily crestfallen. 'I've given up on relationships anyhow.'

She gathers herself up and sets Ella on the floor. 'Okay, well, I'll be off, then, to Hemel Hempstead. Wish me luck. If I'm not back by three call the police, tell them I've been kidnapped for my cosmopolitan taste and good shoes.'

I roll my eyes and Ella waves enthusiastically as we see Dora off. As she is about to leave she pauses in the door frame and looks at me hard.

'I'm not sure I can pretend this didn't happen to you, Kitty, even if you can,' she says.

I smile brightly.

'You can. You have to, for me, okay? It'll be okay, I promise.'

I have never seen her look so sad as in that moment before she turns to walk away.

'Come on you,' I say to Ella once the house is empty. 'We've only got an hour and half to get you ready and go less than half a mile down the road. It's going to be very tight.'

In fact, it is two hours later when I finally ring Clare's bell. I'm sticky, flustered and hot. The sunburn I picked up on the beacon has intensified and reddened as a cruel reminder and I feel uncomfortably huge in this summer shift dress that makes no effort to hold in my stomach or even give me a waist.

'Helloooo?' Clare's greeting through the intercom seems oddly flirtatious.

'Hi, it's me. Kitty.' I add my name as an afterthought.

'Oh! Kitty! God, sorry, I forgot you were coming over. Come up!' Her cheeryness seems to be edged with a touch of hysteria, and as I park the buggy and lug Ella up the two flights of stairs, it occurs to me that maybe she thought I was the man she was so excited to tell me about. Her front door is on the latch and I push it open to hear her finishing a telephone call.

'If you want that, then don't come back here! Okay, okay. I'll see you later,' she's almost whispering. 'Love you. Bye.'

I pause in the doorway, embarrassed to have caught her trysting with her mystery man.

'Hi!' I shout loudly, waiting for a second in the doorway before I go in.

'Hiya. So sorry. Ted and I slept in and I've only just got up. I'd forgotten we were fitting your dress today. Actually, I'd forgotten what day it was. Tea?'

I put Ella on the floor and nod. 'Mmmm, please. So am I going to meet him then?'

Clare avoids my eye. 'Um, oh, eventually, I expect. I, oh Christ, I forgot. I've got no milk! How about a Coke and we'll get started?'

I nod and smile as Ella and Ted begin their usual Mexican stand-off over Ted's musical telephone.

'Soooo, who is he then? How did you meet him?' I call into the kitchen. 'I'm so excited, and to think I was trying to fix you up! You didn't need my help after all, you dark horse.'

'Um, oh, he was . . . at the college when I did my course? We sort of knew each other a bit from around town and we just hit it off. We're just keeping it quiet for now though.' Clare comes back into the room and hands me a glass of flat Coke.

'He's not married, is he?' I ask, scandalised, almost hoping the answer will be yes.

'No! No, it's just . . .' The turmoil in Clare's face seems to

352

resolve itself. 'You know me, I have about as much luck with men as . . . well, I don't know, but not much luck, and I sort of feel that if I crow about it and how happy I am it'll go wrong and I'll be left feeling embarrassed again.'

I shrug. I understand how that feels.

'Fair enough, as long as you're happy. Are you happy?'

Clare's face lights up. 'Oh yeah, I am. Almost too much.' She surveys me critically. 'Right, now get your kit off. The dress is through there on the bed, so if you put it on and then come back out here I can start pinning it.'

For a moment, in the quiet environs of Clare's plainly decorated, corporation-style bedroom, and after the acres and acres of baby-pink netting and satin have settled around me, I pause and look at myself in her wardrobe mirror. It's a fairy-tale dress that Clare has made, and I'm certain that really she's made it for herself. All of the other costumes have been loosely based around the film version of *Calamity Jane*, but this dress is purely Clare's imagination made real. It's her dress, the one she dreams of dancing with her Prince Charming in, and she's had to make it for someone else. It looks wrong on me somehow. I mean it's all the wrong size, but beyond that it clashes with my pale and burnt skin and dark hair. And more than that, its exuberance, its optimistic romanticism, is meant for someone else. Someone who still believes.

On Clare it would look fabulous.

'Come on then!' Clare calls anxiously from the next room. I guess she's got a meeting planned with Mr Mystery later on.

'Oooh, doesn't Mummy look lovely?' Clare asks Ella as I swish into the room. Ella responds by gazing up at me with a dumbfounded expression before returning to beating up Ted's Tellytubbie with a wooden mallet.

I stand on a stool and Clare kneels at my feet as she begins to hem the dress.

'So how are you feeling about Monday, then? Excited?' she asks me through a mouthful of pins.

'Um, excited? No. Sick and terrified? More than you can know. I fully expect to be terrible.' I glance down at the dress. 'It should be you, anyway.'

Clare straightens up and begins to pin in the waist.

'Oh, you've lost a bit of weight since we cut this,' she says with a smile.

I stare down at myself incredulously. 'No I haven't. I can't have. Have I? Do you mean I was fatter than this?'

Clare grins, shaking her head. 'You're not fat.'

I smile, absurdly pleased with myself, and start humming 'A Woman's Touch'. After a while Clare chimes in with the harmony, and before we know it we are regaling our children with the full-length version, polkas around the room included.

We collapse on to her sofa full of laughter and Clare gives me the once-over with a critical eye.

'You look like you're born to wear this,' she says. 'Beautiful.'

'Yeah, right tasty.' Gareth leans in the door frame, his gaze lingering too long on my body. I take a step back, tripping over the hem of the dress.

'Get out!' I say quietly. 'Who the hell do you think you are, following me *here*?!' Get out, you're not welcome.'

Clare looks from me to Gareth to me and then back again.

'I know you fired him and all, Kitty, but steady on,' she says with half a smile, and then to Gareth. 'I thought you weren't coming back till after?'

I close my eyes and hope that I'm dreaming.

'Well, I wasn't,' I hear Gareth say. 'And then I thought I couldn't miss out on the chance to see my ex-boss in all her glory . . . *again*.'

Of course. Gareth is Clare's secret lover. Somehow it seems inevitable that it should be.

'Since when?' I manage to say to Clare, turning my face away from Gareth.

'Well, we've been "together" since the weekend?' Clare allows herself a small shy smile. 'I wasn't lying to you, Kitty, I did meet him after my college course. He just turned up one day and asked me for a coffee and it went from there, didn't it? And then things got a bit heated and we sort of just got together. Ted loves him.'

I stare at Gareth, shaking my head in disbelief.

'You were with Clare when you, when we . . .?'

Gareth shrugs.

'So? Anyway, I thought you wanted to keep it quiet?' The insolent tone in his voice, the indifferent expression on his face, every single thing about him is intolerable. I wish I could find a way to hurt him with my loathing, but somehow I know he's impervious to anything that I might feel.

'What do you mean? What's happened, Kitty?' Clare asks me. 'What were you doing with Gareth?'

I turn away, unable to speak, and pick Ella up. I have to get out of here, I have to get past him and get out of here *now*.

'Nothing, nothing happened,' I say, hoping that if Gareth cares for Clare at all he'll want to make what happened go away just as keenly as I do.

'Gareth?' Clare's voice is tight with anxiety. For a moment he seems to weigh the situation and I feel his eyes on me, waiting, just waiting, for me to look him in the eye. Finally I raise my face to meet his, and he can see me begging him not to tell her what happened.

'No point in hiding it now, Kitty, is there?' Gareth says almost lazily before turning to Clare. 'Kitty and I fucked up on the beacon. You know, the same place I took you the day before?'

A moment of stunned silence ricochets off the walls.

'How could you . . .' I begin, and I reach for Clare.

355

'You bitch, you stupid bitch!' She slaps my hands away and screams in my face. Ted begins to cry and then Ella's clinging on to the material of the dress, hiding her face from Clare's wrath and shaking. 'You just couldn't bear it, could you, to see someone else happy!' Clare lunges for me and I'm forced to grab hold of one of her arms and push her back a few inches.

'Clare, listen to me, I didn't know he was seeing you . . .' It comes out all wrong.

'Oh, so you wouldn't have done it if you'd known, would you? You wouldn't have cheated on your husband and your baby if you'd known? Well, how *big* of you.' Clare breaks free of my grip and backs away from me. 'Having everything not enough for you? Was that the problem? You disgust me. Get out. GET OUT!'

'Clare, please,' I say, trying not to look at Gareth. '*Please*! It wasn't like that, I didn't want to do it, he . . . he wouldn't listen to me when I said I wanted him to stop . . . Clare, he. . .' I can feel that with every fibre of his being Gareth wants me to say the word, he wants me to admit to what he already knows. I won't give him the satisfaction.

'*Get out! Get out now!*' Clare screams, and I pick Ella up and head for the bedroom. 'Now, I said!' Clare is hysterical, gasping for breath.

'But my clothes?' I say desperately. Gareth begins to move towards me, and in the confusion and the noise I'm not sure if he's going to hurt me again or not.

'I think you'd better go, don't you?' he says with a smile, and I just run past him, leaving the door banging open behind me; the last thing I hear is Gareth comforting Clare.

'I wanted to tell you, darling, but she said I couldn't. She was all over me and I just couldn't stop myself. It was nothing, though. She's nothing. You're the one I want. She's nothing.'

★

356

I've dreamt about walking into a classroom – or, when I was older, my office – naked, with everyone staring at me and covering their mouths with their hands. Eventually they can't keep a straight face any longer and chuckles turn into giggles and then into guffaws and I look down and see my inadequate flesh laid bare for their ridicule. Palpitating white and goosebumped all over. Everyone's had a dream like that.

However, I am fairly sure that no one in the thousand-, give or take a century, year history of Berkhamsted had rushed through its main streets and thoroughfares in a half-finished pastel-pink ballgown with a screaming and highly disturbed baby in a buggy. Heads did more than turn as I rushed by, wiping the tears from my eyes – they span three hundred and sixty degrees. People stood and watched me race past, murmuring to each other as I took a short cut past the British Legion and W.H. Smith's. One old man reached out to me as I hurtled by.

'Are you all right, dear?' he asked. 'Are you fund-raising?'

I shook my head and ploughed dangerously across the busy high street, fairly convinced that my visibility factor would never be higher, and cut up past the posh women's clothes shop that Georgina practically funds one-handed and headed into this park, Butts Meadow.

I'm lucky, the schools have not quite chucked out for lunch yet and there's no slouching parade of ruddy-cheeked boys in rugby gear filing back to their dorms nor the inevitable entourage of hiked-up-skirted comp girls flashing their highlights and jewellery at them in the hope of enticing something a bit different for lunch. There is just one woman plodding round the back of the park with her dog at her heel and that's all. Sniffing, I wheel Ella into the children's play area, and, lifting her out of her pram, settle us both on the swing, the skirts of the dress riding up around me like demented fairy wings.

'Mummy's gone and done it now,' I tell Ella shakily, but she's already asleep before the swing has completed its first inverted arc, and I worry that she'd rather be unconscious right now than awake with everything that's gone on. 'Daddy's going to find out about what happened all the wrong way, and Mummy's going to lose him.' My voice wobbles and I add dramatically, 'Don't worry, though, I'll make sure you two always see each other, all the time. You won't miss out. You'll be best friends.'

A woman, her hair bound up under an orange chiffon headscarf, comes out of the back of her house and peers at me conspicuously for a second, clearly debating whether or not a distraught young woman in a huge pink dress falls under her remit as the local neighbourhood watch co-ordinator.

'Are? You? Okay?!' She asks me the three questions loudly and slowly as if she imagines I might be foreign or mad or both.

'Fine,' I manage, and back it up with a snotty smile. The woman peers at me and opens her gate, which backs directly on to the park, before beginning a purposeful march across the field. As she gets closer, the awful truth sinks in. Underneath the scarf and despite the absence of make-up it's clear that it's Caroline, Director-Dictator, Human Megaphone Caroline.

'It *is* you, Kitty Kelly? What on earth are you doing sitting on a swing in my costume like that! I have never advocated method acting, if that's what you think you're up to! What kind of publicity do think you're garnering? Unlike Oscar Wilde, I am a firm believer in bad publicity and . . .' She catches sight of Ella huddled amid the netted up blossom of the skirt that is bunched around my shoulders. 'And frankly this kind of behaviour is intolerable,' she whispers considerately. 'You'd better have a darn good excuse, my lady.'

I push her to the brink of implosion by blowing my nose on the skirt, and turn my red-rimmed eyes to meet her face.

'Well, I have as good as ruined my marriage and thrown away

the only good thing that has ever happened to me, the man I love more than anything, except Ella.' I had meant to say that I was fine and that I was just checking the gown for a range of movements, but it turns out I am too tired to make anything up.

Caroline sighs heavily and holds out her hands.

'Give me the baby: you'd better come in for a drink and tell me about it, I suppose.'

I consider the options. Probably right now, at this very moment, Clare is imparting her new-found information to Fergus and my life is crumbling slowly away to nothing. For all these months I haven't really even been sure if it's the life that I've wanted or was even meant to have, and now that it's going I can't bear the thought of letting go of it. Caroline may very well scare both of us to death in her house, but whatever lies in wait there can't be worse than what won't be waiting for me at home.

'Okay,' I mumble, and I hand her Ella, who she hoists over one shoulder like a sack of sleepy potatoes.

'Never had children,' she informs me as if I couldn't tell. 'Never saw the point in them. Very untidy.'

Caroline's house is rather different than I imagined. I imagined a regimented, tastefully decorated Victorian interior with the odd art nouveau theatre poster framed against Rennie Macintosh-style wallpaper. Instead it's eighties peach and grey, furnished with a beige velour sofa, and the place is covered with magazines and newpapers, cuttings and clippings littering every surface including the floor. At first glance I can't see any link in their content at all, they're not even reviews of the Players' efforts over the years.

'Are you mad?' I find myself asking her, presumably because my basic social skills have finally been eroded to nothing. 'I mean, what's all this . . . crap for?' I gesture at the piles of paper as Caroline clears one of them off the sofa and on to the carpet before laying Ella gently down and wedging her in place with a brown velveteen cushion.

'Mad? No, I am not mad in the sense that I'm insane. I am frequently quite angry, however. No, this "crap" is because I'm writing a novel. I cut things out, keep the things that interest me that I want to use as material. You can't just make stuff up, you know!' She self-consciously touches the headscarf which I can now see is hiding the plastic hairnet which in turn is covering a half-baked concoction of bright red hair dye. 'We'll have to sort you out in the ten minutes – I don't want to go orange again. The last time I went too orange Colin got all uppity and attempted a coup. Tea or whisky?'

'Whisky,' I say instantly, and she hands me a gratifyingly large half-full tumbler.

'Have you nearly finished it, your novel?' I ask her, delaying the inevitable.

'Oh, good Lord, no. I haven't actually started writing it yet. Planning is the key. I'm planning it as we speak. Meticulously.' She gestures to her personal paper mountain. 'So, you gave in and slept with that Gareth chap, the scenery boy, did you?' I blink and take another gulp of Tesco's finest blended whisky. I'd always thought she'd be a single malt woman.

'How do you know!' I exclaim in a splutter as the back of my throat ignites. 'Does everyone know!'

'No, dear, but everyone knows he was after you. I suppose you didn't see it for yourself whilst you were up on stage, but he watched you like a wolf tracking his prey. Those pretty eyes fixed on you just waiting, as if it were inevitable.' She downs her whisky. 'I must say, I'd hoped you wouldn't go for his rather obvious Celtic charms. But I suppose young women are foolish.'

I look at Ella, so like her daddy in repose, and I feel like removing my heart and handing it over to Caroline now. I don't want to be the foolish girl who fell for his obvious charms; that wasn't me.

'I didn't,' I say at last, weary now with the strain of pretence. 'I didn't give into his charms, he forced them on me. Even when I said no, he went ahead and did it anyway and I wasn't scared, not really, or hurt or anything, so I wasn't really sure what had happened, if it was his mistake or his . . . intention. But I do know I didn't want it to happen and he didn't care.' I shrug miserably. 'And now he's managing to convince everyone that it was me that wanted it, and Fergus doesn't know yet but he will, and he'll leave me. He won't even want to look at me, he'll just go.'

Caroline watches me levelly for a long time, her hooded eyes apparently naked of lashes now.

'So you must tell him the truth. Fergus first and then the police.'

I shake my head. 'I can't, Caroline, I can't tell the police. Not days later when I've told no one what happened except for you . . . oh, and Dora. Like I say, there were no bruises, no marks, no evidence. I went with him of my own free will, I let him kiss me. The police won't believe me, and neither will Fergus.'

Caroline taps the side of her glass with a long nail.

'Well, my dear, you must tell Fergus the truth anyway, it's the only thing you have left and it's the only thing worth saying. If he believes you, then he loves you as much as you hope he does, because he'll be able to see the truth in your eyes. If he doesn't, then he was never the man for you. Another whisky?'

I shake my head as Caroline pours out another dram for herself.

'But you're wrong, he is the man for me. He is, but I don't think he'll ever be able to love me again after I've done something so disgusting. If I'd wanted Gareth, if I'd loved him, in a way it wouldn't be so bad. But I let him use me, I let him use Fergus's wife, the woman he cherishes, Ella's mum, like a dirty magazine. Fergus will never get over that.'

We all jump as Caroline's egg timer rings shrilly. Ella's hand flies out in surprise but she doesn't wake.

'You didn't let him do anything, my dear,' Caroline says, poking at her headscarf. 'And at the end of the day all you will have left is the truth.' She reflects on her own words for a moment and then scribbles them down along the empty margin of a newspaper.

'Are you going to put me in your book?' I say sulkily.

'Oh no, dear, my book's about the dark secrets of Berkhamsted.' She taps the side of her nose with her long, bony finger. 'Now, off you go and get out of my costume. If you drop it into Sketchley's this afternoon, I'll pick it up and take it round to Clare's for finishing, to avoid any nastiness. Okay?'

I stare at her and she waves a dismissive hand in my face.

'Have you never heard the phrase "The show must go on?"'

Somewhat numbed by a combination of the Real Caroline Thames and whisky it occurs to me halfway down the street that she could at least have offered to lend me something a tad less conspicuous to wear home, but maybe she liked the poetic justice of it all. The thought of the fairy-tale princess arriving back to her crumbling palace to claim her true love . . . or something. I'm a bit pissed. I think she gave me a quadruple.

In any case, I feel as if this dress is really the only thing I should be wearing today on the last day of my dream of happiness. The intensity of the sun burns right through its faint gauze and I feel my skin prickle and pucker under its heat, stung, intermittently, by the various pin sticks. It is sort of like a fairy-tale version of sackcloth and ashes.

I thank God that I left my bag, with my keys and purse in it, in Ella's buggy when I went up to Clare's, and that I am able to let myself into the quiet cool of the hallway. I'll sit down and have a long cool glass of water and think about what I'm going to do next. With some time and space to myself I might be able to find the right way, the right solution, a way to make everything better. The key is to not jump in without thinking.

I wander, shell-shocked, into the kitchen and for a terrible confused moment I thinks it is Gareth sitting there, but it's not. It's Fergus.

Fergus has beaten me to it. He's sitting with the back door open, staring out at the garden, a glass of iced water in his hand, his shirt unbuttoned at the neck, his tie discarded.

'Oh!' I say softly. He lifts his head and, as he takes in my appearance, his face lights up with delight, but it's a pleasure that is covering some other thinly veiled emotion.

'My God! You always said you'd wear your wedding dress shopping and now you finally are! What's going on?'

I can tell his bravado is false – his sweet smile stops short of his hurt and anxious eyes. My blood runs cold with fear and my mind races. Don't rush in, don't rush in. Take your time to think about what you are going to say . . .

'Oh, this.' I twitch at the skirt with nervous fingers and roll my eyes. 'You'll never believe it – I had this terrible fight with Clare, a stupid one really, and she threw me out. Why are you home?'

Fergus takes a measured moment and I hold my breath until I think my heart might burst with the anticipation and fear.

'Today was the day.' He shrugs. 'I got in and Tiff was already gone. The stupid cow from HR was in my office packing all my "personal effects" into a box. It was like I had bloody died. I had to leave immediately. Six years I've been there, and I couldn't even stay until the end of the day in case I ran off with some industrial secrets. They even took back my laptop. She told me the details of my redundancy package would be in the post and that I shouldn't think of it as an ending but as a beginning. Oh, and that telephone counselling was available until the end of the month, after which I assume we should just go and top ourselves.' He smiles wryly. 'So I came home, only place left to go.'

I know that the relief I feel is a betrayal, but as I go to him and hold him all I can think about is that now I'll have the chance to tell him how things happened my way, in my own time, before anyone else does.

'I feel sort of free in a way,' Fergus says in measured tones. 'In fact, when I came in through that door I was really quite happy. I mean, so what if the house and the home I've worked my bollocks off to keep for you is going on the market in the morning? I've got you and Ella, haven't I?' I don't hear the tightening in his voice until it's too late. 'That's what I thought when I came in? I've got you, haven't I, Kitty?'

I pull back from him hearing the edge in his voice, and I stare into his unreadable and suddenly hard-edged face.

'Of course you've got us. Always,' I say, forcing a smile. 'And it is a new beginning in a way. The one that we need. Fergus, we need to get away from here . . .'

He slaps my hands away from him and shakes his head angrily.

'You were never going to tell me, were you?'

It begins then: the tiniest tear in the corner of my heart.

'Tell you what?' I say, my words dropping dead out of my mouth.

Fergus gets up abruptly and walks into the hallway. I hear the click and whirr of the answerphone, and then Clare's voice, angry, impulsive and vengeful, fills the house.

'I just wanted to say that I'll give you until tonight to tell Fergus you've been fucking Gareth and if you don't I will. It's up to you.' The tear rips right through me then, bisecting my heart. Everything is over.

'Oh that,' I say to myself.

Fergus walks back into the kitchen and without looking at me, he crouches and gently lifts the sleeping Ella out of her buggy, his eyes full of tears, and turns his back on me. For a moment I think he's going to leave with her, run away and leave me behind, and I run out into the hallway with him, but instead he's carrying her up the stairs, kissing her hair as he goes, and holding her so tightly he might even wake her.

I sink on to the bottom stair, waiting for the horror to kill me, but I'm still alive when Fergus returns. He steps over me and walks into the living room and I follow him, wishing that there was something, anything, I could do to turn the seconds back from this moment.

'When?' His voice is low but full of a fury that I never knew he was capable of. There's no point in trying to hide anything now.

'Wednesday,' I say. 'But . . .'

'Wednesday! You went with him and then came home and said all that crap to me. You slept with me after him!' Fergus's face crumbles. 'I don't know you. I don't know who you *are*. Don't you remember how often we talked about what infidelity does to a marriage? How both of us knew that if it happened we could never go back? How we told each other it would never happen to us? Never?'

'But Fergus, let me explain what . . .'

Fergus shakes his head, chopping his hands through the air angrily to silence me.

'How often?' he demands.

'Just once,' I say rushing on. 'Fergus, listen, please listen to me, it was . . .'

He cuts across me, his force of emotion obliterating my voice.

'Don't tell me it was *nothing*, that it meant *nothing* to you, it was a *mistake*. Don't tell me – you were unhappy, curious,

365

vengeful.' His voice is bitterly sarcastic. 'There is no way back from this, Kitty, no way. None.' Finally he looks at me. 'When I came home today it didn't matter about my job or the house because I had you and Ella, and I realised that wherever you two were that was my home. And then I played that message and now I know all I ever had was an empty sham. I have nothing; you've even taken my daughter.'

He reaches behind a chair and pulls out his overnight bag. 'I can't talk to you at the moment, I'm going to Mum and Dad's. In a few days I'll be in touch to talk money and access to Ella . . .' His voice breaks and his face is wet with tears.

Galvanised by panic, I scramble to stop him leaving, to make him hear me. 'But Fergus, I love you,' I say as he heads for the door and turns, unable to look at me full in the face.

'You just tell Ella that I love her, that I love her so much. You just tell her.'

'I will,' I say, and he's gone.

Caroline was wrong. It doesn't matter what the truth is or what you think the truth is, sometimes the universe takes hold of its purity and pollutes it, ruins it beyond all recognition until it is something else entirely. My truth is no good to me now, it's just a reminder of everything I've lost.

'Daddy loves you,' I tell Ella, who's been sitting at my feet for the last few minutes bashing her stacking cups together. 'He loves you, so much, and he always will.' She won't miss him yet, he's hardly been in before eight the last few weeks. It'll be the weekend when she begins to realise he's not here any more.

The front door slams and for a moment I think he's come back and my head lifts . . . Then I remember. Dora.

'Hi, hiya.' She plonks her bag on the sofa and drops to the floor next to Ella and balances a cup on her head. 'Got to tell you, Hemel Hempstead – a bit fuck me new town, but in general not as bad as I thought it was going to be. Pleasantly surprised. Wouldn't move there but wouldn't recommend its immediate annihilation either. Fuck, he's found out about you and the gardener?' She runs the revelation seamlessly into her sentence, keeping her tone even and calm.

I nod, stuffing the hem of the T-shirt I'd changed into into my mouth, not wanting Ella to notice that I'm crying again.

'Only he heard Gareth's version first and now it's just like I said it would be. He hates me for betraying him.'

'How! What happened?' Dora maintains a sing-song voice and rebalances the cup on her head, which make Ella laugh nearly as much as when it slides off.

I tell her about Clare finding out and the message on the answerphone.

'What a scum,' Dora coos. 'Jesus, whatever made you want to go with him, Kits?' If ever I needed Dora the warrior princess it's now.

'I didn't want to, not in the end. I mean at first, when he first came here, he was so gentle, Dora. And sexy and funny and he had this kind of powerful . . . presence. He made me feel like a woman again, instead of just a lump of flesh. Fergus loves me and wanted me, but when Gareth looked at me he just saw a woman, not a mother or a wife. At least, that's what I thought he saw, but actually he was just seeing something he could never have.' I formed each word with a careful calm tone. 'Something he wanted to stamp out.'

Ella lifts her head and looks at me frowning. She crawls towards me and pulls herself up, asking to be lifted on to my lap. I hold her and attempt a smile as she pats my cheeks with her hands.

'Oh, mate, just let me think of who I know, of what I can do to sort him out. I can arrange it, you know.' Dora's stillness is the best indicator of her fury that I've ever seen.

'Dora, don't be foolish, you'd just get yourself into trouble, really.'

Dora's dark eyes flash at me. 'I'm not joking,' she says, her voice cold.

'I know, and that's what scares me.' I manage a weak smile.

'Would he be at Clare's now?' she says with quite menace.

'Dora, no, you can't go round there, you'll make things a hundred time worse and anyway, he'd snap you in two.' I plead with her, lost in the strangely surreal conversation where each one of us is trying to keep the emotional charge out of our voice.

'I just want to talk to Clare, set her straight, that's all,' Dora says. 'Then maybe she can talk to Fergus.'

'No,' I tell her with determination.

'Well Fergus then,' she begs.

'No! God, no!'

Dora comes and sits next to me, taking one of Ella's hands in hers and shaking it.

'Let me do something! Please! You can't let that ... thing ruin what you have. You need Fergus. I need you to have Fergus, you are my family. I can't let that slip away, Kitty. I don't think you realise what it means to me.'

I squeeze her hand and lay my head on her shoulder. 'You are here and that's all I need.'

Dora kisses my forehead and pulls herself up off of the sofa.

'I'm calling Camille, it time to get the musketeers together. The three of us, we'll sort it out. I promise you.' She pauses in the door frame. 'Fergus loves you more than life. This won't be the end. It can't be.'

Camille will be here soon. After Dora called her they spoke for a long time on the phone while I gave Ella her tea, and then Dora came into the kitchen and smiled at me, her kind of gung-ho battle-frenzy smile which means she is making an attempt at looking reassuring. It's unnerving.

'She says she'll be here by seven; she'll phone in sick tomorrow and that gives her five working days off, and then if we need her after that she'll get a doctor's note.'

I breathe a sigh of relief before saying, 'Hang on, don't you have to be properly ill to get a doctor's note? Propping up a terminally tragic friend doesn't count, does it?'

Dora rolls her eyes and, taking Ella's spoon out of my hand, flies it into her mouth with kamikaze special effects.

'You can't be me for as long as I have been,' she tells me mid-dive bomb, 'without getting some official-looking headed notepaper and sick-note pads, duh.'

'Of course!' I say. 'Of course, how could be I be so stupid?'

Dora shrugs and begins to clean Ella up, lifting her out of her chair and wiping her face.

'Can I give her a bath?' Dora says. 'I know the basics – not too much hot water, not too much water full stop, can't leave her alone for longer than a couple of minutes.' I open my mouth in horror. 'Joke – just a minute. Joke! Not at all.'

I press my lips together and cross my arms over my chest.

'One day you can explain this new-found maternal instinct to me. But yes, I guess you can give her a bath, but please be careful. That thing about babies being able to swim instantly – it's a myth.'

Dora and Ella giggle complicitly as if they know differently, and she hikes her over her shoulder and heads for the stairs.

The phone starts ringing in the hallway. I want to know how it happened and when – when this small instrument became so pivotal in the lives of millions. What did they do before the phone? How did people know if their romantic existence was doomed or not? Did whey-faced ladies sit around parlours staring hard at the butler, wishing he'd bring them a note? Did they go to the front door and check the doorbell to make sure it was working? I want it to be Fergus. I want it to be him but I can't bear it if it is.

'Hello?' I pick up finally, before the caller rings off. I hold the receiver in both hands.

'Kitty? How are you? What's going on?'

It's Georgina. He can't have told her what's going on, otherwise she'd never sound so civilised. I'm trying to think of the best thing to say when I hear the sound of my own voice running on without me.

'He's got it wrong, Georgina. He thinks I wanted someone else, that I wanted us to break up. But I didn't want it to happen. I mean, I don't mean that it was a mistake, I mean, it *was* a mistake, of course it was. What I mean is, I didn't want it to happen in the first place. I was angry and I lost my temper, but then things got out of hand and . . . Does Fergus really hate me? I'd do anything. Anything,' I say, out of breath and scrambling up everything I want to say in one frantic speech.

There is a long pause, and I get the feeling that Georgina's hand is over the receiver and that she's talking to someone, maybe Fergus. When she does speak again, her voice is measured, not hostile exactly, but not far off.

'He told me you had an affair. I can't believe it, Kitty, I really can't. I know we've had our differences, but I said to him it didn't seem like you at all, that you may not have been the best at the practical side of things, but that it was plain that you loved him. He said you confessed it, that there was no doubt, and something about a message? I just wanted to hear it from you myself.'

I look up the length of the stairs to where Ella's near-hysterical shrieks are drowning out Dora's experienced rendition of 'What Shall We Do with the Drunken Sailor?'

'It wasn't an affair, Georgina. It was . . . I don't know how it happened. I felt trapped and almost beguiled. It happened only once, it was the most revolting and degrading experience of my life. I only thought that if I told Fergus, if it came out, I'd attach some meaning to it, and I didn't want there to be any. So I tried to forget about it, but, well, everyone knows now. I love Fergus, I love him so much, I'd do anything to make him see that, but at the very least I want the chance to explain it to him.'

Georgina is silent for a moment.

'He's asleep now, has been since he got here. Went up to his room and refuses to come out. He was always like this as a boy – the first hint of worry and he'd take to his bed.' I can hear her nail tapping against the phone. 'Listen, I'm not sure what you're telling me, but whatever happened I do believe that you love my son and that he loves you. I've had a second chance once, and you deserve one. Come and see him tomorrow. He'll be a bit calmer and maybe you'll be able to explain.'

Tears of gratitude prick at my eyes and I swallow hard.

'I never thought you'd be so kind,' I say at last.

Georgina sort of huffs. 'Neither did I,' she says. 'But let me tell you, if it turns out you're lying to me, things will be quite different. Do you understand?'

'I understand.'

As I hang up the phone, feeling faintly buoyed, Dora comes down the stairs with Ella, resplendent in a pair of bear pyjamas complete with a hood, ears and a tail.

'Good God,' I say. 'What have you done to my daughter. More to the point, what have you done with my best friend? You might know her – short blonde hair, skinny, incurable cynic and fatalist with disdain for small children?'

'I know!' Dora coos. 'It's so cute, isn't it? I saw it in the shop in Hemel and it was meant to be a surprise to say thanks for having me. She looks gorgeous, like an ickle bear! Don't you, an ickle-ickle baby bear!'

I stare at Dora, wondering if her years of inebriation have covered up the fact that she's actually Julie Andrews, in which case maybe sobriety isn't the answer.

'Come on mate, let's get your milk on and let Mum have a sit-down.' Dora winks at me as she heads for the kitchen.

When the doorbell rings I pray that it's Camille, somehow miraculously early, and hopefully with an Indian takeaway for six. It isn't – it's Mr Crawley. He looks at me reproachfully.

'Caroline sent me . . . for the dress?' he explains. 'She said she thought the chances of you remembering to take it to the dry-cleaner's were pretty slim under the circumstances, and Sketchley's opens till eight on a Thursday, so she sent me to pick it up.'

I step aside and let him in, marvelling at Caroline's single-minded relentlessness, which she seems to apply to every part of her life except her novel.

'How are you, my dear?' Mr Crawley stops and looks at me so tenderly that I can feel the tears threatening instantly behind my eyes.

'Am I okay? Yep, yep, fine,' I say stiffly. 'Did Caroline tell you anything else?' I challenge him.

'She told me everything else . . .' Mr Crawley begins.

'Oh great!' I fling my hands out in exasperation. 'That's fantastic. The whole of bloody Berkhamsted is going to know about it by tomorrow, aren't they?'

Mr Crawley shakes his head, catches my angry hands, and holds them tight before nodding to the sitting room.

'Let's sit down. Now, Caroline won't tell anyone else. She told me because she knows that you and I are friends, and because, well, she and I are . . . well, we have an arrangement.' He smiles a little shyly.

'You and the she-Hitler are an item?' I exclaim, temporarily diverted.

372

'Well, close friends at least. We choose to keep it under our hats, though, if you don't mind. It's a casual thing, not love's middle-aged dream.'

I shrug and muse that I wouldn't be surprised right now if Colin turned up on the doorstep to tell me he'd been turned straight by Barbara in the prop cupboard.

'So, how are you? Really?' Mr Crawley asks me again.

'Hysterical and not drunk, unfortunately,' I say. 'And oddly all right. You sort of expect the sky to fall in, don't you, when something disastrous happens, but it hasn't and I'm still breathing and talking.' I consider the miracle momentarily before continuing. 'Fergus's mum called me just before you came and, well, I think she's sort of on my side. I mean, she's not totally against me and she's suggested I come round tomorrow to talk to him and to try and explain . . .' I trail off as I wonder what on earth I will be able to say to change the full force of fate that has landed on me like a ton of cosmic bricks over the last week. 'It will probably be a futile exercise, but it's a chink of light to keeping me going,' I tell him with an improbable smile.

'Good. And now what are you going to do about Gareth?' Mr Crawley looks awkward. 'Caroline says you won't call the police?'

I shake my head. 'I know I should, I know I have a responsibility, but I just can't go to the police because when you say it out loud it sounds like nothing happened! It's only here.' I tap the side of my head. 'It's only in here where it's terrible and dreadful. They'll listen to what I have to say, and that'll be that. Just like everyone else, they'll think it's an affair that went wrong and that I'm making it all up to try and get my husband back.' Even I think that sometimes, I think bitterly to myself. 'I'd like to be certain that I was blameless, but I can't.'

Mr Crawley puts an arm around my shoulder and I lay my head gratefully on his.

'I understand. Don't worry about Gareth,' he says as if he's arranging a fishing trip. 'I'll make sure he won't hurt you or anyone again.'

I sit up and look up him. 'Please don't tell me you know the Mafia too?' I plead with him.

He laughs and squeezes my shoulder reassuringly.

'I don't know the Mafia,' he says. 'But I do know how to get rid of a rat.'

Camille rushes into the room like a tropical hurricane, hot and furious.

'Oh baby!' she squeezes me tight, her warm skin branding me. 'Sorry I'm late.'

'Cam, it's okay, it's okay,' I say, disentangling myself from her long arms. 'I'm okay, really I am.'

Clearly disbelieving me, Camille grips my face between her hands and tips my head back, examining me like I'm a horse or something and she needs to see my teeth.

'Christ, you look like shit.' Her diagnosis is typically blunt. 'I'm so sorry I was late but just as I was about to leave . . . oh fuck it.' She clearly thinks better of offering up one of her stock excuses. 'I'm late because I am the sort of person who can never get their arse into gear. It's not my fault. It's genes. Or sheer ineptitude, one or the other.' She delves into her Valentino bag and brings out a half-bottle of brandy. 'I bought this because I thought you probably wouldn't be able to sleep very well.' She glances at Dora as she returns from putting Ella to bed. 'So I thought, Dors, that to make it fair I wouldn't have any either, and we'd just ply her with it until she's blotto and then I'll hide it or something, okay? And because Dora told me what happened and because I'm a coward and I don't know what to say to you, I thought it'd be easier to get you drunk. I'm sorry.'

I shrug and smile. 'Fair enough,' I say.

Camille makes us mugs of hot chocolate and I only have to smell mine to know that it is at least 31 per cent proof. The first sip burns my mouth and throat, but after the third or fourth sip I feel pleasantly numb and distant. Dora and Camille chatter on about anything they can think of that isn't about me, and the requisite number of hours before bedtime is allowed slowly – almost painlessly – to pass.

'This is sort of like old times, isn't it?' Camille says suddenly, no doubt trying to think of one of my nan's silver linings. 'I mean, it's a long time since we've sat around gossiping like this, and I know we've never actually lived together, unless you count that holiday cottage in Blackpool, but it sort of feels like we did, doesn't it?'

Dora eyes the bottom of her mug as if she hopes some brandy might lurk there after all.

There's a long and difficult pause.

'It sort of feels like a Harold Pinter play,' Dora says at last. 'I'm sorry, Kitty mate, but I'm running out of inane and distracting things to say. Shocking, I know.'

I force my mouth to bend into a smile.

'God, poor old Dora, comes down here to be looked after and ends up saddled with Calamity Kitty.' I hold out a limp hand to Dora. 'I'm sorry, mate, I haven't forgotten that scumbag in your flat, you know. When I'm sorted I'll go up there and beat him up for you.'

'Oh, no need!' Camille says as if she's suddenly remembered something. 'Boyfriend went round there yesterday before he had to fly back. Got him out, had the locks changed. Sorted.' She smiles at Dora. 'Sorry, I totally forgot, what with all this.' She gestures broadly and begins to look in her bag again. 'There's a set of keys in here . . .'

'I love your boyfriend,' I say with a slight slur. 'Why did he have to fly back yesterday? Why couldn't he stay and come down here and change my locks?'

Camille holds out a bunch of keys to Dora.

'Well, because you don't need your locks changing and because he flies the plane,' she says with a smile, although even I can see that her smile hides the fact that she misses him terribly when he's not here.

'Is it the absence thing, do you think?' I ask her out of the blue. She looks at me quizzically. 'I mean, that makes you so happy after so long. You've been going out for longer than some people are married.' I find that during the course of that sentence I slip off the edge of the armchair and slide seamlessly to the floor. 'Mentioning no names, of course,' I finish, wondering if Fergus and I really will be divorced before Ella is one.

'Well, I suppose the fact that we don't see other much keeps it fresh, for sure . . .' Camille looks a little wary about discussing her relationship, probably because she's sensitive about upsetting me, but I find that I really want to know how she's done it.

'You know, I don't like to analyse it too much. If I go on about how prefect he is and how much I love him, I'll tempt fate and, God only knows, I've tempted it far more than I should have already. We've just been good together. We knew what we wanted from the start and it works,' she finishes lightly, looking around the room as if casting about for a new subject.

Dora runs a finger around her empty chocolate mug and sucks it clean.

'Well, we should do something,' she says, 'apart from sitting around here getting all maudlin and drunk. We should make a plan of action to get Fergus back for Kitty. Yes, a list of pros and cons, and help her prepare a speech or something . . .'

Camille gets on to her knees and, taking my hands, pulls me into a sitting position.

'Yeah, she's right. Sit up, Kitty, we're going to sort you out and everything will be all right, every cloud has a silver lining.' She smiles brightly and I give her a long hard hug.

'I know, my nan always used to say that,' I tell her.

I stare at the darkened ceiling for a long time, listening for the sound of my mum's voice in the corners of the night. If only I could guess what she'd say now, if only I knew her well enough to know how she'd respond, but as hard as I listen there's nothing there except for shadows.

'Well, I could have told you that was going to happen,' Doris says, admiring her hair in my dressing-table mirror.

I roll over, hoping she'll take the hint and vanish instantly, but instead she just sits beside me on the bed, fixing me with that quizzical, practical stare of hers.

'How did you ever get to be a sex symbol?' I ask her cattily. 'And anyway, if you'd known, I wish you'd warned me or something!' I grumble. 'What's the point of dreaming about musical stars if they don't give you decent advice. Gene Kelly would've.'

Doris presses her shell-pink lips together and tips her head to one side.

'I'm ignoring that ungracious behaviour because I know you are a little overtired. And anyway, I did give you good advice. You ignored it. If you'd been a little more lady and a little less woman, you wouldn't be in this predicament. That's the trouble with you young women of today; you never listen, not even to your heart.'

Something other than my urgent desire to be out of this dream is calling me awake, but the brandy seems to be pressing me ever closer into the mattress.

'Doris, I've got to go,' I say urgently. 'Tell me what you've come to say, and it better not be that crimping my hair is the answer.'

Doris leans close to me and the scent of Dior washes over me. 'It seems to me that you never let your love for Fergus be free, it seemed to frighten you. Open up your heart – sing out how much he means to you. Don't keep your love a secret any more. Oh, and by the way, a wash and a trim wouldn't go amiss.' She winks and is gone. As I blink awake, Ella's cries pull back the bedcovers and compel me to her room before the imagined scent of Dior has fully evaporated.

'Oh Doris,' I say as I lift Ella out of her cot. 'If you insist on showing up, I wish you'd say something at least semi-coherent.' Ella buries her face miserably into my neck and I begin the ritual of elimination by finding some teething gel and rubbing it into her gums. If it's not that then it's wind, or she's thirsty or she just doesn't fancy sleeping right now thanks very much. In this one tiny aspect, though, fate seems to favour me for a change, and a few minutes later she is slumbering peacefully against my shoulder. I consider putting her back in her cot and creeping back to my own empty bed, and I consider taking her back to bed with me, but neither option seems to be quite right, so I sink into Fergus's stupid rocking chair, and as it rocks back under my weight it creaks a greeting.

I pull open Ella's curtain a chink and look down at the empty road and then up at the black presence of the hills that cancel out the stars along their horizon.

Fergus is just a mile or so away somewhere in that darkness.

I wonder if he's sleeping?

Chapter Twenty-three

My entire wardrobe is spread over the living room. Ella has made a sort of den in the discarded items as Dora and Camille road-test everything that I have until we find an outfit suitable for going to see your betrayed husband in. Personally I thought all black with a veil would have been a good idea, but Camille found the deep red top that suits me best and isn't too clingy, whilst Dora picked out some black bootleg trousers, a bit too heavy for the heat that the day promises, but they looked better on my arse than my summer trousers.

'This is obscene,' I say, watching Ella throw my discarded clothes over one shoulder only to spin around on her bum and start the process again. 'This is what you do when you go on a first date, not a last date, and anyway it's not going to help, is it? The way I look is not really going to make a difference.'

Camille stands in front of me, scrutinising my outfit and frowning unnervingly.

'You'd be surprised. I read this article about the fact that men can only understand the world visually, and anyway it will help you feel good about yourself, which in turn will give you confidence, which in turn will . . .'

'Make you come across as an arrogant and unrepentant cow?' Dora adds helpfully, wearing one of my bras on her head to the total indifference of an unamused Ella.

'Help you express your feelings more eloquently,' Camille finishes, flicking a warning glance at Dora.

'Or you could just take your clothes off. I find that is usually the best bargaining tool when it comes to men,' Dora says. 'That and fellatio.'

'Oh fabulous, Dora,' I say, flinging out my arms in despair. 'So, after all your list-making and speech-writing last night, your plan is that I go and offer my husband a blow job in return for his forgiveness? Brilliant.'

Dora shrugs and exchanges an 'oooooh, touchy' glance with Ella, whose head I sincerely hope this entire conversation has gone over.

'I'm just saying get your chops round their bits and they don't usually complain, that's all.' Dora looks a little petulant. 'It's just that when I read the speech we'd written last night it turned out to be drunken hysterical bollocks, and fellatio is my best Plan B.'

'It's your only Plan B,' I tell her.

'Okay, but you have to admit it's a good one.'

Even if there was an alternative route to Castle Kelly I would not choose to take it. I am hoping that as the main body of the town slips away behind me into the valley I will find the secret, the magic words that will make everything all right again.

Gradually the dense network of streets breaks up into detached plots until the countryside stretches out in full view beyond the last buildings, and what few properties there are are so detached that their gardens might as well be referred to as grounds. Castle Kelly is one of these – of course, it isn't really called Castle Kelly – that is my own plebeian nickname for the largest privately owned house that I have ever been in.

It was designed and built, Daniel told me proudly the first time I trembled on the threshold, by an architect in the 1930s, and its central sleek white tower rises a full four floors above the dense copse of mature trees that surrounds the house. As I approach it, the sound of traffic fades finally into nothing and I wonder how the architect would feel about the Virginia creeper that now covers a large part of that tower, spreading thickly over the window to what was once Fergus's bedroom. I can just make out through the plant's mysteriously rippling leaves that his curtains are closed. He must still be sleeping.

For a long time I stand in the porch looking at the deco sunburst cut into the door, waiting for inspiration to come, waiting to know what to say. But nothing comes, except that I realise that the flip-flop sandals Camille has picked for me are biting painfully into the spaces in between my toes. Daniel opens the door and looks at me, his face a picture of perfect neutrality.

'Are you coming in?' he says gently. I hesitate for a moment and step over the threshold. 'He's up there in his old room.' Daniel nods at the gently spiralling staircase. 'He's been there since he came. Georgina's seen him, but I haven't. I went up there last night and stood outside his room, talked through the door, you know? But nothing. You've hurt him badly, Kitty.' He considers me for a moment before saying finally. 'I don't think I was wrong about you, I still think you can make him happy, but please, be careful with him, okay?'

I nod anxiously and take the first step on the sweep of the spiral staircase that leads to Fergus until I'm standing outside his bedroom door.

I knock and wait. Nothing.

'Um, Fergus, it's me?' I pause. 'It's Kitty. Can I come in?' I say quietly, almost hoping not to wake him, desperately resisting the urge to run back down the stairs and out of this house, leaving the front door banging in my wake. When he doesn't reply I try again a little louder.

'It's Kitty!' I call. 'Please let me come in?' Nothing comes back at me but I hold my nerve. I've come this far, I can't turn back now. Doris would say that I mustn't keep my feelings a secret, that I must sing them out. How will Fergus ever know the truth if I don't tell him. I open the door and look in.

He's sleeping, wearing his huge 1980s headphones which are plugged into his old record player. I can faintly hear the tinny back-beat of whoever is on the turntable. His black hair is brushed back from his pale forehead, and even stubbled and unkempt as he is he looks about fourteen: sweetly vulnerable in a dangerous and unpredictable world. I go over to the record player and look at the LP crackling as it spins. The Stranglers. I lift the needle and return the arm to its rest, waiting for him to jerk awake or at least to show some sign of life. Instead he just lies there on his back, his arms flung over his head.

'Fergus, baby,' I whisper as I sit on the bed beside him. 'I'm sorry, so sorry.' I touch the tip of my forefinger to his forehead and trace a line down to the corner of his mouth, holding my breath as he smiles briefly in his sleep. Leaning closer just to be near him, I feel the heat radiate from his body and every moment that I move closer to him passes like a hundred years. I can feel my desire just to be with him vibrating, humming beneath my skin, and unable to resist any longer I kiss him, just touching my lips to his. I don't expect this new alabaster effigy to respond, somehow, but when he does, his mouth parting just slightly under mine, I kiss him again, more deeply. This time a small moan escapes from the base of my throat as I feel his arms surrounding me, crushing me into him, pulling me close, kissing me back, hard.

He opens his startlingly blue eyes and looks at me. 'Kitty,' he says simply before rolling me on to my back and kissing me again, insistently, deeply, his hands already finding my bare skin as he rakes his short nails down my back, kissing and biting gently at my ribs as he pulls my top over my head, pulling the straps of my bra down, ripping the lace away to expose my

382

breasts to his lips and hands. I pull him on to me, pushing myself against the strength of his body, daring to believe that this isn't a dream. I begin to unbutton my trousers but he pushes my hands away and, taking control, pulls them and my knickers down in one rough movement, working at his own fly at the same time until at last we are both naked, limb to limb, crashing and crushing one another with the weight of emotion around us, and he slides into me, strong and hard. I hear my own gasp as I feel him connecting with me on every level of my being.

Finding his face, we look into each other's eyes and I hold his gaze as each wave of sensation seems to weave us into an ever-closer embrace until I cry out, taken by surprise by my climax, clinging on to him. Moments later he follows me and crumples exhausted, breathless, in my arms. I feel the excruciatingly brittle edges of pure perfect happiness hard in my chest, and I allow myself to hope.

'Fergus . . .' I try to speak, try to begin, but he closes his fingers over my mouth, looking away from me before saying, 'Shhhh, don't say anything, please. Let's just have this moment. Let's just have this.'

It's when he speaks that I realise nothing's changed, that he hadn't meant for that to be a reunion.

He meant it to be a goodbye.

For a long time, as we lie in detached silence, I watch the shadow of the creeper outlined against the illuminated orange of Fergus's boyhood curtains, and I wait for him to break the quiet. We are still, side by side, no longer touching, a thin line of disconnection carefully laid between us. Finally he rolls on to his side and brings himself to look at me.

'I'm sorry,' he says. 'I shouldn't have done that. I've confused us both. I just, I've missed you and I wanted to be close to you again. It's so strange, isn't it? When you break up with your best friend, the one person you want to talk to about things isn't there any more.' He half smiles.

I sit up, drawing my knees up protectively over my breasts.

'Fergus, don't make us end like this. We don't have to end,' I appeal. 'Please, I want you to listen to me,' I say. 'I'm going to tell you everything. Just listen, please, because if you're going to let this . . . this *pointless mess* split us up, I want you to know exactly why.'

Fergus looks resigned and crosses his arms behind his head. 'Go on,' he says.

As I talk, I notice that his eyes stray purposefully from my face and fix instead on the blank, curtain-covered circle of window, its filtered light reflecting on the still, white planes of his face. Watching him as I tell him about that morning, I look for anything in his face that shows he's still listening or understanding, but there is nothing there except an ever-increasing remoteness and a quiet, coldly burning detachment.

'Are you listening to me?' I break my narrative, unable to prevent myself sounding like an irritable wife interrupting the Sunday football.

Fergus's bright blue eyes lock on to my face.

'Sorry, did you want me to applaud you or something? Bravo.'

I had thought that the only way to make him understand was to tell the whole truth from the beginning, and that included my decision to go with Gareth that morning instead of getting on a train to London to see him. I'd only succeeded in hurting him all the more.

'Look,' I say, reaching for his hand. 'I know this is hard, but I went with him because . . . because for every day since I met you someone in the world has known where I am. I've been a girlfriend and a wife and a mother. I have never been just me, not for months. It was a stupid, impulsive thing to do, but I wanted to feel free, just for a little while. It wasn't him that I wanted; it was a little open space?'

He pulls his fingers abruptly out of mine and gestures for me to continue.

'So we got up there and it was so beautiful and then I told him about Mum . . .' I begin.

'You told him about your mum?' Fergus interrupts. 'But you told me that you've only spoken about that to people who you trust, who you love. When you told me about that I really believed it meant something between us,' he says angrily, suddenly sitting up, pulling his shirt on over his head and hunting around the floor for his boxers. Odd how even now, like this, we still feel fine to be naked in front of each other.

'No, listen. He persuaded me to tell him. He told me that he'd understand. He told me things about himself that made me think he would, he'd . . .' I see Fergus staring hard at a Smiths poster on his wall and I trail off realising how it must look to him. When we spent that night together talking about how my mum had been murdered, it was almost like I was giving him a gift, a gift of my trust and my faith in him and our future together. All he can see now is that I gave this to someone I hardly knew, someone who for reasons unknown made me feel free even as he entrapped me.

'I don't know why I told him – maybe because I thought he wouldn't pity me. I was right about that, at least. But I do know why he wanted me to. He wanted me to be vulnerable, emotional. He wanted a reason, an excuse, to touch me, to initiate things.'

Fergus sits back on the edge of his single bed with his back to me. I hesitate, but I know I have to say it. 'For a while, I thought that I wanted it too. But it wasn't real. It was just a stupid fantasy, escapism. I never expected it to actually happen.'

I watch Fergus's back but he doesn't move. 'And he did, he

did kiss me and from the moment, the very *second*, it happened, I knew what he wanted and that and I didn't want it, that I only wanted you and Ella and everything that we had together, so I . . .'

'Fucked him.' Fergus spits the word like an assault. The tension across his shoulders speaks volumes as I watch him slipping further and further away for me.

'No. No.' I reach out a hand to touch his shoulder, recoiling from him as he flinches. 'I didn't know what to do. I was in the middle of nowhere, I thought it would be best to sort of put him off, you know, say that I didn't want things to go too fast. That we'd better be getting back. I told him I didn't want it to happen any more, that I just wanted him to take me home. I said I didn't want it, but he didn't listen.' For a moment I find myself caught in the heat and the wind of that moment and my heart panics, clenching tightly. 'I thought I'd got out of it, I was laughing because the whole thing was so absurd. He even said he understood, that it wasn't a problem. As he said that, it happened. It was like he was saying one thing and doing another.'

Fergus snorts in disbelief.

'He raped me, Fergus,' I say quietly. 'It was quick and brutal, it was over even before I knew what it was, but it was rape. I didn't want him, but what I wanted didn't come into it.' I wait for him to understand.

He stands up and goes to the window, pulling back the curtains and throwing it open, and for a moment the bright light dazzles us both.

'Bullshit,' he says, and at first I don't hear him, or I don't want to.

'What?' I say. 'What do you mean? I said that he . . .'

'Raped you. Right.' Fergus looks at me at last, his eyes dark with fury, his face filled with disgust. 'You go up there with him voluntarily. You just told me a second ago that you wanted to go with him instead of coming to see me. You said you wanted to be *free*! You get all cosy and emotional, you even give him the dead mother test!' I stare at him in disbelief as he picks up one of my flip-flops and throws it on to the bed.

'What do you mean? What test?' I ask, astounded.

'The murdered mum test. You only ever roll that one out when you're planning to fuck, darling – I should know.' He starts gathering up my clothes and throwing them at me. 'I mean, you wouldn't want to give yourself to a man who couldn't play up to your perpetual victim complex would you? And then it went wrong, it wasn't how you imagined it, maybe your poor desperate needy husband wasn't as bad in the sack as you'd thought. Or maybe after trying you out he didn't want you any more and you realised that you'd blown it with me and fucked up our family and now all you can come up with, all you can manage is that "he raped me".' He mimics a cruel falsetto. 'Very fucking original, Kitty.' He flings the last of my clothes at me. 'Now get dressed and get out!' He bangs open his door and I hear him running down the stairs.

There's nothing in my mind now as I pull on my clothes and the one flip-flop he hurled at me – just pure rage. Anger at myself, hatred for Gareth, and rage at Fergus. Fury that this man I believed to be the perfect one could be so wrong, so flawed. Outrage that even now, even after each one of those words, I still love him. I almost tumble down the stairs after him, bouncing off the curved walls, and I race to catch him.

'He held me down when I said no!' I scream at him, dimly aware of Georgina and Daniel staring at me from the breakfast table. I hold my forearm across my neck. 'He pressed his arm over my windpipe like this, so that I couldn't move, I could hardly even breathe . . .'

Fergus pushes me hard and I almost lose my footing.

'Get out!' he screams at me, trying to turn away, but I run to him and drag him round to face me. 'He forced me to have sex with him, Fergus, he raped me and I'm sorry, I'm really sorry I haven't got any bruises to show you, or blood. I'm sorry that it's easier for you to believe that I wanted it, but it's the truth!' I scream in his face, and for a second, just a hair's breadth apart, we watch each other; our heaving breaths labouring under the weight of our lives.

'You went there with him of your own accord,' Fergus says deliberately.

'But not to sleep with him, never to do that,' I reply with steadfast determination.

'Then why no police, why when I came home a couple of hours later weren't you a trembling wreck. You were fine, Kitty. You were absolutely fine. Just a bit hungover, that was all, and a bit worried about our fight. At least that's what I thought. You must have been shitting yourself that I'd find out . . .' Fergus spits at me.

'Fergus! Son, please.'

Fergus shakes off Daniel's restraining arm.

'You fucked me after him, and you hadn't even deigned to take a bath. I'd better get tested, hadn't I? God only knows what you might have given me.'

I feel it then, the last thread that holds us together snap and wither away

'You don't understand,' I say finally, exhausted, defeated. 'I told myself it was my fault, that I let it happen, but that it was nothing, nothing when I compared it to how much I love you. I knew you could make it into nothing when you came home, and you did.' I step back from him. 'Maybe I was wrong. I must have been wrong about us, because if I'd been right, if we're really meant to be together, then I know one thing for certain.'

'What?' Fergus shrugs.

'That you'd believe me when I was telling the truth,' I say.

As I head on to the boiling drive Fergus calls after me.

'I want Ella tomorrow. Mum'll pick her up at ten, okay?'

I stop for a second, almost unable to hear him.

'Fine,' I say without turning back, and I head back into the valley. It's only when I've crossed Shooter's Way that I realise I've only got one flip-flop on.

'He didn't believe you!' I notice the tiny crinkle of disbelief between Camille's brows, and blink, sweat stinging my eyes. Since I stumbled in through the front door both of my friends have been looking at me as if they are hoping I might be lying. I didn't cry, I think to myself absently. That's strange. Normally I can cry for England at the drop of a hat. My husband calls me a liar and a whore and I'm dry as the Gobi desert. Weird.

'He's got my flip-flop,' I say stupidly, examining the filthy sole of my bare foot and musing on its significance. There isn't one, of course.

Dora helps Ella build up her recently demolished tower of bricks again, shaking her head.

'But . . . I mean, what?' she says, incredulous.

'He said I was making it up to try and get back with him,' I shrug. The walk in the near-noon sun on the way back has melted all of my fear, frustration and anger into one messy stupor. I can't be sure what I'm feeling any longer.

'But . . . but Fergus loves you. He has to believe you.' Camille says, returning from the kitchen with a glass of cold water. 'I mean, it's you and it's Fergus and he loves you! This is the wrong ending. It's got to be. Things like you and Fergus don't end like this, over something like . . . a stupid mistake. That's not how it's supposed to be!' She looks around the living room as if she can pluck the answer out of the dust-moted air.

'I know,' I say slowly, methodically. 'That's what I thought too. I thought, "Oh well, Kitty, you've fucked up big time, but it's okay because Fergus loves you and you love him and love conquers all, etc. etc." But it turns out it doesn't and he didn't.' I smile wanly at Ella as she holds out one of her beloved bricks to me in a rare gesture of magnitude. 'Who would've thought it, hey?'

Dora shakes her head.

'Well, I don't think it. I know that this world is a different place now. I know that awful things happen to good people, but I know that Fergus loves you, I know he does. He might not believe you for whatever fucked-up reason, but he still loves you because that kind of love, Kitty, doesn't just evaporate into thin air.' She crosses her arms thoughtfully. 'All we've got to do is show him that you're not lying, somehow.'

I smile at her.

'Dora, you don't get it,' I say sadly. 'If he doesn't believe me it doesn't matter if he loves me or not. It's over.'

Camille and Dora look at me and then at each other and I pick up Ella off the carpet and hold her close for as long as she can bear.

'There's no way back from this.'

'What do you mean?' Camille asks me cautiously, as I set the struggling baby down.

'I mean that the whole point of us, the whole point of Fergus and me was that he was supposed to be The One, you know, my perfect match, my other half, my soulmate like in all those books. He was supposed to be the end of the rainbow, and together we were supposed to be perfect.' I looked at Dora. 'You're right, awful things do happen to good people, but in all of this I never really expected, I never *really* thought, he would doubt me. I thought somehow he'd always be on my side, by my side no matter what happened. I was wrong.'

I kick my remaining flip-flop forcefully into the corner of the room. 'There's no way back from this. It's over.'

Chapter Twenty-four

'Good girl,' Caroline whispers in my ear. 'Just try not to think about anything but the show and you'll be fine. Remember, the show . . .'

'. . . must go on, yes, Caroline,' I say irritably. 'Yes, I understand that, but at the time I didn't think it had to go on with me wearing a costume that had been altered for a mystery person who is two sizes smaller than me and quite a few feet shorter!'

The murmur of the crowd behind the heavy curtains subsides and Bill's five-piece band, consisting largely of hungover and ironic sixth formers, begins to play the overture.

It's the last five minutes before the first night of the Berkhamsted Players' Summer Festival production of *Calamity Jane*, and it seems that Clare has wreaked her revenge by altering all my costumes once more so that they don't fit me. In fact, so that they fit so badly that every inch of spare flesh I have (which is many) is bulging out of them in ways I never knew possible, ways that conceptual artists would find inspiring for installation pieces. Why am I still here? Why am I taking the disintegration of my life so blithely? I think it's because I'm not in the least bit surprised.

I always knew it couldn't be me that had the happy ending.

I don't *want* to be here. The moment Fergus threw me out of his mother's house I sort of assumed that I wouldn't *have* to be here, that emotionally and physically wrecked people don't have to perform in local musical productions. I thought I'd have an automatic sick note, like the kind that Dora forges for a small fee. But it turns out that I was the only one who thought that.

For starters, Caroline phoned me and said, 'The show must go one, my dear.' In actual fact she spent about an hour giving me a motivational pep talk, clearly amalgamated from a combination of women's magazines and a sports mistress, but in essence what she wanted to say was, 'Terribly sorry and all that, but blah, blah, blah.'

Somehow, without the aid of an invitation or even a phone call, Mr Crawley had turned up that Saturday evening and brought *Madam Butterfly* on CD and cooked Italian for all of us before telling us about the night he met his wife.

'Was it in Italy?' Camille asked him, already starry-eyed.

'No, it was in High Wycombe, but the town's first pizzeria had just opened and, well, ever since then we loved all things Italian. We went to Tuscany for our twenty-second wedding anniversary.' He smiled at the memory. 'Less than a year later she was gone, but every one of the twenty-two years was a gift.'

I twirled my pasta languidly around my fork.

'Twenty-two years.' I said wistfully. 'I'm not sure that we made twenty-two months . . .'

'Well, of course you haven't,' Mr Crawley said robustly. 'Not yet.'

And not for the first time I wondered why everyone but me refused to see that Fergus and I were over. Surely I was the one supposed to be in denial while they all gave each other 'poor deluded soul'-type meaningful glances over the top of my head. Then I realised that Fergus and I were some kind of flagship of hope to these people, even loved-up Camille and cynical Dora. I realised that maybe they needed the fairy-tale ending even more than I did.

'Perhaps he'll come on Monday, to the show,' Dora said. 'And then everything will work out fine.'

I looked at her, wondering if it were possible for Doris to somehow possess the body of my best friend, but I couldn't see any hint of her lurking in her brown eyes.

'Dora, this is real life not a Judy Garland musical,' I said wearily. 'Firstly, why would my soon-to-be-ex-husband come to watch a show starring his loathed soon-to-be-ex-wife? Secondly, even if he did, how could that possibly translate into "And everything will work out fine" . . .' I trailed off.

'Well, once,' Dora said seriously, 'I had a date with the guitarist from a goth rock band and he wasn't very attractive to me personally – piercing, penis-shaped nose, and on top of that he was a bit of a sexist twat who sprayed fake spider web around his bedroom when it wasn't even Hallowe'en. So anyway, I went to this gig he was playing at, specifically to dump him, and funnily enough when I saw him up on stage for the first time I was suddenly overcome with desire for him. You know, the aphrodisiac of fame and all that. It's the reason why people sleep with any old celebrity. Oh, I know it was only pub-band fame, but you never know.'

I considered her thoughts for a moment and then chose to ignore them for fear that I might actually implode if I admitted to myself and the world that she wasn't joking.

'And thirdly,' I said defiantly, 'I'm not going to be in the stupid show now anyway.' I sulked. 'I only did it to try and be part of this godforsaken town, and now it looks like I'll be moving back to London very soon, so bollocks to Calamity Fucking Jane, I'm not doing it.' I sank my glass of wine and then the rest of Camille's in two easy steps. Mr Crawley fixed me with a very intimidating hawk-like gaze, and for the first time in our acquaintance I realised just how formidable he could be, particularly if you got on his wrong side.

'Yes, you *are* going to be in the show,' he informed me. 'You might be in some personal difficulty, but that does not give you the right to ruin weeks of hard work and preparation by all the other Players. They gave you the chance to *be* part of this "godforsaken town" and you can't throw it back in their faces. Besides, if you go out on to that stage you'll be showing everyone, maybe even Fergus, whether he's there or not, that you have done nothing to be ashamed of. Understood?'

'Understood,' I said meekly.

'Good.' Mr Crawley topped up Camille's wine glass, passing over mine with the air of a headmaster. 'Now, as for everything turning out all right on the night . . . Well, let's just say that things have a habit of doing that when I'm around, so we'll just wait and see, shall we?'

'Yes, Mr Crawley,' Dora, Camille and I said in unison, and so here I am waiting to see.

Of course I hadn't bet on Clare's woman-scorned act or the gut-wrenching fear and pounding of my already faulty heart, possibly exacerbated by the extremely tight clothing which is cutting off my circulation. I look into the wings for Mr Crawley, but he must still be getting his make-up done. Instead I see Clare, her face white and pinched, and behind her Gareth grinning at me from the shadows, his face thrown into sharp relief, making him look like a Punch puppet. I force myself not to look, though for a second holding on to his gaze with every ounce of anger and fury I have. If he wants me to be his victim, then he'll be disappointed. I'll show him that he means nothing to me.

'Anything else you'd like to throw at me,' I say to God through gritted teeth as I climb up on to our kit version of the deadwood stage.

'Yes I have actually,' God says as the curtains creak back, and the first thing that I lay eyes on is Fergus, two rows back, seated firmly between Dora and Camille. It looks like Dora is attempting to put her plan into practice after all.

'Oh Jesus Christ,' I say under the music.

'Exactly,' says God.

The rent in the rear of my suedette trousers as I tip over the side of the deadwood stage is not audible above the music, but it doesn't have to be: the audience's roar of laughter and a quick exploration with my hand is all I need to tell me that approximately half of my arse is now exposed and an unscheduled eclipse of the moon is threatening. That's the bad news. The good news is that it appears everyone thinks it's part of the show. I think of what Doris would say, apart from 'Wear a girdle!' and I'm fairly sure she'd tell me to ham it up. I think of my mum, the living-room net curtains draped over her head like a veil when she made me hysterical with laughter as we sang songs from *The Sound of Music*, and I think of Fergus, probably frog-marched here by my two dear misguided friends in the hope that, quote, 'everything will be all right', and I think, bugger it, if I'm doing this I might as well do it the best that I can.

I can't sing. I can hardly move in these clothes, but it doesn't seem to matter too much. Okay, so the audience are laughing *at* me rather than *with* me, and, okay, so Barbara's secret Botox session only hours before the curtain went up has meant that although she looks the ten years younger than Katie Brown that she should, she can no longer pronounce consonants (a 'ooman's 'ouch is all 'oo 'eed'), and, okay, Bill's sixth form sextuplet seems to be playing the chill-out version of the score, which means that the cast finish each number about two minutes before the band does. But even if half of the audience have their camcorders out in anticipation of a fast £250 from Lisa Riley, they really are enjoying themselves.

Just before act one's curtain, I allow myself to look at the seat where I know Fergus is sitting, hoping against hope that I'll see the same indulgent smile on his face that has let me know so many times in the past that he loves me. Hoping against hope that Dora could be right after all and that mending ruined relationships really is this ea—

His seat is empty and I catch Dora and Camille in the midst of a heated exchange just as the dusty curtain crumbles to a close.

Oh well, it looks like sometimes even Mr Crawley can't work enough magic to fix everything.

I stand in the star's dressing room, which is actually the delicately fragranced disabled loo, and pick out my first second-half costume, the dress. This time Clare's gone the other way and made it too big so that it flops off my shoulders and ignores my approximation of a waist, to skim over my bum and hips. As I try it on and turn around I realise she's made it to fit her. On Clare it would look lovely, on me it fits in exactly all the wrong places, making me look too big for a too-big frock. I shrug and look at the ceiling.

'Bring it on,' I tell the fluorescent light fixture. 'Come on, I'm ready.'

'I'm sorry.'

I turn swiftly on my heel to see Clare looking me up and down, suppressing a smile.

'I was so, I was just so . . . angry.' She advances into the room. 'You already had it all. I just didn't know why you wanted what I had as well.' She shrugs and produces a packet of pins from her pocket. 'Come on, I'll fix it up so no one'll notice.'

I back away from her impulsively. 'Clare, please believe me. I didn't know about you and Gareth.' I think about the way he talked about her, but decide to leave that out of it. 'And you have to believe me, I never wanted what happened to happen . . .' I turn my back on her and begin hastily reapplying mascara in thick sticky globules. 'Oh look, you can think what you like, but I'm sorry.'

Clare puts her hand on my shoulder and turns me around. She has slotted several pins between her lips and extracts one as she begins to take up the straps.

'All these pins might help you hit the high notes if you move too quickly,' she says between gritted teeth. 'And actually, I do believe you. I've been the stupid one, *again*.' I look into her face and see tears standing in her eyes. 'Should have known that nothing like that ever happens to me. I was just so jealous of you, Kitty. I'm not proud of it, but it's true. With your lovely house and your proper family. Even though I liked – like – you so much, there you were with all that . . . easiness at your feet, moaning about pretty much everything you could think of. I know the grass is always greener and all that, but sometimes I just did think you were acting sort of ungrateful. I'm sorry.' Her eyes avoid mine as she carries on her work, and I shake my head, startled by her clear picture of me, which I observe as if standing outside of my own body.

'Don't be sorry, Clare – you're not stupid, I am. You're right. I was complaining about having it all. But you know what I think? It was all such a shock. Meeting Fergus, loving him. The wedding and Ella. All so whirlwind and wonderful that when the fuss died down and I was left with my life I felt sort of disappointed and I felt sort of absent. I should have realised how it must have looked to you. What a stupid cow!'

Clare holds my shoulder and looks at me. 'Yeah, well. None of that excuses what he did to you. None of it.'

Now it hits me – she knows everything.

'But . . .? You were with him just now? Are you okay?' I

397

touch her hand and look at her. 'What's he done to you, Clare?' I ask her, my voice low with anger.

'He's here because he wanted to see you, couldn't believe you'd go through with it. Said you didn't have the guts.' She removes her hand from under mine and carefully inserts another pin. 'I thought he was a bit cold, you know, when it came to sex. But he was always so sweet and attentive in conversation, really romantic, and he said all the right stuff, you know, made me feel special. After you went that afternoon he was fantastic, fantastic until we went to bed, and then it was like he was . . . like I wasn't even there. I thought that, well, things like that take time . . . and then the next day Ted set him off. He was bouncing on the sofa while Gareth was trying to watch the racing on TV. He told him a few times to give over, but Ted's just a baby! He thought it was a game. Gareth just picked Ted up and shook him and threw him back down on the floor.'

Her hand had begun to tremble and I held her wrist still.

'I couldn't believe it. I flew at him – no one touches my kid like that, no one, and he, well, he hit me, Kitty, knocked me on the floor, and then . . . then he left. Ted and me weren't hurt too bad. I was a bit bruised and Ted was more shocked than anything else, but it was so quick, over before it even began. I almost wondered if it had happened at all.' She bites her lip over a cautious smile. 'But after he'd gone and I'd checked us both over, I realised that he wasn't that sweet sensitive bloke I thought he was at all. I realised that maybe you were telling the truth, and, well, it was too late by then, the costumes had already gone.'

We hold each other hard for a moment.

'Oh God, Clare. I'm so sorry I dragged you into this. You've been such a good friend to me. I really think, I really do, that if I hadn't met you I'd have gone insane even more than now! Imagine!'

Clare and I laugh and cry and hug, and in that instant I have an idea.

'Ouch,' I say loudly, and then 'Owwwwww!'

Clare springs back in concern. 'What is it, a pin?' She examines me.

'No, I've sprained my ankle,' I say woodenly. 'Ow. Owwwww. Ouch.' I try louder, hoping to attract some more attention. Clare looks at me askance.

'What are you on about?' she giggles. 'The stress *has* finally sent you mental!'

Caroline opens the door and scowls at me.

'The audience can hear you screeching, you know. Victorian ventilation system.' She eyes Clare speculatively as I press home my plan.

'I'm sorry, Caroline, I just turned my ankle over and it's agony, I'm practically crippled, so there's no way I can go on for the second half. Ow. Clare'll have to do it.'

Clare claps her hand over her mouth, her eyes wide at first with fear and then delight as she catches up with my plan.

'Me?' she gasps, and I suppress a giggle.

'Ow, I mean. And after all, the show must . . .'

There's a pause. 'Very well! Curtain in one minute, get on with it!'

Caroline whirs out of the room as Clare and I hastily begin to pull out all of the pins.

'Oh God, Kitty, oh God,' she giggles as I help her into the dress. I step back and look her up and down. She looks beautiful.

'Why, Wild Bill won't believe his eyes,' I say with a smile. 'You were made to wear pink!'

'Curtain!' Colin hollers down the corridor.

'Thank you, Kitty, thank you.' Clare takes a deep breath and heads out towards the stage.

'Well, it always should have been you, after all,' I call out after her, and I smile to myself in the mirror. Tonight it's been my turn to be fairy godmother.

Standing in my underwear I begin to wash away the thick sludge of stage make-up until my own skin appears in pink patches through the panstick. I start brushing the tangles out of my back-combed hair and dare to let the slightest edge of optimism into my thoughts. If Clare believes me, then it's a start, and maybe, after tonight, I can get her to talk to Fergus and explain, and maybe, just maybe . . . I trail off and examine my hairbrush. What's the point in hoping? If there had been any chance he would have stayed, or he'd be here now talking to me. Fergus has already gone back to his mum's house, back to Georgina, Daniel and Ella, a perfect little family without me.

'I just wish there was a way we could talk to each other,' I say to myself into the mirror. That's the irony of these kind of situations, the cruelty. There's nothing, nothing I'd like to do more than be able to run to him now and tell him about all this, laughing together and holding each other the way we always used to. Even when we argued we were in each other's arms. How can I, though? When the one person I want to confide in is the one who hurt me, the one who doubts and probably hates me? How can I, when I'm the one who kept pulling at the seams of our marriage until it came apart in my hands. 'I can't, can I?' I tell myself. 'I can't do that ever again.'

'I'm all ears, love,' Gareth says over my shoulder. I stand still for a moment, caught between the urges to crumple and cower and to run. Then, in one breath, both of those impulses flee by themselves, leaving me alone to face him. Alone but not afraid.

'What's wrong?' I say, turning to face him, straightening my shoulders. 'No babies for you to bully round here?'

He smirks and closes the door behind him. I catch my breath

in my throat, but I stand my ground. He will not see what I'm feeling.

'Yeah, well, kids should know their place. My dad taught me that, remember?' he says with a matter-of-fact tone as he leans against the wall to look at me. My stomach turns in disgust and I reach for my shirt, trying not to look rattled.

'That's not all he taught you, or did you make up all that crap too?' I ask him, calculating the distance between him, me and the door.

'I thought you understood me, Kitty,' he says. 'I thought that now that Clare and I are over we could pick up where we left off.' He takes a step closer. 'You're looking good. It must be all this misery – helped you shed a bit of that weight.'

I shake my head and laugh, buttoning my shirt with trembling fingers.

'Just leave, Gareth, just go,' I say with as much authority as I am able, but he pushes himself off the wall and takes a step closer, his smile so sweet that for a split second I forget who he is, what he is, before it turns into a vicious leer.

'Come on, baby, I'll make it last longer this time, I promise.'

I don't actually believe that he'll do anything until he's grabbed me and pushed me hard into the spine of the basin, his hands pinning my elbows to my ribs.

'Go on, make a fuss,' he says, and the last part of my courage dissolves. 'I like my women feisty.'

And something incredible happens, something . . . wonderful and terrible. The anger, the pent-up fury that has been eating away at me since that first time, maybe for even longer than that, galvanises in the pit of my stomach and unleashes itself, flowing through my body, licking at my limbs like fire.

In this instant, in this breath, I know I will not let him hurt me; I will not let him touch me. Suddenly I feel a surge of strength, power and certainty that I never knew I had until this moment, and I shove him away from me making him stumble and lose his footing. He crashes to the ground, his head catching the edge of the toilet seat. A long gash opens up before my eyes and begins to bleed. As I watch the blood well and thicken I hear my own heart thundering in my ears, the rasping sound of my own breath, and I know that I am in control.

'You fucking bitch.' He smears the blood away from his eyes and begins to rise. 'You fucking bitch! I'm going to . . .'

I laugh at him, small and bleeding on the floor of the disabled loo. I laugh, and this time it doesn't make him angry, this time it doesn't give him power, it robs him of any that he had. He looks small and stupid. He looks pathetic.

'What are you going to do, Gareth?' I ask him. 'Look at you, you can't do anything to me, not any more. You really are nothing, just some stupid, self-deluded, preening prick. I can't believe I let you bother me, you're disgusting. You're nothing, less than nothing.'

As Gareth's face clouds with a mixture of embarrassment and maybe even fear, the toilet door slams open.

'I may not have been there to stop you the first time,' Fergus snarls, 'but I'm here now and I'm going to stop you now.' He lunges on top of Gareth, his fists already flying, and I realise that Fergus has hit him somewhere in the past few seconds and that he's going to keep on hitting him again and again.

'Stop! Stop it, Fergus!' I scream. 'It's sorted, I've sorted it. Don't!' I shout, not knowing what I'm trying to say, only that I need to protect Fergus from his own rage. The room is full now and I see Mr Crawley and Bill Edwards pulling Fergus back into the corridor and I stumble after him, tripping over Gareth's outstretched leg, so that I fall face first against the opposite wall in a heap at Fergus's feet. Bill and Mr Crawley pick Gareth up by one arm each and fling him back into the loo. I think I hear his head crack against the sink.

'Kitty.' Fergus helps me stand and we cling on to each other for a moment as the world tilts before finally righting itself.

'You're bleeding.' Fergus touches my face and I wince in surprise.

I stare at him in stunned disbelief as Mr Crawley emerges from the toilet, shutting the door behind him, and then finds a dust sheet and wraps it around my shoulders.

'Would you get Dora and Camille. I think I have to go home now,' I ask Mr Crawley in a small voice. 'I think I need to go home.'

Mr Crawley looks at me and then, his arms still resting on my shoulders, reaches out to Fergus and in turn touches his shoulder too.

'It's okay,' he says to us both. And then to Bill, 'You should get back before Clare's big number. You two, why don't you go and sit at the back, watch the end of the show?'

I look at Mr Crawley, his tall and elegantly slim frame, and then at the closed toilet where Gareth is bound to be refuelling his fury even now.

'What about him? . . .' I say shakily, pointing at the door. 'He'll kill you . . .' Mr Crawley smiles and shakes his head.

'There is more than one way to skin a rat,' he says serenely. 'Just leave him to me, Kitty. I'll just have a little chat with him, and I think you'll find he will be out of town before morning, a very different man.'

I open my mouth to protest, but there is something in his quiet determination that makes me realise that I shouldn't doubt him, let alone question him; that when pushed to the limit he can be a very formidable man.

'And how are you going to do that?' a more sceptical Fergus asks doubtfully.

'Oh, I'll just work my usual magic,' Mr Crawley says, and his

403

smile is quite chilling as he goes to open the toilet door. If it was anyone except Gareth in there I'd feel sorry for them.

'Kitty.' Fergus grabs my arm but I shake him loose instantly. My skin feels bruised all over.

'Not now, Fergus.' I can't face him. 'Just let things calm down a bit, okay?'

Fergus looks hurt and angry.

'But I've come to tell you . . . to apologise . . .'

I start walking back to the hall.

'As if you can do that now, just like that?' I say over my shoulder.

Part of me thinks that I should be falling into his arms and kissing him passionately just like the girl does when the hero saves the day, and part of me wants to. But it wasn't the hero, was it? It wasn't Prince Charming on his white charger that slew the dragon. It was me, all alone. I rescued myself. I saved the day, Fergus hadn't believed me, and for now at least I need to be alone to understand that, to feel what it means.

I can't look at Fergus as we sidle into the back of the auditorium. I feel the kind of elation I previously imagined only athletes and fighters know. I've won. I've beaten Gareth and taken back myself. As we walk into the hushed auditorium I'm shouting, singing in my head. I just know that I've got control of my life, maybe for the first time, and that maybe I don't have to wait for someone else to change things. That maybe, no *definitely*, I'm strong enough to change things for myself.

It seems that the audience have hardly even noticed the change in their leading lady, except that instead of laughing and whispering amongst themselves they are sitting in rapt silence as Clare take centre stage.

'*Once I had a secret love,*' she sings, '*that lived within the heart of me . . .*' A sigh ripples through the audience as she begins, her voice as pure and as clear as glass as the song reaches its sweet crescendo, her face illuminated by a delighted smile. As she sings I realise that Fergus is still holding my hand, and carefully I extricate my fingers from his, for all my new-found strength still confused and uncertain by what his apparent volte-face means, or what I might want it to mean.

Clare walks to the edge of the stage, holding her hands out to the audience as she sings the final line. '*Now my heart's an open door, and my secret love's no secret any more . . .*'

Applause ripples through the hall in breaking waves, and soon cheers and shouts for an encore are joining them as gradually the whole hall climbs to its feet.

Clare stands caught in the spotlight, looking off stage, shaking her head and laughing, 'But it's not the end yet!'

'Oh, just sing it again! Give the crowd what they want, girl!' Caroline calls from the wings, and the band strikes up once more.

'But what did you say to him?' Dora and Camille walk slightly ahead of us, their arms linked through Mr Crawley's.

'I rather think it would get lost in the retelling,' he says amiably. 'Suffice it to say that he's gone, and that he knows better than to try anything like that again.'

My friends giggle and flit around him like a couple of butterflies, stepping over the threshold of the front door and leaving it open for Fergus and me. I stop him at the door, my hand on his chest.

'Will you bring Ella back in the morning?' I say.

Fergus looks at me, clearly not understanding. 'But I thought I could give Mum a ring, and she could bring her now . . .?'

His mouth continues to move as if he had another question to ask that he can't quite articulate. 'Isn't it over? Isn't everything okay now?' he says at last.

I shake my head. 'Isn't what over? It doesn't seem like long ago that you told me we were over, and for good.'

Fergus reaches out to touch me, but his fingers hover millimetres above the surface of my skin. I step away and walk back on to the road, away from the welcoming light and warmth of the hallway. 'Yes, I know, but surely we can put that behind us now. Surely you can see that I love you . . .'

'Do you know what day it is today, Fergus?' I ask him, leaning on the gate and letting it swing slightly under my weight. I turn around and face him, seeing him desperately sort through our various anniversaries. 'It's twenty-four years today since Mum died. Since everything in my life went out of control. I thought that when I met you, you were the one who was going to change that for me. But I was wrong. It's got to be me. It had to be me all along.'

I look at his face in the half light and I want to kiss every part of it, bury my face in his neck and just forget about everything that needs to be done just for one second, but I know that I can't, not yet. I owe that much to my mum, to myself.

'I think I've been putting important things behind me without trying to sort them out for too long, Fergus. I don't think we can just go back. If we go anywhere, it has to be forward. I need to think, I need to straighten things out, okay? There's no point in us going back to the way it was, we'd just end up here again – sooner or later. Give me a couple of days to get everything straight here.' I tap my forehead. 'Do you understand?'

Fergus takes a step closer to me and encircles me with his arms briefly before stepping past me, through the gate and back on to the street.

'I think I understand,' he says. 'Do you understand that I'm so sorry, so very sorry, and that I love you?'

I nod my head and watch him for a while as he disappears into the shadows. I almost run after him, I almost call out, but I'm afraid to. I'm afraid of what I might say to him before he's ready to hear it. I know he really means it when he says he's sorry, but what he doesn't realise is that sorry isn't nearly enough to mend our relationship. It's only the hint, the faintest hope of a beginning. The scent of blossom heavy in the trees suddenly swells and seems almost to caress me.

'I understand everything now, Mum,' I say into the soft sweet dark. 'At last I do.'

Chapter Twenty-five

'See, what I don't see,' Dora tells me over a film about cheer-leaders and werewolves which none of us has been watching, 'is that he believes you, he loves you, he wants you. The end. Geddit?' She settles back in the armchair and looks at Camille. 'Don't you think she's sort of lost the plot a bit? This is the "Happy Ever After" bit, right?'

Camille shrugs and purses her lips, looking at me with faint disapproval. I know what she's thinking, I know what they've both been thinking for the last couple of days, they've been wondering why Fergus isn't back home, why they are both still here nursemaiding me and why all isn't right with the world.

'It's not that I'm not on your side, Kits, it's just that haven't you punished the poor man enough?' Camille asks me gently. 'The look on his face when he dropped Ella back yesterday. It was like you'd ripped his heart out and stamped on it. And as for Ella, did you see *her* face?'

I had seen her face, of course I had, I'd felt it in every fibre of my being. I could see her wondering why her daddy hadn't come in with her, why things suddenly weren't the same as they always had been. Maybe she didn't think quite that clearly but she felt it, I knew that she did.

'Look,' I turn to them. 'Don't you think I want us all back together again? But it's just not that easy. This mess isn't something you just sweep up under the carpet and pretend it's all fine. Something'd happen and we'd just be back to square one before you knew it. And I don't want that again.' I find myself gripping hard on to a cushion. 'I don't think I could *survive* it again.'

Camille crosses the room and sits on the arm of my chair, hugging me briefly.

'But what then? You can't just go on in this, in this . . .' She waves her arms in the air. 'This kind of suspended animation. You need to break the spell, Kitty, get things moving again. Makes things right.'

Dora nods in agreement.

'I know,' I tell them. 'It's just I'm sort of scared to. I've lived my life this one way for so long – always in pain, always alone, always expecting the worst – that if I let that go and just let myself be happy, I'm scared of losing myself. That sounds pretty stupid doesn't it?'

Dora shakes her head. 'No, no, I know what you mean. There was a time when I'd rather have killed myself than be happy. Who knows why we're so fucked up, Kits? Maybe there was something in the water when we were kids. After all, Cam seems peachy.'

Camille bites back a smile. 'I have my moments, not quite as life changingly dramatic as yours, but I do have them. We all do at some time in our lives.' She leans her cheek against mine.

'What's the first thing you need to do to get things on the right track again? Maybe Dora and I can help you?'

I reach my arm up around her neck and hug her. 'Oh, God, I wish you could, but you know what? The first thing I have to do is something I have to do by myself.'

Dora and Camille exchange a glance and look the question at me.

'I have to go and see my father.'

★

It's not that I haven't thought about all those things he said to me that day, it just that somehow, with everything that's happened, is seems like for ever and a day since he told me he'd always blamed me for Mum's death. I put off dealing with it initially because that's my preferred way of approaching complex emotional issues, to tuck them away at the back of my mind in the file clearly marked 'denial' and face them when, and only when, circumstances meant I could no longer ignore them. In fact, if it hadn't been for this whole mess, the entire incident might have quietly sat there for years until I'd gone mad or forgotten about it altogether. But my life has turned upside down and those circumstances I was talking about mean I can't go forward – with or without Fergus – until I've found out what exactly is left of my relationship with my dad.

Dora and Camille took Ella out for the day until Fergus was due to collect her. I told them where I was going and they both gave me speeches about rushing into things, running before I could walk, but I told them. Some things can't just be left unsaid, not if I'm ever to be at peace with my future. Some things need to be resolved.

As the train rattled and shuddered its way towards London, I thought of the last time I'd made this journey, full of uncertainty and anxiety, wondering if and when the real me would ever come back. I don't think I realised then that the real me, the essence of me, had vanished in that moment when I found Mum all those years ago, or rather had retreated so far inside myself that it took someone or something like Gareth to make it come charging back out to defend me. As the train pulled into Euston I felt none of the apprehension and misgivings I'd felt the first time, nor the longed-for homecoming that I had thought I should feel. Instead I just felt perfectly relaxed and calm as if I was in the arms of a very old friend.

It was like walking back through time, walking back through my teens and my childhood, until eventually I climbed the steps up to our old flat. It was almost like that final trip home from school on that terrible day, the trees still heavy with late blossom, the air thick with exhaust. Dad was still there, still in the same few rooms where it happened, and in some way, I felt, so was my mum.

I knocked and waited, and then knocked and waited again, knowing that my dad's policy on answering the door was identical to his stance on the phone. Eventually I saw his shadow behind the frosted glass lumbering towards the door.

'ID please,' he called through the letterbox.

'It's Kitty,' I shouted, and I half laughed as I wondered if I should produce a credit card or something. I watched the hunched figure freeze for a second before it straightened and opened the door.

'Kitty,' he said, and stood aside to let me in.

I expected the fear and the memories to come racing to greet me as I trod the familiar path to the front room, but instead the flat seemed clean and bright and, somehow, empty. We stood there looking at each other, for a moment feeling the strangeness of the situation.

'I didn't expect to see you again,' he said simply, sadly. 'After everything I said. It came out badly, wrongly. I was trying to mend things . . .' He trailed off, shaking his head.

'I know. I didn't expect to want to see you again,' I replied. 'But, well, when you came up, a lot of things were going on in my head, and since then I've had a chance to think about what you said, or about what you were trying to say. I wanted to give you the chance to finish what you started. I wanted to give us both a chance.'

He looked at me, and it seemed as if a little colour had returned to his face.

'Do you want a drink? Tea and a Digestive?' he asked brightly, but I shook my head.

'Let's just talk, Dad,' I said. 'After all these years, let's just talk.'

For an agonising few seconds we did not talk. I sat on the same sofa I had made a camp behind all those years ago – the mossy green velveteen worn bare on the arms and corner cushions – and Dad sat in his old chair, looking out of the window across the city, its myriad of lives reflected minutely in his glasses.

'I don't know, Kitty, I feel as if I'm waking up from a long dream, like that fellow, you know, the one who went to sleep under a tree and when he woke up a hundred years had passed?' He looked at me and I nodded. 'It wasn't just meeting Joy that brought it on, it started with your wedding, I suppose. I could see how uncomfortable you were with me there and . . .'

'I wasn't, Dad, honest,' I protested, but too weakly to be convincing.

'It doesn't matter, love. I could see it and I knew you were terrified I'd make a show of you and you shouldn't have had to deal with that, not on that day.'

I closed my eyes for a moment, feeling horribly guilty and ashamed, because he was right, I would have much peferred it if he hadn't been there at all.

'Then when the little one came, and you didn't bring her to see me and I didn't try to go and see her, it was then really that things started to change, slowly. I began to realise how much I'd thrown away. You back then with your scrappy pig tails and that frilly red dress you insisted on wearing every day of the week, the minute you got in from school. I think that's the last time I really felt like I knew you. I thought of your mum, and how furious she'd be with me for letting you drift away like this.' He half smiled. 'Her eyes flashed lightning when she was riled, you're just like her in that respect!'

412

I smiled in return and a moment's silence passed before he spoke again.

'Well, it was then I decided to do something about it, thought I'd try to get out a bit, met Joy at the club and she has been fantastic. She just seemed to be able to listen and understand. It was she who told me that I'd never get you back unless I made a clean sweep of it, unless I told you why or how I was like I was. The thing is, I never got the chance to apologise to you, that day, to say that I'm so sorry. You deserved better than me growing up, you deserved your mum, and someone took that away from us and I'm sorry, Kitty, I'm sorry I couldn't stop it . . .'

'Oh, Dad?' I crossed the room in two or three steps, and kneeling in front of him I held his hands, not quite ready to fling myself into his arms just yet. 'Dad, a lot of things have happened to me recently. Things that have made me realise those fairy-tale endings don't really exist, there's not a magic wand to wave away all your problems or a way to mend relationships overnight. I realise that now, and I feel ready, strong enough somehow, to face those things head on. I think that you and I, we have to get to know each other all over again. But I want to Dad. I want to for Mum's sake. And for mine.'

I'm not sure how long we did talk for, but we didn't stop until the sky darkened and the orange glow of the city rose behind the skyline. Twenty-four years of the things we should have said to each other, the things that had been waiting to be told, asked or spoken, until we talked away the darkness and remembered only the light.

'I wanted to tell you,' I said finally, 'that I was thrilled with the colour TV. I mean, I didn't mean to hurt you, I really didn't. I was ever so proud of it.'

My dad laughed. 'I'd forgotten about that. You were so like your mum. Always away with the fairies.'

I smiled at the comparison and thought of her smiling, dreamy face.

'You understand, don't you now, that when I said all that stuff about blaming you, it was just so I could tell you I was wrong, so that I could clear everything away. Make a fresh start?' He took my hand and held it to his face. 'I've wasted so many years, Kitty, so many years being angry when I should have just loved you, taken care of you the way you needed. At least you've got Fergus to do that now.'

I touched his hand. 'You can still look after me a bit, Dad, it's not too late, and I can look after you.' I kissed him gently on the forehead and sat back in the chair. 'There's something else I wanted to ask you?'

Dad nodded, raising his palms in invitation.

'Well, those "other things" I was telling you about, that were going on at home. A lot of stuff has happened with Fergus . . . and, well, Dad, I think I know what I'm going to do, but I wanted to tell you first.'

Dad leant forward a little in his chair and began to listen closely.

Dora and Camille exchange glances they think we don't see over our heads and Camille nods towards the living room.

'So anyway, we'll, um, leave you to it,' Camille says with studied calm. 'If you need us, Kits, just shout.' She shoots a meaningful glance at Fergus and I nod, looking at him, his eyes bruised with shadows and red rimmed as if he's lost a lot of sleep.

'Are you okay?'

He half smiles and nods and then shakes his head in one fluid movement.

'No, I'm terrible. I loved being with Ella but I missed you, I missed you being there, Kitty. The three of us together.'

I want so much to be able to connect with him now, for him

to be my knight in shining armour again. I want so much to be able to fall into his arms and be all happy ever after again, but if I believed that could happen once I know that it can't now. Fairy-tale endings and trouble-free futures are things that really do only ever happen in books. The question is, do we have any kind of future at all? And after talking with my dad I know the answer.

'What about you? Are you okay? Do you miss me?' he asks me, his voice hoarse.

I nod mutely in reply. I am relieved, even almost pleased, that Fergus found out about Gareth when he did. Vindicated, justified, exonerated are the words that have been flashing through my head ever since. But still, everything Fergus and I said to each other burns like a fresh scald and I keep thinking, if he loved me, if he truly loved me, then he wouldn't have had to wait for it to almost happen again to believe me. He would have stood by me come what may, he would not have abandoned me. For Ella's sake, for Fergus's and mine, I want this to be a new beginning for us, but I have wondered and worried – have we fallen too far apart?

After Dad had finished listening to my plan for the future, he had nodded and said, 'Never let go of the things you love, not if there is still a chance, not ever. You'll just spend the rest of life regretting it.'

'Clare came to me the morning of the play,' Fergus begins, clearly phased by my silence. 'She told me about Gareth and the baby and everything. She told me that she was wrong about you and that I was, too, and that I should give you another chance. Go to the play and see you. And then the girls turned up and practically frog-marched me there anyway.' I look away from him. 'But I was glad I let them. It's been hell without you, Kitty. I'm asking *you* to give *me* another chance.'

The one thing about this town I have always loved is that here you can see the stars wheeling about you in the night sky, moving endlessly over time in a way that the vast, permanently switched-on city never allows. Now I push back my stool and open the back door and step out into the garden. The night air is still warm and the dark sky seems only inches away from the tips of my fingers. I sense Fergus standing behind me, and for a moment I scan the skies looking for something, a sign, a shooting star, even a banking airplane, but everything is perfectly still. For once I think I trust myself to know the right answer.

'The thing is,' Fergus says, 'that I didn't need Clare to tell me what the truth was, I didn't need to see Gareth in action to know what had happened. I didn't need anything, Kitty, except to hear it from you.'

I turn and look at him, thrown for a moment, confused and hurting.

'But I did tell you, I did,' I say. 'Maybe too late. But I told you and you threw me out.'

'Because . . . Because you waited to tell me. Because you kept it from me when I should have been the one you ran to first.'

Fergus digs his hands into his pockets and looks away from me. In the moonlight and the half light from the kitchen his profile is picked out in an etching of fluorescent silver, and just looking at him makes my heart ache.

'I don't know how to say this without making you hate me. I was angry with you for not telling me, I was hurt that you went up there with him in the first place, and I couldn't see past that for a long time . . .' He pauses, pulling his hands free of his pockets and running his fingers through his hair. 'The blunt truth is that I couldn't face it, Kitty. I couldn't face what happened to you. I couldn't bear the fact that I couldn't protect you, the very person I live to protect. And . . . Christ, Kitty, I'm ashamed to say it, but I didn't know if I could love you, I didn't know if I had it in me to love you after that had happened. Not because I didn't want to, but because I didn't deserve to, because I had failed you. I said those things because, well, because it was easier to believe that it happened that way.'

I stand apart from him and concentrate on breathing.

'I should have told you straight away,' I say, breathless. 'I should have told you I was unhappy, but I didn't want to admit our perfect life wasn't perfect. I shouldn't have gone up there with him. I did things that were stupid and wrong, but I never thought you'd let me down when I needed you most. Maybe I took your love for granted. Maybe I thought that whatever I did you'd still be there. I didn't know what you wanted, Fergus, I didn't know if you wanted to us to be together or not, and I didn't know if I could be with you any more. Everything's different.'

Even as I say the words I find myself moving into Fergus's arms, welding myself to the heat of his body, inhaling his scent, desperate to hold on to the ghosts of the past even as I finally let them go.

'Christ knows I love you, but when we met I thought that love was all we needed. Now I don't know that it's enough.' Fergus holds on to me hard, pressing me close into the contours of his body. 'If we do this then we're going to need much more than just a hope and a prayer, we're going to need each other. A proper partnership. You and me working together, sharing the load financially, emotionally, equally.'

'I'm not letting you go,' he says, the first hint of a hopeful smile shadowing his mouth. 'Maybe love on its own isn't enough, but we have so much more than that, Kitty. We have honesty now, and respect, and if we've found a way through this we'll be stronger than we ever were before. And now we've come through this, the next time anyone tries to knock us for six we'll be ready to face them. We know the worst that life can throw at us, we know it's not all fairy tales and romance.' He steps back, one hand on each of my shoulders. 'But what will never change is that we love each other and we love our baby. And *that's* the magic that means we can make it, we really can.'

I smile in the second before his kisses me, and, as I close my eyes, for the first time in months I feel the promise of the future, tender and vulnerable, but there all the same.

'Do you really think that we can beat the world?' I ask him, in a last moment of uncertainty, the taste of his kiss still on my lips.

'I know we can,' Fergus whispers. 'We can do anything as long as we are together.' He lays his palm against my cheek and looks down at me, smiling.

'Please, Kitty. Don't let this be the end.'

Also by Rowan Coleman

Growing Up Twice

Rowan Coleman

'Truly brilliant' Company

Jenny, Rosie and Selin have been best friends since school. Their teenage years were spent drinking too much wine in the park, dressing up for Friday night, and making the wrong choices with the wrong men because tomorrow seemed a very long way off.

Eleven riotous years later, Jenny realises something. After more than a decade of waiting for her real life to begin, nothing has really changed. Here she is, still hung-over in the park, still dressed up in Friday night clothes and about to make her most inappropriate choice of man yet.

But Jenny's not the only one waiting for real life to begin. And when tragedy turns their world upside down, all three friends are forced to realise that the real 'growing up' is still to come ...

Also available in Arrow

Getting Over It

Anna Maxted

'Warm, poignant and very funny' Marian Keyes

Helen Bradshaw, 26, has a lot to get over. A dogsbody job on a women's magazine. An attraction to unsuitable men. Being five foot one. Driving an elderly Toyota.

She is about to ditch the infuriating Jasper when she hears the news that will change her life. Her father has collapsed with a massive heart attack. Initially Helen thinks of this as an interruption in her already chaotic lifestyle. But with his death everything starts to fall apart around her – her relationship, her mother, even her cat. Her flatmate Luke has the tact of a traffic warden with toothache, her friend Tina is in love with her new man, her landlord Marcus is in love with himself, and, after the tequila incident, it looks as though Tom the vet will be sticking to Alsatians.

Seems like Helen will be dealing with this one herself . . .

Running in Heels

Anna Maxted

'Funny and inspiring, you'll be turning the pages 'til the small hours'
Company

'To say that Babs is my closest friend is rather like saying that Einstein was good at sums. And if you've ever had a best friend, you'll know what I mean. Babs and I had such a beautiful relationship, no man could better it. And then she met Simon.'

Now Babs, noisy, funny Babs, is getting married. And Natalie, 27, is panicking. What happens when your best friend pledges everlasting love to someone else?

As the confetti flutters, Nat feels her good-girl veneer crack. She teeters into an alluringly unsuitable affair that spins her crazily out of control and into trouble – with her boss, Matt, and with Babs.

Caught up in the thrill of bad behaviour, Nat blithely ignores the truth – about her new boyfriend, her best friend's marriage, her mother's cooking and the wisdom of inviting Babs's brother Andy – slippers and all – to be her lodger. But perhaps what Nat really needs to face is the mirror – and herself . . .

Virtue

Serena Mackesy

Saints, sinners and the mere mortals in between.

What do you need to be a saint these days? Ambition, determination and good PR. But what do you do if your mother's a saint and you just want to be human?

Anna and Harriet share a burden: hellishly saintly mothers. So armed with a wicked sense of humour, they set out to paint the town red. And for a while life goes swimmingly. But when they tread on one toe too many, they find that they have only their worst instincts – and each other – to rely on.

Be good. And if you can't be good, be careful . . .

The Nanny

Melissa Nathan

It'll take more than a spoonful of sugar to sort this lot out . . .

When Jo Green takes a nannying job in London to escape her small-town routine, complicated family and perfect-on-paper boyfriend Shaun, culture shock doesn't even begin to describe it . . .

Dick and Vanessa Fitzgerald are the most incompatible pair since Tom and Jerry, and their children – glittery warrior pixie Cassandra, bloodthirsty Zak and shy little Tullulah – are down-right mystifying. Suddenly village life seems terribly appealing.

Then, just as Jo's getting the hang of their designer lifestyle, the Fitzgerald's acquire a new lodger and suddenly she's sharing her nanny flat with the distractingly good-looking but inexplicably moody Josh. So when Shaun turns up, things get even trickier . . .

Order further Arrow titles from your
local bookshop, or have them delivered direct
to your door by Bookpost

☐ Growing Up Twice	0 09 942768 0	£6.99
☐ Getting Over It	0 09 941018 4	£6.99
☐ Running in Heels	0 09 941019 2	£6.99
☐ Virtue	0 09 941475 9	£5.99
☐ The Nanny	0 09 942797 4	£5.99

FREE POST AND PACKING

Overseas customers allow £2 per paperback

PHONE: 01624 677237

POST: Random House Books
c/o Bookpost, PO Box 29, Douglas
Isle of Man, IM99 1BQ

FAX: 01624 670923

EMAIL: bookshop@enterprise.net

Cheques (payable to Bookpost) and
credit cards accepted

Prices and availability subject to change without notice
Allow 28 days for delivery
When placing your order, please state if you do not wish
to receive any additional information

www.randomhouse.co.uk